Color of the Sea

Color of the Sea

John Hamamura

Thomas Dunne Books
St. Martin's Press   New York

This is a work of fiction. All the characters, organizations, and events portrayed in this book are fictitious or are used fictitiously. Although aspects of the story told in this novel were inspired in some respects by actual events, those events have been completely fictionalized, and this book is not intended to portray, and should not be read as portraying, actual events.

THOMAS DUNNE BOOKS.
An imprint of St. Martin's Press.

www.stmartins.com

Design by Phil Mazzone

Library of Congress Cataloging-in-Publication Data

Hamamura, John.
    Color of the sea / John Hamamura.—1st ed.
       p.   cm.
    ISBN 0-312-34073-7
    EAN 978-0-312-34073-5
    1. Japanese Americans—Fiction.   2. Japanese Americans—Evacuation and relocation, 1942–1945—Fiction.   3. Hiroshima-shi (Japan)—History—Bombardment, 1945—Fiction.   4. World War, 1939–1945—Secret service—Fiction.   5. World War, 1939–1945—Japan—Fiction.   6. Americans—Japan—Fiction.   7. California—Fiction.   8. Hawaii—Fiction.   I. Title.

PS3608.A549436C65   2006
813'.6—dc22

                                                                2005016611

First Edition: April 2006

10   9   8   7   6   5   4   3   2   1

For

Shizuo Hamamura,

Kiyoko Inagaki Hamamura,

and

Chizuko Hamamura

with

Gassho

Acknowledgments

To my agent, Scott Hoffman, for putting the ball through the hoop. To my editor, John Parsley, for your steadfast commitment to the heart of the story. To my copyeditor, Karen Richardson, for your sharply honed attention to clarity and exactitude. To everyone at Thomas Dunne Books and St. Martin's Press whose energy went into this book. To Donna Galassi for your invaluable suggestions. To JB, Barb, Niko and Jessie, Karen, Chris, Brian, Alex and Kelly, Douglas, Pat, Karl, and the Sansei Legacy Project for your love and encouragement. And most of all to Susie Knight, my first reader, editor, critic, muse, and loyal friend. With deepest thanks and many blessings, I bow to you all.

Katatsumuri

> *soro-soro nobore*
>> *Fuji no yama.*

Snail,

> slowly-slowly climb
>> Fuji mountain.

>>> —Kobayashi Issa (1763–1827)

Part 1

JANUARY 1930–DECEMBER 1938

Snow Dance

JANUARY 1930

THE BOY'S BREATH STEAMS IN THE GRAY WINTER LIGHT AS HE RUNS TO-ward Ogonzan hill. Black school cap askew, uniform jacket flapping unbuttoned over a blue and white padded cotton kimono, his thin bare legs and feet flashing, he runs. The clacks of his wooden clogs echo off the houses and walls along the narrow rain-wet streets of Honura village.

Isamu spots them—Mama, his brother, Bunji, and sister, Akemi—beyond the houses on an exposed section of the trail that climbed through the pine and bamboo forests of Ogonzan hill. Before he can shout or wave, they disappear into the trees. Isamu runs harder. On either side of him, deep stone-lined gutters gurgle with clear water rushing downhill.

When Isamu comes to the bend between the last house and the edge of the forest, he gives two long hoots, cranks his arms, and runs puffing like a train around the curve. Slowing to catch his breath, he considers jumping off the tracks onto the secret fox trail that he and his friends had discovered. But this afternoon the bamboo groves look dark and spooky. In the cold still air he can hear water dripping like rain off the long thin leaves. Isamu shivers and decides to keep to the main path.

He catches up with his family just before they reach the cemetery. Three-year-old Akemi beams and puts out her arms. Isamu kneels. She climbs onto his back and wraps her chubby arms around his neck. Straightening and lifting her, Isamu speaks with the unself-conscious authority of a Japanese eldest son. "Hang on tight, Akemi, here we go." Six-year-old Bunji trotting at his side and Mama following closely, Isamu leads them up the steps through the terraced graveyard until they come to Grandfather and Grandmother's stone.

Three days of rain have washed the tall stone clean; nevertheless, they ladle water over it as they have always done. The children sweep away fallen leaves and bits of debris around the base. The boys dump out the two water cups and fill them with fresh water from a nearby cistern. Mama gives Akemi pine boughs to place in the cups, then lights sticks of incense, which the children carefully poke and stand in the wet sand and ashes of the incense bowl. Then they all put their hands together and bow.

Close behind them is a small temple dedicated to Kannon, the goddess of mercy. The humble wooden structure has only one bare, unadorned room. Leaving their grandparents' stone and approaching the temple, the children see that today the temple doors are chained and locked shut. Mama gives each child a coin to drop in the offering box, and she lights sticks of incense for them to place in the temple's incense burner.

The children put their hands together, dip their heads, then immediately run to peek through cracks and knotholes in the unpainted wooden walls of Kannon-sama's temple. Akemi tugs at her big brother's jacket. "I want to see!" Isamu lifts her to a knothole. She moves her head from side to side, surveying the empty interior. Gray light falls through gaps in the roof, through cobwebs sagging from the beams, to the wooden floor carpeted with dust and shriveled leaves, where it glistens on the surface of several small rain puddles. Isamu lowers his sister to the ground. She gives a little sigh of disappointment. "No one home."

From the front of the temple, it is only a few steps across the clearing to Kannon-sama's bell. Four sturdy posts support a black tile roof. Under the shelter of the roof hangs a beautiful old bronze bell. One after the other Mama lifts Akemi then Bunji, helping them take hold of the rope and swing the suspended log against the side of the bell.

Isamu waits for his mother and takes his turn last. He loves ringing the bell. He loves the depth and age and purity of its voice. Especially today, his last full day in Honura village, he savors the bell's song. Eyes closed, Isamu lets the final reverberations soak into him like *sumi* ink into rice paper.

In the stillness left by the bell, Isamu becomes aware of a soft chattering. Looking down, he discovers the sound comes from his brother's teeth. Bunji is shivering like a wet puppy. Isamu removes his school cap and drops it crookedly onto Bunji's head. Then Isamu takes off his uniform jacket and holds it while Bunji slips his arms into the too-long sleeves. Isamu wraps and smooths the jacket over Bunji's chest, then together the two brothers close the brass buttons.

Isamu feels his mother's hand on his shoulder. He turns to look at her face and sees the bell and temple behind her.

"Isamu, you are nine years old and starting a great circle in your life. Someday you will return to close that circle and begin a new one. We will be waiting to welcome you home."

Isamu nods. But feeling the ache growing in his heart and wanting desperately not to break into tears, he points at Kannon-sama's temple. "Maybe you'll be here, but I bet that creaky old temple will have fallen down."

Mama blinks, taken aback, then understanding her son's need for bravado, she smiles gently. "One of your ancestors built the first temple with his own hands. It will stand as long as Kannon-sama lives in it."

Akemi and Bunji turn to stare at the temple. Quickly Isamu knuckles the tears from his eyes. Akemi's voice chimes sweetly as crystalline bells in the still air. "Mama, I always look for her, but I never see her."

"She's in there right now."

Bunji shakes his head. "No, she's not. It's cold and dark and empty inside. And the doors are locked."

"Yes, but she didn't lock them."

Bunji grows agitated. "You're saying that Kannon-sama's in there right now?"

"Of course."

Akemi hides behind her mother and peeks timidly at Kannon-sama's temple.

"But how do you know?" demands Bunji. "How do you know she's in there?"

Suddenly Akemi lets go of Mama's hand and begins dancing in circles. "Oh, look! Look!"

"Ah, there . . ." says Mama. "The goddess has sent you a sign."

Open-mouthed, Isamu and Bunji stare at the locked temple and the last wisps curling from their incense. They look from their mother's knowing smile to the radiant wonder in Akemi's face as she laughs and twirls and lifts her tiny hands to catch the enormous snowflakes drifting silently down from the ash gray sky.

Spear

JANUARY 1930

THE FOLLOWING MORNING, ISAMU KNEELS ON THE STATION PLATFORM and says good-bye to his little sister. Akemi sobs, locking her arms around his neck, refusing to let go. He hugs and gently pats her on the back. "I'll send you a letter from Hawaii."

"Really?"

"Yes. I'll put your name on it and write it just for you."

"But you always read to me. I can't read by myself."

"Mama will read it. I'll paint and draw you pictures."

"I can do that, too. I can make pictures. Of Mama and Bunji and me."

"Then Mama will teach you how to mail them. I'll be waiting." Isamu inhales deeply, wanting to absorb everything about this moment: the blade blue morning light; Akemi's wavering smile; the weight of his mother's hand on his head; the face of his younger brother, Bunji, awestruck in the damp wind washing over the platform as the snow-clad locomotive pulls in, all whistle, bell, and hissing steam; the smell of burning coal, hot iron, and grease; Akemi's icy hand in his; his own hand sizzling slick with sweat, cooked pink with fear and excitement; his heart hammering—leaving home, leaving home . . . Leaving Japan. Leaving Mama, Bunji, and Akemi. Leaving Honura village. Going to Hawaii with Papa. To live on the sugarcane plantation where the twins sleep in the cemetery on the grassy slope between the black volcano and the sudden cliffs, the wind-washed sky and the dream-dark sea.

The train rolls toward Tokyo, Yokohama harbor, and the waiting ship. Father and son, Yasubei and Isamu, sit in the dining car. Yasubei slips his silver cigarette case from the pocket of his navy blue suit coat, tips his white Panama hat to shade his eyes. The winter sun slanting through the window glints off his gold tie clip. Squinting through cigarette smoke, Yasubei sips sake and frowns at his son. At the boy's new white shirt dusted with rice-cracker crumbs, striped burgundy and navy tie askew, collar gaping around a scrawny neck. Yasubei focuses momentarily on Isamu's hair, shiny as a raven's wing, bangs and sides scissored to resemble an inverted bowl—*Can't do a damn thing about those pink cheeks, but maybe a short haircut will make him look a little tougher.* Yasubei searches for signs of himself, but in the boy's soft, moist mouth and big innocent puppy-dog eyes, all he can see is his fragile, long-suffering wife.

Yasubei sighs. "Your mother came to me as a twenty-one-year-old picture bride. She arrived in Honolulu on the same day the *Titanic* sank. An old Hawaiian woman told your mother it was a bad omen. That's why your mother moved back to Japan after you were born, and why she refuses to leave. She's hoping all her bad luck lies buried with the twins in Hawaii.

"Two babies lost. Ten years slaving in the cane fields until we saved enough to return to Honura village and build our house. But then I couldn't find work . . . well . . . none that I could stomach. So I returned alone to Hawaii and sent money home. I've worked my way up from field hand to assistant manager of the plantation store. But now no matter how hard I try, I can't climb any higher. *Haole* rules and laws block me.

"But you, Isamu, you were born in Hawaii. By birthright you're an American citizen. That makes you our family's winning lottery ticket. First you will go to school and master the English language. You will study hard and excel in all your subjects. After high school, you will go to university on the mainland."

"America?"

"Yes, America. You will plant the Hamada family crest on American soil."

"I'll try, Papa."

"Isamu, you are the eldest son of a samurai family. We speak once, then live or die according to our word. Understand?"

The boy nods solemnly. "I *will* do it."

"Good. As the final expression of my destiny, I will throw you like a spear . . . all the way to the American mainland."

Isamu beams, sits tall, puffs out his chest, eager, proud, ready.

Haole

FEBRUARY 1930

IN YOKOHAMA THEY CHECK INTO A SMALL INN. THE OWNERS KNOW Yasubei well—each time he returns home for a visit, he stays with them. Passing through inbound from Hawaii last month, Yasubei had posted flyers on the announcement board outside the inn and at shops, restaurants, and bars in the neighborhood. The innkeeper tells Yasubei, "Lots of fish in your net!"

Yasubei lights a cigarette. "Any keepers?"

The innkeeper shrugs and smiles politely.

In the morning after a breakfast of miso soup, broiled sole, pickled radish, and rice gruel, Isamu peeks outside at a line of men extending down the street and around the corner. He sits at a table next to his father while the men shuffle forward to be interviewed. By lunchtime Yasubei has signed twenty new workers for the sugarcane plantation. The next day they board a ship called the *Taiyo Maru* and steam out of Tokyo Bay. Two weeks later they exit Customs in Honolulu and catch an interisland ferry to Hilo, where Yasubei, swaggering like a samurai warlord, leads his ragtag army down the gangplank.

"Aloha!" Exposing crooked tobacco-dyed teeth in a hard tanned face, Papa's best friend, Kojiro, waves from the shade of a flatbed truck parked on the Hilo docks. "Hey, Yasubei, you brought your boy? Welcome to the Big Island."

Yasubei's work gang begins loading supplies onto Kojiro's truck. The new field hands, grateful to be on solid ground, glad to flex the sea-stiffness from their bodies, work eagerly, bare arms glistening with sweat.

Isamu, all knobby joints and twig limbs, dances around them like a colt among draft horses. Isamu, spinning in a cloud of loud voices, laughter, tobacco smoke, and body odor, bouncing on his toes, wanting to help and trying to get out of the way, trips and sprawls facedown at his father's feet.

Yasubei glares, reaches down with one big hand, grabs the boy by the belt, shakes off the dust, sets him on his feet. "That's it. Everyone in back."

The men jostle past Isamu, toss their suitcases and cloth-wrapped bundles over the boy's head and scramble aboard the flatbed.

"Isamu, in front."

Sitting between Kojiro and Papa, Isamu can barely see over the dashboard.

Yasubei removes his Panama hat and wipes his brow. He loosens his tie and unbuttons his collar. Kojiro turns the key. The engine roars, backfires. A rasp of gears, a neck-jerking lurch, and they're off.

Kojiro drives through Hilo, leaves the town behind. Over the truck rattle and engine noise, Kojiro and Papa shout the latest news, gossip, and dirty jokes. They laugh and hawk and spit out the windows. Isamu hugs the moment to his heart, thinking he is learning a great secret: *This is how men live when they're away from women.*

Isamu is both thrilled and intimidated by Papa and Kojiro's powerful voices and crude language. Reinforced and amplified by the growling jouncing truck, the energy emanating from the two men seems edged and volatile as the vanity of drunken samurai. Isamu peeks at his father. Yasubei snaps open his ornately engraved silver cigarette case, lights two cigarettes, gives one to Isamu to pass to Kojiro. From Papa's hand, rough as tree bark, Isamu lifts the cigarette, and Kojiro snaps it away with callused crab-claw fingers, leaving Isamu pondering the silky softness of his own small hands.

Inhaling deeply, reveling in the tobacco smoke and humid wind pouring through the wide-open windows, Isamu stares out at the vegetation, dense as a tunnel around the winding road. Amid enormous leaves, black branches curl like snakes in the shadows. Strange flowers glow in shafts of sunlight.

Then the truck rolls out of the jungle onto a vast tilting landscape of sugarcane rippling like green fur under the stroking hands of the wind. They pass beneath a lacework of timber supporting an aqueduct two hundred feet above the road. Isamu bumps his head against the dashboard as he cranes his neck to marvel at it. Papa's voice deepens with pride. "The Awaopi'o high flume. Kojiro and I helped build it."

Kojiro leaves the main road, climbs through the cane toward the immense cloud-capped volcano. They rumble by a graveyard. "That's where your brothers are buried." They pass a branch road lined with houses on both sides, a village, but with a name unlike any back home. First, Yasubei calls it "Awaopi'o Camp," then "Japanese Camp." "Over that way are Filipino Camp and Portuguese Camp."

They turn onto a road where the houses are bigger, more generously spaced, pass them and arrive finally at the largest and finest house, isolated above the rest. Squinting through the smoke of a cigarette dangling from his lower lip, Yasubei removes his coat, rolls his sleeves, then helps Kojiro and the men unload supplies from the truck. Yasubei, Kojiro, and the new workers maintain a loud friendly banter as they walk leisurely back and forth, stacking crates, sacks, and barrels on the back porch.

Isamu wanders, finds two horses, a roan mare and a magnificent black stallion tethered in the shade just around the corner of the house. Isamu is staring at the horses, when a voice thunders through an open window, "You there. Boy!"

Yasubei calls, "Isamu! Back in the truck!"

The screen door swings open, and two *haole* men descend the back stairs. The first carries a black whip coiled at his hip. The second wears a pith helmet and a British Army officer's uniform complete with Sam Browne belt, riding breeches, and leggings. His gray beard reaches to his sternum.

Yasubei pulls on his jacket, straightens his collar and tie, adjusts his gold tie clip.

The new workers need no explanation. They withdraw into silence, work faster, bow and dip their heads as they scuttle by Gray Beard and Whip.

Gray Beard strides past the truck and glares at Isamu. Isamu thinks Gray Beard's eyes look like pale blue gemstones. Gray Beard puffs on a cigar, and Isamu grimaces when the smell hits his nose. The boy's focus darts from Gray Beard to the whip attached to the other man's belt.

Gray Beard and Whip mount their horses and ride past the line of laboring men. Isamu hears the clink of glass as Kojiro and Yasubei appear around the truck with more crates.

Gray Beard snaps, "Be careful with those!"

Kojiro and Yasubei grin apologetically, bob their heads. "Yes, sir, Mr.

Boyer." They speak almost in unison, bowing repeatedly as they carry the boxes carefully up the stairs, doing their best not to make another sound.

Watching from the truck, Isamu feels like he has been stabbed in the heart.

As they ride away from the big house, Papa's voice sounds parched and thin. "That was Mr. John T. Boyer, the plantation manager. The other fellow was Mr. Bidwell, one of the foremen. We call them *luna*."

"John T. got a new racehorse," says Kojiro.

Isamu cannot look at Papa and Kojiro, and the pain inside him deepens and spreads. Both men have shrunk. Their pride, their boisterous male energy, their strength . . . reduced to smoke blown away in the wind.

Yasubei lights a fresh cigarette, and Isamu notices his father's hands trembling slightly.

Isamu struggles to understand what cowed his father, how that gray-bearded old man's frost blue eyes could cut down two strong samurai like Yasubei and Kojiro. Crumple them into cringing monkeys.

Isamu recalls what his mother told him: "In Hawaii the *haole* rule. Native Hawaiians, Japanese, Chinese, and Filipinos are their slaves. Your father was the last samurai in his family. You don't know the humiliation he endures to send a little money home each month."

Isamu feels like sobbing and spitting. Pushed and pulled by alternating waves of grief and contempt, shame and rage, he swallows and keeps his eyes straight ahead. *Monkeys! Shrivel-shouldered, cave-chested, cringing little monkeys . . .*

They ride down the hill and stop in front of a large barnlike building. Yasubei and Isamu climb out of the truck. "This is where I work—the Awaopi'o Plantation store." The men unload more supplies, their mood considerably subdued. Then with waves from the new workers and a toot of the horn, Kojiro drives off and leaves Isamu and his father standing beside their luggage.

A gang of barefoot boys, all deeply suntanned, jog by and stare at Isamu. They chatter in a patchwork language, only partly Japanese. One boy points at Isamu and says something that makes the rest laugh.

Eyes lowered, shoulders slumped, Isamu follows his father into the store.

A fair-haired freckle-faced man sits reading behind the counter. Another *haole*. Isamu tenses, watches Papa, waits for the trembling servile monkey to reappear. But this *haole* is different. He puts down his newspaper. "Hey, Yas, welcome back." With a genuine smile the man comes around the counter and pumps Yasubei's hand.

"My son," says Yasubei.

The man puts out his hand. Shyly, Isamu shakes it. His first *haole* handshake.

"Isamu, this is my boss. His name is Mr. John Edward Weight. Say that: Mr. John Edward Weight."

"Mr. John Edward Weight," says Isamu.

Mr. Weight grins. "What's your name, lad?"

"His name is Isamu," says Yasubei.

The corners of Mr. Weight's blue eyes wrinkle. "Well, from now on let's just call him Sam."

"Say, 'Yes, sir. Thank you, Mr. Weight.' "

"Yes, sir. Thank you, Mr. Weight," says Sam.

English

FEBRUARY 1930

IT IS RAINING WHEN YASUBEI AND SAM LEAVE THE STORE. THEY RUN across a side street to a small house on a narrow wedge-shaped lot. Yasubei kicks open the white picket gate, and they run through the yard to the shelter of the porch. Yasubei leaves the bag of groceries in the kitchen, carries his suitcase into his room, and hangs his suit to dry. In his underwear he returns to the kitchen and finds Sam waiting next to the groceries. "The other bedroom's yours. Here, take this." Yasubei hands Sam a pot, opens a cupboard and points to a sack. "You know how to wash and cook rice? No? I'll teach you. It'll be your job from now on."

Yasubei gets a drinking glass and bottle of sake. His hands shake as he pours and pauses, savoring the longing, letting the saliva build in his mouth.

His nostrils flare as he inhales the fragrant rice wine, then he downs it in one long swallow. Sighing with the sad pleasure of a drunk about to binge, he refills his glass. "It's stuffy in here. Open the windows."

While the rice cooks, Yasubei sits at the kitchen table in his underwear. He smokes, drinks, and reads a newspaper. Sam sits across the table and stares down at his hands. Neither speaks. The rain stops, and Sam listens to the soft bubbling of the rice pot and the distant voices of children playing.

Yasubei staggers to his feet, dumps some vegetables on the table. "Chop these." After another glass of sake, he lurches across the room and takes a cast-iron skillet off a nail in the wall. He drops the skillet on the stove, pours in oil, covers the bottom with bacon. "Next time don't cut everything so damn small." Yasubei throws the neat, perfectly sliced onions, carrots, tomatoes, and eggplant into the skillet, lets them sizzle while he has another drink, then cracks six eggs and stirs everything with his chopsticks. Finally, he splashes soy sauce over the mix and puts the skillet and rice pot on the table.

Yasubei eats quickly, refilling his sake glass several times. "When you're done, wash the dishes and go to bed. Tomorrow the plantation siren will wake us at five."

Sam gets up and carries his father's empty plate to the sink.

"Hey, why so glum?"

Sam shrugs. He puts down the plate so carefully, there is no sound.

That night Sam dreams that he and Akemi are stalking fireflies in the garden of their house in Honura village. They already have two in the bamboo-and-mosquito-net cage their mother made. Sam captures one more. Akemi claps her hands with delight.

Sam awakes dream-befuddled in his unfamiliar bedroom. Tiny, bare-walled, smelling of dust and damp wood. Window half-open. Paper shade rolled unevenly, torn edge askew; ring, dangling on its string, tapping the wet glass. Pinprick moons in each droplet, rain calmed to slow steady plops below the eaves. Bedroom door ajar, rimmed with yellow light from the kitchen, where Papa, hoarse and blurry, sings.

Sam thinks tomorrow he will write a letter to his mother, enclose the NYK shipping schedule for Bunji. And for Akemi, he will paint the steamship with its massive black hull, white superstructure, and two smoke-stacks. Sam knows Akemi will think they are the best part of the picture—he will take special care to get them right—two red stripes on a wide white band around the upper half of each big black smokestack. Dark blue sea, light blue sky, white clouds, gulls . . . Does Papa have paints that he can use? Sam starts to cry, tries to stop himself, covers his face with hands still smelling of greasy eggs and onions.

The sound of a chair scraping the kitchen floor. Footsteps. Yasubei appears in the doorway. "What's wrong?"

Sam sits up in bed and fights to stifle his sobs.

"Homesick? You miss your mother and sister and brother?"

Sam nods.

"Don't feel ashamed. We all went through the same thing."

Sam tries so hard to regain control of himself, he feels like he is choking.

"You look around and nothing's familiar."

"Even my name," whispers Sam. "Stolen from me."

Yasubei snorts. "You don't understand. It was a gift. Your new name will help you fit in. Help you build your future. Today an American name. Tomorrow school. Your mother told me you were an excellent student . . . far ahead of the rest of your classmates. I'm proud that you can read and write Japanese. But tomorrow you must make a new start. You'll be in first grade until you learn English. When you go in the classroom, the children will be younger than you, and you won't understand a word. Don't panic. Just sit there and behave yourself. I'll find you a tutor. Education. That's the key. Else you'll end up a stinking laborer like Kojiro or a clerk like me. What you saw today sickened you, yeah? Remember it. I don't want you to have to grovel like me. Not ever."

Sam lowers his gaze. His crying eases, but the ache in his chest doubles, and the last tears he sheds are for his father.

Yasubei returns to the kitchen.

Sam listens to the chair thump and creak as Papa settles himself. Then the clink of the sake bottle against the drinking glass.

In the weeks and months that follow their arrival, Sam's teachers report to Yasubei that the boy has a gift for languages. Back in Japan, Sam's favorite school subjects were reading and writing; he loved practicing calligraphy with *sumi* ink and brush. Now like a patron alternating between two very different restaurants, Sam savors words and phrases on his tongue; to him Japanese tastes familiar, aged and subtle, warm and salty. In contrast English seems youthful, sweet, effervescent, surprising him with pockets that snap, releasing ticklish bubbles.

But under mounting pressure from his father, Sam is not allowed the luxury of feasting like a gourmet. Instead he gorges like a contestant in an eating contest. Sam tries to swallow the English language whole. Month after month he eats, drinks, inhales it, until he feels choked, bloated, bursting. Finally striking a wall, scraping himself raw to claw through, bleeding not blood but words and phrases of English, unable to absorb or retain any more, scared, desperate, and lonely, hunched over the kitchen table one Sunday afternoon, he weeps and curses himself, self-judged and convicted, a failure.

Papa, passed out drunk, snores in the bedroom. Papa's jacket and necktie are draped over the back of his kitchen chair. The gold tie clip and silver cigarette case gleam on the table. Blinking through a blur of tears, Sam stares at the design engraved on the lid of the cigarette case. Amid flowers and ornate curlicues, Sam suddenly notices English letters. He looks closer. They spell out . . . his father's name! *Y. Hamada.*

Sam picks up the cigarette case and turns it over. He has admired the engraving many times, but today the graceful curving lines on the back of the case blossom. The mysterious door called language opens before his eyes.

The engraved lines are not just decorative. They are English calligraphy!

Softly, he unravels the words, feels them resonate like poetry, like sacred text. *Compliments of J. E. Weight, Awaopi'o, Hawaii, August first, 1914.*

An enormous radiant smile filled with clarity and hope spreads across Sam's face. "Yes," he whispers in English. "I can do this."

Engagement

MAY 1930

LEAPFROGGING FROM AMBUSH TO AMBUSH, THE BOYS FIGHT THEIR WAY down the trail through the dense Hawaiian forest. It begins to rain. Realizing the climactic battle has begun, the little soldiers are no longer willing to die honest deaths. Those shot repeatedly at point-blank range jerk spasmodically as the imaginary bullets tear through them. They stagger in circles, curse their enemies, then fall into the nearest puddle.

But the instant their killers' attention is diverted, the dead leap to their feet and fight again. When bullets prove impotent no matter how loudly or repeatedly they are fired, the boys throw down their stick rifles and resort to hand-to-hand combat. Squealing and grunting like wild pigs, they crash through the rain-spattered foliage. They beat upon each other with huge bright flowers, which they pretend are flaming torches. They leap and grapple on the wet, spongy carpet of fallen leaves and delicate ferns.

They tumble down through the forest toward the sea, until they leave the trees behind and fight on the beach under a dark and grumbling sky pelting them with rain. Ready to call a truce, they discover a wide, shallow basin of mud. Joyously they push and drag one another into this new arena and fight on. Finally, panting and dizzy with exhaustion and laughter, they stagger arm in arm into the surf to wash their bodies and clothes.

The rain squall passes. Clean, hot sunlight returns. The soldiers whoop reborn from the sea and resume their combat.

Out past the eastern end of the beach, on the rocks on the far side of Awaopi'o Arch, an old man is fishing alone. His name is Fujiwara, a master carpenter and stonemason held in the highest esteem by the plantation community. Listening to the children playing at war, Fujiwara-san's gaze grows distant with memories of his own boyhood games. Until his father began his formal training—then he spent years practicing with sword, spear, bow, and bare hands. The old man loves the energy in the voices of the children warring on the beach. But he prays none will ever experience the real thing.

"I'm not afraid! Come on! I'll fight you all!"

Fujiwara-san wonders which boy made such a bold declaration. He runs his tough dark hands through his white short-cropped hair, shields his eyes, studies the wiry, coltish child standing alone on the crest of a dune, recognizes the son of Hamada, the store clerk. The other boys form a line and charge. Sam does not hesitate or retreat. He attacks the center of the line. A smile appears on Fujiwara-san's lips. The gang closes around Sam, swarms over him, wrestles him to the ground.

———

During a rest break, the boys spot the man fishing on the rocks beyond the arch. Deciding to investigate, they leave the beach and march along the ridge and cross over the rock arch. They come to the edge of the cliff and climb single file down the steep narrow trail.

Sam follows his new best friend, Fish Mouth Enzo, who warns Sam, "That's Fujiwara-san. He's crazy."

Fujiwara-san is down on his knees. The boys draw near, and the old man puts one finger to his lips. The boys freeze, crouch and watch. The old man holds a thin bamboo pole tipped with a tiny noose of thread. Five feet in front of him, a small crab suns itself on the rocks. With delicate precision, Fujiwara-san drops the noose around one of the crab's protruding eyestalks. Instinctively, the crab jerks in its eyestalk, tightening and trapping the thread. The old man grabs the captured crab, deftly peels away the back shell, and cracks the body in half. He takes two legs, buries the point of his hook in one of them and ties the other to the hook shaft with sewing thread. Then he sets his feet firmly on the rocks, swings the stout hand line several times around his head, and casts far out into the waves.

After the boys watch Fujiwara-san for a while, they grow bored and restless. But as they are about to leave, the old man pulls in his line. "I'm done fishing. I want to go for a swim. Will someone please carry my gear?"

"Looks heavy," says Fish Mouth Enzo.

"I'll give you one flagtail and half a blue jack."

"Good eating. Deal!" Fish Mouth takes Fujiwara-san's gunnysack and fishing tackle.

Fujiwara-san strips to his white cotton loincloth. He rolls his clothes, ties them with his belt, and gives the bundle to Fish Mouth. Fish Mouth passes it to one of the younger kids. "Carry this."

"I'll meet you on the other side of the cove." Fujiwara-san tightens his loincloth, walks into the water, and splashes his chest and arms.

Sam throws his shirt to Fish Mouth.

"Hey," says the old man. "What do you think you're doing?"

"I'm going to swim with you."

"It's farther than it looks."

Sam studies the distant shore.

"There's a current. And the water's cold out there."

Sam shrugs.

"Let's have a race," says Fish Mouth. "You guys swim; we'll run the trail."

"Wait," says Fujiwara-san. He looks sternly at Sam. "What color is the sea?"

Without hesitation Sam answers, "Blue."

"What's the distance from here to the other side of the cove?"

"Fifty yards, maybe sixty . . . I don't know."

"You're not ready to swim with me. Go with your friends."

Sam glances at the boys, then glares at the old man. With a defiant snort, Sam runs past Fujiwara-san and leaps off the rocks into the sea.

"The race is on. Last one to the other side's a dead pig's fart," yells Fish Mouth, and the boys scamper across the rocks and up the trail.

Sam swims so fast that he feels like a flying fish skimming over the surface of the waves. He exhales curses into the water. He'll show that arrogant old man. They'll see who's the best swimmer. And he kicks up a wild, frothing wake behind him.

He squints down; the shallow sloping bottom reflects a friendly pale green warmth up into his face. Just ahead he sees the rim of light dropping away into darkness.

Suddenly, he swims into a current so cold he gasps with surprise.

He looks up. The opposite shore seems very far away. Below him, the depths absorb all the light. He cannot see the bottom. He looks back. He is shocked at how far out he is.

There is no sign of the old man.

Fighting his fear, Sam visualizes a long white rope stretching between a big tree ahead and Awaopi'o Arch behind him. The imaginary rope marks his course. He swims, pushing himself to his fastest pace and holding it until his breath grows irregular, and he accidentally inhales water. Coughing and sputtering, he raises his head. The opposite shore seems no closer. He looks back and realizes he is off course.

The current is carrying him away from shore.

Silence Within

MAY 1930

TEETH CHATTERING, SAM TREADS WATER. HE CAN NO LONGER SEE HIS tree. Scanning the distant forest, he feels the current pulling him. He spots a big tree but is not sure if it is the correct one. It doesn't matter. He swims for it.

He swims until his arms, legs, and lungs burn. He swims until he is crying and his spirit cowers like a baby monkey alone in the corner of a damp steel cage.

The shoreline looks farther than when he last checked. There are no big trees in sight. He looks back. Above the waves, he can barely see Awaopi'o Arch.

Just then, he hears singing coming from the open sea. Sam cannot make out the words, but he sees old man Fujiwara calmly breaststroking amid the waves.

Sam stifles his tears. "Hey! I'm . . . I'm tired."

"Tired?" Fujiwara-san swims to the boy. "Rest. Float on your back." He puts a hand under Sam's head for support. "Breathe in through your nose and out through your mouth. And say: 'I inhale strength, I exhale fear.' "

"The current's taking us away from shore."

The old man's voice is clear and calm. " 'I inhale strength, I exhale fear.' Say it."

Through chattering teeth Sam quickly mutters the peculiar refrain.

"Good. Again. Slower."

"I inhale strength, I exhale fear."

"Inhale deeply, exhale fully. And say it again."

"I inhale strength, I exhale fear." From the corner of his eye, Sam peeks at Fujiwara-san. The old man is floating on his back and gazing at the clouds.

"Say: 'My breath is the sky, my body's the sea.'"

"My breath is the sky, my body's the sea."

"Say: 'My strength is without limit, my spirit is filled with gratitude.'"

"My strength's without limit, my spirit's filled with gratitude."

Sam realizes that his breathing has returned to normal. He rolls over. The shoreline looks terribly far away.

Fujiwara-san yawns. "Such a nice day for a swim. Let's not hurry." He strokes gracefully, effortlessly forward. Sam has no difficulty matching the old man's pace.

"Let's study this current. Let's see if we can merge with it and ride it."

"It'll pull us out to sea."

"It's not strong enough to do that."

"It isn't?"

"Didn't we just breathe in all the strength of the sky?"

For a moment Sam says nothing. Then he mutters, "That was just words."

"Really? Then we'll probably both die out here."

Shocked, Sam stares at Fujiwara-san. Fish Mouth was right. The old man is crazy.

Fujiwara-san strokes slowly, speaking in a calm, untroubled voice. "When you're caught in an overpowering force, you can move with it or break. Moving with it may feel frightening; however, you do not have to move haphazardly or helplessly. Just remember that nothing in the universe travels forever in a straight line. Sooner or later everything bends or curves. Everything changes. Impermanence is the law. Once you merge with a force, the force cannot find you. Once you learn its rhythm you can move within it, and it cannot hold you. Move to its rim, and you can ride it. Move to its axle, and you can spin it like a wheel on your finger."

"I don't understand what you're talking about. All I want to do is go home."

Fujiwara-san laughs. "Home? We are home."

They swim at the old man's pace. To his astonishment and relief, Sam watches the shoreline growing closer. "Hey, where's the current?"

"It's wearing us . . . like a tattoo."

Because he no longer fights the current, Sam is not sure of the exact moment they leave it behind. However, he notices the water growing warmer and the shoreline drawing closer. Sam grins with an overpowering sense of accomplishment. He wants to swim fast now, a final exuberant sprint. But the old man grabs his arm. "Stop."

"What's wrong?"

"Don't move. Just be still and float for a moment."

Sam senses the movement of something huge and dark. He thinks it is the shadow of a cloud. Then he realizes that the darkness has passed *under* them.

"What was that?" whispers Sam.

"A shark."

"Did he go away?"

"No. He's circling." The old man's voice is calm but serious. "They say a shark won't attack something larger than himself. We're about to learn if that's true. We'll make no jerky motions. We'll make no awkward splashes. I'll be right behind you. Whatever happens, don't look back and don't stop until you've reached shore."

"But what if the shark—"

"We are a sea turtle. You're the head and front flippers. I'm the body and back flippers; and this is"—he unwinds his loincloth—"our long white beard."

Sam begins swimming. Fujiwara-san's voice is right behind him. "Good. That's right, nice smooth strokes. Ah, yes . . . and there he is. Hello, Mr. Shark."

Off to his left Sam sees a tall hooked fin moving parallel to them.

"Mr. Shark, we respect you, but do not fear you. You are a child compared to us. We are the dream and wisdom within the waves, an ancient sea turtle, one thousand years old."

Suddenly the dorsal fin veers toward them and submerges. Sam feels and sees an immense darkness rippling just below him. His instinct is to draw in his arms and legs or to flail the water to frighten the monster away. But the old man's calm voice keeps his strokes smooth and steady. "We are the salt, and we are the water. We are the sound and the motion. We are the light and shadow within the kelp forest, the texture within the coral and lava, the silence within the smile of the Amida Buddha."

The shark turns. This time Sam is certain it will strike. He hears the old man praying. "*Namu Amida Butsu, Namu Amida Butsu, Namu Amida Butsu.*"

They are almost to shore. But as he rises and falls with the swells, Sam does not alter his stroke in any way. Suddenly, he feels something coarse scrape hard against his knees. He cries out, thinking the shark has got him. Then he realizes it is sand.

He stands up. A small wave strikes him, and he stumbles and falls. He stands up a second time and walks out of the water on trembling legs. He looks back and sees old man Fujiwara standing naked in knee-deep water. Holding one end of his long white loincloth, Fujiwara-san is gazing toward the open sea.

From the edge of the cliff high above the narrow beach, Fish Mouth Enzo's voice descends. "Hey, you guys!"

Sam looks up and sees his new best friend silhouetted against the sky. Fish Mouth has both arms stretched way out. "Did you see the shark?"

Colors

SEPTEMBER 1930

ON A RAINY FRIDAY AFTERNOON EIGHT MONTHS AFTER ARRIVING IN Hawaii, Sam returns from schools and puts his books on the kitchen table next to Papa's big pale blue bottle of sake. On a whim Sam pours himself a drink, followed by another and another until he passes out on the kitchen floor.

Yasubei shakes his son awake.

Sam laughs and belches in his father's face. "Papa, I feel like rubber. It's wonderful! Now we can drink together."

Yasubei takes off his belt and beats his son bloody.

The following day, Yasubei, sober and nauseated with shame, takes his bruised, limping son to Fujiwara-san's house. Yasubei drops to his knees before Fujiwara-san. Yasubei bows until his forehead touches the floor. He begs the old man to take Sam as a student, to develop the boy's character, to save him from becoming a miserable drunk like his father.

When Sam tells his friends that he has started working after school for Fujiwara-san, they laugh. Nervously. "I'm afraid of him," admits Fish Mouth Enzo. "I wouldn't work for him in a million years."

"Never mind your friends," says Papa. "Fujiwara-sensei's skill is beyond their comprehension. Play with your friends, practice English with them. But when you're with the old man, speak your best Japanese and mind your manners. Do whatever Fujiwara-sensei tells you. Pay attention. Remember his every word. Watch him."

Sam shrugs. What's there to see? An old man, barely five feet six, with a sturdy laborer's body of perhaps 140 pounds. Short, snow-white hair. Except for the hair color, the description fits most of the adult Japanese males on the plantation.

The first day Sam shows up to work in Fujiwara-san's vegetable garden, the old man hands the boy a hoe. "What color is the dirt?"

"Brown."

The old man waits, disappointment gathering in his eyes. "Start hoeing. And don't forget to breathe."

"How could I forget to do that?"

"I want you to breathe with your belly. Inhale down to your toes."

Sam sputters and laughs. Biology is one of Sam's favorite school subjects. With a voice full of pride and authority, Sam describes the anatomy of lungs. "And they end right about here," he concludes, cupping both hands on his rib cage.

Fujiwara-san nods. "Inhale all the way down to the soles of your feet and up to the tips of the hairs on the top of your head." He turns and walks away.

Sam laughs and calls after him, "I told you. Air can't travel that far."

"Air?" The old man pauses at the gate. "We're not just talking of air."

After six months of working in Fujiwara-san's garden and carrying his carpentry toolbox all over the plantation, Sam concludes, "He's harmless."

Fish Mount Enzo shakes his head. "He's still asking about colors?"

"Yeah. He never stops. What color's the river? What color's the back of your hand? What color's that cloud? It's just a stupid game. The more colors I name, the more points I get."

"But there's more to it than that."

Yes, thinks Sam. *There's the stillness.*

Sam has never met anyone more profoundly calm than Fujiwara-san. Walking, standing or sitting, even laughing or talking, within and surrounding the old man there exists a constant field of tranquillity. But it isn't just that he always seems calm and relaxed. There is a deeper quality that captures Sam's respect and imagination. The old man is like a clear, still night.

A pond smooth as a black mirror reflecting the full moon.

Absolute serenity.

But aware of the softest breeze.

Old Enough

APRIL 1933

THE JAPANESE-LANGUAGE TEACHER, IMAGAWA-SENSEI, WRITES A LIST OF words in English on the blackboard, and the young students begin writing the words in Japanese using brush and *sumi* ink. Sam, the assistant teacher, walks the aisles between the desks and helps the students—correcting their strokes, reminding them to lay down each stroke in proper order, checking their calligraphy for stroke length and width. Sam loves Japanese calligraphy, so simple and so complex, the look of the dense black ink on stark white paper. He takes his seat beside the teacher's desk and writes the words.

Imagawa-sensei checks Sam's work. Sam's brushwork expresses his nature and his growing character—energetic, bold, developing some grace but not yet shed of the awkwardness of youth. Imagawa-sensei dips his own brush in red ink and lays down a few strokes on top of Sam's. "Everything you've written is correct and perfectly readable, but you must be mindful of balance and proportion. . . ."

Sam nods. "Oh, yes, I see what you mean."

Imagawa-sensei smiles and hands Sam a book. "For next month's special assignment, I want a three-page report. Choose your favorite passage or chapter and tell me why you liked it."

Sam takes the book and opens it.

"No, don't start reading now. Today we are practicing our writing. We have about thirty minutes of class time remaining. Why don't you write a letter home to your mother?"

Sam puts away the book and gets a fresh sheet of paper. He stares at the blank page for a moment then starts.

Friday, April 28, 1933

Honorable Mother, Bunji, and Akemi,

It has been three years and four months since I left Japan. Next month I will be thirteen. I am busy all the time. I go to school, and some afternoons I work in the store with Papa and Mr. John Edward Weight. Other afternoons I work for Fujiwara-san. And the rest of the time I am a teaching assistant at the Japanese-language school—I know that probably sounds like bragging. But of course the reason is that even though almost all my friends can speak Japanese, I am the only child in my class who was taught to read and write in Japan. They call me a kibei—one educated in Japan.

Most Sunday afternoons I play with my friends.

I am not complaining. I am satisfied with every part of my life, except the time I spend working for Fujiwara-san. I thought Papa and Fujiwara-san had an agreement. I thought Fujiwara-san was supposed to teach me martial arts. But he has not. Not a single kick or punch. Nor said one word about fighting or swords or anything like that. Whenever I try to talk about it, he changes the subject or ignores me. I think he just wanted free help with his chores. Maybe he was a great samurai when he was young. But now he is too old and crazy to teach anything to anyone. Or maybe he doesn't want to teach. Maybe he wants to keep all his knowledge for himself. My friends are taking jujitsu lessons from a man who has a black belt from a school in Osaka. Fish Mouth Enzo has been urging me to join the class. His parents bought him a uniform. When I saw Fish Mouth wearing it, I felt sick with envy. I wanted one, too. I never wanted anything so much in my life. My friends are becoming really strong. They are learning how to fight. They are leaving me behind.

This week Papa has gone to Honolulu on business for the plantation store. I am alone, and I've had time to think about things. I have de-

cided to quit working for Fujiwara-san. I have kept his garden weeded, and swept his house, porch, and walkways spotless. I've lugged his heavy toolbox all over the plantation. I've sawed and hammered and pulled nails. I've carried lumber and mixed cement. I've shoveled tons of dirt and sand and gravel. And talk about wasting time—I cannot tell you how many hundreds of hours we have spent playing name the colors! I can't stomach it any longer.

Papa may be displeased. But you know how impatient he is. He would never have waited this long. I really like Fujiwara-san. That is the only reason I have not already quit. I want to join the martial arts class with my friends. Maybe Papa will buy me a uniform for my birthday. Thirteen! Old enough to make some decisions for myself.

I will not quit until Papa comes home from Honolulu. Or maybe I will wait until after my birthday in May. But I have made my decision.

With my most humble respect, Isamu

Blue *Ulua*

APRIL 1933

SUNDAY AFTERNOON. THE BOYS RUN ALONG THE TRAIL TOWARD Awaopi'o Cove. They carry rope, fishing line, and baling wire. They plan to collect logs and build a raft. When they arrive at the beach, they see Fujiwara-san fishing from the rocks beyond the arch.

"You guys start the raft," says Sam. "I need to talk with him."

"Going to tell him you quit?" asks Fish Mouth.

"Yeah." Sam jogs away across the beach and climbs the rocks toward the old man.

When Sam joins him, Fujiwara-san smiles and passes the boy the hand line. "Maintain the tension. Can you feel the little fish nibbling on the bait?"

The line vibrates rhythmically. Sam watches the waves surging back and forth, and he realizes the vibration is the background music of the sea. Within that hum are intermittent snaps and pops like someone plucking sharply at the fish line.

"Feel those? Little fish stealing bits of bait."

"Why don't you try to catch them?"

"I never try to catch anything. I just wait until a fish swallows the hook. I use big hooks. Won't fit in a little fish's mouth. Any fish that can swallow the hook, it's exactly the right size."

"I bet you don't catch a lot of fish that way."

"You're right. Sometimes I wait all day while little fish nibble away the bait, then I pack up my gear and go home and eat rice and pickled vegetables."

They stand silently beside each other. Sam takes a deep breath. *This is it. I'm going to tell him I quit.*

Just then the old man asks, "What color is the sea?"

The boy sighs. *Okay, one last time.* "I see light blue and dark blue and gray and green and black and white and yellow and orange. I see green. Gray-green, dull green, bright green, yellow-green, blue-green." He goes on listing each color he sees in, under, and on the water.

The old man smiles as if the boy is reciting a favorite poem. When Sam stops, Fujiwara-san says, "Any more?"

Sam looks for a while. Then he points out the creamy tan stains in the white foam. The old man nods as if he and the boy are involved in a deep philosophical discussion and Sam has just made an especially profound observation.

The fish stop nibbling. Fujiwara-san tells Sam to pull in the line. The hook comes up clean and shiny. The old man cracks crab legs, baits his hook. He casts the line, hands it once more to Sam. Fujiwara-san kneels, rinses his fingers in a tide pool; a tiny film of oil spreads across the surface. It looks pale purple and blue and pink. Sam mentions the iridescent colors; Fujiwara-san nods and smiles gently.

Just then the line twangs and runs out through Sam's fingers. Sam grabs the line tight with both hands. The line zips out fast and hard, burning and cutting his flesh. "Ow!" Sam lets go. "Sorry. I've lost it."

The line suddenly jerks taut with an odd sound. The end of the line is tied to an automobile inner tube roped to the rocks.

Sam grabs the line, begins hauling it in. "It's huge!"

The old man nods with satisfaction. "Just the right size."

Sam never realized a fish could be this strong. Hand over hand, he struggles to bring in the line.

Sam hears Fish Mouth Enzo yelling from the cliff trail. Sam ignores him. Within moments Sam's friends appear on the rocks beside him. Dancing excitedly, they yell encouragement and advice.

Fujiwara-san does not say a word. He stands very still, watching.

"Let me help you," says Fish Mouth Enzo.

"No! Keep your hands off it."

The boys yell conflicting advice. "Pull it in. No, ease up. Don't let the line go slack. Pull harder. Watch out, you're pulling too hard. You'll tear the hook loose."

The line zigzags through the waves. Hand over hand, Sam draws the fish closer. It jumps out of the water. Fish Mouth shouts, "It's a blue *ulua*!"

In the midst of the boys' screaming, old man Fujiwara leans close and speaks directly into Sam's ear. "What color is the shadow of the fish?"

The fish is streaking back and forth. Sam can barely see it moving over the shallow coral rocks. "What? The shadow?"

Just then the line goes slack. Sam staggers backward. The boys groan in unison. "Aw, you just lost the biggest blue jack I've seen all year!"

"The color of the shadow," repeats Fujiwara-san.

Sam stares into the water, but the *ulua* has disappeared. "I can't see it anymore. It's gone."

"Close your eyes."

Sam shuts his eyes. Instantly, he sees the blue jack. Sees it leaping once, bright and vivid, falling, blurring back and forth. He sees the taut line, beads of water bouncing off to sparkle momentarily in the sunlight. He sees the *ulua* and the ripples ripping across the surface of the water. He sees a sliver of darkness flitting against the coral. "The shadow had no color. It just darkened the colors it passed over."

"And what were those?"

"Tan. Pink. Purple. Black. Orange. Blue-green, emerald green, and a kind of brownish-reddish-purple seaweed color."

"Yes!" Fujiwara-san claps his hands and laughs with delight. Sam opens his eyes.

Fish Mouth Enzo, face red with rage, screams, "You crazy old man! What are you cackling about? The damn fish got away."

"True," says Fujiwara-san, "but the boy caught the shadow."

"Huh?" says Fish Mouth. All the boys stand about in slack-jawed confusion.

Fujiwara-san pulls in the line, puts fresh bait on the hook. He gives Sam a pleased smile, leans close, and speaks softly, gently: "Isamu, today you passed an important test. But now you and your friends go play. You're all too agitated. You'll scare away the fish."

Fish Mouth gives the old man a wary sideways glance and grabs Sam. "Come on, let's go work on our raft." Walking back to the beach, Fish Mouth gives Sam tips—things he should remember next time he hooks a big fish. Sam nods politely, but really, Sam hardly hears him.

The boys roll logs together. Sam works as hard as any of them, but every once in a while, he stops and puzzles over what has happened. And he finds himself looking around in utter amazement at the profusion of colors he is seeing. In the logs, in the faces of his friends, in the beach and the forest and the shadows of the clouds passing slowly over the water.

Sam decides to go back and ask Fujiwara-san some questions, but when the boy looks over at the rocks, he sees that the old man has gone.

Mu

MAY 1933

MONDAY, MAY EIGHTH, SAM'S THIRTEENTH BIRTHDAY. HE WALKS alone up a red dirt road through fields of green cane bowing under the wind. He crests a hill, looks back, and pauses a moment with the realization that almost everything he sees belongs to the plantation—the cane fields, the sugar mill, the plantation store, the workers' houses, the contracts of the workers themselves. . . . Light and color shimmer in the cane. From the cliffs overlooking the sea to the barren slopes of the snowcapped volcano, the cane ripples in rhythmic hissing waves.

He resumes walking. The road narrows, the tall cane closes around him until he feels like a mouse in a maze. The terrain drops steeply, and the road switches back and forth. The air grows hot and still. Sam hears the wind dying in the cane and then the rush of water from somewhere ahead.

Sam rounds a bend, sees Fujiwara-san standing with his legs wide apart, one foot on the bank and the other on a rock in the stream. His right arm hangs relaxed at his side, a hammer in his hand. He is building a support form for a small bridge; bags of cement are stacked nearby, waiting to be mixed and poured into the wooden forms. The old man waves at Sam. Sam holds up a cloth-wrapped bundle. "Lunchtime."

During lunch, Sam pokes at his food with his chopsticks. Finally, unable to eat, he speaks. "I'm sorry."

Fujiwara-san, mouth full of rice, pauses, waits for the boy to continue.

"I know a true samurai never breaks his word. I told my mother and my friends that I was going to quit working for you."

"Why did you make that decision?"

"I got impatient. I thought you weren't . . . teaching me anything. I didn't understand that your lessons had already started. I'm sorry it's taken me so long to appreciate you. Thank you for being patient and not giving up on me. My decision to quit working for you was a mistake. Do you think it's okay for me to break my word to Mama and my friends? I really want to continue working for you."

"If one makes an error in judgment, the honorable path is to admit it and work to correct the mistake. Isamu, broken promise or not, what would you call a person who proceeded along a path they knew was wrong?"

"A fool! But Papa says samurai spoke once, then lived or died according to their word."

Fujiwara-san nods. "Which explains why samurai spent so much time scowling and practicing with their weapons and so little time talking."

It takes a moment before Sam realizes the old man is joking. Sam laughs with relief and bows deeply. "From now on, I promise I'll pay closer attention."

The old man puts down his bowl, lunch finished. "Go home now."

"Why?" the boy stammers. "Are you mad at me?"

"No. First, stop at the plantation store. Your father has a birthday present for you."

Sam's face lights up with a shy surprised smile. "Really?"

Fujiwara-san continues his instructions. "I want you to run all the way. Run slowly, so you can maintain the same speed for the entire distance. But don't loaf. Breathe deep. Be sure to empty your lungs. Feel your sweat. Before you touch your birthday present, take a bath. Wash yourself thoroughly, your hair, your teeth. Purify yourself. Then go to my house. Wait for me in the backyard."

Sam stands.

"And there is something I want you to memorize while you run."

The boy nods.

The old man takes a paintbrush from his toolbox. He dips it in the stream then writes an ideogram on the side of the empty bridge form. Even as he writes, the water soaks into the warm wood and is evaporating, fading. "*Mu*: nothing, no thing. Emptiness. To throw away."

"*Mu?*" says Sam.

"And along the way, if you see any bees or butterflies . . ."

"Yes?"

"Contemplate them."

Sam gathers the lunch things and begins the long jog down the hill. *Another of the old man's riddles. Mu . . . What does it mean? Nothing. No thing. Emptiness. To throw away. To throw away what? If you have nothing, how can you throw it away? Maybe mu is the emptiness left after you throw something away?*

Yasubei looks up as Sam enters the store.

Hands on his hips, Sam paces back and forth in front of the counter. Sam drips sweat, gasps for air.

"What's wrong?"

"Nothing, Papa. Just been running. Fujiwara-san sent me. He said, uh . . . you had . . . a birthday present. Please."

Yasubei smiles. From behind the counter he takes a bundle wrapped in plain brown paper, tied with white cotton twine. "Happy birthday."

Sam holds the bundle awkwardly.

"Open it."

"Fujiwara-san told me to take a bath before I touched it. Please, could you open it for me?" He hands the bundle back to his father.

Yasubei sets the gift on the counter between them. He unties the knot and spreads the paper.

Sam's eyes widen. A jacket, pants, and a belt. All made of coarse white cotton. A martial arts uniform. "Papa . . . Thank you. Thank you so much. I . . ." His voice cracks, his eyes fill with tears.

"Your mother sewed this uniform for you. Your sister, Akemi, made the belt."

Sam is too choked to speak.

"Well, what're you waiting for? Try it on."

"I'm sorry, Papa. I'm not supposed to touch it until I've . . . purified myself."

"He told you that?"

Sam nods. "Then I'm supposed to go to his house and wait."

Yasubei nods, gazes deep into his son's shining eyes, then says the same words his father once said to him. "Today you begin your training."

An hour later, scrubbed pink, dressed in his new white uniform, Sam waits in Fujiwara-san's backyard. Sam paces and hops, kicking and punching. He watches bees in the garden. Listens to them buzz, wonders what they have to do with *mu*.

The old man appears wearing a martial arts uniform, his hair wet from his bath. He helps Sam retie his belt. "Watch how I make the knot. Like so . . . Not too tight. Not too loose. It rides low on your hips, the knot about a hand's width below your navel." Fujiwara-san steps back, inspects Sam.

Sam feels like a racehorse waiting for the starting gun. What will the old man teach him first? How to kick? How to punch? Maybe a throw?

"Today," says Fujiwara-san, "we practice bowing."

"Bowing?"

"Yes. How to bow. How to stand. How to sit."

Sam nods vigorously, bounces on his toes, unable to suppress his excitement. "And then you're going to teach me jujitsu?"

"No."

"Karate?"

"No."

"What then?"

"Let's call it *mu*."

"I don't understand. What kind of fighting style is that?"

Old man Fujiwara shrugs. "The name bothers you? Change it. Call it bees-and-butterflies."

A look of intense disappointment crosses Sam's face.

"What's wrong?"

"My friends are going to die laughing." Sam sighs, then brightens—*Let the old man call it whatever he wants. Today, this moment, my training begins!* Sam grew up in Japan; he knows that every martial arts class begins and ends with a bow. Eagerly, Sam bows to his teacher.

Fujiwara-sensei returns the bow, then shakes his head. "Again. Not just to me, Isamu. To the training."

An hour later, Sam is still bowing. Off to one side the old man sits on a wooden bench. "Again, Isamu. Calmly." Sam stands bowing toward the vegetable garden, where bees work in the golden haze of the late-afternoon sun. The old man shakes his head. "Too stiff. Try again."

Sam bows.

"Again. From your center. Express your deepest humility. Allow respect to suffuse your whole being."

Sam bows.

"Again. Hello and *sayonara* in the same motion."

Sam giggles. "Hello, bees. Good-bye, bees."

"By the end of next month they'll all be dead. Gone and replaced. But see how hard they work for the survival of their clan? With selfless diligence each performs her duty—"

"Her?"

"Worker bees are all female. Didn't you know that?"

Sam shakes his head.

"They're samurai women. To protect their hive, they unsheath their swords and attack, even though they know that to use their swords once means to die."

"Do they know that?"

"What do you think?"

"I think they don't know."

"Would it matter to them? Would they refuse to attack if they knew it would mean throwing away their lives?"

"No, I don't think so."

"Do you hear any complaints, any fear or sorrow in their voices?"

Sam listens carefully. "No, they sound happy. And"—perhaps it is a trick of the breeze harmonizing with the barely audible buzz—"it sounds . . ."

Sam feels a mysterious electricity shiver up his spine. "It sounds," he whispers, "like they're singing *mmmmmuu*." Without thinking, the boy bows slowly toward the bees.

"Perfect," says the old man. "That's how you should bow each time."

Sam practices bowing for a month. Then Fujiwara-san teaches him how to fall—fall, tuck, and roll like a ball. Constantly admonished to protect his head and spine, Sam practices falling from various heights in every direction. The old man pushes and shoves him forward, backward, sideways, slowly and gently at first, then quicker and harder. Each session the falling becomes more demanding. Sam sprints across the yard and dives headfirst over a four-foot hurdle. Curving through the air, he tucks and rolls on the grass. They move the hurdle, and Sam practices landing on sand, then pea gravel, then a canvas tarp spread over crushed lava. Even when alone, he practices. Running to and from school or the plantation store—from the moment his training began, his instructions have been to run whenever possible—he drops his books and flings himself through the air to land and roll onto his feet in a single, fluid motion.

He is introduced to his first throw. The old man walks Sam through the setup, entry, execution, and follow-through. Again and again they move through the steps, slowly as dancers immersed in glue. Each time the old man allows himself to be thrown. Building speed and power, until Sam feels like he could topple a tree or toss a horse over a house, Sam executes the movements, and Fujiwara-san falls.

Without warning the old man spins Sam like a wheel on a frictionless axle. Over in a blink, it is the most amazing sensation Sam has ever experienced—his body flipped and spinning through the air. Without conscious thought, his body reacts. He lands perfectly and painlessly. Even as the grass is springing back, the boy rolls leaping to his feet to face his sensei with eyes full of wonder and respect.

Sam had felt *it*. The magic. He could have read a million books, watched a million demonstrations and never understood, never even grazed the knowledge that had just been injected permanently into the marrow of his bones. The feeling. The tiniest whip crack of energy, pure, devoid of anger or desire to defeat or conquer; and yet immense, the force of the sun spinning planets and comets into orbits of perfect balance; weightless and invisible, his own flesh and bone lightened to a puff of wind so far beyond transparent . . . no wonder the old man called *it* empty. Force without force, mass rendered weightless and spun around a void of absolute stillness, all of it whole, all of it nothing.

Once shown that such magic existed as a real human possibility—that it was . . . what? A *skill*? A thing that he himself might be able to master? Sam wanted *it*.

He embraces his training. Tracks, hunts, chases after *it* with wholehearted devotion. And the longer he seeks *it,* the more elusive and mysterious *it* becomes. As he dives ever deeper into the mystery, digging and sieving for the essence, the training shapes his body, mind, and spirit.

Bamboo

MAY 1934

On his fourteenth birthday, Sam receives a practice session that carries him beyond the limits of his endurance. He is being tested on his favorite throw. But today, it does not work. No matter how quickly, carefully, or powerfully he tries, the old man does not fall. Nor will Fujiwara-san allow Sam to stop or rest. "Again, Isamu. Try again."

Sam's limbs tremble and burn with fatigue. With a lurch and lunge, Sam tries the throw for the 417th time.

"Again. Spin. Spin like a wheel. Crack like a whip."

Four hundred eighteen. "Again." Four nineteen. "Don't cheat. Give yourself totally to the throw, each throw your first and last." Four twenty. "Try without trying. Let the throw come through you like a breath or heartbeat." Four twenty-one. "Don't think. Don't plan. Just move." Four twenty-two. "Again." Four twenty-three. "Eyes open. Remain clear. See the colors." Four twenty-four. "Again." Sam's body runs slick with sweat.

"Again." His arms and legs are molten lava. "Again. Again. Again." Sam's mouth hangs open, throat and lungs scorched raw. But the old man will not let him quit. "Again." Four fifty-nine. "Again."

They move across the lawn together. Sam feels like he is dancing with smoke. Fujiwara-san yields to every push or pull as though he has no substance. *Mu.* Whenever Sam attacks, he encounters either cloud or mountain, either he's grasping at fog or trying to lift a mountain with a core of iron. "Again." Four hundred ninety-seven failed attempts.

Every fifty tries, Fujiwara-san throws Sam. Even though he knows it's coming, each time, it catches Sam by surprise. High, low, moving left, right, forward or back, the throw strikes sharp as a bee sting, then is gone like a secret whispered in a dream.

"Again." Sam has lost count. "Again." Sam's pulse thunders like *taiko* drums in his ears. "Again." He blinks, sweat burning his eyes. "Again." The old man's voice calm, gentle, patient. "Again, Isamu. Don't give up."

Sam attacks and the old man evades and counters forcefully, slamming the boy to the ground. Stunned, Sam is momentarily unable to rise.

Fujiwara-san kneels, leans close to Sam's face, gazes steadily into Sam's eyes. "Someday . . . when you are beaten and exhausted and all is lost . . . you will hear my voice in your ear. *Isamu, go the distance.*"

"Yes, Sensei . . ." Sam pants hard for every word. "I will." He rises and attacks. Again and again he tries. Now barely conscious of his movements. And no strength left. "I . . ." Arms gone. Legs and back going. "Will."

"Again."

"Again."

"Again."

And suddenly, there *it* is. Tiny. A raindrop striking the sea. Sam feels the effortless spinning sensation, assumes he's been thrown. But to Sam's amazement, Fujiwara-san hits the ground. Smoothly, the old man rolls onto his feet and steps back. "Good."

Gasping, panting, Sam raises both fists, crows, "I did it! I got *it*!"

"You did nothing. Except finally get out of *its* way."

"What? What do you mean?"

"Isamu, stop talking."

"But—"

"Be still, Isamu. Be still."

Sam stares at his sensei. Where is the praise? He finally got *it*.

"Isamu, you want to hold *it* in the light like a diamond. You want to drink *it*, savor *it*, allow *it* to soak into you. You want to grab *it*, hug *it*, breathe *it*, feel *it* in every part of your body, even to the tips of your hair and the roots of your teeth. But you cannot. You don't own *it*, nor can you ever own *it*. Because *it* is nothing. *It* is *mu*."

"Sensei—"

The old man's fist blurs and his knuckles rap sharply on top of Sam's head. The boy snaps into a state of startled, speechless attention. Fujiwara-san bends from the waist. Automatically, Sam returns the bow. "Happy birthday, Isamu." The old man turns and walks away, leaving the boy standing alone in the garden.

Another year of school, work, teaching, and practice. Another birthday. Fifteen and cocky as a rooster, Sam follows Fujiwara-san up a narrow trail into a bamboo grove. They stop. Not in a true clearing but an open space little more than enough to fit them both. Sam is instructed to stand with his eyes closed. He cannot see the old man moving around tying strips of fabric on the bamboo. "Isamu, are you ready to be tested?"

"Yes, Sensei."

"When you hear my sword, dodge it and open your eyes."

Sam waits, moving his head slowly from side to side, listening to the noise of the wind in the bamboo. Then hears a soft sudden *whoosh* and feels the old man's bamboo sword tap his left shoulder. "There!"

"Too late. Keep your eyes closed."

Sam waits. Again the barely audible *whoosh* followed instantly by a gentle tap on his right shoulder. "Too late," mutters Sam.

Again and again and again the tiny whisper and tap. *This test is impossible.* Sam feels an overwhelming urge to peek. But he refuses to cheat. He knows the old man will never give up on him. The old man has faith that he can do this. With this certainty in his heart, Sam stands there aching to pass the test. But with each *whoosh* and tap, he fails and fails and fails, until his muscles and nerves are like a pane of glass twisted to the edge of shattering.

"Isamu, you travel in the wrong direction. You've lost yourself because you're holding yourself too tightly. Reclaim yourself by throwing yourself away. *Mu*."

Sam draws a deep breath, relaxes. *Whoosh,* tap. "Better," says the old man. A long pause. *Whoosh,* tap.

"Sensei, I can't do it. My ears aren't good enough."

"Did I . . ." *Whoosh,* tap. ". . . say anything about using your ears? Keep traveling. You're moving toward your center now. Find the stillness at the core."

Whoosh, tap.

Stillness at the core. Birdsong and bamboo creaking, rustling, hissing. *Whoo*—Sam moves left, and the bamboo sword flashes past his right shoulder. His eyes snap open.

Instantly, the old man's voice calls, "Red!"

Sam's eyes target the bits of colored fabric tied in the bamboo all around him. His hands and feet blur. He counts each piece of red fabric he kicks or punches. "One-two-three-four-five!"

"Stop!"

Sam freezes. He returns to the ready position. He closes his eyes.

"You missed two and four."

Sam nods and waits. *Whoosh,* tap. He breathes deeply, slowly. *Whoosh*—Sam pivots clear of the bamboo sword.

"White and brown!"

"One-two." Sam counts his hits. "One-two-three."

"And black."

"One-two-three-four!"

"And red."

"One-two-three-four-five!"

"It's not enough to hit your targets. Maintain proper form. Strike with focused power. Back to ready."

"Yes, Sensei."

June 1936. Sixteen, tanned and lean and hard, reflexes honed sharp as a samurai's sword. Stripped to a white loincloth, Sam stands, eyes closed in the bamboo grove with his sensei. Wind and rain gust through the thin leaves and swaying branches. There is no sign of tension in the boy's stance. Water runs down his neck, down the smooth muscular curves of his chest, shoulders, and arms.

The old man's wooden sword slashes through the rain, and Sam leaps clear.

Sam's hands, feet, knees, and elbows strike the scattered hints of color—now no longer pieces of cloth, but mere bits of thread tied to the bamboo. Counting the strikes, Sam's voice is calm and certain.

Kiai

JUNE 1936

SAM AND FUJIWARA-SAN WEAR WHITE UNIFORMS IN THE MIDST OF A tropical rainstorm. The belt tied low on Sam's hips is jet black. They stand barefoot on the rocks at the seaward base of Awaopi'o Arch. They face into the rain and wind. The old man shouts to be heard. "Sometimes, you cannot defend yourself physically. Then all you have is the strength of your *ki*. Today, we test your spirit against the storm. Give voice to your *ki*. Use the cry called *kiai*. Make your voice cut through the roar of the surf like a lance piercing silk."

Sam tries. *"Eeeiiii!"*

"Your well is too shallow. Go deeper. Grip the rocks with your toes. Let the cry come up from the core of the earth. Even though it burns your throat like a volcano, shape it and throw it with the full force of your spirit."

"Eeeeiiiiii!"

"Too weak. Much too weak. Your spirit wavers like an uncertain breeze. Focus your *ki*. Make it sharp and hot and hard."

"EEEEEEEEEIIIIIIIIII!"

"I didn't say louder."

Sam looks uncertainly at the old man.

Just then a huge booming wave strikes the rocks in front of them. Old man Fujiwara's *kiai* hurls itself against the wave.

His cry opens a hole of silence in the wall of water. For an instant Sam is deaf. He hears nothing. Not a single sound. Then the world snaps back to normal. Gulls shriek, take flight. Rain and wind howl into Sam's face, and the shattered wave comes splashing down upon him and the old man like applause.

Butterflies

MAY 1937

AT SEVENTEEN SAM IS A STRAIGHT-A STUDENT. AFTER CLASSES, HE DIvides his week—two days as a teaching assistant at the Japanese-language school, two on construction jobs and martial arts training with Fujiwara-san, and two clerking for Papa at the plantation store. Sundays are spent cleaning boilers at the plantation sugar mill—a job Sam got through Papa's best friend, Kojiro. Each morning before Papa awakes, Sam goes outside and practices the strict and formal choreography that martial artists call kata.

Walking along carrying Fujiwara-san's toolbox one afternoon, Sam reviews his weekly routine and complains to the old man, "I wish I could spend more time practicing martial arts. The only good thing about being a teaching assistant is that I'm getting paid for it. Teaching basic Japanese calligraphy to a bunch of bored kids is a waste of my time."

Fujiwara-san smiles. "Isamu, the waste is that you are too bored to learn the lessons your students can teach you. A true artist finds stepping-stones to enlightenment in every part of their life. From hammering nails to stacking canned goods to teaching Japanese calligraphy—in every act, act once. Each nail hammered straight and true. Can on can. Brush touches paper, ink bleeds. No hesitation. One chance. One stroke. Brush or sword. The same."

Eyes lowered, chagrined and thoughtful, Sam follows his teacher up the long sloping driveway to the house of the *O-luna*, the head foreman of the Awaopi'o Plantation, Mr. James A. Bidwell. Sam carries Fujiwara-san's tools in a long rectangular wooden box with rope handles. Sam figures it now weighs close to fifty pounds. Every time the load begins to feel comfortable, the old man adds, "Just a few more nails. We don't want to run out."

Fujiwara-san knocks on the front door. No answer. They go around to the back where a big bay gelding is tethered. *O-luna* Bidwell is sipping whiskey and reading a newspaper in the shade of the veranda.

"Hello, boss. I've come to study the foundation repairs."

Bidwell ignores them.

Fujiwara-san gestures for Sam to put down the toolbox. They stand waiting at the foot of the stairs while *O-luna* Bidwell continues to read. Bidwell is a fair blond, a lean six foot three, drinking whiskey for lunch.

Bidwell puts down his newspaper and gestures for Fujiwara-san to come up to the veranda. The boss gives the old man a sheaf of blueprints to unroll. Bidwell measures Sam through gray-blue eyes. Bidwell's expression, his entire manner, oozes contempt.

Sam looks away and studies the backyard; in one corner a vegetable garden languishes full of weeds and small blue butterflies.

The screen door swings open and a young, pretty Japanese woman in a pink and white cotton dress steps onto the veranda. Seeing Fujiwara-san, she bows, then politely asks in perfect Japanese, "Would you care for some tea, coffee, or ice water?"

The old man beams. "Thank you, Yuriko-san. If it's not too much trouble, a cup of tea would be wonderful, please."

Yuriko turns to Sam, speaks in English: "Would you like something to drink?"

Sam stares at her bright red lips, wonders how old she is. "No, thank you."

"Really? How about a big glass of ice water?"

Sam hesitates, then nods shyly. Yuriko smiles and goes into the house.

"Boss," says Fujiwara-san, "these are the wrong blueprints."

Bidwell checks them. "Damn it! Wait here." He goes into the house.

Fujiwara-san turns, finds Sam staring at the back door. The boy has a slightly dazed look in his eyes. "Isamu, are you ready to be tested?"

The boy snaps to attention. "Yes, Sensei!"

"Bring me two butterflies. One in each hand."

Sam bows and moves like a stalking cat toward the garden. The old man smiles. It is a pleasure to watch the boy, to teach and challenge him.

When Yuriko returns carrying a tray, she finds Sam bowing to Fujiwara-san. She puts down her tray. Sam glances at her, then holding out his hands to the old man, opens them proudly.

"No," says the old man softly. "I did not say to bring them to me dead."

Sam lowers his eyes and drops two crushed butterflies onto the grass.

Yuriko hands Fujiwara-san a cup of tea. Then she walks to the veranda rail. "Here's your ice water." She leans down, holding the glass.

Sam raises his eyes from the dead butterflies on the grass to the glass of water sparkling in the hot sunlight. The shade cast from the roof cuts across her wrist. Sam looks up toward her shadowed face but never gets past the sight of her smooth, young breasts exposed above the drooping neckline of her dress.

Just then Bidwell comes out carrying blueprints. He tosses them to Fujiwara-san and moves up behind Yuriko. "What're you doing?"

Sam notes a subtle slur in Bidwell's speech. Bidwell carries himself without a hint of unsteadiness, but Sam recognizes instantly: *The boss is a drunk just like Papa.*

Bidwell grabs Yuriko's shoulder. "Hey! I'm talking to you."

"Oh!" The wet glass slips from her fingers.

Sam's hand shoots out, catching the glass in midair, spilling half the ice water over his hand and forearm. He looks up at her, their eyes meet for an instant, and she throws him a quick tiny smile. Then she jerks her arm free of Bidwell's grasp, turns and retreats into the house.

Bidwell rests his hand on the black whip coiled at his belt and glares at Sam.

"Boss, who made all these changes?" Fujiwara-san rattles the blueprints. "This new section will double the costs."

"What?" Bidwell shifts his attention to the plans.

Sam sips ice water. He faces the men, but out of the corner of his eye, he can see the woman. Yuriko stands in the kitchen, just out of Bidwell's line of sight. She is looking through the screen door at Sam.

Stripped to the waist Sam stands alone in Fujiwara-san's garden.

Eyes closed, motionless.

Butterflies flutter all around him.

Sam opens his eyes, begins moving with fluid grace. Arcs and circles endlessly blending into one another, he dances with the butterflies. His right hand cups around a blue butterfly in midair. Instantly, his hand opens again, and the butterfly veers off.

Finally, Sam stops, naked torso glistening with sweat in the day's fading light. He opens his hands. Two butterflies flutter up from his palms. One lands on Sam's head and preens itself before flying away.

Scrubber

JUNE 1937

THE AWAOPI'O MILL STANDS A HALF MILE UP THE ROAD FROM THE PLAN-
tation store and Sam's house. The sugar boilers look like water tanks, ten
feet high, ten feet in diameter, welded steel wrapped with asbestos, sheathed
in varnished wood bound with metal straps. Saturday evening, after the
cooked syrup is pumped out, the hatches are opened on top, and the boilers
are allowed to cool.

On Sunday, Sam arrives with the other scrubbers. They strip to white
loincloths and tie cotton sweatbands around their heads. Through the hatch
Sam lowers and sets his ladder, checks hose and sprinkler, hooks an insu-
lated work lamp, then climbs down into his boiler, hot, sweet, burnt air billowing into his face.

The floor is perforated with thousands of holes, each fed by a two-inch
copper pipe. Live steam, entering through the pipes, cooks crushed cane
juice down to a syrup to be spun into brown sugar. If the boiler man burns
the juice, the steam pipes become encrusted with black, burnt syrup. Sam's
job is to scrub out the insides of the pipes. His cleaning tool is a half-inch-
thick steel bar, hinged into three sections. The business end is a foot-long
steel-bristled brush.

Sam turns his job into a martial arts exercise. Under constant rain from
the sprinkler, he swishes the film of cooling water with his bare feet over the
hot, sticky metal floor. Using his toes to keep track of the holes already
cleaned, he shoves the brush into a hole, pushes it down until it hits bottom.
Then he pulls upward, hand over hand, three times, and the brush pops
out. Sam skips no holes; he makes sure each and every pipe in his boiler is
clear. Finished, he climbs the ladder and shimmies out the hatch.

On this particular Sunday, *O-luna* Bidwell is giving his young Japanese mistress a private tour of the Awaopi'o mill. Through his office window, they see Sam emerge from a hatch onto a boiler roof.

Sam is facing away, he does not notice them. In a shaft of sunlight falling through an open skylight, he stands tanned golden and naked except for his white loincloth, muscles pumped and flushed, skin glistening with water, syrup, and sweat. Heat steams off him. He unties his headband, shakes out his raven black hair, bends, lifts a full bucket of water with both hands and inhales the fresh air, inhales down to his toes, then pours the cold water slowly over his head and body, and roars with pleasure.

Yuriko stares, mesmerized. Bidwell grabs her arm and pulls her away. From somewhere on the far side of the boiler room Fujiwara-san's voice rings out, "Isamu."

"Yes, Sensei!"

"What did he call him?" *O-luna* Bidwell asks Yuriko.

"Sensei. It means teacher." She sneaks a quick peek back over her shoulder, but the top of the boiler is empty.

The vision of Sam, golden and shining, inflames Yuriko's fantasies. She cannot stop thinking about him. A month later, she sees him at the plantation store. A shipload of fresh goods has arrived, and the store is filled with shoppers. Yasubei is at the counter. Papa's friend Kojiro and his field gang loiter nearby, smoking, inspecting the merchandise and the women. Across the store from the men, Sam is on his knees, busy stocking shelves; he can see but cannot hear Kojiro.

"Great ass," murmurs Kojiro. "You see how the ladies are snubbing her? That's because her mother runs a brothel in Hilo. When she was just a toddler, Mama-san sent her to live in Japan and get a good education. Finished school last year and returned to Hawaii. Not long after she arrived, she and her mother had a big fight."

"I heard she wanted to manage the place," says another man. "But all the girls objected and threatened to leave. That's what caused the fight. People could hear the whores screaming half a block away."

"You got it wrong," says a third man. "I heard the girls wanted her to work there, said she'd make a great junior mama-san, but her mother wouldn't allow it."

"She's really pretty. What's her name?"

"Hey, shut up. She's coming this way." The men stare as she walks by, ignoring them.

Sam hears footsteps, feels a tap on his head. He looks up.

"Can you help me?" says Yuriko.

Sam rises, wipes his hands on his apron. She turns. Sam follows, while Kojiro and his friends snicker and make lewd gestures.

Yuriko leads Sam along the aisles until she reaches the back of the store. She seeks privacy but finds none. She grabs a shirt off a shelf, shakes it out, holds it up to Sam, backing him until he bumps against shelves, pins him there. "You do yardwork? My garden needs weeding."

She goes up on her toes, leans closer as if to check the fit at his neck and shoulders. She smells like flowers, her breath tickles his ear. "Tomorrow afternoon."

Then she backs away, frowning at the shirt. "Thank you." She tosses him the shirt and leaves.

Sam blinks, swallows, and folds the shirt with shaky hands.

In the aisle two older women, eyebrows raised, watch him walk away.

Weeding

JULY 1937

SAM ARRIVES TO WEED YURIKO'S GARDEN. OVERCOME WITH SHYNESS, he cannot bring himself to knock on the door. Instead he simply starts working.

When Yuriko sees him through the kitchen window, she comes running out. "Stop! If you do too much, he won't believe I did it myself."

Sam drops a handful of weeds onto the pile at the end of the row.

Yuriko walks right up to him. She is barefoot, wearing a dress with a pink and white Hawaii orchid print; her lipstick looks shiny and wet. Yuriko stands so close, he feels like stepping back. At the same time he wants her to move even closer. He risks a quick peek down the front of her dress. She wears a lacy pink slip.

"I'll pay you now," she says. "Wash your hands, then come in."

He enters through the back door and waits just inside the kitchen.

"In here," she calls.

He removes his work boots, leaves them by the door next to her shoes. He walks through the dining room, notes a wall rack filled with rifles, shotguns, and pistols.

He finds her in the bedroom. She has unpinned her hair and is brushing it with long, firm strokes. Under the floral scent of her perfume, there is another smell—a warm, dark, mysterious, human smell. He waits at the threshold.

She puts down her brush and studies his face. "You're a virgin."

Shyly, Sam nods.

She walks on bare feet across the room to him. Her dress looks different, looser, more graceful. She has removed her belt and slip. She stands in front of him. Very close.

Their eyes meet, and he realizes with a start that she cannot be much older than himself. He looks down into her dress. He sees her small smooth breasts. He sees her nipples.

She takes his hands, hers cool and dry, his warm and damp. She places one of his hands on her breast and the other between her legs.

Through the thin cotton of her dress, he feels her nipple harden. His other hand feels heat and moisture. He is barely breathing. His heart is drumming, loud, deafening. His throat feels swollen, thick, dry. He takes a shaky breath, and Yuriko closes her eyes. She makes a soft sound, almost, he thinks, like a wild dove.

She moves slowly against his hands. She removes her hands from his.

His hands remain, one on her breast, the other between her legs. Grabbing, he pushes toward her.

She backs away.

Instantly, he stops, then eases the grip and weight of his palms and fingers until her dress slips and slides, caressing the contours of her nipple and sex. And she resumes her slow, soft, dove-moaning dance, rubbing herself against the smooth cotton, fitting herself to his hot, firm, cloth-covered hands.

He stands still, rock solid, breath quaking as her hands go to his belt, undoes the buckle, slowly slips the leather tongue free, unbuttons his pants, slides the zipper down, lets the pants slip off his hard, narrow hips to sag around his lean, muscled thighs.

Yuriko raises her arms. "Take off my dress."

Sam lifts the dress up and off her in one smooth motion.

She reaches down into his underpants, grasps his erect penis and squeezes it hard.

"Ow . . ." Pain and pleasure jolt up his spine and down his thighs, nearly collapsing his knees. Straightening, he stares into her eyes.

She stares back. Easing her grip but still holding Sam with one hand, licking the fingers of her other hand, she pulls him toward the bed.

He shuffles forward clumsily, crumpled pants wrapped around his knees.

They pass the open window. They hear a horse nicker.

Instantly, they freeze, eyes widening with panic.

Sam pulls up his pants, flies out of the bedroom, buckling his belt as he passes the gun rack in the dining room, into the kitchen where he hears *O-luna* Bidwell's footsteps thudding up the stairs.

Sam grabs his work boots and backpedals, collides with Yuriko in the dining room as the screen door slams open and Bidwell enters the kitchen. Sam rushes into the bedroom as Yuriko greets Bidwell in the kitchen. "You're home early. You want a drink?"

"Yeah." Bidwell's footsteps move heavily into the dining room, continue toward the bedroom, where Sam is at the window.

Both hooks to the screen are paint-stuck.

"*O-luna!*" calls Yuriko from the kitchen doorway. "You know how many tricks a woman can do with one of these?"

Bidwell's footsteps pause just beyond the open bedroom door. "A carrot?"

"Come into the kitchen."

"Show me in here."

"You're not interested?" Yuriko's voice fades into the kitchen. "Forget it."

"Hey, wait, come back!" Bidwell's footsteps thump quickly away from the bedroom door.

Sam breaks both hooks loose, opens the screen, flings out his work boots, climbs through and drops next to the bay gelding, grabs his boots, and sprints down the hill away from the house.

He glances over his shoulder.

He is not certain, but he thinks he sees a person at one of the windows.

Pele

JULY 1937

ONCE OUT OF SIGHT OF BIDWELL'S HOUSE, SAM PAUSES LONG ENOUGH to put on his work boots, then runs the rest of the way home.

A white horse is tethered outside his house. Papa, Kojiro, and a crowd of men stand in the yard. Sam veers away, but they spot him and wave him over. Helplessly, he jogs down to them.

"Well?" demands Papa.

Sam works at catching his breath. *Do they know?*

"Well?" says Kojiro with a huge grin.

Yes, they know. "I—"

Before Sam can blurt out an apology, Kojiro and his friends start talking excitedly. "Your papa just won a racehorse!"

"Ain't she something? Yasubei won her in a card game over in Hilo."

"We're all going to get rich off her," says Papa. "I'll retire to Japan. You'll go to university on the mainland."

Sam laughs so hard that Yasubei's temper flares. "You doubt me? I know she looks small, but she's got heart."

Sam inhales deeply, forcing himself to concentrate on the gentle sleepy-eyed mare. "Papa, she's beautiful."

"Damn right! Her name's Pele. Goddess of the volcano."

Yasubei enters Pele in a Japanese festival race in Awaopi'o Camp. Of the five horses competing, the favorite is the black stallion belonging to the plantation manager, John T. Boyer.

To Sam's astonishment, Pele finishes first. Old Graybeard, John T. himself, comes by after the race to shake Yasubei's hand. "Congratulations, Mr.

Hamada. It was a fine race. A close one. Would you be interested in selling your mare?"

"No, sir, Mr. Boyer. I plan to run her in Hilo in September."

"The big Hilo race? Well, she'll be up against the best on the island. I'm planning to run my own horse there."

"Then he and Pele will meet again."

"Aye, I'm looking forward to it already. Good luck to you, Mr. Hamada."

"Thank you, Mr. Boyer, sir. Good luck to you, too, sir."

Yasubei's friends are respectfully subdued until the boss is out of sight and hearing, then they begin whooping and dancing with Yasubei on their shoulders. Sam swells with pride. Somebody hands Yasubei a bottle of sake. Yasubei, reeling, bobbing, guzzling and spilling sake, waves to his son as the crowd carries him away.

It takes Sam a month to work up the nerve to return and finish weeding Yuriko's garden. That night he and Papa sit at their kitchen table, Sam doing homework, Yasubei drinking and sharing snippets from the newspaper. "Still no sign of Amelia Earhart, who disappeared last month during her flight over the Pacific . . . Japanese troops now occupy Peking . . ."

The house is dark except for the light above the kitchen table. The windows and doors are open; moths whir and bump against the screens. Sam fidgets in his chair, sniffs Yuriko's scent on his fingers, souvenir of the loss of his virginity, inhaling until his head buzzes as softly as the moths at the screens. *Today I became a man.* He wonders if his light-headedness means he is in love. The way he and Yuriko touched each other that afternoon . . . the look on her face when she asked him to come again tomorrow . . . was this love? This fuzzy dullness in the brain, this rich salty potato-water perfume on his fingers?

"Who is she?"

Sam jumps slightly, glances up but does not answer.

"I can smell her from here."

Sam lowers his eyes to his notebook and maintains his silence.

Yasubei refills his sake glass. "Just remember to pull out before you come. Otherwise, you'll get her pregnant."

Unable to think of a suitable reply, unaware that Papa's advice is flawed, Sam neither moves nor speaks. But inwardly he celebrates this moment as the first man-to-man talk he has ever had with his father. He waits for Papa to say something more. But Yasubei resumes drinking and browsing through his newspaper. "Japanese bombers and warships shatter Shanghai. American women and children evacuate the city. U.S. cruiser *Augusta* hit by Japanese shell. Japan's next target: Nanking . . . Biggest Nazi rally held in Nuremburg . . ." Yasubei puts down the paper. "The whole damn world is going mad." He grabs his bottle and takes it with him to bed, leaving Sam alone at the kitchen table.

Squall

SEPTEMBER 1937

YASUBEI RIDES PELE UP THROUGH THE CANE FIELDS. HE LEADS A STRING of three mules delivering supplies to a new camp high on the slopes of the volcano.

The morning is hot and humid. Sweat runs down Yasubei's face. Red dust sticks to his skin and clothes. He ignores his discomfort. This is nothing compared with how it was when he and his wife labored in the cane. In those days, before the flumes were built, they loaded the cane onto sleds dragged by horses and mules. He remembers the smell of the burnt fields, the sound of his broad blade chopping through thick cane, hands blistered raw, itching inside filthy gloves, twisting cane leaves into cords, bundling and tying the stalks, everything black and sticky, bodies aching, covered with scratches, insect bites, cane juice, dust, and ash.

Every morning back then, they carried the newborn twins into the fields, raised a tarp to shade them from the sun, and left them. At lunch his wife, Ohatsu, hurried back to brush the bugs off their faces and feed them.

After the twins died, Ohatsu's hair turned gray, and Yasubei dove into a sea of sake. Ohatsu became sad and serious, talked incessantly about returning to Japan. She bore him a son. But every time Isamu sneezed, she panicked. She began avoiding sex. When they did make love, she did not respond. Did she think that numbing herself would keep her from getting pregnant? When she stopped making noises, that, more than anything else, killed things for him.

It was almost impossible for Yasubei to speak of such things, but he tried to explain to her how important it was for him to hear her moaning and crying out in passion. Embarrassed, she turned away. When she continued to remain inert and silent in bed, he tried again to tell her how much it meant to him, how most people lived through their eyes, but to him, hearing her was equal to touching her or her touching him. She looked at him as if he were crazy. He was fighting to keep his passion alive, but she didn't seem to understand or care. He persisted. He, Yasubei Hamada, a man who spoke little, who almost never asked anyone for anything, struggled to explain what he needed from her. "The music of your passion. You used to sing . . . so beautifully. Please, could you not sing for me again?"

Her embarrassment turned to rage. She snapped at him, "All you do is drink. I want to go home to Japan, and you spend everything on sake, tobacco, and cards."

"I'm not talking about Japan. I'm talking about our lovemaking."

"Our baby sleeps in the same room with us. I don't want to frighten him. I don't want him to think you're hurting me."

Yasubei built a second bedroom onto the house. But still she refused to "sing" for him. His lovemaking grew more vigorous, crossed into brutal. He would make her cry out. He would hear her voice, even if it was in pain. She thought he had the sex drive of a beast; her silence hardened. His drinking increased. She preoccupied herself with the baby Isamu. When she became pregnant with Bunji, she began packing, said she was going home even if it meant leaving Yasubei. Realizing he had no choice, Yasubei relented and returned to Japan with her.

After he left Ohatsu in Japan with the children, and he was alone in Hawaii, he had time to sort out their problems: the loss of the twins, his drinking, the backbreaking field labor, the poverty, the racial discrimination, anger, fear, homesickness, and brutal silent sex. Sometimes he grasped pieces of it, but the more he thought about it, the more it exposed his own helplessness and shortcomings. To escape his unbearable shame and regret, he numbed himself with drink.

Pele sneezes. Yasubei pats her neck. "The dust tickling you?" They climb uphill. The air cools. The last mile to camp, a breeze sweeps down into their faces. Pele delights in it, tosses her head, prances. Powdery red dust puffs around Pele's hooves. Yasubei restrains her. She's already had her morning run. In Hilo in another three days, she can run her heart out.

Yasubei rides past a gang of men clearing a field of rocks. When he arrives in the camp, a Filipino woman and several runny-nosed children help him unload the mules. The Filipinos' ragged clothes and drooping canvas tents depress Yasubei. After the twins were born, Yasubei moved his family into a house rented from the plantation. Seeing the Filipinos' tents, Yasubei is reminded of when he and Ohatsu were first married and lived in a tiny dirt-floored hut, the grass shack of Hawaiian songs. When it rained, their hut looked like a pile of rubbish. Despite that, in the beginning, they had some happy times.

After unloading the supplies, Yasubei leads his mules down the mountain. It starts raining. In Hawaii every new laborer is told, "It's all right if you forget your lunch, but never your raincoat." The standard raincoats, which the Japanese called *kappa,* taken from the Hawaiian *kapa ua,* were made of unbleached muslin treated with many coats of oil. Yasubei unrolls his *kappa* and puts it on.

Cold rain falls in rhythmic waves. *I blamed my wife, but it was my drinking. And my brutality. And my holding her here like a prisoner. It's my fault our marriage went bad.* The rain grows heavier. Yasubei feels like he has ridden into a waterfall.

Then, abruptly, the rain stops. Yasubei unbuttons his raincoat. Shaking off water, he turns in his saddle to check the mules. Behind them the peak of the volcano is curtained with rain. He can see individual rain clouds like huge dark jellyfish drifting on the wind. High above the rain clouds, the sky is completely overcast, a smooth iron-gray ceiling. Looking around from this steep section of trail, Yasubei can see for miles across the cane fields, all the way down to Awaopi'o Camp and the tiny flecks of red on white that mark the roof and walls of the plantation store, and beyond to where the land ends at the cliff edge and a towering thunderstorm—massive ink blue cumulonimbus spiked with lightning and the dark blur of rain—marches in from the sea.

Pele makes a nervous sound. Yasubei leans forward and pats Pele's neck. "It's all right, girl. I've been through hundreds of these rain squalls. Don't worry." Yasubei puts music into his voice. "It's just noise and water. It can't hurt you." He feels Pele relax under him. Yasubei clicks his tongue, and they resume their journey down the mountain.

Stoically, Yasubei watches the monstrous wall of rain approach. So tall it scrapes the high, gray, overcast ceiling, so wide it appears to be swallowing the sea, it floods over the coast, and the land below dissolves into darkness. Greater than any tsunami, the storm rolls across the cane fields toward him. Yasubei loves the approaching crackle and boom of thunder. Birds arrow past, thrilling him with the soft urgency of their wings. Heart thumping faster now with surging excitement and a hair's tickle of fear, Yasubei glances around, even though he knows there is no cover anywhere.

A gap opens in the clouds overhead. A shaft of sun strikes Yasubei, igniting ten thousand diamonds in the sweet wet cane around him, flooding his heart with joy. His eyes fill with tears of gratitude. To be here at this moment. Alive. Alive!

High and exposed astride Pele, Yasubei arches back, stretches his arms wide, closes his eyes, and grins into the blazing sun, feels the heat fade, watches the red dimming against his eyelids as the rent in the clouds closes. Inhaling deeply, he straightens and faces the oncoming wall of blue-black rain, tugs his raincoat shut, buttons it tight, clicks his tongue. "Let's go, girl."

Pele's hooves slide in the mud.

She lurches to catch herself. Yasubei pitches awkwardly in the saddle, loses his balance, feels himself falling. Trying to catch hold of his saddle, he inadvertently pulls hard on the reins, jerking Pele's head around. Abruptly, Pele slips, toppling sideways into the ditch beside the trail. Yasubei lands on his back, dazed, cursing, tries to stand, keeps slipping and falling, smearing his pants, raincoat, and hands with slick reddish-brown mud.

Frightened and splashing in the ditch, flailing on her side, Pele kicks the legs of the lead mule. The mule jumps, gets kicked again, slips and falls across Pele's legs.

Yasubei hears two quick ugly cracks. Pele screams.

Yasubei stands unsteadily, arms extended for balance. All around him the cane is hissing, the air swarms with bits of wet debris stinging his face. A tremendous wind blast flattens the tall cane, snapping stalks, knocking Yasubei to his hands and knees, and then the rain is on him, sudden, heavy, driving him facedown against the slick film of red mud and the lava-hard rib bones of the volcano.

Rain. Lightning. Thunder. Pele screaming.

On hands and knees Yasubei crawls toward Pele as she thrashes in the cane beyond the ditch. Yasubei reaches her. She is up, trembling, on three legs. Jagged bones protrude through the skin of her left foreleg.

Yasubei tries to take hold of the reins, but Pele shies, slips and falls again. Crushing cane, she struggles upright. Eyes rolling and crazy, shivering in the rain, she hobbles away, stands staring at him from deep in the cane and screams.

Yasubei abandons her.

Slipping and sliding, he runs through the storm down the mountain toward Awaopi'o Camp. Pele's voice echoes in his mind. Yasubei has never heard any living thing utter a sound so filled with terror and pain.

Shark Eye

September 1937

THE AFTERNOON SUN SPARKLES IN THE WET CANE. YASUBEI, KOJIRO, Sam, and Fujiwara-san ride a narrow flatbed wagon drawn by two mules. Pele stands where Yasubei left her. The three pack mules are a short distance up the trail.

Fujiwara-san holds out a rifle. Yasubei takes it and shoots Pele once between the eyes. She drops onto her hind legs, then flops over on her side. Using a block and tackle, they haul Pele up a ramp onto the wagon.

Sam retrieves the mules, ties their leads to the back of the wagon. Then they go down the mountain. All around them birds sing in the fragrant glistening cane.

They pass solemnly through Awaopi'o Camp. People stare, whisper among themselves, but no one speaks to the men on the wagon.

Kojiro drives to the cliffs near Awaopi'o Arch. The men drag Pele from the wagon, roll her off the cliff into the sea. Pele does not sink when she hits the water, she floats, and the waves carry her back and forth, rocking her in their blue-green arms. Pele's mane and tail sway like sea grass as the ocean washes the mud and blood from her white coat.

Then old man Fujiwara points. "Ah! There! He comes."

A curved fin rises above the waves. It cuts unerringly toward Pele.

Sam's throat goes dry, his bowels turn to water.

An enormous shadow slides just below the surface. The scarred snout comes up as the great white shark rolls and clamps its serrated teeth on Pele's belly. Then the shark turns and carries Pele out to sea.

"I saw the eye," whispers Yasubei. "It looked at me."

That night Yasubei burns with fever. He sees the eye of the shark, the protective eyelid lowering just before the jaws close. Yasubei rocks his head fiercely from side to side, throws off his bedcovers, but cannot shake free. He moans as he tries to push the shark away. But the shark is too strong. The shark drags Yasubei bleeding into deep water. Finally, the jagged teeth release him, and the whole attack begins all over again. And the noise! Lighthearted birdsong, snake hiss and wolf howl of rain and wind, granite-crushing thunder, and Pele screaming and screaming.

From a deep dreamless sleep, Sam opens his eyes. He sits up. Did Papa call? Sam hears muffled thumping. He goes to his father's bedroom.

Yasubei thrashes on the bed. "Shark! Shark!"

"I'll get Fujiwara-san."

Sam returns, finds his father shivering, disheveled blankets clutched to his chin, wide eyes staring at the ceiling. Fujiwara-san feels Yasubei's pulse, shallow and deep, on both wrists. Then the old man unfolds a cloth packet and withdraws a set of acupuncture needles, a box of matches, and a paper envelope full of dried *mogusa*. "Isamu, fetch Yasunaga Sensei."

Sam is not sure he heard correctly. The Buddhist priest?

"Isamu, your father is near death."

When Sam arrives with the Sensei, they find Yasubei sleeping peacefully and the room pungent with burnt mugwort. "He lives," says Fujiwara-san. Neither Sam nor the Sensei dare to ask for how long.

Fujiwara-san and the Sensei speak with members of the Japanese community. Everyone who had planned to bet on Pele donates money to send Yasubei home to Japan. Gaunt and sallow, Yasubei slowly packs for his journey home. "Isamu, I'd like to take you with me, but there's only enough money for one. Anyway, it's better that you stay with Fujiwara-san. You're doing well here in Hawaii. Good part-time jobs. The respect you get because you're a teacher at the Japanese-language school. And you'll graduate from high school in less than a year. Isamu, don't forget your promise. College on the mainland."

"But, Papa—"

"You come from a samurai family!"

"Yes, Papa. We speak once, then live or die in accordance with our words."

"That's right. And if anything happens to me, I expect you to look after your mother and brother and sister." Yasubei's gaze is stern, unwavering. "You understand?"

"I promise to protect and care for Mama and Bunji and Akemi."

Yasubei leaves for Japan, and Sam moves into Fujiwara-san's house. The first night after supper, the old man asks, "Do you play *shogi*?"

Sam shakes his head. "What's that?"

"Japanese chess."

The game becomes their nightly ritual. After Sam's homework, they play *shogi*.

One balmy April night seven months after moving in with Fujiwara-san, the old man pauses in midgame. "Oh, I almost forgot. Isamu, a letter came for you today. From your mother. It's over there under the newspaper."

Sam retrieves the letter, presses the fat envelope to his forehead like a fortune-teller and grins at Fujiwara-san. "Papa has recovered his strength. Now he's restless." Fresh understanding flickers into Sam's eyes. "The streets of Honura village feel too narrow. Papa's lungs miss the sweet Hawaiian wind. Despite the contempt of the *haole,* Hawaii is where he belongs. Somehow he's raised enough money for a ticket. He's taking the next steamship back." With this final pronouncement, Sam tears open the envelope.

Yasubei's gold tie clip drops into Sam's hand.

Monday, February 14, 1938

Isamu,

    I am very sorry to tell you that your father died of a heart attack on the night of Saturday, the twelfth of February. He was out drinking with friends—they said it looked painful, but that it was over quickly. The funeral and cremation will begin within the hour. Your brother

Bunji will offer prayers and incense in your place. Bunji and Akemi and
I send you our love and condolences. I wish you were here with us.
Please try to be strong. Your father would not want his death to dimin-
ish you. Guard your health. I will write again soon.

I am enclosing the letter your father was writing to you. It is un-
finished. He was working on it just before his friends took him out
drinking.

> With deep sympathy and love, Mother

February 12, 1938

Sam,

No matter what happens, do not return to Japan for the time being.
It's not safe. Two months ago Japanese troops committed unspeakable
atrocities when they overran Nanking. Last month the army occupied
Tsingtao. Last week Adolf Hitler named himself the Supreme Commander of the German armed forces. If you come home, I fear you might
be drafted. Stay with our plan—go to the mainland. Attend university
and get a good education. In the meantime behave yourself in
Fujiwara-san's home. Give one-third of your earnings to Fujiwara-san
to pay for your maintenance, save one-third for college, and send one-
third home to your mother. As soon as you graduate from high school,
go to the mainland. Until you are accepted into a college, we have
arranged for you to live and work with your mother's stepbrother, Genzo
Matsuyama, a farmer in Lodi, California. Pay him a third of your
earnings for your upkeep, send one-third to your mother, and save the
remainder for college.

You are the eldest son. When I die, you will inherit my property,
my responsibilities and debts. You must send money home every
month without fail. You must pay for any house repairs and property
taxes. Thus far, you have lived a soft life. You are prone to dreami-
ness. You are conceited and arrogant because you are smart and get
good grades.

But now you must learn to work in the real world. You must be *mindful of every word and action. You must atone for the shame and failures of your father. Now, more than ever, you are the hope for the future of this family. Remember—you are my winning lottery ticket. You are my spear. After I am fully recovered, I will—*

Pig Gun

OCTOBER 1938

O-*LUNA* BIDWELL IS CERTAIN HIS MISTRESS IS CHEATING ON HIM. PER-haps with more than one man. Yuriko is careful, but *O-luna* Bidwell is intent on vengeance. He makes himself a lookout in the tall cane on the slope above his house. There he waits with whiskey, a long brass telescope, and a pig gun—an ugly brutish shotgun, stock and double barrels sawed down to hunt wild pigs in deep brush.

The scent of the rut rolls off his woman; he knows he only has to wait.

Her lover comes in the morning, shortly after Bidwell leaves the house. The man runs swiftly to the house, enters without knocking through the front door. Bidwell leaves his horse hobbled and tethered to a stake. Close-set eyes burning with blue-hot fury, Bidwell works his way down through the cane. He will blow the man's legs off, drag him screaming into the yard, and whip him to bloody shreds.

In the front yard Bidwell pulls on gloves, uses a leather thong to wrap his fist tight around the gun stock. He fingers the triggers, cocks both hammers. He hears Yuriko moaning in the bedroom as he climbs the front steps. Last week he had a carpenter nail down every loose plank and oil the door hinges. He unlatches the front door, hears the lovers panting, bedsprings creaking, headboard thumping the wall.

Suddenly there is a sharp *whack* on the bare floor of the front hall.

Someone had propped a broom against the front door, and it has fallen.

Bidwell rushes now, no longer concerned about making noise. Only wanting to get to the bedroom before the fox goes out the window. Last week the carpenter reported the broken hooks when he nailed the screen shut, according to Bidwell's orders. That should slow the bastard for a step or two.

Bidwell bursts into the bedroom, sees Yuriko wide-eyed and naked in bed. Her mouth opens into a glass-shattering scream as a naked man hurls himself across the room toward the doorway. The *O-luna* has the sawed-off shotgun aimed low, intending to take the man's legs off at the knees. But the man is already in the air, flying high and fast as a human spear. Bidwell's breath bursts out as the man slams a full-bodied kick into Bidwell's breastbone.

Bidwell, knocked forcefully off his feet, sails out the bedroom door. He crashes onto his back in the dining room. His head thuds against the wall, rebounds, trapping the twin muzzles of the shotgun in the soft slack flesh beneath his jawbone. Stunned and panicked, he jerks his arm to move the pig gun away, but he flinches, and his finger spasms against the double triggers. The shotgun goes off, both barrels blasting Bidwell's chest, neck, and face, splattering and tearing ragged holes in the wall paneling and gun rack, jarring weapons loose.

Shotguns, rifles, and handguns avalanche onto Bidwell.

Shame

NOVEMBER 1938

O-LUNA BIDWELL IS DEAD. THE ONLY WITNESS, HIS MISTRESS, A young Japanese whore, swears it was suicide, says Bidwell was a drunken jealous lover, that he wanted to marry her and killed himself when she refused. An autopsy shows alcohol in his system and a liver so diseased it would have ended his life within a few years at most. Which leads some to conjecture that Bidwell committed suicide because he knew he was dying. It appears he shot himself while lying flat on his back in the dining room. Odd, but there are no signs of a struggle. And a drunk will lie down anywhere.

Then Bidwell's horse and whiskey bottle are found in the cane fields along with his brass spyglass. Obviously he was watching the house. Why? Perhaps his jealousy was not unfounded? Was there another man?

"Other man?" Yuriko sticks to her story. "There was no other man."

"But you're a whore. There must have been hundreds."

"No. I am the daughter of a madam, but I have never been a whore."

The cops, the plantation owner, bosses and workers, the town officials, all know and respect Yuriko's mother. The mama-san has always been good to them. Many even remember Yuriko from when she was a baby. No one ever really liked James Bidwell. He was an arrogant bully and a mean drunk. But he was a *haole,* and Yuriko is a Japanese whore.

The community is perplexed, angered, divided.

The Japanese consulate conducts its own investigation. Documents are checked. Yuriko was born in Hawaii, but her birth was never properly recorded; legally she is not an American citizen. The consulate orders Yuriko to return to Japan, where the investigation will be completed. Deeply shamed, the Japanese-Hawaiian community takes up a collection, buys Yuriko a one-way steamship ticket to Japan.

Some *haole* are disgruntled, but when they are apprised of Japanese police interrogation techniques, their objections fade into horrified silence.

"What the hell were you thinking?" says Fujiwara-san.

"Nothing. I wasn't thinking anything," says Sam. "I was just having fun. You know. A fling. And she really . . . comforted me after Papa died."

"We must get you away from here."

"I should tell the truth about what happened."

"No! You will not."

"But—"

"A Jap boy, a Jap whore, and a dead *haole* O-*luna*? You and Yuriko would end up shot or hung. It's a tragic mess, but I will not allow you to throw away two more lives and whatever honor remains in your family name."

"Honor? I wronged that man."

"Yes. And you will carry that shame for the rest of your life."

"No. I can't live like that. I'm going to the cops."

"If you do, you will destroy yourself and your family. Imagine how your mother and siblings will suffer. Imagine how this could damage our Japanese community. And you will disgrace me as your guardian and teacher."

"I have no other choice. I'm sorry."

"I am the one who should apologize. I promised your parents that I would care for you. Your father asked me to build your character. I have failed." Fujiwara-san stalks out of the kitchen, returns carrying his *wakizashi,* draws the short blade from its sheath. "I will atone for my shame here and now."

Sam leaps forward and grabs the old man's wrists. "Wait, Sensei! Please. Stop. Please don't do it."

"Are you asking me to live with my shame?"

"Sensei, please—" Sam stares into the old man's eyes. Sam expects rage. What he sees instead stabs him to the core. Fujiwara-san is weeping with pain and love and sorrow.

"Isamu . . . You want us both to live with our shame?"

"Yes."

"Then you will tell no one."

"Whatever you say, Sensei."

"Say it."

"I will tell no one."

"Not ever."

"I will take the truth to my grave."

Sayonara

DECEMBER 1938

Fujiwara-san throws Sam a belated graduation and bon voyage party, announcing the boy is leaving for college on the mainland. Kojiro and others harbor suspicions about Sam's involvement with Yuriko, but out of loyalty to Yasubei's memory and fearing *haole* retribution, no one asks, no one speaks. Sam finds himself cloaked in protective silence.

Sam and Yuriko see each other one last time. On the Honolulu docks as they wait to board separate ships that will sail in opposite directions, they sneak glances at each other. Barely twenty yards apart, they cannot touch or speak because they are under the constant scrutiny of those who have come to see them off. Yuriko is with her mother, a handsome, dignified mama-san, several gaudy prostitutes, and consulate and police escorts. Sam, festooned with flowered leis, stands with Fujiwara-san, Kojiro, Fish Mouth Enzo, and other friends and classmates.

A prostitute waves to Kojiro and comes over to him. Kojiro appears both embarrassed and pleased as she coyly draws him aside. They whisper briefly then approach Sam. "This is Ai-chan. When I told her you were Yasubei's son, she said she wanted to meet you."

Everyone watches Ai-chan congratulate Sam on graduating from high school. She wishes him safe journey and good luck. She shakes his hand and passes him a scrap of paper.

Ai-chan mentions Sam's father, what a fine man he was, how sad to hear of his death, and Sam slips the note into his pocket.

But Ai-chan doesn't leave. She chatters on, red lips smiling, dark eyes sharp, waiting.

Finally Sam realizes that she is waiting for payment, not money, but something, a lover's word, some sign of devotion. Flustered, wanting so much to do the right thing, he rubs his hands against his chest, fusses with his flowered leis, his tie. Once more he thanks her for her kind words, grabs her hand, shakes it, then bows deeply.

Ai-chan returns his bow.

While both their heads are lowered, caught in the rush of the moment, his voice covered by a long low blast from the ship's horn, Sam blurts in a staccato whisper, "I'll send for her. I want her to be my wife."

They complete their bows, Ai-chan's eyes glittering. She retreats, dipping her head to Kojiro, Fujiwara-san, and the others. She crosses the dock to Yuriko, delivers Sam's two promises. "He said he would send for you. He said he wanted to marry you. And he sent you this." Ai-chan opens her hand. Gleaming in the sunlight is Yasubei Hamada's gold tie clip.

At the ship's rail Sam takes the piece of paper from his pocket, unfolds it, reads Yuriko's hastily scribbled, *I love you. Write to me,* accompanied by Ai-chan's address in Hilo.

"Isamu!" Fujiwara-san's shout rises from the docks.

"Sensei!"

"Are you ready to be tested?"

"Yes, Sensei!"

The old man raises one hand, his gaze clear and steady as a hawk's.

Sam strains to hear through the racket of the crowd, waits for the old man's instructions. Then he realizes Fujiwara-san has no more words to give.

The test has already begun.

Sam cups both hands around his mouth and shouts, "I'll do my best! Thank you, Sensei! *Sayonara!*"

Part 2

DECEMBER 1938–JUNE 1940

Golden Windows

DECEMBER 1938

Dawn. Sam shivers at the bow rail as the ship pushes through fog toward the bright disk of the rising sun. The fog thins and the ship emerges into a clear morning. Ahead lie coastal hills, low, sensuous, draped in blue gray chaparral and winter emerald grass. Sam inhales down to his toes and up to the tips of his hair.

California! A new land. A clean page in his life. Another chance to get things right.

Escorted by tugboats the ship passes slowly under the newly completed Golden Gate Bridge. Sam stares, dizzy, reeling with awe. If Fujiwara-san could see this bridge! A dream blossoms in Sam's heart. He will study to be an engineer. Someday he will design and build a marvel like this, graceful, powerful, useful to all.

Delivered across the long rolling swells of the Pacific into the calm waters of San Francisco Bay, Sam feels the morning sun penetrating and warming him, sees it mirrored golden in the windows of the city. Sam Hamada, eighteen years old, sharp and bright as a naked sword, eldest son, bearer of his family's crest, his father's spear reaching the mainland . . . the United States of America . . . He inhales deeply. He bows.

Lodi

New Year's Day, 1939

Carrying a single suitcase, Sam steps off the train in Lodi, a small farm town in the San Joaquin Valley between Stockton and Sacramento.

A man reaches out to him. "Genzo Matsuyama."

Sam shakes his uncle's callused hand. Like Sam's father and Fujiwara-san, Genzo Matsuyama is an *Issei*, a first-generation Japanese immigrant. Tall, thin, tough. Tanned face, friendly, intelligent eyes sparkling with curiosity and enthusiasm. Peeking from Genzo's shirt and jacket pockets are pens, pencils, dog-eared books, and a tightly rolled wad of newspaper clippings bound with pink rubber bands.

"This is my son Dewey and his best friend, Al Yanagi." Two teenagers in matching blue jeans and white T-shirts. Sam's cousin, Dewey Matsuyama, is tall like his father, wiry, chewing gum with a wise-guy grin, hair gleaming with oil, combed high and showy, bouncing on his feet to an inner jitterbug beat. Al Yanagi has sleepy, soulful eyes and a shy smile. Thick and solid through the body and with wide shoulders, his left hand sheathed in a well-worn baseball glove, Al extends his right hand to shake Sam's—nothing shy or soft about Al Yanagi's grip.

"Boys, this is Sam Hamada, my nephew. He graduated high school in Hawaii, but before that he went to school in Japan. He's a *kibei*—a person educated in Japan. He's going to be your new Japanese-language sensei."

An old glove, contoured by time, body oils, and sweat, to exactly match one particular hand. This is how it feels to Sam—entering into the lives of these two families, the Matsuyamas and Yanagis in Lodi, California—his hand sliding into a comfortable old glove, a perfect fit.

Instant family and new best friends, they walk from the station, across several sets of tracks, past long fruit-packing sheds, onto the almost deserted main street of Lodi's Japantown.

A peculiar sensation takes hold of Sam. Perplexed, wondering, he walks beside his uncle Genzo. Al and Dewey move into the street, begin playing catch. The odd feeling inside Sam grows stronger. What is it? Like . . . *being in the bamboo grove with Fujiwara-san.* Suddenly every sense in Sam's body is wide awake, alert as the full moon reflected in a pond; absolutely still, responsive to the merest hint of wind, he waits for the signal that will set him into motion.

Danger? No. Something else . . . *What?*

Genzo stops in front of a noodle shop. "This restaurant belongs to Al's father, Shoji Yanagi, my oldest and dearest friend. We were classmates back in Japan. We came to America together." Genzo opens the door for Sam.

Sam feels like he is walking into a dream. There is something so familiar about the noodle shop. It is empty except for one man sitting at a table with a teapot, cup and cards laid out in a game of solitaire. The man smiles, rises to his feet as a woman comes from the kitchen with a big platter of sushi covered with wax paper. "Shoji Yanagi and his wife, Kuwano," says Uncle Genzo. "Here, Kuwano-san, let me carry that for you."

Shoji is an older version of his son Al, gentle eyes, a big solid bear of a man.

Kuwano, plump, obviously busy but not scattered, focused, clear-eyed, measuring Sam in a quick foot-to-head sweep, extending the proper New Year's greetings, listening, immensely pleased by Sam's perfect Japanese response, smiling, bowing, returning to the kitchen.

Genzo puts down the platter of sushi, pulls a little bag of Bull Durham from his shirt pocket. He and Shoji roll cigarettes. Sam stands watching them. Genzo offers him the tobacco.

Sam shakes his head.

No. This is not it. Not yet. Something else. Wait. Sam's every sense alert, calm, clear. He waits, patient as the emptiness in the center of a gold ring. *Mu.*

He rotates slowly, looking at the tables, the neatly pushed-in chairs, the immaculate floor, old clock, new calendar, announcements and artwork on the walls . . .

Behind him, Sam hears the striking of a match as the men light their smokes.

"Hi. I'm Keiko."

Sam spins. The girl in the blue dress has taken him completely by surprise. She stands there holding a blue and white porcelain plate of sushi, and her smile blinds him. Literally, for an instant Sam cannot see anything else around him or around her. Just her smile, simple, sweet, natural, relaxed, and as Sam stares at her face, he feels the gentle tap of Fujiwara-san's bamboo sword on the crown of his head. Sam opens his mouth, but his mind fumbles the words, drops them like loose paper, and his voice comes up empty. Helplessly, he dips his head.

Keiko blushes, returns his bow, and carries her sushi out the front door.

"My daughter," says Shoji Yanagi.

"What?" says Kuwano, coming out of the kitchen with a third dish of sushi.

Uncle Genzo is studying Sam. "She'll be one of your students."

"Who will?" asks Kuwano as they all leave the noodle shop and climb into Genzo's battered old pickup, Kuwano in front between her husband and Genzo at the wheel. Keiko and the boys climb in back. Al and Dewey sit, knees up, their backs against the cab. Sam and Keiko are on either side, facing each other between the rear wheel humps. Sam stares at her, and as the truck begins to move, he feels like all the weight within him is turning to smoke. Soon nothing will remain of him but a hard thin hollow shell. What is this? *Mu*? He blinks, and then he has the oddest feeling—as if he is watching himself through the eyes of another.

Rolling out of town and gathering speed through the wide, flat vineyards, Shoji turns, looks through the rear window. His daughter, Keiko, eyes momentarily shut, faces into the cold wind like a hunting dog, her long hair streaming. Dewey and Sam are staring at the front of her dress, at her breasts, nipples erect and perky under the blue cotton. Anger flares in Shoji. Before he can stop himself, he raps sharply on the glass.

Everyone looks up at Shoji.

Flustered, he gives a little wave. The truck hits a pothole, Shoji's wire-rimmed glasses bump against the window. *Look at how she's grown.* He straightens his glasses. *How old is she now? Fifteen? No . . . sixteen. Sixteen already.*

Keiko, satisfied with her brief invigorating splash of icy wind, buttons her sweater, closes her wool coat, lifts the collar.

Shoji notices her sleeves are frayed. He should buy her a new coat. She deserves it. She's a good girl. He'll take her to San Francisco and buy her new clothes.

Keiko catches her father staring at her. She gives him a big happy grin, a smile radiant with pure youthful innocence.

The new boy cannot take his eyes off her. Shoji, the man, knows instantly and instinctively what is happening to Sam Hamada; Shoji, the father, refuses to acknowledge it.

Unable to match his daughter's dazzling smile, Shoji gives the best he can manage in the moment, a shaky smile muted with the subtle colors of age and experience. Then suddenly feeling like he might start weeping, he turns and looks out the front windshield at the road ahead.

As soon as Keiko's father's eyes are off them, Sam draws a huge breath, feels his lungs expand against his rib cage. The claustrophobic shell enclosing him—desiccated and brittle from the despair and stress of his father and Bidwell's deaths, bile-bitter with the shame he caused Fujiwara-san, fractured by the helplessness of being separated from Yuriko—disintegrates and scatters like confetti in the fresh California wind.

Sam is suddenly giddy with a sense of total release. Blinking, he looks around at the unfamiliar landscape. But instead of freedom, what he sees whipping past are long rows of winter-pruned grapevines, leafless and gray, like gnarled stumpy ill-formed bonsai. And it occurs to him that shame is a shell that grows back, that forgiveness and grace are not so easily won, that he is only out on bail from the courtroom of fate. Determined then to savor every moment of respite and beauty, he stares once more at the young woman sitting across from him, and he drinks her radiance like a toast to this first day of the new year.

Keiko sees Sam looking at her.

When she meets his gaze and steadily holds it with open and innocent curiosity, Sam's heart fills with gratitude and inexpressible tenderness. Wordlessly, Sam bows his head to her.

Without any way of knowing what he is thinking or feeling, Keiko smiles shyly and dips her head, politely returning his bow.

Mochi

JANUARY 1939

WHEN THEY REACH HIS FARM, UNCLE GENZO TURNS OFF THE COUNTY road and pulls up next to a line of cars and trucks parked in front of his barn. Al, Dewey, and Sam get out. Sam turns to extend his hand, but Keiko is already in motion. She lands lightly next to him. When she notices his hand, she tosses him a grin before running off to join her girlfriends. Al and Dewey lead Sam toward the house and around to the side yard, where a gang of young men are making *mochi*. Standing upright on the ground is a stout two-foot oak log with its top hollowed into a bowl. In the bowl is a big lump of cooked rice. From either side two young men pound the rice with long-handled oak mallets while a third fellow reaches in between blows and turns the rice. The beaters swing rhythmically, smacking the rice, compacting it blow by blow into a dense heavy dough.

"Hey, aren't you guys done with that batch yet?" The question comes from the women waiting at a makeshift table propped on sawhorses. Keiko and her mother put on aprons and rub white flour onto their hands. Keiko and her two best girlfriends walk over to the rice beaters. "That's good enough, boys," says Mitsy.

"Yeah, you guys. Quit showing off and start on the next batch," says Haru.

"Wait!" yells one of the beaters. "Let's go!" And they work up to a final burst of high-speed pounding. Finally, the beaters give up, breathless, their arms and bare torsos flushed, glistening with sweat.

Haru lifts out the dough and places it onto the floured tray Keiko holds. One of the beaters gives Keiko a wink and a grin. "There you go. Perfect."

"It better be," warns Mitsy, looking past the speaker and straight at Sam.

Keiko carries the dough to the table. Her mother throws down a handful of fresh dry flour, and the other women and girls spread it over the tabletop. Keiko places the dough in the center of the table. The women squeeze off pieces of dough, roll, pat, and smooth them into the small round rice cakes called *mochi*.

Dewey rushes to the mortar, dumps in a fresh mass of steaming sweet rice.

Al pulls off his shirt, grabs a mallet. He nods toward Sam. "This is Dewey's cousin, Sam Hamada. He just arrived from Hawaii."

The guys say hi, hello, welcome to California and, "We assume you can hula, but can you pound *mochi*?" They laugh, and Sam strips off his shirt.

Someone whistles. "Hey, George, look at those muscles. You better cut the wisecracks before the hula dancer pounds you." The guys laugh, and Al and Sam begin pounding while Dewey turns the dough.

Back at the long table the women want to know, "Who is he?"

"Sam Hamada," says Keiko.

"He speaks perfect Japanese," says Keiko's mother. "Genzo says he was born in Hawaii, but raised by his mother and educated in Japan."

"He's our new Japanese-language teacher."

Haru gives Keiko a wide-eyed look. "He's our new sensei?"

"He's *really* good-looking," says Mitsy.

"He's Genzo's nephew."

"Is he going to be staying here?"

"No. Genzo got him a job working over on the next farm."

"You mean the Widow Franklin's place?"

"Yes. Sam will be living in the old foreman's cabin."

"Mmm . . . he can work for me anytime."

"Mitsy! Hush!"

The women, young and old alike, pause to check out the new man in town, roll their eyes, squeeze and pat the *mochi* dough, sputter, giggle, and laugh out loud.

Japanese-American Girl

JANUARY 1939

FOR ONE HOUR, FIVE DAYS A WEEK, AFTER REGULAR PUBLIC SCHOOL, the Japanese-American children of Lodi attend Japanese-language classes at the Buddhist temple. Sam is the youngest sensei who has ever taught there. His uncle Genzo told everyone that Sam is *kibei,* Japan-educated. Sam needs the job, so he refrains from adding that although he did learn to read and write in Japan, and he was the most advanced student in his class, he was only nine when his father brought him to Hawaii. Growing up on the plantation, Sam, like most of his friends there and his new friends here in Lodi, spoke Japanese at home and with the older members of the Japanese community. But Sam's considerable Japanese-language skills were developed over the years by self-study and monthly special assignments from the teachers he assisted at the Japanese-language school in Hawaii.

Sam is only a few years older than his Lodi students. The difference between them is Sam's far higher level of comprehension and fluency, especially in the breadth and depth of his reading and written vocabulary. Every week since leaving home, he has written a letter to his mother and Bunji and Akemi. And now he has added Yuriko and Fujiwara-san to his weekly Japanese correspondence list. Except in Yuriko's case, hating the idea of having his letters forwarded through Yuriko's mother's brothel in Hilo, he stores them for future mailing.

After vacationing over the Christmas and New Year's holidays, then two additional weeks to allow the new young sensei to settle into his job at the Widow Franklin's, the students return in late January. Sam arrives for his first class in Uncle Genzo's old pickup, driven by Dewey. Sam has spent the day in Mrs. Franklin's vineyard. He wears work clothes, boots caked with mud. At the classroom door, fiddling with the lock, he stands momentarily beside Keiko Yanagi.

Keiko feels a wave of heat coming off Sam's body and catches his scent—a blend of clean, healthy sweat, grapes, and wood smoke. And she infers that he's been pruning and burning cuttings. Keiko finds the smell delicious, intoxicating. Before she can stop herself, she leans closer and takes a deep whiff.

Sam swings the door open and steps aside to let her enter. He gives her a big smile.

Keiko blushes, dips her head, scoots past him.

Sam begins his first class by conversing in Japanese with each student for several minutes. Next, he tests their reading ability. Then Sam opens a newspaper and asks his students to write a Japanese translation as he reads in English: "January twenty-third, 1939. Denmark, Latvia, and Estonia have signed a nonaggression pact with Germany. Norway, Sweden, and Finland have refused. . . ." Another item catches his eye. "The German Reich has issued an order forbidding Jews to practice as dentists, veterinarians, and chemists. . . ." Finally, Sam asks the class to write something on their own. "Tell me how to bake a cake or play baseball. Describe someone you know or the dream you had last night. Have fun. Write me a letter, a story, or a poem."

"I'll write about my dream husband. . . ." says Mitsy.

Al perks up hopefully.

"Cary Grant," says Mitsy.

Al deflates, the class laughs.

After the end of his first day of teaching, Sam sits at his desk in the empty classroom. Leafing through the students' writing samples, he comes upon the poem written by the girl with the special smile, Keiko Yanagi. When he first saw it, he had to pause and collect his wits before he could read it to the class without stumbling over his own tongue. Sam felt like her words had been aimed directly at him. Keiko had titled her poem "A Japanese-American Girl."

Speaking to me on the telephone,
who would know the color or shape of my eyes?

Who knows what it is to be
a Japanese girl in America?
Who can see past my polite smile?
In a sunny autumn vineyard
who sees the color of the shadows?

Sam puts Keiko's poem on top of the stack of writing samples. On the level of daily conversation, most of his students are quite fluent, but as soon as they attempt to discuss anything complicated, they flounder. He had seen it in Hawaii; here on the mainland it is the same. His students are *Nisei*, second-generation, born and raised in America, the children of first-generation *Issei* immigrants. More than anything else, his *Nisei* students want to be one hundred percent American. In clothing, speech, and attitudes, his students mimic young Caucasian Americans. Especially now, with Japanese military imperialism advancing across Asia and anti-Japanese sentiment mushrooming throughout the United States, Sam's *Nisei* students resist identifying themselves as Japanese living in America, but rather as Americans cloaked in Japanese skins and Japanese names.

In their quest to be accepted as genuine Americans, his students risk losing their Japanese heritage. The more fluent they become in English, adopting every new bit of American teenage slang, the more his students distance themselves from their Japanese-speaking parents.

Sam remembers his first day of school in Hawaii. He was nine, humiliated and panicked in a classroom of staring first graders. The *haole* teacher's mouth moving, forming words Sam could not understand. Like a maddening form of deafness. Learning to communicate in English was like being reborn. Like breathing after drowning.

Sam knows his students consider the Japanese classes a boring waste of time and irrelevant to their lives. In Hawaii he desperately wanted to learn English. How can he get his students to want to improve their Japanese? How can he get them excited?

With the next class Sam begins developing a new curriculum. He retires the battered old textbooks and focuses on deepening his students' ability to communicate with their *Issei* parents. Each week he gives his class a new vocabulary list, then makes them practice their new words and phrases in provocative make-believe scenarios—sobering, tense, improvisational minidramas. And he adds one final twist that triggers some of his students' deepest insights. When Sam assigns roles, he swaps genders. "Al Yanagi, you're an *Issei* mother, you think you're pregnant, but you haven't told anyone yet. Mitsy, you're the *Issei* husband; if this crop fails, you will lose the ranch. Keiko, you're the only son, your dad expects you to take over, but you hate farming, you want to go to college and be a poet. Dewey, you're the daughter, you want to go to Hollywood and be an actress." Everyone laughs. "Okay, you're sitting at the dinner table. Start talking. In Japanese only. Let's hear what comes out."

In class after class, what comes out catches them all by surprise. The last teacher taught reading with children's books; Sam assigns poetry, short stories, and novels. The last teacher taught them how to ask a stranger for directions to the post office; Sam gives them the vocabulary of family members working through hard times and life-altering decisions.

One afternoon Al, momentarily swept away by his role of an *Issei* wife, turns to Mitsy, his *Issei* husband, and shouts, "Damn you. Stop ignoring me! You may be the master of this house, but I'm its heart." Al yells at his children, "You're the future of our family, but I'm the ground on which our past and present are built. Your survival, all of you, has been paid for by the sacrificing of my life. You've taken your pleasure and sustenance and comfort from my flesh and my spirit. You've ignored me, mocked me, disobeyed me, lied to me. You think I'm stupid and dull and weak. While I work and clean and cook to maintain our lives, you drink and gamble and play. On Mother's Day, an American holiday, you give me a card with words of praise or gratitude. But the printed words aren't even your own. And they're in English, a language I can't read. When have you ever thanked me? When have you ever stopped to think about how I feel?"

In tears Mitsy throws her arms around Al. "Oh, Mama, I'm so sorry!"

Al pats Mitsy's shoulder. He blushes with pleasure at being in her arms and from the blossoming of thoughts and emotions he hadn't known he possessed.

Anger, resentment, fear, hope, frustration, and love surface in the students' improvised dramas. They shout and curse like foul-mouthed drunkards—for Sam has given them that vocabulary, too. They weep. And laugh until they are limp.

Sam's students admire and respect him. The girls develop crushes on him. Dewey and Al are his new best friends. Dewey in his work shirts and blue jeans reminds Sam of a lanky Japanese-American cowboy. Keiko's younger brother, Al, is handsome verging on pretty, especially when he flashes his shy million-dollar grin. Al's laughter sounds like music.

Haru is Dewey's girlfriend. Al adores Mitsy. But Mitsy, her sweet virginal body swelling into womanhood, her quick and clever mind realizing that grown men have begun staring at her, decides to use Sam for target practice. She fires arrow after flaming arrow—wetted lips parting into smiles, sultry sleepy-eyed looks, pouts, winks, head tosses, hip wiggles, and even glimpses of cleavage—every technique of flirting or feminine seduction she can conjure. Her inspiration comes from novels, movies, romance magazines, and radio love songs. She doesn't know what she is doing, but she works hard at it, like someone new to fishing, eagerly testing every bait and lure.

Keiko's affection for her lifelong friend cools. She thinks Mitsy is acting like a cat in heat, and watches Sam for the first glimmer that Mitsy's efforts have raised a positive response. Al suffers the torments of jealousy conflicting with friendship. To his and Keiko's relief, Sam never gives any indication that he finds Mitsy attractive.

No one realizes the effort that Sam puts into maintaining his placid exterior. He struggles to hide how much Mitsy's little games flatter and excite him. But it is even more difficult for him to conceal his reactions to Keiko Yanagi. Keiko never flirts like Mitsy. Her behavior blooms straight from her heart with a spontaneity that constantly surprises him. "No," he says in class one afternoon. "That was incorrect."

"Well, then," Keiko's voice softens into a low imploring purr, "teach me."

Sam drops a box of chalk on the floor. The girls giggle; the guys grin. Keiko blushes. Sam gathers his chalk, retreats to his desk. Later in the midst of a quiz, sitting quietly grading papers but feeling swollen and distended by all the sexual energy boiling within him, Sam looks up, finds Keiko staring at him, her gaze both innocent and curious. A guilty blush spreads over his face. Keiko responds with a big goofy smile that illuminates the whole room.

Such a smile! It overwhelms Sam's defenses, triggers a reaction as natural as squinting under bright sunlight; his heart swings open in a way that he has never before experienced. Unbidden, his heart invites Keiko to enter.

Then Sam's conscience rebukes him. Has he forgotten? His heart has been promised to Yuriko. His honor will be destroyed if he breaks his word. Waves of sorrow and regret pass through him.

Once again his eyes meets Keiko's. He feels her looking directly into his heart. He watches her expression soften, and he realizes that she has seen the pain within him. And he also realizes that he made no effort to hide it from her. He wants her to know him.

Obon

JULY 1939

BEDROOM CURTAINS DRAWN AGAINST THE SEVEN O'CLOCK SUN, HER skin aglow in the ninety-eight-degree heat, Keiko stands naked before her bedroom mirror. Holding Mitsy's movie magazine open to a picture of Katharine Hepburn, Keiko slowly rotates, examining her face and figure. She hears Mama coming. Quickly, she hides the magazine and puts on her panties and new bra.

Kuwano comes into the bedroom with a large package.

"Oh! Is that it, Mama?" Keiko reaches out with trembling fingers and touches the brown string tied around the package. "It came in time!" She studies the Japanese characters in the return address. "From your older brother, Nobutaro-san, in Nagoya."

"Yes. You can see by the calligraphy that he's a man of strength and character."

Keiko has waited over a year for this moment, but knowing that her mother finds impatience vulgar, Keiko fights the urge to tear into the package. Gifts demand a proper show of appreciation, respect, and humility. Keiko opens the fabric-covered sewing box she made in her high school home economics class. She lifts the scissors with a trembling hand. "Mama, I'm sorry I'm so American, but I can't stand it." Keiko snips the string then tears off layer after frustrating layer of paper until she comes to the cardboard box. When she opens it, light seems to emanate into the bedroom. They both exclaim in unison, "Oh! Oh, my!"

Keiko lifts the kimono from the box. Exquisitely subtle pastels—purple, green, blue, and the palest pink of twilight—hand-painted on fine silk, fill the bedroom with the hushed glow of wisteria cascading over flowing water.

Keiko can hear the colors like music in her heart.

"I told you," says Kuwano, wiping tears from her eyes. "I told you my brother would not fail you."

Her face radiant with joy, Keiko gently hugs her new kimono. She brushes the silk against her cheek, inhales deeply. "Oh . . . it smells like Japan."

Kuwano helps Keiko dress. "You are pretty as a butterfly," she says as she wraps the obi, the wide silk brocade sash, around Keiko's waist. "Lift your arms."

"Wait. I'm trapped." Keiko pulls her long sleeves free of the obi. "Mama, I can hardly breathe. How can women in Japan wear kimono every day?"

"The skin around my mother's waist was discolored because of her obi."

Just as Kuwano finishes knotting the sash, Mitsy arrives with her makeup case. Kuwano frowns. "Not too much. I don't want my daughter looking like a . . . well, you know what I mean."

Mitsy winks at Keiko. "No. What do you mean?"

Keiko giggles, and color lovelier than any powder rises in Keiko's cheeks.

Kuwano gazes at her daughter. *There,* she thinks, *that's what I mean. Women paint their faces hoping to duplicate that blush. . . .* "To cover her face with paint would be a crime. Mitsy, just look at her! She's beautiful!"

Keiko and Mitsy are both amazed. They have never heard Kuwano speak this way. Keiko's eyes fill. Immediately, Mitsy scolds her. "Keiko! Don't you dare start bawling! Your eyes will get all red and puffy."

Kuwano heaves a huge helpless sigh, shakes her head, and leaves the bedroom.

Several hours later, smiling in the warm summer twilight, Keiko and her girlfriends in their beautiful silk kimono stand before a square stage set in the middle of the street in front of the Lodi Buddhist temple. The street is barricaded at both ends and lit with strings of gaily colored paper lanterns. From the stage the Buddhist priest addresses the crowd through a PA system. "Obon is a festival in which we celebrate life and show appreciation to our ancestors. When I was a boy in Japan, on the day of the Obon, we went to the cemetery and burned incense before the gravestones of my ancestors. At nightfall we lit paper lanterns to guide their spirits home. Some families built bonfires of welcome in their front yards. For one day the dead and the living would be together again.

"After dinner, we gathered with relatives, friends, and neighbors just like we've gathered here tonight. And we danced. Oh, how we danced! We danced with aliveness burning like bonfires in our hearts to show our ancestors how gratefully we carried the life energy they had passed on to us.

"When I was a child, I loved the *taiko* drums and the joyous singing. It felt good to thank my ancestors in this way. It felt good to invite them to return and taste the food and drink of the earth. When I grew older, I loved how it was such an earthy festival, full of flirtatious womanly smiles and swaggering male cockiness."

The crowd laughs and murmurs with delight to hear these words coming from their normally somber Buddhist priest.

"While we celebrate here tonight, let us put aside our daily complaints and worries, just as our ancestors did the moment they died. As Buddhists we accept the truth that life is suffering. But for tonight, let us not worry or quarrel about anything. Let's dance and enjoy our aliveness and the aliveness of our families and friends."

The Sensei puts his hands together in *gassho*. The people join him, their voices blending into the ancient music of the holy words, *"Namu Amida Butsu . . . Namu Amida Butsu . . . Namu Amida Butsu."*

The Buddhist priest descends from the stage. Mitsy, Haru, and Keiko wait at the bottom of the wooden steps and bow as he passes. Then the three young women take the stage and begin a classical dance, which they have practiced for months. Their teacher smiles proudly from the street below. Mitsy cannot restrain herself. She loves the spotlight, and her movements sparkle with excitement. Haru dances with perfect, precise motions. But Keiko is transformed, lit from within by an unearthly radiance. The spirit of the Obon has entered her.

Keiko's mother, eyes shining with tears, glances around at the crowd, at the rapt admiring faces. But then her eyes narrow, and she frowns when she notices that the most ardent of Keiko's admirers is the new young Japanese-language sensei.

After the classical dance, two musicians leap onto the stage. One beats the *taiko* drums, the other plays a bamboo flute. Folk music, music of the Obon. Keiko, Mitsy, and Haru remain dancing on the stage, while down on the street, the crowd dances around them in three concentric rings.

Sam dances in the middle line of celebrants slowly orbiting the stage. He studies Keiko with a martial artist's eye. She moves with grace and clarity, centered and comfortable in her body. She possesses flexibility and stamina. Sam values and admires these traits.

Keiko becomes aware of Sam's unwavering gaze. Color flares in her cheeks. She glances at him, her eyes alive with excitement.

Sam continues to study her movements. He sees that she knows he is watching her, yet she does not grow flustered or stiff or change speed or do anything different. Nothing in her dancing changes. She remains clear and centered. Sam's respect for her deepens.

They are doing a dance that requires a half-circle turn to the right and then to the left. Swinging toward him, Keiko meets Sam's eyes for an instant with a look so bold that Sam falters and takes a misstep.

She smiles at that, then rotates away from him.

Sam is shaken. He realizes Keiko has just given him two martial arts lessons. The first is a reminder of the power of a focused gaze. The second lesson is so subtle, it amazes him down to his toes. A lesson in motion, a way of rotating the body in a confined space without imbalance, without surrendering or jeopardizing one's protective boundaries. Turning and exposing one's back in a way so imbued with awareness that it offers no opening for attack.

When Keiko rotates a half-circle back, Sam turns away from her, and shows her what he has just learned.

For Keiko observing him, it feels as if Sam has developed eyes between his shoulder blades and can still see her.

When the dance ends, Sam faces Keiko. He bows to her as he would to a martial arts sensei, bows with such genuine respect, she is taken aback. She returns his bow and gives him a shy smile.

People are laughing, talking, wiping sweat from their faces, children with sparklers run between the street dancers, and Haru announces the title of the next song. But Keiko cannot take her eyes from Sam's. He stands holding her gaze. Keiko feels she is about to float off the stage, drift past the strings of glowing paper lanterns and up into the warm summer sky, her long silk kimono sleeves dangling from her outstretched arms until she is just a moth-like silhouette against the full moon.

Only Sam's eyes tether her to the earth.

But then Sam feels other eyes on him, and he glances around. Keiko's mother and father are watching him from the far side of the stage. Sam bows to them and smiles. Keiko's mother looks so serious. Sam wishes he could hear what she is saying to Keiko's father.

A new song begins. Sam dances, but now he does not look at Keiko.

"I'm not an ogre," Kuwano says to her husband. "You think I disapprove because he's poor. But there's something else. I don't trust him. He acts like a man with something to hide. And Kei-chan can't see it."

Shoji gazes at his daughter, so young and fresh and pretty. But no, she is more than that. Far, far more than that. Keiko is breathtakingly, achingly beautiful tonight, dancing in her new kimono under the paper lanterns, her innocent heart tumbling in the bittersweet winds of first love.

Kuwano stares at Sam. Their eyes meet, and her gaze is so distrustful and hostile that Sam flinches. Breaking out in panicked sweat, he feels as if Keiko's mother has just discovered the secret room of his shame. She sees him bowing to that gaudy whore Ai-chan on the Honolulu docks, overhears his urgently whispered declarations—*I'll send for her. I want her to be my wife.* Sees Yuriko naked in the bedroom doorway, Yuriko cringing with horror and back-stepping to keep her toes clear of the blood pooling from *O-luna* Bidwell's corpse. Sam douses the light in his eyes, sweeps every emotion from his face, turns his face away from Kuwano's.

Kuwano's gaze narrows. Sam has eyes she does not trust. She must protect her daughter from him. He could hurt her.

The dancers turn and turn again. Keiko does not understand. Sam seems no longer interested in her. Even when he is facing in her direction, he does not look at her. His eyes are distant, mouth set, body stiff, movements jerky and robotic. He seemed so happy a moment ago. What's happened?

The song ends. Keiko watches Sam leaving, the line of dancers adjusting themselves, filling the void he left. He carries his shoulders high and hunched, like a man protecting himself from blows on the back. But before he disappears into the darkness beyond the crowd, just on the edge of light from the paper lanterns, he looks back.

Their eyes meet. He sees her hurt and bewilderment. And he cannot stop himself. He allows her a glimpse of something he would never show her mother or any other human being.

Keiko has a single heartbeat to read his eyes: his regret and apology, his fear, anger, pain, and shame. And something more. Something like a wish, a yearning, a wanting . . .

A question.

Yes! Keiko feels herself respond with a spontaneous, joyous, full-body blush.

Yes, Sam. Yes!

Samurai Jitterbug

OCTOBER 1939

THE AUTUMN GRAPE HARVEST BEGINS, AND JAPANESE-LANGUAGE classes are suspended. Sam works in the vineyards eighteen hours a day, seven days a week. Japanese migrant farm laborers flood into Lodi's Japantown. The shops and restaurants remain open twenty-four hours to serve the army of farmworkers, almost all single men with harvest pay in their pockets, who come to eat, drink, gamble, and whore in the four square blocks of Japantown.

Before and after school, Al and Keiko help their parents. Shoji spends every waking moment making noodles, and Kuwano shuttles between the restaurant kitchen and the boardinghouse that she and her husband manage.

After a month of nonstop work, the harvest peaks and concludes. The migrant laborers move on, and Japantown's permanent residents collapse from exhaustion. Even the storefronts appear to sag, as if expelling a collective sigh of relief.

To celebrate the successful harvest, a dance is held at the Buddhist temple in late October. The Obon had been a Buddhist festival of traditional Japanese folk dancing. This dance is all-American. Jitterbug! Slow dancing, close and dreamy.

Keiko arrives early, ready to be swept off her feet.

After the Obon, Sam seemed cool and distant in class. During the grape harvest, when classes were suspended, Keiko missed him terribly. She had told him that she would be working in the restaurant and kept waiting for him to stop by and visit her over a bowl of noodles. But he never appeared. The day classes resumed, Keiko was so eager and happy to see him. She felt crushed when he seemed to be taking extraordinary care to treat her exactly like all his other students; no . . . in fact, he was colder and more critical of her than the others—admitting it to herself alone in her bed that night, she wept. The best explanation she could conjure, the only one that calmed her enough to sleep, was that Sam didn't want anyone, especially her mother, to know that he had feelings for Keiko. *That's why he's been so aloof.*

But not tonight. Tonight is going to be different.

She has been fantasizing about dancing with Sam, both of them glittering like Hollywood movie stars. But now in the big hall, jammed with frenetic young dancers, music booming, Sam is withdrawn and awkward. She confronts him. "Sam, what's wrong?"

Sam dredges for something to tell her. Something true. Tonight she won't settle for anything less. "I never learned to dance."

"That's unacceptable. I'll teach you."

"It looks complicated."

"It's called the jitterbug, and there's nothing complicated about it."

"People . . . will stare at me."

She has never seen him this hesitant. Then she understands. *Ah! Loss of face.* "You'll survive." Keiko takes his hand and leads him onto the dance floor. She teaches him the steps. He makes mistakes, begins clowning. Keiko won't have it. "Stop that! How would you feel, Sensei, if I acted like that whenever you tried to teach me something new? Is this how you learned the martial arts?"

Sam reels like he's been slapped.

Keiko fears she has overstepped; instead she hears respect in his voice. "Sorry. Show me one more time?"

"Sure. Listen to the music. Hear the beat? Okay, here we go."

After that, he learns quickly. But Keiko is bothered by the glowering ferocity of Sam's concentration. Finally, she grabs and shakes him. "Hey, relax! This isn't a matter of life and death. It's supposed to be fun, okay?"

He nods. "Okay."

She smiles. "I think you've invented a new dance. We can call it the samurai jitterbug."

The song ends. The next is a slow dance. Keiko takes Sam's hands and positions herself so he can watch her feet. They dance like that for a while, then she says, "I think you've got it. Okay . . . Look at me, not your feet."

Sam raises his eyes to hers, and she senses something like an electrical buzz pass between them. A weak zap fading to nothing. His eyes are on hers, but his mind is in his feet. Understandable. But what surprises Keiko is her anger. She was caught off guard by Sam's initial shyness and vulnerability. Then she began enjoying their role reversal—she liked playing the teacher for a change. And now she likes touching him.

But this is not enough for her. She is not happy.

She wanted a Japanese Clark Gable, cool and self-assured. Instead, she has a sweat-soaked country bumpkin slow-dancing for the first time in his life. Then he tells her he'd been so afraid of appearing inept, he almost didn't come to the dance. *Losing face* . . . His fear of losing face in such a public arena and of not measuring up to her expectations has reduced him to a frightened little boy. And Keiko is astonished and ashamed at her own impatience and intolerance. *Connection.* That's what she wants. She and Sam are physically closer than they have ever been. They are touching, yet totally out of touch.

Sam is so overwhelmed, he can barely form a coherent thought. He has no desire to talk, but even if he did, his teeth are clenched so tightly that he fears his jaws would crackle if he opened his mouth. Seeking his center, his point of balance, he struggles for a deep breath.

Dancing in Sam's uncomfortably stiff arms, Keiko discards the last of her tattered fantasies and ruined expectations, and feels herself awakening to the astonishing reality of her own lithe body. With all her senses clear and with feline grace she moves into Sam. She fits her body to his and holds him. Their feet stop moving. They sway gently with the music. His body feels hot, his shirt damp, but she rests her cheek on his chest and inhales his clean salty scent. She had come to the dance expecting a dream. What she holds in her arms could not be more real. Not Gable, but . . . *Oh, he smells delicious!*

She feels life flowing into his stiff arms and hands. His chest swells, and she realizes he has been holding his breath. The song ends, but he does not release her. They stand hugging. Someone announces the next dance is lady's choice.

Keiko and Sam hear excited female voices rapidly approaching them. They step away from each other and find themselves surrounded by the girls in Sam's Japanese-language class. Mitsy grabs Sam and jitterbugs away with him.

Mitsy is a flashy dancer. She moves every part of her anatomy provocatively, aims her body mostly at Sam, but she's generous and draws looks from others around them. When the song is over, Mitsy is mobbed by guys wanting to dance with her. Keiko's brother, Al, manages to outmaneuver them. But before Al whisks her away, Mitsy grabs Sam's arm. "Hey, Sensei, let's do at least one slow dance together, okay?" She winks. "I want you to hold me like you were holding Keiko. Ooohhh . . . it looked sooo hot!"

Sam retreats from the floor. He seeks refuge with two guys leaning against the wall. He doesn't know them, and they ignore him, but he remains there through the next several numbers. All the guys want to dance with Keiko, Mitsy, and Haru. Keiko looks over at Sam from time to time. Sam winces at the storm warnings in her eyes.

The guys next to Sam finally work up the nerve to start dancing. That leaves Sam alone and exposed. He looks around for a fellow sufferer. Anyone will do. His cousin Dewey jitterbugs over to him. "Get ready to grab Keiko as soon as this song's over. And while you're dancing with her, make sure you ask her to save the last dance for you. The bases are loaded and you've got two strikes. If you dance with Mitsy again before you dance with Keiko, you're dead." Lanky limbs flailing, Dewey gyrates wildly away from Sam.

Sam sighs and shakes his head at Dewey. He leans miserably against the wall, crosses his arms, lowers his chin to his chest, withdraws deep into himself, and immediately bumps into the image of his old sensei. Sam wanted to learn to fight like a samurai, and Fujiwara-san sent him chasing butterflies. Sam remembers how long he had to practice before he was able to catch and release them unharmed. He remembers how he had learned to track, then merge, then disappear into their flight paths. Butterflies, dancing, and *mu*— nothingness, to throw away the self. Why? Because self gets in the way of the constantly flowing *ki,* the magic *it.*

Keiko has been watching Sam. She can't decide if he's a drunk asleep on his feet or a Zen monk in deep meditation. But she's had enough. To hell with him.

Sam raises his head, searches the crowd. He spots Keiko and pushes off the wall.

Keiko sees him walking deliberately as a tiger toward her. Their eyes meet, and a jolt of velvet-soft lightning crackles from her eyes to the soles of her feet.

There seems to be no transition between the end of the jitterbug and the beginning of the slow dance. Sam comes up, not elbowing or shoving, but guys waft away like smoke on either side of him. Sam asks her to dance, but she has no sense of hearing his voice. She just finds herself swaying in his arms as though it were a condition of nature. She sighs deeply, and he does, too. Forget Clark Gable, she is dancing with a Zen tiger. What a surprise! *Mmm, this is wonderful . . .* And she snuggles into him.

Such an insignificant act on her part, but it gives Sam a sudden erection. When Keiko feels it against her, she is so startled, she looks down and blurts out, "Oh, dear!"

Sam leaps back, collides with the couple behind him. "Excuse me." Blushing furiously, he sidesteps away from the couple and Keiko. "Please save the last dance for me. Excuse me. I'm sorry. I . . . please excuse me." And he's gone.

Sam hides in the men's room, waiting for his erection to subside. It proves stubborn, and he begins to fear the dance will be over before he can come out. He splashes cold water on his face and curses himself.

The moment he returns to the dance floor, Mitsy ambushes him with a quick grab, and they begin jitterbugging. Sam is relieved. He thinks maybe if he diverts most of his blood into his muscles, there might not be enough left over to fuel his unruly penis. Sam begins dancing with great gusto. He dances near Dewey and tries to copy his cousin's moves. Dewey laughs.

Mitsy is delighted.

Keiko is furious.

The next dance is slow and Mitsy says, "Yes, I'd love to," even though Sam hasn't spoken a word. Mitsy's idea of slow-dancing is so erotic, it makes all the young men watching her salivate and want to howl at the moon.

Sam needs to be touched like this, and he almost loses himself. He feels his sexual heat rising but catches Keiko staring at him. He tries to give her a reassuring smile, one that says, *It's okay. Mitsy's just being Mitsy, and I'm still yours.*

Just then Mitsy makes a sly move that rubs her hipbone along Sam's penis. Sam's expression changes. He frowns and a chill encircles his heart; in his mind he hears huge black doors close with a resounding *boom.* His penis stays limp.

Keiko sees it all: Mitsy's bump and grind, Sam's initial reaction, then the glacial ice engulfing his face. It satisfies her but also frightens her. A man who can block out someone as sensuous as Mitsy—how can she, Keiko, hope to reach and hold such a man?

After dancing with Mitsy, Sam makes an effort to dance with each of his female students. When the last dance is announced, Sam has to walk past Mitsy to get to Keiko. Mitsy sees him coming toward her, and she smiles at him. He returns her smile, but keeps going until he stands in front of Keiko.

They dance.

Keiko is dizzy, so many unexpected feelings, so many new questions,

thinking, *But for now, for this one last dance, just hold him and be happy.*
She closes her eyes. An image comes to her. A hill. A smooth round hill covered with tall yellow grass and clusters of oak. High up, just below the crest, there is a scar where the earth has eroded, exposing jagged gray rock. The outward appearance of the hill is a lie. Inside, it's knife-edged granite. *I'll never break through. He will never let me in.*

Sam is tense and knows she can feel it in his body. He wants desperately to relax. But he fears becoming sexually aroused again. *This is the last dance, fool. Throw yourself away. For her. Do it. Now.* He closes his eyes, draws a deep breath. He exhales and feels his heart open. And the truest, gentlest part of himself, terrified at the sudden exposure and height, falls.

Into Keiko's arms.

Falling to his doom, caught by an angel, Sam whispers, "Thank you, Keiko."

She feels the change in him. She is too young and inexperienced to understand it, but she loves it—the feeling, dark, mysterious, deep. Sam rests totally in her hands, she can break him with a finger snap; if she drops him, he will shatter. But she doesn't know it.

The song ends.

They let go of each other, step back, trade smiles, survivors of a storm at sea, surprised to find themselves intact, shaky on their legs but back on solid ground.

Love Secret

OCTOBER 1939

AFTER THE DANCE, SAM WALKS KEIKO HOME TO THE BOARDINGHOUSE her parents manage in exchange for free rent. Only three blocks. Barely enough time to say how much he enjoyed dancing with her. And thanks again for being such a good teacher. He feels an overwhelming need to talk, he wants a million insignificant words to fill the air between them, to settle like snow, to cushion the real sounds of their real shoes against the real pavement, to build some distance between himself and Keiko and reality.

Balanced against Sam's agitation is the steady warmth of Keiko's serenity. She feels calm and clear and sure of herself. Several hours ago while preparing for the dance, she had prayed Sam would walk her home. And here it is, but it's not the dreamy, walking-on-air feeling she had imagined. She finds herself listening to Sam's nonstop monologue as if she is an animal unfamiliar with human speech. She ignores the meaning of his words and listens to the tones in his voice. What she hears is distress and distance. What she senses is a struggle—a deep yearning to approach and touch, combined with a fear of allowing that to happen.

They pass her parents' restaurant. Closed, but with lights on in the kitchen and over the basement stairs. Papa is making fresh noodles for tomorrow.

When they come to the boardinghouse, Keiko and Sam pause on the sidewalk. Keiko touches Sam's arm. "The next time that happens," she glances down then quickly away from his crotch, "don't run. I hate people who run like mice. You don't need to hide from me."

Overwhelmed and off balance, Sam does not hear Keiko's last sentence correctly. "I'm not hiding anything from you," he says.

Instantly, Keiko knows he is lying.

But before the next heartbeat, she dismisses her feeling as unacceptable and impossible. Keiko tips her head to one side, looks at him, perplexed. Her mind circles around Sam's lie. She splits in two, stands on opposite sides of a square black table. In the middle of the table is a sheet of paper inscribed with the words, *I'm not hiding anything from you.*

One side of her mind speaks in Sam's defense. It babbles on and on. The other side remains silent, calm and sure. The speaking side says, "He must be telling the truth. He *must* be. He couldn't lie to you. He loves you." The speaking side grows more and more defensive, edged with hysteria.

Then from the other side of the table comes a single pronouncement: "Maybe he lied *because* he loves you."

Keiko's mother opens an upstairs window, scolds Keiko for standing around talking in the street at night. Keiko and Sam look at each other. Sam starts to say something. But Keiko's hand flies to his face, lightly touches his lips. Her voice is quiet, almost a whisper. "Whatever you're hiding from me, whatever you're keeping secret, is okay. It's your business, not mine. Just don't ever lie to me. Please."

Sam stares at her. Finally, he says the only thing he can: "I'm sorry."

Keiko's smile is sad but full of gentleness. Again her mother calls.

Sam stands, unable to move. Keiko's eyes are soft, clear, wise. She is in full possession of herself, and at the same time, she seems to be giving everything to him.

"Good night, Sam."

"Good night, Keiko."

Keiko goes in and closes the door. Sam stands paralyzed on the sidewalk. He hears his old teacher chuckling in his ear. *"Now you know."*

"What?"

"She's a samurai woman."

Sam cannot think of any way to respond to Fujiwara-san in Japanese. Only English will do. *"Wow . . ."*

Tie Clip

October 1939

THAT NIGHT IN HIS CABIN, SAM LIES AWAKE IN BED. EYES BURNING WITH fatigue, he lifts his head from the pillow and checks his alarm clock—almost three-thirty in the morning. He groans and lets his head drop. Once again, as he has every day since he left Hawaii, Sam wonders why Yuriko hasn't written to him—is she in prison, sick, dead, or has she fallen in love with someone else? Almost a year has passed and no word. What will happen when Yuriko arrives in California . . . and he marries her? Marries her? How can he do that?

Keiko . . . She unsettles him. Hell, she terrifies him. She forces him to admit how much of his persona is a shield conceived and maintained to keep people away from his real self. But Keiko is able to see straight into his heart. She speaks with a boldness and honesty that reduces his own words to the babbling of an idiot. Her actions are decisive as a sword stroke. How can a woman so young be so wise? How can a woman so delicate and graceful be so powerful? A samurai woman . . .

Maybe he can get Keiko to back off? Fat chance. She appears to be in love with him. Are the gods blessing or toying with him? Being with her is bliss and terror. Can he measure up to her? Can he hold her? Naked? Yes! No! Absolutely not. She will burn him; she will burn him to cinders. And how he aches and hungers for that . . .

He has no right entertaining such thoughts. He has given his word to Yuriko.

The word of a samurai. His bond. Sam is exhausted and feverish. Dazed, falling asleep, starting to dream. Of promises. And ropes. The promises he made to Yuriko are the twisted fibers of a hemp rope tying them to each other. Sam dreams he is dangling over an abyss. No matter how tightly he holds on, he is sliding down. The hemp is frayed, breaking, burning and cutting his hands. He aches with the desire to let go, but he feels the rope tightening like a python around his body and neck. And he realizes that a promise can bind even when broken.

Slipping deeper into sleep, Sam dreams of a single white silk thread connecting him to Keiko. Their love is a promise he hopes will hold forever. He hears Keiko whispering, *"Sam, our love is the only promise we must never break."*

Sam opens his hand, intending to release the rope to Yuriko. He hears the sharp twang of a freed bowstring. And he flies, arcing high into the air. Naked and winged, he soars, hovering at the apex, his spine toward heaven and his groin exposed to the earth.

And though he does not see Keiko anywhere beneath him, suddenly he feels her, the long smooth caress of her skin and the hot sting of her rigid nipples against his chest as he descends into her. As he gasps awake in midorgasm, Sam's eyes snap open. Moonlight slants through the window. He takes his cock in his hand, and the firm slippery feel of it is neither poetic nor dreamlike. Crowbarred by his own flesh, pried from his dream wings and dumped onto his bed of snarled, sweaty, semen-spattered sheets, Sam stares at the guillotine blade of moonlight cutting across his wall, and he knows he must make a choice.

Daylight. Sam sits at the table in his little farmworker's shack, the floor littered with crumpled paper—in front of him is a sheet bearing two columns: one for Yuriko, the other for Keiko. Hoping to bring order to his confusion, he had begun the comparison with a notation that Yuriko was a Japanese-*Japanese* woman and Keiko was a Japanese-*American* woman. He went on to list and grade qualities like physical features, personality traits, education, skills, intelligence, imagination, sexuality, grace, sense of humor, courage, self-sacrifice, and diligence . . .

Sam massages his temples. Think! Think this through. Logic. Reason. Damn! What is it? This thing. This thing he has for Keiko. Sam groans. *Thing?* Isn't it enough to be an idiot? Must he add timidity and cowardice to the list of charges against him? *Love,* damn it. Call it by it's proper name. It's love. But wait—is it? How can he be sure? What does he know of love? He sincerely believed that what he had felt for Yuriko was love. What if after going to bed with her, the love he feels for Keiko turns out to be no different than what he first felt for Yuriko? He must not forget that right now with Keiko there is the added zing of unavailability. Self-imposed, because he is the only one blocking the way. Which brings him full circle. Back to his promise to marry Yuriko, his samurai code of honor at stake.

He cannot pursue Keiko . . . unless . . . what? How? How can he make this work?

Forget it. No. Think! Think it through. All right. Just answer one question: Why? Why does he love Keiko? He closes his eyes, meditating on the question. Yes . . . Keiko has a good heart and she's beautiful. And smart. No . . . she's more than smart; she's sharp, quick, intuitive, in touch with a deep natural wisdom. She has the attributes of a samurai warrior woman—calm under pressure, clear-eyed and fully present, willing to stand or fight when confronted. She has a strong, supple, graceful body. . . .

Again Sam begins to groan, but midway the sound moving up from his chest softens into a moan of pure animal longing. He opens his eyes and crumples his list. The answer cannot be calculated numerically. The sum of all Keiko's finest attributes do not add up to the reason for his love. Keiko did not outscore Yuriko; Keiko does not measure higher than any other woman because of her positive traits. Now Sam breathes deep and slow and the certainty growing inside him is as real as the air moving in and out of his lungs—

no one, man or woman, *earns* a love like this. One either has it or doesn't have it . . . or more precisely, a love like this either comes into your life or it doesn't.

There is no reason for this love. There is no *why*. And that is the answer.

He had hoped to clarify his choice with reason and logic. But love does not care about reason, logic, or choice. Love will not fit into tidy columns, will not be quantified or measured.

Keiko has not won his love. Yuriko has done nothing to lose or deserve it less.

Love does not recognize his good intentions or samurai code of honor. Like yin and yang, love is the other half of *mu;* instead of nothingness, it is everythingness; it fills Sam's heart and mind without regard to his dismay at what is being squashed or displaced. It is not his to control. Only to betray and lose.

But how do you know? How can one be sure? Certainty? Is that what you're asking for? Yes. Certainty, damn it!

What would his old teacher say? He would say, *Isamu, are you ready to be tested?*

Sam closes his eyes. Waits.

Isamu, what color is your promise to Yuriko-san?

Sam sees his father's old cast-iron skillet. Black, both shiny and dull . . . varying shades of gray, two tiny pits of rusty orange. Burnt-oil smoke rising, it sits on the stove. Smoking-hot skillet. Empty of food.

What color is your love for Keiko-san?

Sam's closed eyelids flutter. His mind floods with light. He sees an autumn vineyard ablaze with color. An enormous sky, windblown clouds, two hawks high up and circling, tiny against a fierce sun. Their cries, wild as naked swords, slice into his heart.

That's it.

He is sure.

He cannot marry Yuriko. He will write and tell her the truth.

Sam breathes a huge shaky sigh of relief. He is close to tears.

"Sam! Sam Hamada, hello?" Mrs. Franklin calls to him from the main house.

Sam jumps up and opens the door of his shack. "Yes, ma'am, I'm coming."

He walks past the vegetable garden and orange trees, across the dew-speckled back lawn, and along the brick path between Mrs. Franklin's prizewinning roses. The old lady stands on the back porch. She holds one hand up, shading her eyes from the morning sun.

Alberta Franklin reminds Sam of a snow white egret. She is seventy-three, and her hair, which she keeps cut short, is pure white. She is tall; her neck, arms, and legs are skinny, her shoulders somewhat hunched; and she looks about with eyes that alternate between a hunter's focused attentiveness and a kind of stately bemused distance. Her voice quavers. But her pride and dignity are rock solid. "Your uncle came by to see you yesterday. But you had already left for the dance. Ah! The dance. Did you enjoy the dance?"

"Yes, ma'am, I did."

"I'm glad. I used to be a wonderful dancer in my day. I could have danced all night, every night of the year, and never gotten bored. More than once I went to bed with blisters on my feet. But they were worth it."

"Yes, ma'am."

"Whenever there's a dance, you go to it. When you get to be my age, you'll be afraid to move for fear of falling down and breaking something. Get in all the dancing you can while you're young."

"Yes, ma'am, I'll try. To tell the truth, last night was my first dance."

"Really?"

"Yes, ma'am. I learned to jitterbug."

"I used to love to waltz. Did they play any waltzes?"

"No, ma'am. I don't think so. I don't know how to waltz."

"No? Well, you must definitely learn to waltz. I'll teach you."

"You will?"

"Yes. We could bring the Victrola out on the back lawn."

"It sounds like fun."

"Oh, yes. It will be fun, Mr. Hamada. You'll love it. The waltz is the natural dance of the heart in the first days of springtime. The waltz is the scent of roses and the colors of all the prettiest flowers you can think of. When I was young, I could dance a waltz that would bring tears to your eyes."

"Then I couldn't ask for a better teacher."

"That's right."

"Mrs. Franklin, I'd be forever grateful and honored if you'd teach me to waltz."

"We'll do it, Mr. Hamada. We'll do it for sure."

"Yes, ma'am. Thank you."

"Oh, my! Look what time it is. I'll be late for church."

"Yes, ma'am. I'll get the car ready."

Mrs. Franklin turns to go into the house.

"Uh, pardon me, Mrs. Franklin? What did my uncle want?"

"Oh, dear!" She laughs. "I forgot all about him. He brought you this letter." She reaches into the pocket of her dress, pulls out an envelope, and hands it to Sam.

A letter from Japan. From Yuriko. It takes all Sam's willpower to wait until Mrs. Franklin disappears into the house before he rips open the envelope.

September 28, 1939

Isamu-san,

I was sent to prison. I was sentenced to ten years. But luckily it was a token gesture to placate the Hawaiian authorities, so I was released after only three months.

Now I am working at a nice restaurant in Tokyo. I live upstairs with the owner, who is an old friend of my mother.

I have something to tell you that I hope does not displease you.

I have given birth to your son. He was born on the morning of June fourth.

I am sorry I took this long to inform you. I was already about three months pregnant when we parted in Hawaii. But I did not know if the baby I carried was yours or Bidwell-san's. I felt it was your baby, and I prayed very hard that it would be, but I could not be sure. With your permission I thought we could name him Yasubei after your father.

When the baby was born, I was going to send you a letter immediately, but he became very sick shortly after he was born. Everyone feared he might not survive. I waited until he was well before writing to you.

I hesitate in asking you this, because I don't want to burden you, but I had to borrow money to buy medicine and pay the doctor. Please send me some money as soon as possible. After all my debts and loans are paid, we can begin saving money to bring your son, Yasubei, and myself to America.

Please take good care of yourself.

With my deepest love, Yuriko

Stunned, clammy sweat soaking through his shirt, Sam stares at the photograph. Yuriko is dressed in a kimono. She sits holding a baby on her lap. The baby wears a floppy white cap. It looks like a knitted or crocheted sailor's cap. Clipped to the front brim, throwing off a glint of light from the dead center of the photograph, is Sam's father's gold tie clip.

Umetsu Chubei

OCTOBER 1939

SAM WALKS INTO THE CLASSROOM. SEVERAL OF HIS STUDENTS ARE wearing Halloween masks or costumes. Mitsy wears movie star dark glasses, Haru is dressed as a witch, and Keiko pretends to lick her paws and clean her homemade cat ears. Sam gives them a weak smile and announces a surprise quiz. The students clear their desks except for pens, paper, and dictionaries.

Sam faces the class. "I'm going to tell you a story that relates to my life. When I'm finished, you will write an essay about how the story relates to your own life.

"Once upon a time there was a samurai named Umetsu Chubei. One night he was alone on sentry duty, patrolling a trail along a cold and windy ridge. Below him he could see the lights of a village. Mist blew across the trail, and through the mist, he saw someone approaching. He called for them to halt.

"It was a woman with a baby in her arms. The woman was beautiful, and she wore white robes that billowed in the wind. She bowed and said, 'Please forgive me for bothering you, but I need to ask a favor. There is an emergency, and I must hurry down to the village. If I leave this baby here by the side of the trail, would you please watch over it until I return?'

"He said, 'The ground is cold and damp. I will hold the baby until you return.'

"She thanked him and handed him the infant. Then the woman leaped off the trail.

"Umetsu Chubei was shocked because the lady went down the cliff of jagged rocks and tangled bushes faster than he could have run on level ground. Her movements seemed effortless, like she weighed less than a silk scarf twirling in the wind.

"Just then the baby stirred. Umetsu Chubei saw that its eyes and mouth were shut tightly. *Such a tiny baby,* he thought, *it can't be more than a few days old.* Cradling the baby in the crook of his left arm, Umetsu Chubei resumed his patrol. Then the baby moved again. Umetsu Chubei looked down and thought the baby seemed to have grown bigger. But that was impossible. He felt the baby jerk once more, and he realized the baby was not growing in size, but in weight. The baby stirred again, and now there was no doubt. The baby was growing heavier and heavier with each passing second. Sweat ran down the samurai's face. He stuck his spear into the ground so he could use both arms to hold the baby, whose weight continued to double and double and double again.

"Umetsu Chubei listened to the wind hissing in the grass and he thought, *That lady was from the spirit world. She's trapped me, and now I'm doomed.* Clouds darkened the moon, and now with each beat of its heart the baby grew hotter as well as heavier. Soon Umetsu Chubei felt like he was hugging an iron cauldron full of red-hot coals. And he realized that he was about to die. Most people would have simply put the baby on the ground. But Umetsu Chubei could not. Why? Because a true samurai speaks once, then lives or dies according to his words. Umetsu Chubei had said he would hold the baby until the woman returned. Now he was down on his knees. He was gritting his teeth and panting. And the baby was crushing and burning the life out of him. But Umetsu Chubei did not whimper or cry out in fear or rage. Instead, he hugged the baby with all his strength and composed his mind to die.

"Suddenly, the moon broke free of the clouds, and the baby disappeared from Umetsu Chubei's arms. The samurai scrambled to his feet and looked up and down the trail and into the tall grass. But he could not find the baby anywhere. Then he saw the woman in white coming toward him. He bowed deeply. 'I'm sorry. I don't know how it happened, but I've lost your baby.'

"The woman answered in a clear and gentle voice, 'I am Kannon, the goddess of mercy, and I came to this village because I knew a woman was going to have great difficulty in delivering her child tonight. For her sake I needed to borrow your physical and spiritual strength. Her first son now sleeps at her breast. As your reward, you may keep what you found within yourself tonight. For all the days of your life on earth and through your blood to your posterity, for as long as it is not abused, you may keep what you have found.' Then the goddess began to glow brighter than the moon. Umetsu Chubei shielded his eyes, and she was gone.

"And it came to pass that Umetsu Chubei's stature as a samurai grew, and his feats of strength and perseverance became legendary throughout Japan. Umetsu Chubei's strength, even when he became an old man, honored and beloved by all, never faded, and his samurai spirit remained steady and shining and pure."

The students work on their essays. At his desk Sam sits reading a newspaper—the headline proclaims, NAZIS ATTACK WESTERN FRONT. Keiko longs to go to him; clearly something is wrong, but she is the only one who notices. She heard the strain in Sam's voice while he told his story. She saw the pain in his face. *Umetsu Chubei . . . what is he trying to say? That I need to be strong and persevering? That Sam needs to borrow my strength? Or maybe Sam wants to lend me his? Is it about honoring his word to the death? Maybe he gave his word to someone, and it is killing him?*

Sam raises his head. Their eyes meet, and Keiko sees such bitterness and sorrow that she almost bursts into tears. But there is no time. For a fleeting moment he exposes his terrible grief. This is his unspoken farewell to her. Then he chokes off all signs of feeling. He commits a form of emotional suicide, and she watches him bleed to death.

It is over in seconds.

She is looking into his eyes, but he is no longer there. The cold, dead husk that he left behind begins grading papers.

Dazed, Keiko lowers her head. *Why is he acting like this? Did I say or do something to offend him? At the dance? After? He's so angry. He hates me. But why?*

She does not understand what she has just witnessed, but she knows it was final. Heartbroken, Keiko bites her lip as tears roll down her cheeks.

Tag

NOVEMBER 1939

In the days that follow, Sam's body performs the chores of daily life. He mouths the words people expect to hear, he smiles and they smile back. But behind the facade his spirit wanders over a landscape of bare rock and howling wind.

Dewey and Al notice the change. Awkwardly, they try to draw Sam out, but he resists. They sense he is adrift in turbulent waters, but being young, possessing only rudimentary maps of their own inner seas, they retreat to known shores, guy talk—sports, politics, and work—thus helping Sam to build an even thicker layer of isolation around himself.

Keiko is disgusted with Al and Dewey. "Baseball? That's all you talked about?"

"And Hitler," says Dewey. "We talked about the war in Europe. The Nazis have invaded Poland. Britain and France have declared war on Germany. There are reports of terrible atrocities at a Nazi camp called Buchenwald."

"But what about Sam? You're his best friends! He's drowning, and you're standing there like a couple of big dumb dogs, wagging your tails and barking about sports and politics."

"He can't drown; he's a fish," declares Mitsy. "Yes, indeed, he's a cold fish, and I'm throwing him back in the river where he belongs."

"Mitsy, how'd you like a punch in the mouth?"

"Hey, sis, calm down. He'll be okay. Whatever it is, it'll pass."

"Yeah," says Dewey. "And really, it's none of our business."

"Right. Let's forget it," says Mitsy.

Keiko, furious, turns and leaves them.

Dewey lowers his voice. "Was she crying?"

"I told her not to get involved," says Mitsy.

Thinking Sam needs time and space to work out whatever is bothering him, Keiko gives him until after Thanksgiving. When she turns her calendar page to December, she decides to confront him. She plans her ambush with care. She wears a warm sweater and reties the laces of her saddle shoes. If he chooses to walk, she'll walk with him. If he wants to stand out in the cold and talk, she's ready. After class, she waits in the empty lot next to the Italian gambling house at the south end of Japantown. Here comes Sam, walking alone, lost in thought. He passes, and Keiko falls into step beside him. "Tag! You're it."

Startled, Sam gives a little sideways skip.

"Sam, what's wrong?"

"You surprised me."

"That's not what I meant. Something's bothering you. I want to know what it is."

"I don't want to talk about it."

"Was it anything I said or did? That night after the dance, I said some things . . ."

"No. This doesn't have anything to do with you."

Keiko heaves a sigh of relief. "You're not mad at me?"

"Oh, no, I'm not mad at you."

"That's good, because I thought maybe my knowing you had a secret made you hate me."

Sam flinches. Warily, he studies Keiko. She appears fresh, focused, and full of compassion.

"Don't be afraid, Sam. I won't betray you. Tell me what's wrong."

"Nothing. Nothing's wrong."

Keiko doesn't say a word. She waits and watches him with deeply caring eyes.

"I'm tired . . . and I've got a lot on my mind."

"Like what?"

"Like . . . oh, I don't know. My mother and sister and brother in Japan."

Keiko considers this for a moment. "Anything else?"

Sam shrugs. "Politics. You know . . . the war. Japan's formed alliances with Germany and Italy. The Nazis are bombing England. Japan's invaded Indochina. It worries me."

Keiko nods.

"Look," he says, "I've really got to go."

"Sam, tell me your secret."

"Keiko—"

"It's poisoning you. It's poisoning both of us."

"I can't."

"You must."

"Damn it! Please, Keiko, if you love me—" He is shocked at what he's just said. And the expression blossoming on Keiko's face rips his heart in half. "I mean . . . if you care about me, please don't ask me any more questions." Looking into her eyes, he is astonished—his own emotions are in chaos, but she is calmly weighing his plea.

This is the first time that Sam has ever asked her for anything, and Keiko takes it as a challenge and a chance to prove her love. "All right. I promise. Just stop giving me the cold shoulder."

"Okay, I'll try not to."

"You'd better do better than try, Buster."

"That sounds like Mitsy talking."

"Mitsy's not the only gal in town who can talk tough."

"She may talk tough, but you're the samurai woman."

Keiko smiles uncertainly. "What's that supposed to mean?"

"It's the highest compliment I've ever given a woman."

Keiko's face lights up. "Really? Well . . . thank you. Thank you very much."

Just then Dewey pulls up in Uncle Genzo's truck. "Hey, Sam, want a ride home?"

"What about me?" says Keiko.

"Sure. We can drive you home first."

Keiko sits between Dewey and Sam. When they arrive at Keiko's boardinghouse, Sam gets out. She waits until he reaches up to help her down. She gives his hand a little squeeze before she lets go. Keiko waves as they drive away. Then she jitterbugs across the sidewalk. She pauses. Would a samurai woman jitterbug? Keiko didn't ponder long. A Japanese-American samurai woman would. Yes, indeed. Especially at a moment like this. Keiko grins and jitterbugs toward her door.

Sam looks back and watches her jitterbugging as the lampposts go on.

Baby Picture

New Year's Day, 1940

Dawn. Sam is alone in the vineyard behind his cabin. In white uniform and black belt, his breath steaming in the frosty stillness, Sam practices the kata, the fluid and exacting movements of his martial art. Parry, kick, strike. Turn, parry, double strike. Finished, standing with the sun at his back, Sam bows, whispering New Year's blessings toward Hawaii and his former teacher. Sam strips and washes with cold water at the big outdoor pump. Getting dressed he glances around his cabin—one room with a single bed, a table barely big enough to seat two, an electric two-burner hot plate, homemade bookshelves. Everything washed, swept, and dusted the day before according to Japanese custom—to carry none of last year's dust into the new year.

Sam leaves his cabin, glances back at Mrs. Franklin's empty house, reminding himself that he is scheduled to pick her up at her daughter's home at nine that evening. Sam hikes away from the big white house with its green doors and window shutters. He walks through Mrs. Franklin's dormant Tokay-grape vineyard, hops the fence, and crosses the dirt road that marks the boundary of the acreage Uncle Genzo leases from her.

At Genzo's house Sam is greeted by Dewey and Al. They take Sam around to where the other men are gathered, preparing to pound *mochi*.

Through Genzo's kitchen window, Keiko and her mother watch Sam removing his shirt to join the men in their work. Walking through the kitchen, Uncle Genzo pauses for a moment to study the faces of Keiko and Kuwano.

Spooked by all the curious eyes observing him, Sam avoids Keiko all day.

Putting on her sweater to leave after helping wash dishes, Keiko goes out the back door and finds Genzo feeding scraps to his two German shepherds.

"Watch this," says Genzo. "Guard! Suke-san, Kaku-san, guard," and the dogs run to the porch, positioning themselves on either side of the door. "My samurai guards," says Genzo, proud and pleased that they had remembered their latest trick.

Keiko laughs and claps, and the dogs perk up their ears and wag their tails.

Across the yard Keiko's father and the other men are disassembling tables and carrying them into the barn, working quickly under the darkening sky.

Genzo leans close to Keiko. "You're in love with him, aren't you?"

"What? Who?"

"Him." Genzo nods toward Sam.

She blushes and cannot keep the confused emotions from showing in her eyes.

"Well . . ." says Genzo. "One thing's for certain—he loves you."

"You think so?"

"From the moment he met you, Kei-chan."

"Really? Do you really think he loves me?"

"It's more than that. He *knows* with absolute certainty that you are the one great love of his life."

"Uncle Genzo, how did you become so wise?"

"Hah! Easy to say when I'm telling you something you want to hear."

Keiko kisses him on the cheek.

"Hey, sis," yells Al. "Give us a hand with this."

Genzo watches her run to join the boys, the dogs bounding on either side of her. A gust of wind catches her blue dress, briefly exposing her legs all the way up to the curves of her white cotton-clad buttocks. *Oh, sweet children,* thinks Genzo, *be careful. Please, please, be careful.*

Sam and Keiko stand alone under the light behind Genzo's barn. Sam is nervous, glancing at his watch. In the last five minutes he has told her three times that he needs to fetch Mrs. Franklin at her daughter's house. They hear people calling good-bye and trucks and cars leaving, headlights sweeping the trees and vineyard. Sam starts to go, but Keiko presses one hand firmly on his heart, and he pauses, smiling. She takes a deep breath then speaks in a quiet, gentle, serious voice. "Sam, I want you to tell me what's bothering you."

Under her open palm she feels Sam jump then freeze. "Sam, I'm in love with you. And I think you love me. There's nothing I couldn't forgive.

There's nothing my love couldn't accept. This thing is like a wall between us, Sam. We can't allow it."

"You promised not to ask me."

"I know. And I haven't forgotten your story about Umetsu Chubei. I'm sorry I'm breaking my promise. But I have to. I can't live without the truth, and neither can you."

Sam nods. Breaking her promise is an act of honor and integrity. Keeping her promise would only be enabling him to maintain his collection of hidden lies. By her example Keiko has taught him a lesson Fujiwara-san, and even Papa, would have respected. To respond to her with anything less than complete honesty would be like spitting in all their faces.

Keiko is surprised at how sad and solemn Sam becomes.

He takes out his wallet and hands her an envelope. "What's this?" She unfolds it. "A letter from Japan?" They had recently practiced names and addresses in Japanese-language class; Keiko thinks Sam is testing her. "Don't give me any hints, okay? I can read this. It's from a Yuriko..." Keiko slowly works her way through the Tokyo return address. "How was that?"

"Perfect."

"That's because I have a great sensei." Keiko smiles and carefully repeats the name and address on the envelope. She opens it and takes out a photograph. "Is this Yuriko-san?"

Sam nods.

"What a cute baby..." Suddenly, a chill starts in Keiko's chest and sweeps through her entire body. All the odd pieces are falling into place. Pieces of ice, forming walls, a box to hold her heart. "She's pretty."

"I met her in Hawaii. She was with a man named Bidwell. She was his mistress, and he was the head foreman of the plantation. But he . . . I was in bed with her. And he caught us. He and I got in a fight, and he accidentally shot himself."

"You and this woman were lovers?"

"Yes. The day I left Hawaii, I promised to send for her and marry her."

Now Keiko can barely breathe. "And the baby?"

"Mine. My son."

Keiko hears her mother calling from the driveway. Sam puts the photograph back in the envelope. Keiko and Sam walk around the barn to where Mitsy's father's car is idling. "Hurry up, sis, we're getting a ride home with Mitsy." Al grins. "Isn't that great?"

"Such a bother. Are you sure there's enough room?" says Kuwano.

"It'll be fine," says Mitsy. "I'll sit on Al's lap."

Their words steam in the icy air and blow away on the wind. Keiko is freezing in her sweater and coat. Al wears only a white cotton shirt over a T-shirt. But he stares at Mitsy and wipes sweat from his forehead. Everyone begins a final round of thanks and good-nights. Keiko speaks all the proper words but keeps her gaze lowered.

Sam faces Keiko. "Thank you for everything, Keiko. Good night."

She raises her eyes to his. "Good night, Sam."

He bows to her, and she bows back.

"My, my," says Al, "aren't we formal tonight." Everyone laughs, and Keiko climbs into the backseat next to her mother. Al and Mitsy follow her. Mitsy settles against Al. "Isn't this cozy?" They sigh in unison. Keiko stares past Al's and Mitsy's faces, out the window at the stark winter vineyard as Mitsy's father drives slowly away.

Bowing good-bye to his guests, Genzo stands with his dogs on the edge of the driveway. He had been watching Keiko and Sam. All day she seemed lighter than air. But when she and Sam appeared from behind the barn, her grace and sparkle were gone. Genzo heard the finality in their voices when they said good night. He noted the burden of unspoken emotions in their bows. When Keiko got into the car, Sam's face was set hard as stone, but his eyes were soft and welled with unshed tears. Genzo watches Sam walking quickly through the vineyard toward Mrs. Franklin's place. Genzo kneels, strokes his dogs, whispers to them, "Such beautiful fragile youths, why must they break each other's hearts?"

Widow Franklin's Waltz

APRIL 1940

Sᴀᴍ's ᴜɴᴄʟᴇ Gᴇɴᴢᴏ ʜᴀs ʀᴇᴘᴇᴀᴛᴇᴅʟʏ ᴅᴇᴄʟᴀʀᴇᴅ ᴛʜᴀᴛ ʜᴇ ʙᴇʟɪᴇᴠᴇs one should not interfere in the personal affairs of others. Except for advice. Which every soul in the county's Japanese community knows he offers with lavish generosity. In the case of Keiko and Sam, Genzo displays what for him is an extraordinary degree of restraint—he maintains what he himself considers a Buddha-like vigil of compassionate silence. For three months. After which he concludes that he must speak because no one else will. He senses that two lifetimes' worth of regret and sorrow balance at the tipping point. Knowing he risks rejection, anger, humiliation, and that once again he may be cursed as a meddling old fool, he finds it fitting that the day of his intervention falls on April first.

Genzo parks his truck in front of Mrs. Franklin's house. He hears the sound of an orchestra in the backyard. Timidly, not wanting to intrude but overwhelmed with curiosity, he follows the music and comes upon a sight that makes him blink in wonderment and delight. Alberta Franklin is teaching Sam Hamada to waltz.

On a table under the orange tree the Victrola sits, iridescent colors flashing off the record's spinning surface. On the lawn Mrs. Franklin carries herself with all the dignity of her seventy-three years. The joy in her face is so rich and subtle, Genzo's heart aches to see it. It is the happiness of an old person, Genzo realizes, a joy of such muted and pastel colors that the young might pass it by, too involved with their serious work or raucous frivolity to bother with the perfume lingering in the heart of a single wilting rose.

Mrs. Franklin, in a navy blue dress with a long full skirt, and Sam, in jeans, white shirt, and work boots, waltz; they float around and around the newly mowed back lawn. Behind them are the tall white house with green shutters and two trees filled with big bright navel oranges.

The music ends. Genzo claps while Mrs. Franklin leans on Sam's arm. She gasps for air. Sam grows alarmed and asks if she is all right. It takes her a while to get the words out, but she is finally able to say, "It was worth it."

Genzo grabs a wooden lawn chair and brings it to Mrs. Franklin. Sam runs to get her a glass of water. When she catches her breath, she asks if Genzo has come to speak with her. Genzo shakes his head and says he's here to visit Sam.

"Before you two go off to talk," says Mrs. Franklin, "give us a moment to review our dancing lesson. Mr. Hamada, you have it in you to be a first-rate dancer. You're gifted with a natural sense of rhythm, and you move with the power and grace of a panther. However, I sense that you're holding back a very important part of yourself.

"When you dance the waltz, you must open your heart. You must be like a house with all its doors and windows opened wide so the music can flow through every room like a warm breeze. And remember this—when you're dancing with a woman who loves to dance, you must dare to challenge her with your strength. And if she truly launches herself into the dance, you must be courageous enough to go with her, beyond her if you can, and help her to explore the limits of her capacity to dance.

"Of course to learn to do that, you'll need lots of practice and a much younger partner. If I tried, my heart would give out. But I'd die happy, Mr. Hamada. I'm sure all those stiff old fools in my church would be appalled to hear me talking like this. But they've never seen, never experienced, never even dreamed of dancing like I did when I was young. Well, my daughters would understand. My daughters used to peek down through the banisters and watch me dance. And when they were old enough, I taught them to waltz. I wish their husbands weren't so stuffy and self-conscious.

"Don't allow that to happen to you, Mr. Hamada. Practice the waltz. Open your heart."

Sam nods.

"Well, don't feel badly if you find it difficult at first. It takes time. But you have it in you. I can tell. Just trust yourself."

Suddenly, the wind begins to blow. Mrs. Franklin turns her face into it and inhales. "Here comes the storm, gentlemen. And it's going to be a roof-shaker. We had best seek cover." She rises slowly to her feet. "Oh, my, I feel light-headed. I think I'll go in and lie down for a while. Mr. Hamada, would you please carry the Victrola into the house? And could you pick a few oranges for me? I feel like having some fresh juice after my nap. Mr. Matsuyama, it was very nice seeing you again. Please give my regards to your son. Oh, and do help yourself to some oranges. They're very sweet this year."

Genzo bows. "Thank you very much, Mrs. Franklin."

Sam picks up the Victrola.

A big gust of wind whips at Mrs. Franklin's skirt and blows strands of her loosened hair across her face. "Whoa!" she says, staggering a bit.

Genzo goes quickly to her and offers his arm. She takes it with a smile, and he helps her across the lawn. "Mr. Matsuyama, do you dance?"

"No. But after watching you today, I want to get a book and learn."

"No book can teach you to waltz."

"Maybe I can watch next time you teach?"

"Yes, of course."

"Thank you very much, Mrs. Franklin."

"You're most welcome, Mr. Matsuyama." She pauses to listen to the crackle and roll of approaching thunder. "I just love lightning storms, don't you?"

Genzo helps Mrs. Franklin up the stairs and holds the door open for her and for Sam, who carries the Victrola into the house. Genzo takes out his Bull Durham, huddles for a moment on the porch and rolls a smoke. Sam comes out with a bucket, fills it with oranges. In the somber darkening light, the oranges glow with an exuberant gaiety. *Like the innocent confidence of youth,* thinks Genzo, *or the irrepressible song of life in the face of approaching death.*

Sam leaves the oranges in the kitchen then follows Genzo down the driveway to the truck. All the plants, from weeds to the highest branches of the huge oak trees along the driveway, shake with the wind. It begins to rain. The men take shelter in Genzo's truck, listen to the drumming and spattering, lightning and thunder crackling and booming overhead.

Sam waits silently. Genzo smokes his cigarette. Both men have their windows and side vents open slightly, but the air in the cab grows hazy with blue smoke.

"The Yanagis are leaving for Japan as soon as the school year's over at the end of May," says Genzo. "Shoji's selling the restaurant and quitting his job as manager of the boardinghouse. Al will be living with me until he finishes high school. The plan is for Al to continue his education, get a diploma from a good American college. But Shoji, Kuwano, and Keiko are going to Japan to stay."

"I know. Al told me."

"Did he tell you that Shoji and Kuwano are furious with you? Did you know the whole town's talking about you?"

"No . . ."

"Keiko's moping around like a widow in mourning. Her parents believe it's because of something you did or said. But Keiko refuses to say anything bad about you. She insists she's only nervous about going to Japan. She speaks about you in the kindest, most respectful terms imaginable. Clearly, Keiko's in love with you."

"I'm sorry."

"Well . . ." Genzo scratches his head in embarrassment. "I apologize, too. I lied. No one in town knows about this. I just wanted your full attention. Shoji and Kuwano *are* angry with you. But in spite of that, Shoji has great respect for you. And don't you take that lightly. He doesn't give his respect easily."

Sam nods. He cannot look at Genzo.

"Sam, they're going to Japan to find Keiko a husband."

"Yes, I know."

"I'll drive you there right now. Shoji is my oldest and dearest friend. I will stand by you. I will act as your go-between. You must tell Keiko that you love her. You must ask her not to leave you."

Sam shakes his head. "Uncle Genzo, it's already too late."

Genzo stares at Sam, then slowly, with great difficulty, he speaks. "When I was young, I abandoned a woman who loved me and whom I loved. She was looking straight into my eyes, and I turned my face away from her. And at the moment I shunned her, I knew I was making a terrible mistake. *I knew it.* But I did it anyway.

"Years later I went to find her, but it was too late. I'd waited too long, and I lost her forever. No one except Shoji knows about her, and he knows only because he was there. When I look at you, I see my own stubborn face. Don't repeat my mistake. You must not forsake Keiko. You must not betray the one true love of your life."

From gut to throat Sam is a tangled knot of barbed wire. Tears trickle down his cheeks. "Thank you for your wisdom and kindness. I'm sorry, Uncle Genzo. I can't. I can't help it." Sam clenches his fists, but his tears will not stop. "*Shikataganai.* There's nothing anyone can do about it." He bows; then, before Genzo can say another word, Sam flings open the door and runs out into the rain.

Two Dreams

MAY 1940

ABOVE A RAIN-SOAKED LANDSCAPE THE FULL MOON FLOATS AMONG clouds shaped like mythical sea creatures slowly unfurling their tentacles and fins between heaven and earth. It is a night of dreams and tangled sheets, of voices whispering from caverns, ghosts vibrant as actors spotlighted on a stage.

Sam dreams he is in bed with Keiko. Both naked. Her eyes closed. His chest swollen with gratitude, joy, wave after wave of love. "Keiko, I'm sorry." She opens her eyes, moves away from him. "Wait, Keiko—"

She shoves him. He tries to hold her, but she slips away. He grabs, misses, and she is on her feet, running for the door. "Wait!"

Sam leaps. Catches her, throws her on the bed. She kicks at him. He struggles to restrain her. She will not quit fighting. He tries to talk to her, to tell her how much he loves and wants her, not just physically, but in every way. He holds her down and pleads with her to listen to him. But she turns her face away, refusing to look at him. Finally, she rolls onto her stomach, hides her face in the pillow. Behind Sam's eyes, between his ears, something—a leather strap, a belt, a whip—cracks like a gunshot.

He begins spanking her. Horrified and thrilled, he can't stop himself. She squirms and twists, but he holds her down on the bed. Self-control, restraint gone. Compassion, forbearance, understanding, all gone. Harder and harder he spanks her, raging in a voice he barely recognizes as his own. "Why did you leave me? Damn it, Keiko. I love you. Don't you know how much I love you?"

Sam awakes with a gasp, his body trembling, sweating, muscles like stone. He staggers into the bathroom, his rigid cock throbbing against his belly. He splashes cold water on his face.

With dream-dazed eyes Sam looks out the window. Bizarre, dragonlike clouds partially obscure the moon. The moon's blue light penetrates his eyes, diffuses through the smoky shadowed rooms of his mind. All the doors, locked and sealed during his waking hours, stand open. What he glimpses in the moonlight, as the doors begin closing, he neither recognizes nor understands. What he feels is fear and loneliness. And helplessness and rage. All the power and energy of his young male body cannot win what he most desires.

He grips his erect penis and growls hoarsely, "Keiko . . . Keiko, can you hear me? I want you . . . body, mind, and soul. I want you totally!"

At that moment Keiko is dreaming that she and Sam stand facing each other in the courtyard of a Japanese temple. She wears a kimono, he is dressed as a samurai. Keiko moves toward him. But he shouts, "Stay away!" And he draws his sword in a motion so smooth, tracing an arc so pure, Keiko's lips part in wonder.

"Go to him," says a woman's voice. "He loves you."

Keiko looks around, but sees no one. Sam gives no sign that he heard anything. Once more Keiko hears the woman's voice: "Touch his heart with your hand, and he'll be yours forever." Keiko takes a half step forward, straight at the sword aimed at her heart.

"Take care," says the voice of an old man. "If he cuts you . . . if he makes you bleed, even one drop, tragedy will follow for seven lifetimes."

"Blood means death to a man." The woman speaks into Keiko's left ear. "But it's blood that makes you a woman. Go claim your life. Touch his heart."

"The sword of a samurai knows neither pity nor compassion," says the old man into Keiko's right ear. "Beautiful kimono, priceless paintings, the love of a woman, flesh or bone, silk or bamboo—the sword doesn't care."

"He speaks of the reality of steel. I speak of the spirit in a woman's heart, which is equally real."

"Ignore my warning, and you will be punished."

"Men control women with fear. Fear of pain, anger, loss of love or safety or respect."

"You want love? From him? Don't you see what he holds out to you? That's not love. That's death."

Keiko realizes that she alone hears the voices. She takes another half step forward. Sam growls, the muscles of his bare arms knotted, glistening with sweat. But his eyes cup the fear and sorrow of a little boy. She thinks that in his pain and bewilderment he could hurt her, even kill her.

"Yes," says the woman's voice. "He carries the fears of a child. Admitting this truth to himself, exposing it to others, causes him such shame that it makes him want to run and hide or push others away . . . even at sword point. He is terrified of being known. What you know, he wants no other to know. Can you live with his secrets? Can your love overcome his fears? How true is your love? What will you risk? Keiko, how much do you believe in yourself?"

Half step by half step, she moves toward Sam. Her arms at her sides, hands relaxed, head raised, back straight, her eyes never leaving his. As she closes the gap between them, he raises the sword until the tip is level with her mouth.

She feels her lower lip touch the razor-sharp sword tip, pauses, holding herself perfectly still. She gazes steadily into Sam's eyes. Then, gently, she opens her heart and presses slowly forward. A spot of blood appears on her lower lip.

"No," he cries. "Keiko, no!" And he draws back the sword, swings it around behind him. Then he moves to her, leans down, tilts his head and licks the tiny wound on her lip. His voice trembles. "You want me, Keiko . . . You want me that much?"

"Yes," she says, feeling a sudden soft explosion of the purest sexual energy. "Yes, I want you that much."

"And you trust me that much?"

"No," she says, waking in tears from her dream, "it's myself I trust."

Touched

JUNE 1940

ON THE MORNING BEFORE KEIKO AND HER PARENTS ARE SCHEDULED TO leave for Japan, rain clouds and sun share the sky. Windshield wipers squeaking and thumping, Sam pulls Mrs. Franklin's big Pierce Arrow to the curb in front of the Methodist church. He gets out, opens Mrs. Franklin's door, holds a black umbrella against the rain. "After the service," she says, "I will spend the day with my older daughter's family. Please pick me up at her house at nine o'clock this evening."

From the church Sam drives to Japantown, parks outside the Yanagis' restaurant. His stomach knotted, light-headed, vision blurred around the edges, he opens the door and enters. Tables are pushed against one wall, chairs stacked on top. Carrying a box of blue and white porcelain bowls, Keiko's father comes out of the kitchen.

Sam lowers his head in a respectful bow. Shoji Yanagi returns Sam's bow, but the look on his face is not friendly. "My son and daughter aren't here. And they aren't at the boardinghouse, either."

"I've come to say . . . *sayonara* . . . to your daughter. May I wait?"

Shoji studies Sam's eyes. "No. I'm about to lock up."

"Well then . . . Yanagi-san, thank you for all the kindness you've shown me. May you and your family have a safe trip and the best of luck in Japan. I'm sorry for any bother . . . or trouble that I may have caused you or your family. Truly, I meant no harm or disrespect to anyone. I'm sorry." Sam bows deeply.

Shoji returns Sam's bow and sighs. "My children won't be back until dinner. Keiko went to say good-bye to one of her teachers. We're having a farewell party tonight at seven-thirty at the Jade Garden Chinese restaurant. If you want, you may attend."

"Thank you very much, sir, but I'll be working then. I have to pick up Mrs. Franklin at her daughter's house."

"Perhaps that's for the best." Sam turns to leave, and Shoji says, "I know it wasn't easy for you to come here. I'll tell Keiko that you came to say good-bye."

"Thank you, sir, but I'd rather you didn't mention it."

"As you wish." And they bow to each other one final time.

Sam drives out of town, splashing along the county road to Mrs. Franklin's house. He enters the driveway and continues around to the back. He is surprised to see Uncle Genzo's truck parked next to the barn. Sam pulls alongside the truck and rolls down his window.

Dewey is at the wheel. Beside him sit Al and Keiko. "Hi," says Keiko, "I came to say good-bye to my favorite sensei."

Sam parks in the barn. He hears the truck start and Al's voice calling, "Okay, sis, we'll be back for you in one hour."

Sam comes out of the barn, sees Keiko standing with her umbrella in the soft rain. She frowns at her wristwatch. But when he puts his arms around her, she looks up into his face and smiles. He kisses her then, quickly, before her smile can fade or weaken. A long gentle kiss, filled with inexpressible longing.

They go into Sam's little cottage, and he fills a kettle for tea. But before he can turn on the hot plate, she stops him, and they disrobe and lie in bed together. Fearful of the aggression exposed in his dream, fearful of the rage submerged in his blood, Sam touches Keiko's virgin skin with infinite tenderness. Keiko responds with a boldness born of her dream and opens herself completely to him. But when they are breathless and burning, deep into the realm of aching readiness, Sam does not attempt to enter her.

Finally, she understands. "You aren't going to?"

"No."

"Why?"

"I've made so many mistakes. Yuriko was a mistake. But I didn't know. I didn't know any better. And then I lied to you. Humiliated you before your parents. I'm so sorry, Keiko. I'd kill myself before I caused you to lose face again. When you're in Japan, on your wedding night, your husband will have no reason to disrespect you."

"But, Sam, I want you . . . I want you to be my first lover."

"Thank you. And I want to. I want to so much." His voice strains and cracks. "But I mustn't. I won't."

Keiko smiles, and her eyes fill with tears. "Do you . . . Do you . . ."

"What?"

"Nothing. Never mind."

"Yes. Yes, Keiko, I love you. I will love you forever."

They rest, glowing like molten glass. Keiko nestles close. Sam on his side, right hand gently stroking her body. Her shining black hair like calligraphy against the white bed linen. She gazes deeply into his eyes and smiles, radiant, happy, centered.

Sam thinks: *I will never forget this moment. On my deathbed this image will flash across my mind's eye.* He is adrift on a calm sea, then a huge shadow rises and a shark's serrated teeth bite down on his heart. Not blood but shame, fear, bitterness, and rage spill out. He does not want her to see these in his eyes, so he rolls abruptly away from her.

And she responds by softly pressing herself against his back, her hand on his shoulder. "Shall we get up now and have some tea?"

"What?"

"I want this to be easy for you. I don't want you to feel guilty or afraid to touch me. I'm here because I want to be. And you don't have to do or be or feel anything more or less than what's natural and real and true for you."

Here it is again—the pride and mettle of her samurai blood. Sam is touched, shaken to the depths of his soul. He turns to her, bows his head between her small, perfect breasts and kisses her heart. *I'm yours forever, Keiko. I'll love and respect and protect your memory for as long as I live.* But he says nothing. He looks into her eyes and kisses her mouth and says nothing. Even later, when her cries and moans burn his ears, and he is drunk-spun with passion and love, he says nothing. He has said too much already. He has broken too many promises, dishonored himself enough. His soul is naked, defenseless, and terrified, knowing that letting go of Keiko is the most courageous and cowardly thing he has ever done, knowing he is making the biggest mistake of his life.

Dewey and Al drive into the yard, honk, and wait a discreet distance from Sam's cottage. After a moment, the front door opens, and Keiko and Sam come out. They pause and bow to each other. Then Keiko turns and walks the rest of the way alone.

The rain has stopped, the clouds have scattered. The yard is filled with a sunlight so clear and bright that it hurts Keiko's eyes. Everything is wet and sparkling. She knows her face is flushed and tears are streaming down, but she doesn't care. She walks with her head up and a trembling smile on her lips. From the marrow of her bones to the tips of her hair, she is alive. From the deepest, most mysterious reaches of her soul to the widest edge of the universe, she is ringing, she is touched. Al and Dewey have never seen her look more beautiful. She climbs into the truck with them, and they are dumbstruck and shy as two little boys.

Sam raises his right hand. Keiko raises hers.

Dewey turns the truck, and they rattle out of the yard down the driveway to the county road and off to the farewell banquet at the Chinese restaurant.

Streamers and Doves

JUNE 1940

SHIKATAGANAI. HOW MANY TIMES HAS KEIKO HEARD THAT? ABOUT the weather. The price of grapes. The banks closing. The bigotry and prejudice against Japanese. *Shikataganai*. The utterance of a resigned heart. *There's nothing I can do about Sam. All my life I've thought the* Issei *were cowards when they said,* Shikataganai, *nothing can be done. Now here I am, taking my turn—trying to taste some comfort in this bitter, bitter tea.* Shikataganai. *Truly, absolutely nothing can be done.*

Suddenly, Keiko realizes that everyone in the banquet room is staring at her. Mitsy and Haru hand her a gift wrapped in gold paper, topped with a red bow. A Kodak camera and a dozen rolls of film. She holds up the camera, the crowd claps and cheers as Keiko weeps. Everyone assumes it is because of her gift and the sorrow of parting from her childhood friends. No one is surprised to see her tears. No one thinks anything is wrong. Just the grief of parting. It is natural. It will pass.

Keiko recalls what Mitsy once said about a newlywed woman whose husband was killed in a farming accident. "I think it makes her more interesting, even kind of glamorous. After all, now she's a woman with a past."

Through her tears Keiko smiles. *Mitsy. What a crazy girl! How could she say something so outrageous?* Keiko begins to laugh. She gives Mitsy a big hug.

"Watch out, Keiko, your mascara's running. Don't get it on my sweater."

Keiko laughs and cries and hugs Mitsy with all her strength. Then she hugs Haru and Dewey while all the guests clap and take out their handkerchiefs and dab their eyes and blow their noses.

———

The first morning beyond the Golden Gate, Keiko awakes, climbs down from her bunk, takes three steps, passes out and collapses on the floor. The ship's doctor says it's exhaustion and influenza.

Hovering in her fever-dream, Keiko looks down at her heart. It is covered with something white and soft. Mold? No, the covering moves, undulates, a piece breaks free, rises toward her. A white dove brushes her cheek with its wing as it flies past. "Sam!" Somehow the bird and Sam's name are intertwined.

"What did you say?" asks her father.

Keiko opens her eyes. "Nothing." Closing her eyes, she finds a red silk scarf tied loosely around her neck. White doves keep rising from her hidden heart; each carries Sam's name to her lips. She holds the scarf over her mouth.

Everything was so hot and still; where did this sudden wind come from? In her hand the red scarf flutters and flaps. The scarf grows long and thin. It turns into a bunch of crepe paper ribbons. She stands at the ship's rail. On the dock Genzo, Dewey, Al, and Sam hold the other ends of the long red streamers. "Don't let go," Sam yells to her. "Keiko, don't let go."

"I must."

"It's your heart. It's your one true heart!"

She releases the streamers, feels them slice like sword blades pulling across her palm. She looks at the long, deep diagonal cuts and the bloodred streamers falling away, fluttering down like the tails of kites abandoned by the wind.

She raises her bleeding hand, waves to the last of the white doves flying swiftly away, distant specks fading into the sky.

Sayonara, *Sam*. Sayonara *forever*.

Part 3

JUNE 1940–DECEMBER 1941

Misa

JUNE 1940

KEIKO SLEEPS FOR TWO DAYS. SHE AWAKES DRAINED, LIMP AND FRAGILE as a newborn baby. Her father is overjoyed when she eats a bowl of rice gruel with a salty red *umeboshi*. Still light-headed, Keiko imagines the soft white rice will replace her lost doves, and the pickled plum is her new heart. She eats slowly, with great tenderness.

Recuperating, Keiko takes long walks alone, exploring every deck open to passengers. One day, lonely and sad, she hides in a toilet stall and muffles her sobs with her handkerchief. When she comes out, a young woman in a kimono asks if Keiko is all right. "Thank you," says Keiko with a bow. "I'm fine."

"You're an American Japanese?"

"Yes."

"You must be homesick. Do you miss your friends?"

"Yes." Tears run down Keiko's cheeks.

"I know how you feel. When I left Japan, I cried for a month."

Keiko smiles. "And now you're going home."

"Yes. My family and I are returning to Tokyo."

"How lucky you are."

"Yes." The woman smiles gently. "And someday you, too, will go home."

"I'm going to Japan to get married."

"Oh . . ." The woman's brow wrinkles. "I am, too."

Keiko's heart is burning with pain. She barely parts her lips, and her secret slips out like smoke. "But the man I love is in America."

"Oh, I see." The woman's eyes fill with empathy and compassion. "Perhaps he will come to Japan to claim you?"

"No." Keiko shakes her head and sighs deeply. "Thank you for your concern. I feel much better now."

The woman smiles. "My name is Misa. Let's be friends. We can talk."

"Yes," says Keiko, "let's be friends."

Keiko and Misa stroll the deck together. "Tell me about the man you're going to marry," says Keiko.

"The marriage was arranged by my grandparents. The man is an army captain." Misa shows Keiko a photograph of the prospective groom.

"He looks very stern."

Misa laughs. "All Japanese Army officers make that face when they get their pictures taken."

"Must be their samurai face," says Keiko, thinking of Sam.

As their friendship deepens, Keiko begins to see that Misa has lived an extremely sheltered life. Misa does not exaggerate when she confesses that most of her information comes from books. Misa's naivete triggers Keiko's natural boldness. One day, while Keiko and Misa sun themselves on deck, Keiko mentions that she hopes their new husbands will be passionate and skillful lovers.

"Oh . . ." Misa's expression wavers between befuddlement and innocent pleasure. "Yes, I've read about that. It sounds very poetic and lovely . . . *the dance of rain clouds over the earth.*"

Sighing like a woman with a past, Keiko says, "I'm glad Sam and I had a chance to go to bed together."

Misa's eyes grow enormous and she covers her mouth with both hands. "But that's terrible! He ruined you. How can you get married now? What if you're pregnant? And even if you're not, what will your future husband and in-laws think if . . . if you're not a virgin?"

"Don't worry; technically, I'm still a virgin."

"You are?"

"On my wedding night I'll still paint red peonies on my sheets."

"But—"

"Sam didn't ruin me. Even though we both *really* wanted it. Misa, someday you'll understand about the *wanting*."

Misa's voice is barely a whisper. "Then . . . what did you do . . . in bed?"

"Everything a man and woman in love could do. Everything except *that*," says Keiko grandly.

"Oh . . . oh, dear." Misa swallows and blushes. She seems so flushed and huddled up and wide-eyed, Keiko thinks she looks like a little pink mouse.

After a long solemn silence, Keiko says, "What will become of me? Will I live in Japan for the rest of my life? Will I ever see Sam again? I can't disappoint my parents. They've suffered enough disappointment in their lives. I'm trapped. My life's not my own. My future's no longer mine. And my heart . . . Even though I've resolved to forget him, Sam still holds my heart. I love him, and he loves me. He said so. Misa, that day in his bed, he swore he'd love me forever."

Fireflies

JUNE 1940

IN CALIFORNIA, KEIKO WAS A *NISEI*, A SECOND-GENERATION CHILD OF immigrants in a family that numbered four souls total. In Nagoya, Keiko discovers she has more relations than she can keep straight. Uncles, aunts, cousins, their spouses, children, and in-laws. Mama's eldest brother, Nobutaro, overjoyed to have his sister home, throws a huge party, a celebration that rivals Lodi's Japantown on a Saturday night during the height of the harvest. Family, friends, and neighbors eating, drinking, laughing, and talking. Keiko's parents loving the attention, talking themselves hoarse. Sitting beside her mother, Keiko, smiling and sweating in the spotlight cast by all the unfamiliar eyes, bull's-eye of a thousand whispered asides. *Ah! So she's the daughter? She's pretty. Pretty? She's beautiful! Returned to find a husband. No problem, bet she's married in a week. How about your son? You're joking! My son married to an American girl? Talk to her. Ask her something. Ask her about her clothes. Ask her about her undergarments. Ask her what she thinks of Japanese men. Ask her if she can cook. Does she eat rice? Idiot! Look at her, she's eating rice right now. Maybe she's just being polite. Ask her.*

"Keiko-san, do you like rice?"

Keiko, mouth full of rice, blinks, nods.

"Ah, yes, but do you prefer rice over bread?"

Instant breath-held silence in the room.

"I like both equally. But I prefer toast with breakfast, and rice with dinner."

Toast? What's that? Burnt bread. Burnt bread? Idiot! No one eats burnt bread. Even I know that. "Ah, Keiko-san, could you please explain *toast?*"

Uncle Nobutaro's big old house sinking on its foundations like an overloaded boat, passengers squirting out portholes, spilling overboard. Keiko thinks, *Enough!* And that's when the musicians arrive, and the house starts rocking on its keel. And still more. Nobutaro's neighbors' relatives and in-laws, Kuwano's former teachers and classmates, people arriving in waves, bringing more food and drink, flocks of children who peek and run. Blur. Heat. Song. Dance. Laughter. Exhaustion. Stuffed. *No, thank you, not another bite. Oh, look, more guests!* A gang of men rising, tripping over one another, bowing, laughing, heading for the door. But, no, they aren't going home. They take Papa to the local bath house, where they scrub one another's backs, soak, and continue talking. Refreshed, they return to the party, and the next group heads down to the bath house.

Thank the gods for Kodak! With her new camera in her hands, Keiko discovers she can impose a kind of order onto the chaos. She points the Kodak, and people realign themselves. Short of the perfection of a box of new pencils. But the transformation from sprawled drunks into rows of not-quite-perpendicular rosy-cheeked gentlemen amazes Keiko. As for the women, when Keiko feels they are about to smother her and she will fall encircled by beaks pecking her to death with questions, she sweeps them back with her magic Kodak broom, sweeps them up against a wall, their attention instantly diverted from her hair to their own. *Allow me to fix that for you, there, that's fine. All right everyone, hold still.* Click. *Wait. One more, please.* Click. *Thank you.* And Keiko escapes, snapping and moving, snapping and moving, until she is outside, alone in the garden, hiding behind a tree, gazing at the crescent moon.

Finally it is time to sleep. Most of the guests leave. Keiko's aunts spread bedding on the tatami floors. Keiko, sandwiched between two little girls, listens to the slumbering house, the near and distant snoring; one old man, a retired teacher, lectures a class in his dreams.

Japan. *How strange and wonderful to be here.* Surprises for every sense—the known and the unexpected side by side. Japan does not smell like America. The wooden houses: a bit musty, a bit like incense. In the beautiful countryside, along with pine and bamboo forests, are rice fields reeking of excrement. She had known what they used for fertilizer, but it had never occurred to her how the reality would assault her nose.

She will write to Al, Dewey, Mitsy, and Haru about the scenes she glimpsed through the train window. The calendar images and painted scrolls they grew up with: graceful bamboo forests, narrow ravines, footbridges over rocky streambeds, farmhouses with thatch roofs—they are real.

She wants Al to know how it felt to meet their relatives. She wants to tell him about the mysterious power of blood ties. How it felt: the instantaneous and instinctive marrow-deep bond. And how she wept when she first stood on the soil of Japan.

Now she understands why salmon and geese return to their birthplace to mate and bear offspring. When the earth of home calls, flesh and blood answer.

First predawn's pale gray, then the warm tones of sunrise filter through paper doors into the room, illuminating the face of the little girl asleep next to Keiko. A rooster crows. A distant temple bell sings, ancient bronze solemn and beautiful, calming and comforting Keiko's heart. The child stirs but does not wake. Gently as mist enfolding a mountain on a morning without wind, Keiko drifts into sleep.

Keiko's parents rent a two-story house in Nagoya. Two bedrooms upstairs, Keiko's in front with a sunny, southern exposure and a window overlooking a tiny garden and narrow shop-lined street. Uncle Nobutaro gives her a low table that she places next to the window. He also gives her a lamp and a framed photograph of her cousin, Nobutaro's firstborn son, Masanobu, clear-eyed and handsome in his naval fighter pilot's uniform. At her new table Keiko sits on the tatami floor and does her homework. And she looks out over the garden wall at people and traffic passing on the street; at night the street is aglow with paper lanterns and lit storefronts; during festivals, food and trinket stalls crowd the temple yard at the end of her street, and floating in through her window, the music of *taiko* drums, flutes, and strollers clip-clopping by on the wooden clogs called geta.

Shoji goes for long walks at night alone—something he rarely felt safe doing in the United States. He returns, grinning like a boy, loaded with treasures: books to send to Genzo, potted chrysanthemums or pink azaleas for his wife, a glass globe with a single fat goldfish or a bamboo-and-mosquito-net cage containing three live fireflies for his gentle sad-eyed daughter.

Hollow

AUGUST 1940

SAM AND HIS JAPANESE-LANGUAGE STUDENTS MISS KEIKO TERRIBLY.

As military and political conflicts escalate in Asia and Europe, so does Sam's concern for Keiko's safety. One afternoon in class, Sam takes out a letter from his sister in Japan. He skips the first paragraph in which Mama and Akemi thank him for the money that he has been sending them every month since Papa's death. "My sister, Akemi, says that my younger brother, Bunji, was drafted into the army. He's seventeen and being sent to Manchuria." Sam flips to the last page of the letter. "Akemi enclosed one of her poems. As I read it to you, first I want you to write down her words in Japanese, then I want a written English translation."

SHELL FRAGMENTS

Some lie co-mingled with broken skeletons
draped in rags of cloth and flesh.
Others are flayed clean by the surf,
polished to pearl-sheen and rainbows.
Both are nails in the hands of
the carpenters named Life and Death.
The supply is endless as the fence
they build over the dunes of our hearts.

The students dig into their translations.

Refolding Akemi's letter, Sam remembers Bunji shivering and his little sister dancing under the first snowflakes of winter. He remembers his mother and the vacant one-room temple with locked doors.

Sam stares at Keiko's empty desk.

He listens to the soft scribbling of pens and pencils on paper.

He listens to his heart echoing . . . echoing . . . in his chest.

Samurai Girls

SEPTEMBER 1940

KEIKO BEGINS HER SENIOR YEAR AT A PRIVATE HIGH SCHOOL FOR GIRLS, academically demanding, but with a policy that none of the girls is ever flunked. They graduate, marry men from good families, and bear children. But while they are students, the trials of married life seem distant. Chattering happily, they pick newly sprouted leaves from the school's tea bushes and serve the fresh tea to one another during lunch hour.

Keiko's subjects include geometry, science, calligraphy, literature, English, music (Japanese and European—she learns to sing *"Donao No Kawa"* which she recognizes as "The Blue Danube Waltz" with Japanese lyrics), art, home economics (cooking and sewing complete with pattern making and custom fitting), and physical education.

With the exception of her gym instructor, Keiko's teachers seem gentle and refined. B-sensei, with his head shaved bald and drill-sergeant attitude, seems completely out of place in a girls' school. In the U.S., Keiko would simply have asked, "What kind of name is that? And what's his problem?" But trying to act like a proper Japanese, Keiko phrases her questions more tactfully. Her classmates explain that when B-sensei was a student he loved baseball. The *B* in his nickname came from the *B* in Babe Ruth, *Bay-boo-san,* B-san. In November 1935, when Japanese troops attacked Shanghai, Peking, and Tientsin, B-san enlisted in the army. He would have flunked the physical because he had a history of epileptic attacks, but left that off his medical questionnaire and made it into uniform. On night maneuvers during basic training, he had a seizure. The noise drew the "enemy," and his unit was "decimated." Deeply shamed, he almost killed himself except for the intervention of his commanding officer, who said that even though B-san could not be a combat soldier, he could serve on the home front by preparing the youth for war. B-san hung his head. "But, sir, I only teach at a girls' school."

"A soldier makes his stand no matter where he is stationed. Some are sent overseas. I am here, you are at a girls' school. If we are invaded, mothers will defend their children. Japan's a nation of samurai women. They already possess the will and courage. What they need is someone to train them. A sensei like you. Without training they will be killed like rabbits."

B-sensei returned to the girls' school, hung his commanding officer's photograph above his desk, and threw himself into his new mission—to transform his students into skilled warrior women.

"You! Yanagi Keiko! You're the new girl from America?"

"Yes, Sensei."

"America: a rich, fat, spoiled brat of a nation. One that constantly whimpers and whines for special treatment rather than standing and competing gut to gut with Japan. Tell me: Are you Japanese? Or are you American? Where do your loyalties lie?"

The gymnasium is totally silent. All the girls wait for Keiko's answer. Keiko thinks, *Just say "Japan" and be done with it.* Her fear, her eagerness to please and fit in, makes her want to say it. But she knows everyone will sense her ambivalence. *In America, racist children threw rocks at me and adult bigots called me a dirty Jap. Now here in Japan, are they going to call me a dirty American?*

"Why are you hesitating? Answer! Are you American or Japanese?"

"Sensei, the truth is: I am both."

"Unacceptable. If Japan and America were at war, which side would you support?"

"Sensei, my parents and I live here in Japan. My grandparents, my uncles and aunts and cousins are all here." Keiko feels like crying, and her voice wavers. "But my younger brother is in the United States, as are my best friends, former classmates, and teachers. For their sake, and for the sake of all the Japanese and all the American people, I hope such a war never happens."

Momentarily speechless, B-sensei stares at her. "Some would call those kind and gracious sentiments. Others would call them evasive and weak. Europe is at war. Japan is at war. One day soon you will have to decide. You're either Japanese or American. You cannot be both. Japanese, American, or nothing."

"I am not nothing. I am both."

"Yanagi Keiko-san, the nail that sticks up gets hammered down."

And you, with your shaved head, look just like a hammer. B for ball-peen.

B-sensei completes roll call. A classmate hands Keiko a wooden staff with a gracefully curved tip. Keiko is so upset, she accidentally lets it slip through her fingers. The staff hits the gym floor with a loud echoing clatter.

B-sensei reprimands Keiko for her clumsiness. He tells the girls to imagine they are holding sacred samurai weapons.

"What? This stick?" mutters Keiko.

B-sensei overhears her. "That stick represents a *naginata*. You will practice with it until you've memorized the movements, the forms we call the kata. This is a real *naginata*." B-sensei takes the weapon from a rack on the wall. The long black *naginata* looks heavier than the unpainted practice weapon Keiko clutches. B-sensei removes the sheath and displays a gleaming curved foot-long blade. He turns the *naginata*, making the blade catch the light. "For your final exam, you'll be required to perform a selection of kata with this *naginata*." B-sensei replaces the sheath. It clicks as it locks into place. "With this you can defend yourself against attack. Used properly, it is a powerful and devastating weapon. You can even defeat a man attacking you with a sword. Keiko-san, why are you smiling?"

"Pardon me, Sensei, but I was just thinking how unlikely it would be for me to be attacked by a man with a sword. And even if that should ever occur, it's even less likely that I would just happen to be carrying a *naginata*."

"What an impudent girl you are!"

"I'm sorry, Sensei. I didn't mean to be rude. I guess I'm just a modern, practical sort of person, and *naginata* seem so . . . scary and old-fashioned to me."

"I see. You were just being practical and modern."

Keiko nods. "I'm sorry if I offended you, but when you asked why I was smiling, I wanted to tell you the truth."

"I see. The truth." B-sensei senses that most of the girls agree with Keiko. He sighs deeply. "You're all so young and naive. You haven't learned yet that your modern, practical truth is like brightly colored merchandise displayed for sale. It's part of the facade that everyone agrees is 'the truth.' But the real truth hidden behind the curtain is not so pretty. The reality is this: every day of her life, beginning from the moment she's born into this world, a woman is attacked by men with swords. Mostly not to kill her, mostly only to cut, to wound, to bleed and weaken her. Do you understand? Or am I being too philosophical, too metaphorical, for you?

"Let me put it to you in practical, modern terms. Right now Japan's at war in China and Korea. Japan has entered the Axis pact and is pushing into Indochina. Less than three months ago, German troops occupied Paris. Last month the British withdrew from Shanghai, leaving the city to the Japanese Army. The tides of war are unpredictable. However unlikely it may seem, it's possible that someday our homeland might be invaded. Imagine enemy soldiers with bayonets on their rifles attacking you and your family. If that happens, what will you use to defend yourselves and your loved ones? No one will issue guns to you. If we were invaded, I would, without hesitation, sacrifice my life in the defense of Japan, my parents, my students. That's right. I would die for you. Keiko-san, if you saw your parents about to be gutted by an enemy's bayonet, if you had this *naginata* in your hands, would you use it to defend them?"

"Yes, Sensei."

"Truly? Do you mean that?"

"Yes. I would die to save the lives of those I love." Keiko bows deeply. "Sensei, please forgive me for not understanding the value of what you were trying to teach. Please teach me to use the *naginata* so I can defend those I love."

"And your homeland?"

Keiko hesitates for an instant. "Yes." *Both my homelands,* she thinks.

Frowning, B-sensei stares intently at Keiko.

Protection

September 1940

Keiko returns exhausted from her first day at school. She finds Uncle Nobutaro standing on a stool in the doorway of the room where they eat their meals. Keiko's parents are watching Nobutaro mounting what appear to be two long black curtain rods above the doorway. "There have been several burglaries in our neighborhood," says Keiko's mother. "Nobutaro-san's loaning us some protection."

Nobutaro unsheathes the weapons for Keiko's inspection. "The one with the straight point is a spear, it's called a *yari*. The other, with the curved blade, is a—"

"*Naginata*," says Keiko. "Used properly, it can defeat a man with a sword."

Keiko's parents look at her with surprise.

"That's what I learned in school today."

"Kei-chan," says her father, "I don't want you handling those things. They're too dangerous for girls."

"Hah!" says Kuwano. "When the burglars come, Papa can hide upstairs. Kei-chan will grab the *yari*, I'll take the *naginata*, and we'll chase them away."

"You're more likely to cut off your own foot," warns Shoji.

"I remember when our mother gave you lessons," says Nobutaro to Kuwano. "But that was long ago. I bet you've forgotten the kata."

Kuwano smiles but says nothing.

"Mama," says Keiko. "Do you remember all the movements?"

"Those weapons are sacred family heirlooms. Do you think my brother would loan them to someone who didn't know how to handle them?"

"Show us," says Nobutaro.

"No," says Kuwano firmly. "It's time to eat dinner. Besides, it's unmannerly for a lady to demonstrate her martial arts before such a rowdy audience."

"What?" says Nobutaro. "Who's being rowdy? Not us. If we were any quieter, we'd all be asleep."

"You were born noisy. It's not just your voice, which is loud enough to rid the house of mice. It's your spirit. You have a rowdy spirit."

"If I promise to sit meekly in the corner," whispers Nobutaro, "will you demonstrate your skill? I appreciate your modesty, but frankly, as your older brother, I need to see that you won't hurt yourself. I'd never forgive myself if I left these here for your protection but instead filled your house with grief."

"Since you put it that way . . ." From the pocket of her apron, Kuwano takes a braided cord and quickly ties back her kimono sleeves. She climbs onto the stool and takes down the *naginata*. "Back up. I don't want you jumping the wrong way in your excitement."

Nobutaro grabs the stool. "Leave it," says Kuwano.

"Don't you want us to move the table out of the way?" asks Shoji.

"Will the burglars wait while we rearrange furniture?" With a click and an incredibly smooth motion, Kuwano unsheathes the *naginata*. "The space to be defended is cramped and there are obstructions. The height of the ceiling inhibits vertical movements. Therefore I will use the kata called 'Autumn Leaf Spinning Downstream.'" Kuwano bows and begins the kata taught to her by her mother.

Shoji's jaw drops. Keiko's eyes widen. *Mama?* Nobutaro's naturally ruddy face grows several shades darker, and his eyes sparkle with delight.

Kuwano dances gracefully around the dining table, she swings and thrusts, making the *naginata* whoosh and hiss. There is no space in the room where a burglar might take refuge, no angle from which to attack her. Kuwano's movements are fluid yet solid, light as a floating leaf, powerful as a rushing river.

Kuwano ends the kata. With a click she sheathes the *naginata* and bows. She climbs on the stool and replaces the *naginata* on the pegs over the doorway. "Kei-chan, will you help me serve dinner?"

Keiko hurries after her mother. "Mama! You never told me you could do that."

Shoji watches his wife and daughter disappear into the kitchen. His mouth is still open. He is speechless.

"She looked just like our mother," says Nobutaro, his voice filled with pride.

In the kitchen Kuwano puffs slightly, catching her breath. "You know, Kei-chan, my mother chased six burglars out of her house one night with that very *naginata*."

"Six men? And they ran away?"

"If you were a man, and you saw a woman do what I just did? And if the woman uttered a piercing battle cry and thrust that razor-sharp weapon at your genitals? I ask you, if you were that man, wouldn't you run away?"

Keiko laughs. Then for a moment she sees her mother through the eyes of an intruding burglar. Kuwano is no frail, weak-kneed old lady. Kuwano is a smart, tough, clear-eyed woman. To defend her home and family, she would be as fierce as a mother tiger, she would fight to the death. "Mama, can you teach me?"

"Of course. You can help me protect your father."

"Papa didn't know you could do that, did he?"

"Men are comforted by weak women. It's one of their more disgusting traits."

"But don't some men value warrior women?"

Kuwano narrows her eyes. "Are you thinking of anyone in particular?"

Keiko tries to look innocent. "Of course not, Mama."

"By the way," says Kuwano, leaning over the rice pot, "Nobutaro-san brought word of a marriage proposal."

"What? Already? But it's too soon."

"The young man is eager to meet you."

"But, Mama, I'm not ready to get married."

"Nobutaro-san brought a photograph."

Keiko rushes into the front room, where Shoji and Nobutaro sit smoking cigarettes. "Papa, where's that photograph?"

"What? Oh, it's on the *tansu*."

Keiko goes to the chest of drawers. She takes one look at the picture then throws it down. "He's ugly. I hate him!"

Kuwano comes in carrying dishes. "He's from a very good family."

"They're in the jewelry business," says Nobutaro.

"He's ugly," says Keiko. "He looks . . . like a frog."

"When do we meet him?" asks Kuwano.

"The go-between suggested the second Saturday afternoon of next month. That way Kei-chan would have plenty of time to get ready," says Nobutaro.

"I refuse," says Keiko.

"Are you serious?" asks Nobutaro.

"Of course she's not," says Kuwano.

"I'm serious."

"Just go and talk with him and meet his parents," says Kuwano.

"No! I won't." Keiko runs crying upstairs.

"I didn't think a man's looks were so important to women," says Nobutaro.

"They aren't," says Kuwano.

"Ha!" says Shoji. "I told you. I know my daughter better than anyone. I told you she'd never agree to such a match. She's right—the man looks like a damn frog."

"Oh, be quiet," says Kuwano. "I'll talk with her. Nobutaro, you go ahead and arrange the meeting."

"Why won't you listen?" yells Shoji. "Your daughter said no."

"She can't decide something this important on the basis of one stupid picture."

"Perhaps I should wait awhile before I talk to the go-between," says Nobutaro.

"No," says Kuwano. "Don't wait."

"Why?" demands Shoji.

"He might get away."

"So what?"

"He's rich."

"Ha! So that's it."

"Yes."

"We've never had much money," says Shoji, "but we've lived a good life, haven't we? Why are you suddenly so money-conscious? Has our poverty been so burdensome and terrible for you?"

"Yes. Yes, it has."

Shoji is stunned into silence. Nobutaro lowers his gaze.

"And I won't have it for my daughter." Kuwano turns her back on the men and goes into the kitchen.

Mr. Frog

October 1940

Feel the motion through your whole body. From the soles of your feet to the crown of your head. Commit yourself to the moment. Only this moment." B-sensei's voice resonates through the huge cold gymnasium as Keiko and her classmates swing their *naginata* through the arcs of the ancient drill. "Swing forward! Swing back!

"Become one with your weapon. Project your *ki*. For your final exam you will be graded not only on your technical skill, but on the purity and strength of your *ki*. I expect you—" Keiko waves her hand in the air and asks for a definition of *ki*. The class comes to an awkward halt, several girls accidentally whacking one another with their *naginata*. No one is hurt, but to B-sensei the lovely choreography of the girls all moving in unison is ruined. Grinding his teeth impatiently, he tries to answer and begins to stutter. He stops, and after taking a mind-clearing breath, says, "*Ki* comes from within. If you're truly Japanese, you don't need me to explain it. In fact, you'd know that words could never explain *ki*. If you're not Japanese, no amount of explanation will suffice. To a non-Japanese, *ki* must remain forever mysterious . . . and unattainable."

With perverse pleasure B-sensei notes Keiko's befuddlement. This American girl is an intolerable disruptive force. She has no sense of proper feminine modesty. Her attitude and behavior are contaminating the other girls. And most unforgivably, she has eroded his authority and caused him to lose face in front of his students. She needs to be put in her place. In the history of the school, no girl has ever flunked a class. He decides that Keiko will be the first.

At home Keiko fights with her mother about meeting Mr. Frog, but in the end Keiko relents. What hooks Keiko is her curiosity, not about Mr. Frog, but the adventure, the experience of attending a marriage meeting.

Once Keiko consents, her mother and aunts sweep into action. After debating traditional kimono versus Western-style clothing, they buy her a new dress suit. Keiko loves it. It is dove gray wool, and she wears it with a new white silk blouse. They buy her a new hat, handbag, shoes, and her first garter belt and nylon stockings.

On the morning of the meeting, her aunts take her out to have her hair done. When she arrives home, her mother has laid out all her new clothes. Despite herself, Keiko thoroughly enjoys the fuss and pampering. But when she and her parents and Uncle Nobutaro step out of the taxi in front of one of Nagoya's best restaurants, her knees turn to jelly.

She had imagined herself walking in with her head held high. At dinner the evening before, she had entertained her father and uncle and infuriated her mother by demonstrating how she intended to march into the meeting like a majorette waving an American flag and whistling "The Star-Spangled Banner."

But now that the moment has arrived, Keiko finds herself overcome with shyness. She walks into the restaurant with her eyes lowered. She bows to her prospective parents-in-law and murmurs the correct polite phrases in a voice so soft she can hardly hear herself.

They are seated in a private room apart from other patrons, a traditional Japanese room with two facing rows of small low black lacquer tables. Keiko has such a roaring in her ears, she has trouble hearing the conversation.

Women in kimono enter carrying trays loaded with small bowls and dishes. The menu includes: shiitake-mushroom soup; "snowdrifts" of steamed red tilefish fillets; sole and scallop tempura; eggplant with miso and sesame dressing; marinated and fried tofu on autumn maple leaves; egg custard with shrimp, lily-root, chestnut, and ginkgo-nuts; sweet potatoes with *hijiki* seaweed; vinegared shellfish, crab, octopus, and chrysanthemum-cut turnip; *nashi* pear and mandarin orange slices . . . and more.

Keiko forces herself to sit up straight and face her prospective in-laws. One peek at Mama Frog, however, and, terrified, Keiko drops her gaze. She feels helpless, vulnerable, and homely as a rough stone under a gem cutter's loupe.

Nobutaro proposes a toast. Keiko raises the sake cup to her lips. Her hands are trembling.

People talk about the weather and the food. The men begin to speak of war and politics, and the go-between changes the subject. The men lapse into silence while the women comment on the lovely garden outside their room. Keiko raises her head to peek at the garden and finds Mr. Frog staring at her through thick round black-rimmed glasses that magnify his eyes. Keiko gives him a tiny smile, and he chokes on his rice. She lowers her gaze and listens to him coughing, sputtering, and being pounded on the back by his father.

She risks another quick peek. Shaken by his father's repeated blows, dust rises from his back, but Mr. Frog's heavily oiled hair remains glued tight and shining to his scalp. Not a hair stirs to ruin the perfectly symmetrical central part.

Riding home in the taxi, Keiko sits dazed and mute. Her mother and uncle are in good spirits. They laugh and repeat how well the meeting went. They praise Keiko for her excellent performance. "You were perfect," says Nobutaro. "Demure and refined. Not a bit coarse or loud. You said just enough. And every word you spoke . . . your voice was soft and sweet as cherry blossoms in spring."

"But the next time you see him," says Kuwano, "talk to him a little more."

"You were so . . . so . . . Japanese!" says Nobutaro.

"I never felt so out of place in my life," says Keiko.

"He was obviously impressed by you," says Nobutaro.

Finally, Shoji speaks. "He looks even more froglike in person."

"Yes," says Keiko. "I despise him."

"Nonsense," says Kuwano. "You never even looked at him."

Keiko starts crying softly.

"Stop that," says her mother. "People will see you."

"Leave her alone," says Shoji. "Kei-chan, you look lovely in your new clothes. I always enjoy seeing you get dressed up. You remember the first time you and I went shopping in San Francisco?"

Keiko smiles and her eyes brighten. "Yes, of course, Papa. I was nine, and you bought me a whole new outfit. That was such a special day."

Shoji hands her his handkerchief. "If you don't like him, he can go to hell."

"What are you saying?" says Kuwano.

"I want a man of substance for Kei-chan," says Shoji. "I want a man who makes my daughter happy. A man who will cherish her and protect her. That fool couldn't even eat without spitting rice on the floor."

"I don't care if he dumped his whole bowl on the floor. He's rich."

"Not rich enough. Not for my daughter. You saw how that frog leered at

Keiko? She barely glanced at him, and the fool was drooling all over himself."

"That's good," says Nobutaro, "that's what we wanted."

"That's the way men are," declares Kuwano.

"If Kei-chan can get a man as rich as Mr. Frog with such little exertion, just think of how big a fish she might land if she tried."

"Ho-ho . . . I see your point," says Nobutaro.

"You mean . . ." says Kuwano.

"Bigger fish!" Nobutaro laughs with delight. He and Kuwano immediately fall to speculating between themselves.

Shoji whispers to Keiko, "I guess we took care of Mr. Frog."

"Thank you, Papa."

When the go-between brings word of Mr. Frog's formal marriage proposal, Keiko rejects it. Kuwano fusses, but Shoji has learned which strategy worked best, and he sticks to it. "Don't worry. She'll land a bigger fish."

"You really think so?"

"A prince of a fish."

"But what if no others show up, and this one gets away?"

"Would you rather catch an ugly little frog or a great big fish?"

Kuwano relents.

That is when the go-between discloses that Mr. Frog's mother disapproved of Keiko. Mr. Frog proposed over Mama Frog's protests.

Nobutaro's wife tells Keiko that she is lucky she decided against Mr. Frog. "Life with a disgruntled mother-in-law is hell on earth."

"Let's slow down this marriage search," says Shoji. "Kei-chan must finish her schooling first."

"Yes," says Keiko, "that's a battle all by itself."

Uniformity

NOVEMBER 1940

B-SENSEI STANDS WITH HIS BACK AGAINST ONE OF THE COLUMNS FLANK-ing the school's entrance. He squints against the early-morning sunlight, hazy and golden in the street.

A troop of young middle-school boys comes jogging around the corner. Arranged military fashion in rows of twelve, six abreast, huffing steam into the chilly air, they run steadily up the street. B-sensei notices pedestrians and shopkeepers bowing as the boys draw near. Then he sees that one of the boys in front is carrying a framed photograph of the emperor. Instantly, B-sensei steps forward, comes to rigid attention, and salutes the picture.

As the troop passes, B-sensei completes his salute and steps back. Crack-ling his knuckles, he shivers. Not from cold, but the intensity of his patriot-ism. It feels good, the emotion coursing through him, heating his gut, chest, and arms. Better than alcohol. But dangerous. He must calm down. He takes long, slow, deep breaths . . . and lets the heat go. Overtaxing his nervous sys-tem might trigger an epileptic fit. This is the fear that rules him. Without con-trol over every aspect of his life—from his daily schedule to the way his fingernails are trimmed—an attack might strike him. Down, thrashing . . . the girls cringing in horror . . . and later, all those eyes filled with pity and disgust.

Humiliation. Loss of face. He lives with the moment-by-moment threat. And every molecule of his being is directed toward keeping the attacks at bay.

The girls find B-sensei rigid and aloof. None knows that he has studied martial arts since he was six, his proud samurai grandfather insisting that a warrior's regimen would overcome the epilepsy. B-sensei grew up assuming that he would become a soldier. He tried his best, but the epilepsy ruined his dream of military glory. That path was now closed to him. And what of love? Marriage and a family of his own? Here at the finest girls' school in Nagoya, he is surrounded by beautiful young girls, and he is resigned to never being married—after all, what sort of woman would risk marrying a man who might inject such a shameful infirmity into the family bloodline? Here and now all he wants to do is protect his girls, to teach them how to protect themselves, how to harness their inner strength. This is the last dream remaining in his heart. He wants the girls to gain the pride and self-confidence that come with a strong, supple body. He wants them to discover the samurai spirit that slumbers in their blood.

But the girls, his precious girls, do not understand. Most disdain the *naginata* lessons as tiresome and silly. His better students see his drills as an archaic set of calisthenics. His best students enjoy the *naginata* lessons as a form of dance.

Not one, not once, has ever truly realized that the *naginata* is a lethal weapon, that they are being trained in how to cut through flesh and bone. To kill.

All his girls are too . . . sweet. And innocent. If, just once, one of his students could understand what he is trying to teach them. Just once, if a girl could feel her *ki* flowing . . .

B-sensei rouses himself from his reverie. The girls are beginning to arrive. Soon the front walkway is a stream of chattering schoolgirls. They bow as they pass, wishing him good morning, but none pauses to speak longer, none has ever asked why he stands there every morning. They do not understand how much he wants to protect them.

Like an army drill instructor B-sensei inspects their uniforms, the shine on their shoes, the neatness of their hair. . . . Order is good. Order is safe. Each time he sees a student with everything neat, polished, and in place, he smiles. Inwardly. On his face he shows no emotion.

He spots the girl from America approaching. For a moment their eyes meet.

Keiko does her best to smile and dips her head and says good morning as she approaches him. As Keiko passes him, she notices B-sensei scribbling something in his notebook. An hour later Keiko is summoned to the *kocho-sensei's* office. B-sensei is there, his notebook open on the principal's desk.

The principal looks up, adjusts his glasses, and peers across his desk at the self-declared "modern girl" from America. Her bow appears normal. She seems respectful and demure. Her smile is full of light and innocence. He feels hopeful. Tentatively, he begins. "Tell me your name and class."

"My name is Yanagi Keiko, and I am a senior."

He thinks she has a nice voice with a clean, musical quality to it. "Do you enjoy singing? Have you joined the school choir?"

B-sensei interrupts. "*Kocho*-sensei, her uniform . . ."

"Ah, yes, her clothes."

"Yanagi Keiko-san," says B-sensei, "why have you altered your uniform?"

Puzzled, Keiko looks down at her school uniform: a navy blue blouse with a midi collar and scarf, navy blue skirt, white socks, and black leather shoes. Everything looks fine. "I'm sorry, sir, but I don't understand what you mean."

"Don't be impertinent! By deviating from the dress code, you've insulted your school, your classmates, and your instructors."

Keiko is speechless.

"How dare you place yourself apart from your classmates? It's a senior's duty to present a good example for lower-grade students. By flaunting the dress code, you've disgraced yourself, your classmates, and your family name."

Keiko is stunned. The color drains from her face.

The principal looks pained. B-sensei's voice and manner have always grated on his nerves, but this latest tirade is a new level of torture. "You see, Yanagi-san, we want harmony in our school. You understand, don't you?"

"Yes, sir."

"When everyone's uniform is correct, it encourages all the students to behave as one, harmonious group."

"Just like an army," says B-sensei. "We think and act as a group. That's our strength. Uniformity of appearance, thought, and action!"

The principal grimaces. "Well, of course we are not an army. We are the best girls' school in the city, and we must maintain our standards. I'm sure this oversight on your part is just because you're new here. You'll try to do better, won't you."

"Yes, sir." Keiko feels so ashamed and humiliated, she can barely speak.

"She should apologize publicly to the entire school," says B-sensei.

"No. That's going too far. Keiko-san, apologize to us and fix your clothes. Then you may return to your classes."

"Yes, sir. I'm very sorry." Keiko's eyes well up. She bows deeply and humbly. "I'm very, very sorry."

"That's fine. Now fix your uniform," says the principal.

"Yes, sir. Right away." She looks down at herself. Suddenly, she feels trapped in a nightmare. The room is deathly quiet. Both men stare expectantly at her.

"Are you defying the *kocho*-sensei's orders? Fix your uniform! Do it now!"

"I'm sorry. Please, I don't know what's wrong."

"What? Are you mocking us?"

"No, Sensei. I . . . I really don't know."

"Come over here. Look." B-sensei points at a framed photograph on the wall. "Is this your class picture?"

"Yes, Sensei."

"That person there. Is that you?"

"Yes, Sensei."

"Well?"

Light slanting through the tall windows glares off the glass of the black-framed photograph. The glare and Keiko's own reflection in the glass partly obscure the image. She tips her head trying to dodge and focus past her ghostly reflection. She locates herself among the rows of identically clad students. "We all look the same."

B-sensei screeches in her ear, "Are you blind?"

"No, Sensei. Please, really, I don't see what you mean."

"It's obvious. Just look. First, the knot on your scarf is tied at least five centimeters too low. Second, your school pin should be one finger width above and one finger width to the right of the top of your breast pocket. You see? Everyone has their knots tied properly and their pins in the correct position. Your knot is too low and you've got your pin in the center of your breast pocket. Just as you do this very moment. It's shameful. Unforgivable. Sloppy dress leads to sloppy morals. You should—"

"Enough," says the principal. "Keiko-san, fix your uniform."

Using her reflection in the glass, Keiko reties her scarf. She adjusts her school pin several times until she gets it exactly right. Anger flares within her. *All this stupid fuss for this?* She clenches her teeth. Finished, she takes her place in front of the desk. She keeps her eyes lowered, but the men sense the change in her.

"So the wind has shifted," says B-sensei. His voice has an oily tone. "Sir, this is exactly what I was talking about. This American girl is purposely and maliciously trying to destroy the social fabric of our school. She looks Japanese, but she's a fake. Test her. Let's hear her apologize once more. Keiko-san, give us your most sincere, most heartfelt apology."

Keiko's jaw is clamped so hard, she thinks her teeth might break.

"Enough," says the principal. "She's already apologized. Keiko-san, you may return to your classes."

Keiko bows.

"Wait one moment, please. I have something more to say." The principal gazes out the windows and considers his words. "Through the ages many great teachers have counseled us to seek tranquillity within and to express harmony in our daily lives and in our interactions with others. I personally do not equate harmony with uniformity. Furthermore, in our zeal to be good teachers, we may sometimes place too great an emphasis on exactitude and correctness. Keiko-san, I do not believe that you acted out of conscious disrespect. However, please pay special attention to your appearance and conduct. When one is unfamiliar with the ways of a new and different place, one must take care not to inadvertently cause discord."

"Yes, sir." Keiko bows deeply. "Thank you very much, sir."

Tule Fog

FEBRUARY 1941

SAM BOWS. YIN AND YANG. GENTLENESS AND VIOLENCE. AN ICE BLUE moon dims and brightens behind billowing curtains of fog. Alone in the pale blue mist, Sam works out behind Mrs. Franklin's barn. He has built himself a striking post and collected scrap lumber, which he mounts up and down either side of the post. Focusing on his targets, there is something inhuman, machinelike about his eyes, stance, and movements. He tenses, coiling ever tighter into himself, then holds and holds, compressing the energy until suddenly it seems to explode on its own. Fists and feet blur, each strike breaking the wooden targets into kindling.

With each blow pain shoots through him, electrical shocks from the point of impact along his extremities to spine and skull then back to hand or foot. But no matter how hard he hits, no matter how many boards he shatters, he is unable to eclipse the greater pain in his heart.

Keiko is gone, but she has been in his thoughts every day since she left. He let her go, yet he holds her with every breath he takes. Does she think of him? Does she believe his actions were based on loyalty to Yuriko? That was true in the beginning, but at the end everything he did, or did not do, was for Keiko. He told her, but did she really hear? He would not be the cause of Keiko losing face on her wedding night.

Sam stares at the pile of cracked and splintered wood at his feet. He wipes his hands on a rag. His battered hands remind him of gnarled winter grapevines, graceless and ugly. After so many vicious blows, there is not much blood. He is not surprised. His hands are not the only parts of him that have callused and hardened.

No mercy nor love. No whining. No complaints. No needs. Not for him.

With a formal bow Sam ends his practice and heads toward his cabin. The tule fog rolls in, hugging the dank earth. Hands outstretched through moonlight-suffused mist, Sam gropes his way forward. Ambushed by a feeling of blind impotence, he starts kicking and punching his way through the fog. Yin in its yielding, balancing perfectly the yang of Sam's bitterness and rage, the tule fog enfolds him, caressing and wetting his face in place of the tears he refuses to shed.

Hands, feet, and heart aching and throbbing, Sam washes at the outdoor pump. Before Keiko left for Japan, he had tried to trick and outsmart love with secrets and lies, had tried to think his way through its maze. And failed. Now that she is gone, no matter how hard he strikes, he cannot beat love into submission nor eject it from his heart. Perhaps someday after Yuriko has arrived and they are married and busy with building a home for their child, perhaps then the pain of losing Keiko will fade. Instead of comfort, this idea bites him like a snake.

And it comes to him—muted as the full moon glowing through the tule fog—the truth within all his suffering. Yin and yang, bliss and pain, are the two halves of love. Body reality, head reality, and heart reality are not the same. This awful grinding ache that his head abhors and his body cannot escape—is precious to his heart. He stares blindly into the fog, and with grief and gratitude tells himself, *As long as I hurt, Keiko is not completely gone from me; our love has not run out of time.*

Two-san's Sister

MARCH 1941

THE GO-BETWEEN RETURNS WITH A SECOND PROSPECT. KUWANO ASKS, and to Shoji's relief the go-between answers, yes, prospective groom number two did indeed come from an even wealthier family. Two-san's photograph is passed around.

With all eyes on her, Keiko does her best to keep her expression blank. "Well . . ." she says finally, "he's certainly not ugly."

"He's very handsome," says Kuwano.

"He looks even better in person," says the go-between.

"He looks intelligent," offers Shoji.

"He graduated in the top ten percent of his class," says the go-between.

"Tell him I'll think about it," says Keiko haughtily. "Come back in three days, and I'll let you know if I'll meet him." With that she leaves the room.

The go-between's mouth drops open.

Kuwano is mortified by her daughter's rudeness. She immediately begins bowing and offering apologizes.

Nobutaro frowns and crosses his arms tightly. "American women!"

Shoji laughs. "Without a degree of challenge, a man like Number Two-san would surely become bored. By making him wait for an answer, Kei-chan adds the spice of uncertainty to the match. She's not being rude. She's being clever."

"Ho-ho . . . Like a business deal, right? Exposing eagerness puts one at a disadvantage during bargaining."

"Exactly."

Kuwano's anger cools to a simmer. "If that's what she was thinking, she should have said so, instead of putting on such airs."

"She's just going on instinct," says Shoji. "I think she likes him."

"Really?" Kuwano and the go-between are delighted.

"When you return in three days, I bet she'll agree to the meeting."

Kuwano sighs with relief.

"But don't let the other side know that," Nobutaro says to the go-between.

"You can trust me," says the go-between. "This will be the biggest and best match of my life." She rubs her hands together.

Kuwano looks quizzically at her husband. "When did you become such an expert on arranging marriages?"

"I caught you, didn't I?"

Startled and flustered by Shoji's words, Kuwano retreats into a pleased silence. Color rises in her cheeks.

The following afternoon Keiko is home alone. She is in the midst of practicing with her *naginata* when a visitor appears at the front door. The woman's name is Natsuko, and she is Two-san's older sister. "Please, come in," says Keiko. "My parents are away, but they should return soon."

"Actually, I came to speak with you."

Keiko and Natsuko sit at the low dining table. Keiko serves tea.

"Please," says Natsuko, "try to be open and honest with me. I need to know your true feelings about marrying my brother."

"I don't have any feelings about your brother. I've never met him."

"My brother's a good man, but he's very old-fashioned. I think he'd be happiest with a traditional Japanese wife. Since you grew up in America, I'm concerned that your values and expectations might conflict with his."

Keiko nods. "I worry about that, too."

Natsuko sighs. "Good. Then we have some common ground. We can talk."

"Yes, let's talk."

"I've read that American women are strong and independent. Do you truly feel that you can live in this country for the rest of your life? Can you adopt all of our ways? Do you really understand what it means to be a traditional Japanese wife?"

"Well, I'm not sure. Sometimes I'm bothered by the idea that I must go directly from being ruled by my parents to being ruled by a husband."

"A husband who is a stranger to you. Ruled by him *and his parents*. You understand that, don't you? When a Japanese woman marries, she switches her loyalty from her own family to the family of her husband. You must treat your new parents-in-law with your most humble respect and obedience."

"Yes, I understand."

"My brother will expect you to raise his children, run his household, and help with the family business."

Keiko nods.

"I have eight brothers and sisters. My brother also wants a large family."

"I see. . . ."

"My brother loves to go out drinking with his men friends. My brother is a lot like my father. My father keeps . . . a mistress. And he occasionally runs off with geisha—they go to hot springs together, sometimes for two weeks. This has caused great pain for my mother. And my brother, well, as I said, he's just like my father. My brother loves sake and women." She sighs. "I love my father. Sometimes I can even smile at his romantic flings and roguish behavior. But the main reason I'm still unmarried is that I'd rather die than live in silent pain like my mother. I truly love my father, but I would never marry a man like him."

"In America," says Keiko, "we believe that people fall in love then get married. Without love and some romance, a marriage grows stale and dies."

"In Japan," says Natsuko, "marriage has traditionally been more like what you might call a social contract. Love and romance are separate, although with time, love usually blossoms in a good marriage. However, when my father fell in love with one of his mistresses, it almost destroyed his marriage and our family. After that, he learned to act with greater discretion, and my mother learned to blind herself to the truth."

"Passionate, romantic love was a disruptive force to your parents' marriage?"

"Yes, that's it exactly."

"Your parents don't love each other?"

"They do. They care about one another. They're kind and devoted. But as for passion and romantic love . . ." Natsuko shakes her head. "Materially speaking, my mother and we children have always been well provided for. My brother's even more generous than my father. You would live in comfort and relative luxury. But now that you understand my mother's life—could you be happy with a similar one? Do you think you could make my brother happy?"

"No."

"Thank you for your honesty."

"Thank you for yours, Natsuko-san. I know how difficult it must be for you to speak so candidly about your family."

"It's because I love them. And I'm devoted to their happiness."

"Natsuko-san, you say American women are strong. The strongest women I know are all Japanese. When I listen to you, I realize how much strength it takes for a woman to remain true to herself. I don't know if I'm strong enough to marry a Japanese man. I don't know if I'm strong enough to live here without losing myself."

Natsuko smiles. "Don't give up. Japan is changing. Every day I read things that surprise me. Once this war is over, things will be much nicer. Find a Japanese man with modern attitudes. The traditional ones aren't for you."

"Natsuko-san, I wish I had an older brother for you to marry. I think you could make him very happy."

She laughs. "Yes, I should be the one searching for a Japanese-American spouse. Not my brother."

Keiko rejects the marriage meeting with Two-san. She keeps her promise to Natsuko and does not mention their talk. Kuwano rages until Shoji, in the name of family harmony, begs his daughter for her reason. Keiko blurts out the first thing that comes to mind. "I'd have to work in the family business."

"What's wrong with that?" says Shoji. "They have a machine shop. They make parts for airplanes."

"That's right!" says Keiko. "And my teacher, B-sensei, says Japan and America may someday be at war with one another. I refuse to work in a business that might build a weapon that might kill . . . Al or Dewey." Keiko is so horrified by what she has just said, she bursts into tears.

Shoji and Kuwano are stunned. It is a long time before any of them can speak again. "I wish you had told us sooner," says Kuwano. "I wouldn't have nagged you. Please don't mention this to Nobutaro-san."

"Yes," says Shoji, "we must not mention this to anyone."

Ki

MAY 1941

WITH HER *NAGINATA* EXAM LESS THAN A MONTH AWAY, KEIKO PRACtices at home every afternoon with her mother. One night at dinner, Papa hands Keiko a small parcel from Genzo. Keiko tears it open and finds a letter and an old book with a broken spine and loose pages. Two thick red rubber bands wrapped around the book hold it together. Leaving the bands in place, Keiko struggles with the title. "It's a Japanese philosophy book on the subject of *ki*."

Shoji chuckles. "In my last letter I told Genzo you were having some trouble in school. I asked him if he could explain *ki* to you."

Kuwano laughs. "Asking Genzo-san if he can explain something is like asking a rooster if he likes to crow in the morning."

April 2, 1941

Dear Kei-chan,

I have enclosed a wonderful book about ki. Since you may find it difficult to read, I will summarize the main points for you:
1. Ki cannot be defined in words.
2. If you are concerned about results, ki will not flow. That is, if you are worried about failure, if you are burning with desire to succeed, if you are desperate to win, ki will not flow. If you want to appear clever, powerful, beautiful, better than your classmates, ki will not flow.

3. *Once it is flowing, if you pause to look at it, it will instantly disappear.*

Kei-chan, I hope this helps.

My son Dewey says to tell you he has taken up weight lifting. Your brother Al says his grades are good and his baseball team is in first place. There is no hurry about returning my book. Any time after your naginata exam would be fine. Please give my best regards to your parents. Tell your father I will write to him soon.

Your American uncle, Genzo

Late that night after finishing her homework, Keiko reads Genzo's letter again. What on earth is he talking about? B-sensei said that non-Japanese could never understand *ki*. Perhaps she is too American. Sighing wearily, Keiko takes the book to bed with her. She removes the red rubber bands, and along with several pages a letter drops out. She recognizes the handwriting instantly. "Oh, it's from Sam!"

April 3, 1941

Dearest Keiko,

Uncle Genzo mentioned that you were studying the naginata and wanted to know about ki. I'm no master, but I thought I might pass along some of what was taught to me.

But first, the news. Last week Mrs. Franklin sold her farm and went to live with her youngest daughter. I have moved in temporarily with Uncle Genzo. I sleep in the barn, which is fine with me because Dewey and Al both snore. Before looking for another job, I took a few days off to see about getting into the University of California in Berkeley. I learned about tuition and fees and how to apply. And they assigned a professor to be my advisor. Professor Knight is wonderful. He's a real scholar, but not the least bit stuck up or stuffy. He told me he grew up in a little town in northern Michigan, so he understood how intimidating a big university could be. He gave me several scholarship applications, but told me not to get my hopes too high. He said because I was Japanese, I would most likely be rejected. He came right out and said it, just like that. And he looked real sorry, too. Then he told me about an essay contest. The subject is "The Power of Mass Communications in Current International Relations."

Professor Knight had a huge collection of German and Japanese government propaganda. He even had Japanese and Russian propaganda from the Russo-Japanese War of 1898. He showed me a pamphlet written for Japanese consulate personnel. I translated it on the spot—he scribbled it down as fast as I could read it to him.

He offered to loan me some of his Japanese propaganda to use in the essay contest. I got very excited. But when we reread the contest flyer, it stated that the judges wanted only the most up-to-date examples, anything over a year old was unacceptable. Unfortunately, everything in the professor's collection was well over two years old. I may still submit an essay. The prize money would cover my tuition and fees for a year. Professor Knight said he would try to get some funds from the university to pay me to translate all his Japanese propaganda.

Just before I left Lodi to visit Berkeley, Genzo lent me a new black leather briefcase which he'd gotten for Dewey. Dewey refused to use it because he said it made him look stupid. I put the contest flyer in the briefcase with my enrollment forms and scholarship applications, then I walked around the campus. I can't tell you how excited I felt!

But now to the subject of ki. As you know, I practiced martial arts in Hawaii. Shortly before I left for the mainland, my sensei heard that his friend, a sensei in Hilo, was preparing to test his top student, so Fujiwara-san decided to test me at the same time. It was an endurance test. The other student, Kazuo, and I were to fight three thousand matches in three days. I bet that sounds crazy to you. It was an ordeal and a privilege that I'll never forget.

A thousand matches a day. I doubt that either of us got anywhere near that number. And I don't think anyone kept count. Fujiwara-san's friend had a big class, and he also got a bunch of guys from at least two other classes. Kazuo took half the floor, and I took the other. We never fought each other, just all these other students. Kazuo and I weren't supposed to try to conserve our energy. We were told to give our best to every match. A variety of weapons and attack styles were thrown at us. As soon as one match ended, win or lose, the next opponent came forward and attacked us. Sometimes our sensei sent two or three men at once against us.

I began the first day full of self-confidence and energy. At the end of the second day, Kazuo's urine was stained pink, and they made him stop. I was so bruised and sore and exhausted I told my sensei that I didn't think I could make it through the last day. Fujiwara-san took me for a long walk. He led me to the cliffs overlooking the sea. He told me, "Look at the sunlight on the water. See the shimmering light? How many stars do you see?" I told him I saw many. "How many?" I said, "Hundreds, thousands, the number changes as the waves move." He said, "There is only one star." He said, "The light of our one sun dissected by the small teeth of the sea becomes the dance of ten thousand stars. Your kata, all the movements, the routines, the forms, the tactics you've practiced—these are the breaking light, these are the sparks of the sun in the waves. Pieces. Fragments. This dancing light laughs at all who would possess it. This light has been and will continue dancing until the sea runs dry or our sun burns out. The secret of the dancing light hides in its heart. Like you, it has but one."

He said, "Now you must seek your own wholeness. You must claim what you already are—a star. One star. Do not be overwhelmed by fragments; find the core of light within yourself. The core is compassion. The light is wisdom. Do not be taken by the false and sparkling surface. We are not here to win contests. We are not here to defeat enemies. We are not here to look or sound good. Open your mind. Open your body. Open your spirit."

I told him I didn't know how to do that. You know what he said? "Breathe. Just breathe."

Keiko, I learned that physical strength and technical skill can only carry you so far. After that, there is only ki. On the third and final day, I was panting and gasping so hard that my breath tasted like boiled burnt rags. My muscles felt like melted rubber. But ki flowed up from the artery at the core of the universe and flooded through my body and sent my attackers flying like chaff in the wind. They told me rivers of tears ran down my face, but I don't remember that. They said I cackled like a madman, but I don't remember that either.

As for your naginata, first you must practice the kata. You must *practice each routine until every movement is correct and automatic as tying your shoelaces. Then you must practice the kata until in every instant of every movement you are totally conscious and present—present without pride or any desire to impress or look good. And finally, you must practice the kata.*

When I was nine, on the night before I left Japan, I was writing thank-you and farewell notes to my classmates and teachers. I was feeling very sad. My mother pointed to the full moon rising over Ogonzan hill above our house. She held my hand and said, "Do you see the moon? When we look at the same thing together, it's like we're touching. Even when we are half a world apart, we will see the same moon. The world is not so big after all. No matter where you are, we share the same ki."

It's not the size of your muscles or how hard or fast you swing your naginata. Everywhere you look there are big strong men with weak ki. Fujiwara-san was a tiny old man, but his ki could flatten six big guys all at once. Wham! Just like that.

Have faith in yourself. Ki is not unattainable nor limited to Japanese. Every living thing on earth contains it. It's the energy of life. You already have it. You've always had it. I've seen it and felt it moving through you. So don't worry. Just practice your kata. Practice. And breathe.

I realize this is a very long letter. But once I started writing, I felt like I was talking with you, and I didn't want to stop. Right now as I write these words, I'm imagining your beautiful eyes reading, and I wonder if you can hear my voice in your mind. Darling Keiko, I miss you so much. I think of you all the time and hope you are happy. I hope your future is filled with good fortune. Thank you for everything you taught me.

Love, Sam

Keiko puts down the letter. She wipes tears from her cheeks and feels warm energy surging through her. "Ah," she sighs, "my *ki* is flowing."

Lightning and Wind

JUNE 1941

KEIKO SITS ON THE BLEACHERS WAITING FOR HER TURN.

One by one the girls are called to the gym floor and told which kata to perform. Keiko closes her eyes, imagines sunlight sparkling on the surface of the sea.

Keiko is the last to be called. She descends from the bleachers, and the previous girl, her friend Mieko, hands the *naginata* to Keiko with a quick smile. Keiko turns and faces B-sensei and the rest of her class.

"Perform kata seven, nine, thirteen, twenty, and twenty-seven," says B-sensei.

Keiko notices two Imperial Army officers sitting in the first row of the bleachers. Beside them are the principal and several other teachers. When had they come in? So many people are staring at her. Keiko begins to panic.

"What are you waiting for?" asks B-sensei.

Heart pounding, breath shallow and ragged, the *naginata* slipping in her cold, sweaty hands, Keiko lowers her head.

A soft, anxious murmur goes through the girls on the bleachers.

"Too late for prayers," whispers B-sensei.

Keiko thinks: *Their eyes are the waves of the sea scattering my core of light into a thousand tiny fragments. B-sensei, you are not my teacher. I have sensei more powerful and far wiser than you. Mama, Papa, Uncle Genzo, and Sam, I dedicate this to you. Breathe. Just breathe . . .*

Keiko opens her eyes and bows. Her voice rings clear: "Seven, nine, thirteen, twenty, and twenty-seven. Beginning with the seventh kata, the kata called 'Lightning and Wind.'"

B-sensei smiles broadly; Mieko raises both hands and gives Keiko an eight-fingered wave. Keiko ignores Mieko.

Then Keiko does something no other girl has ever done. Looking straight into B-sensei's eyes, she gives the *naginata* a quarter turn in her hands, aiming the blade's edge straight at him. A movement so subtle that only a martial arts expert would notice and catch its lethal implication. B-sensei's grin disappears. Instinctively he sucks in his breath, his eyes widen.

Keiko steps forward and slices downward—the naked blade flashes like lightning. Smoothly, balanced perfectly, she turns and swings the *naginata* powerfully around with the sound of wind. Keiko is present in every movement, she burns in every flowing instant, eyes bright as rain lit by lightning. The *naginata* is an extension of her body; and her body crackles with energy from the soles of her bare feet against the wood floor to the tips of her hair swinging through the cold gym air.

The *ki* pouring through her feels hot and stormy, but the way it expresses itself in the movements she has practiced so many times is anything but wild. Keiko's actions are spare and clean, without hesitation or egotistical flourishes. Her movements are full of authority and power, but everything is pure. Her anger toward B-sensei is gone. Now what she feels flooding through her is joy. Joy, gratitude, and love. Kata seven, nine, thirteen, twenty, and twenty-seven; without pause she performs them one after another. The last kata ends like wind and distant thunder fading into silence.

The gym is absolutely still. Keiko bows.

One of the army officers begins to clap. Immediately, Keiko's classmates join in the applause. Even the principal is clapping, smiling and nodding at something a teacher is saying in his ear. After the applause, B-sensei clears his throat. "Well, I must admit that I've never seen a better demonstration of the eighth kata. However, what I requested first was the seventh kata."

Keiko feels like her face has been slapped. That explains B-sensei's crooked smile and Mieko's frantic waving. Keiko feels utterly defeated. She wants to hide her face in shame. Then very clearly, she hears Sam's voice in her ear: *We are not here to win contests. We are not here to defeat enemies. We are not here to look or sound good.* Keiko draws a deep breath and levels her head. Her shame fades, leaving behind a gentle sadness. She feels humble. And everyone can see it.

B-sensei taps his grade sheet. "You failed one-fifth of your examination. Twenty percent. It's as if I asked you to draw a picture of five fish, and instead you drew four fish and a tree. If technique was the only thing we were interested in, I would have to fail you. However, there's the matter of *ki*. *Ki* is something so immeasurably important and so . . . rare. Confronted with the real thing, one can only bow respectfully before it. The *ki* you just displayed was real. It could not have been faked."

B-sensei's voice falters, softens. "I've waited so long for a student. . . ." B-sensei hesitates and clears his throat. "I have no choice but to give you the highest possible mark on your exam. To do otherwise would betray everything I've tried to teach. Thank you for your performance. And thank you for the invaluable lesson you've taught me." Clearly shaken, B-sensei lowers his head to Keiko.

Instantly, she returns his bow.

Triggering a fresh round of applause. Class dismissed, Keiko finds herself surrounded by smiling, excited classmates. Mieko grabs Keiko's arm and pulls her to where the two army officers are talking with B-sensei and the principal. Keiko recognizes the older, higher-ranking officer as the man in the photograph over B-sensei's desk. He is the one who started the applause. The younger officer turns out to be Mieko's brother, Aki.

"That was the best, most decisive, most graceful *naginata* demonstration I have ever seen performed by a student," says the senior officer. "Your sensei trained you very well."

B-sensei beams, choked and pleased to the edge of tears. Swallowing hard, he admits, "*Ki* cannot be taught," and he bows to Keiko. "I was wrong about you. Please forgive me for the unkind remarks I've made. What you just did . . . it was . . . magnificent!"

Returning his bow, Keiko feels a blush spreading across her face and throat. She smiles and tugs at Mieko's sleeve. Bowing repeatedly, the girls retreat toward the dressing room.

Aki calls to his sister, "Is she the one from America?"

"Yes!"

Mieko and Keiko run into the dressing room. Neither of them sees the change in the expressions of the army officers.

In the dressing room Mieko and the class president tell Keiko that they have never seen B-sensei so impressed with a student's performance, nor ever heard him publicly apologize to a student. Mieko and the class president watch Keiko remove her gym blouse. They see Keiko has embroidered two small flags onto her undershirt—one Japanese, one American.

On her way home from school, Keiko walks by a wall plastered with government propaganda. Until she received Sam's letter, she had ignored all such posters and leaflets. She especially hated reading bad things about the United States, just like she had hated reading negative things about Japan in the American press. But now that she has started a collection for Sam, finding new propaganda delights her.

She is carefully peeling off one of the flyers, when a policeman stops her. While he is scolding her, accusing her of vandalism, a black car pulls to the curb. Mieko's brother Aki sits in the front passenger's seat. "What's the problem?"

The policeman snaps to attention and salutes. "Sir, this girl was defacing government property."

B-sensei sits between Aki and the driver. "Keiko-san, why were you doing that?"

Keiko shows him her brightest smile. "I'm collecting, uh . . . government announcements."

B-sensei frowns with concern. "That's not a good idea."

The rear window rolls down. There are two men in the backseat. One is the senior army officer. The other, sitting closest to the window, is a man dressed in a black business suit. "What's the purpose of your collection?" he asks.

Something about this man, something deeper than his dead eyes and Hitler mustache, makes Keiko shiver. She fights to maintain her smile. "I want to learn more about mass communication in international relations. When I finish school, I want to work for a newspaper or radio station."

The man narrows his eyes. "Really?" He points a finger at the policeman.

"Yes, sir. What should I do, sir?" asks the policeman.

"Let her keep the flyer. But escort the girl home. Make a list of the 'government announcements' in her collection. Write down her address and the names of her parents and deliver your report to my office."

"With your permission, sir, which office is that, sir?"

"The Kempeitai."

"Yes, sir." The policeman stiffens to attention and salutes.

"Wait," says the senior officer. "Miss, after the officer has finished his list, I suggest that you destroy your collection. In these troubled times your actions could be misunderstood." He pauses and looks to make certain that both Keiko and the Kempeitai are paying attention. "I'm positive that you mean no harm. You are just a very naive young schoolgirl."

———

Walking home, Keiko asks the policeman, "What's the Kempeitai?"

"You don't know?"

"No."

"The secret police."

Keiko and the policeman arrive at her house. To Keiko's immense relief, her parents are out. The policeman follows Keiko upstairs to her room. He sits at her desk and starts a list of all the propaganda she has collected. When he fills the last page of his notebook, Keiko gives him more paper from her own notebook. Eager to get him out of the house before her parents return, she sits next to him and helps him make the list. He is grateful for her assistance.

When he is leaving, he says, "I'm sorry I yelled at you. You don't seem like a bad girl after all. Be very careful about how you conduct yourself from now on. Mind what you say and how you act, even when you think you're alone. The Kempeitai have eyes and ears *everywhere*. Your neighbors, the shopkeepers, your teachers and classmates . . . Be very careful. Warn your parents."

He lowers his voice to a whisper. "You'll be watched."

Fireworks

JULY 1941

FOURTH OF JULY FRIDAY. IN A SECLUDED NOOK ON THE BANKS OF THE Mokelumne River, close to but out of sight of Lodi Lake, Sam kneels in the shade of a sycamore. He pushes back a branch of tiny elderberry flowers and spreads a clean white cloth. On the cloth he arranges a framed photograph of Fujiwara-san, a two-inch statue of the Amida Buddha, a basket of strawberries, and a Mason jar of roses from Mrs. Franklin's garden. The final item is an envelope containing a letter from Fish Mouth Enzo informing Sam that Fujiwara-san has died.

Sam lights incense and sticks it in the sand in front of his makeshift altar. He puts his hands together and bows. "Sensei, I see dragonflies and redwing blackbirds in the cattails along the riverbank. The water is mostly brownish green, but in the open where it reflects the sky, its surface gleams like Papa's silver cigarette case, and where the water runs deep in the shadow of the cottonwood and willow trees, it is brown and dark as Mama's eyes.

"Sensei, I am surrounded by a feast of colors. Even if I fail to name them all, I will do my best to see them all, as you have taught me. Sensei, every day my life is enriched because of something you taught me."

Sam bows once more then begins naming colors. The list flowing past his lips sounds like the palette for a Tibetan Buddhist sand painting, a mandala of compassion and gratitude. Sam's grief settles like summer heat in his chest, his ribs glow like limbs in a fire. The love he feels for his former teacher blossoms like a lotus illuminating the earth and all its creatures, living and dead. Sam's murmured chant of colors goes on and on, praising the iridescence refracting off the wings of a wine red dragonfly, the dusky gray-blue of a heron stalking the tule shallows, the pollen baskets on the legs of bees hovering over the ripe strawberries.

The summer twilight descends slowly. Sam remains seated, cross-legged in meditation and prayer, moving only to light more incense. With darkness comes the noise of distant whistling, crackling, booming, and cheering from the lake.

He sees fireworks bursting beyond the black treetops lining the riverbanks. Colors flare in Sam's eyes, but instead of naming them, he inhales them. They illuminate his heart from within like a candle in a paper lantern. He hears old man Fujiwara exclaiming: *Oh! Isamu, do you see? Vibrant and ephemeral as life.*

"Yes, I see. Thank you, Sensei. Thank you."

Dr. Joe

JULY 1941

THE GO-BETWEEN BRINGS KEIKO WORD OF A THIRD MARRIAGE CANDI-date. Three-san is a doctor. Keiko can hardly believe his description. Dr. Three received his medical education in the United States and Germany. He runs a clinic established by his father. Keiko stares at his photograph—movie-star handsome, smiling, not stiff. According to the go-between, the doctor is intelligent, funny, speaks fluent English and German, and loves everything about America.

Keiko consents to a meeting, and the arrangements move ahead quickly and smoothly. The meeting is held at the same restaurant as the first one. When Keiko and her family get out of the taxi, young Dr. Three meets them at the curb. He bows respectfully to Keiko's parents and Uncle Nobutaro while the go-between introduces them. Then he gives Keiko a firm hand-shake and greets her in English. "Call me Joe." He speaks with an accent, but Keiko has no trouble understanding him. "My name is Joichi, but in the States everyone called me Dr. Joe."

During the meeting, Dr. Joe and Keiko speak in English. Dr. Joe asks if Keiko likes living in Japan. He talks about someday going to America to visit Niagara Falls and the Grand Canyon. He also wants to revisit Berlin, Paris, and London. "I want my children to know the world. People who've lived all their lives in one country never understand how much they share with people from other nations. They don't understand humanity. They judge others ac-cording to their own cultural beliefs, and they're blind to their own flaws. One must leave home in order to fully understand the meaning of home and the kinship of all the peoples of the earth."

"Yes," says Keiko. "I understand exactly how you feel."

The go-between cuts into their conversation. She is delighted with the way things are progressing, but she believes too much conversation between the prospective pair on a first meeting is unmannerly.

"What sort of work did you do in America?" Dr. Joe's mother asks Shoji.

"We had a restaurant. I made fresh soba and udon."

"Oh. Noodles." She arches one eyebrow. "I see. And what do you do now?"

"I haven't decided yet. We sold our business before we left America. And we've been living off the proceeds."

"Such a long vacation. It must have been a prosperous establishment."

"No. It was small. But of course I was paid in dollars, and the exchange rate is quite favorable."

"I see."

"I imagine you're glad to be back in Japan," says Dr. Joe's father.

"America is such a barbaric place," says Dr. Joe's mother. "My cousin went there on business and someone spit on him."

"Mother, there are racists and bigots in every county," says Dr. Joe, "including Japan."

"I don't like foreigners. If you weren't my son, I wouldn't have let you in the house when you returned from abroad. You smelled like a foreigner!"

He smiles and winks at Keiko. "She didn't approve of my British cologne."

"And you'd lost all your fine manners."

"I made the awful mistake of walking off the ship and giving her a big hug before I bowed. And then I insisted on toast and coffee for breakfast."

Keiko laughs, then quickly covers her mouth with her hand and dips her head as any proper Japanese woman would.

Two days after the meeting, the go-between reports the doctor was favorably impressed, but his parents have reservations. Out of respect for them, Dr. Joe has asked for another meeting. The go-between warns Keiko and her parents that it might take several more meetings before the doctor makes a decision. No matter how eager he is to settle the match, Dr. Joe will exercise restraint. He is a dutiful son.

Shoji shakes his head. "His mother's convinced we're too low-class for them."

"The way we made our living in America might seem humble to her, but she would have done no better," says Kuwano.

"I think her son understands that," says Keiko.

"Yes," says Shoji. "He's very intelligent. Genzo would like him."

"I think they'd get along wonderfully," says Keiko. She feels herself blushing and turns away before her mother can see.

Tanabata

JULY 1941

THEIR PAPER FANS WAFTING LAZILY, KEIKO AND UNCLE NOBUTARO, dressed in light cotton *yukata*, stroll behind her parents through the warm humid night. Paper lanterns glow along both sides of the street. "The ancient god of the earth had a beautiful daughter," explains Nobutaro. "Some call her Orihime Boshi, others prefer Tanabata-sama. She spent her days weaving garments for her father. One day a peasant led an ox past her window. The young man and Tanabata-sama's eyes met, and in that moment love blossomed and illuminated both their souls.

"When Tanabata-sama's father became aware of her unspoken wish, he gave her the youth for a husband. Lost in nuptial joy, Tanabata-sama and her new husband, Hikoboshi, had no attention for anything or anyone besides themselves. Her loom was silent. The ox wandered far out across the heavenly plains.

"Displeased, the god separated the pair forever, putting the luminous river of heaven between them. He granted them only one night together each year. On that night if the skies are clear, all the winged creatures of heaven fly close. They touch and support one another with their gentle strength, and form a bridge over the silver stream. Then Hikoboshi walks across the singing bridge to his wife.

"But if it should rain on that night, the river of heaven rises and grows too wide to span, and husband and wife must remain apart. According to the whims of the weather, years may pass between their meetings. But their love remains eternally youthful and patient. Each day they fulfill their respective duties while their hearts maintain a love that yearns, abides, and hopes for that one special night of bliss.

"If the sky is clear on the seventh night of the seventh moon reckoned by the ancient lunar calendar, and if the star Kengyu shines brightly, there will be good rice crops in the autumn. If the star Shokujo looks brighter than usual, there will be prosperity for weavers and for every kind of women's work. But if it should rain on that night, the rain is called *Namida no Ame*— the rain of tears.

"Tonight, we will have a happy Tanabata festival." Uncle Nobutaro gestures skyward toward the weaver star, Vega, her husband, Altair, and the Heavenly River, which Keiko had previously known as the Milky Way.

Freshly cut bamboo decorates the roofs of the houses in the neighborhood. Tied to the branches are paper strips in assortments of five or seven colors. The strips carry personal wishes and poems praising Tanabata-sama and her husband. After the festival, the bamboo, together with the attached prayers and poems, will be thrown into the nearest stream.

Keiko and her family join the crowd wandering among lantern-lit stalls displaying trinkets, crafts, and food. Kuwano stops at a booth selling small weavings and stitchery. She waves and Nobutaro goes to see what she has found.

Keiko draws her father aside. "Papa, I love you. I'd do anything for you. Papa, I need to know—do you want me to marry Dr. Joe?"

"Kei-chan, all I want is your happiness. What do you want?"

"To be honest, I still love Sam Hamada. And I need to set my heart at rest about him. I was wondering. . . . Papa, could I please have some traveling money?"

"Traveling money? Are you going to run away from us?"

"No, Papa, I would never do that. I just need some time alone. I want to visit my friend Misa in Tokyo. Do you remember her? We met on the ship coming over. She just sent me a letter. She's married now, but her husband's been shipped off to Indochina. She's lonely, and she invited me to visit her. I would only stay a few days."

"Let me think about it. I'll give you my answer tomorrow."

"Thank you, Papa."

Unseen Children

JULY 1941

KEIKO GETS OFF THE TRAIN AND FINDS MISA WAITING ON THE PLAT-
form. They hug, and Keiko says, "Misa, I need your help. I want to locate a
woman who lives here in Tokyo." Walking through the station, Keiko hands
Misa a piece of paper. "This is Yuriko-san's address."

"Are you sure? I've never heard of this district."

"I only read it once. But I'll remember it until the day I die."

Keiko and Misa exit the railroad station. An old woman is sweeping
black dust off the grimy concrete steps. Keiko checks her own white cotton
blouse and brushes tiny black cinders—fallout from the coal-burning
locomotives—from her sleeves.

Jostled on the crowded sidewalk, Keiko and Misa thread between men in
Occidental suits and traditional Japanese *haori-hakama*, women in dresses
and kimono, uniformed schoolchildren boarding a bus. Misa shows
Yuriko's address to a taxi driver who nods and waves them into his car. Driving away from the station, the taxi jerks to a halt; all traffic has stopped for
an infantry division marching through the intersection. Once their taxi
starts moving again, Keiko and Misa find themselves in a funeral procession
following an ornate hearse—a gold-gilded temple built onto the rear of a
long black car. After a half dozen blocks, they come to a fork and part ways,
the taxi veering up an avenue of shops and restaurants, the hearse leading its
string of mourners toward the multiple curved roofs of a pagoda. Beyond the
temple yard, Keiko sees a factory, four tall smokestacks spewing white
smoke into the summer sky.

Twenty minutes later, Keiko pays and Misa steps to the curb as the taxi
shudders, buffeted by a passing trolley. Keiko and Misa pause on the side-

walk. They scan the storefronts—a bookshop, a tiny grocery, several restaurants, a tea wholesaler—walls and utility poles covered with posters and flyers.

Misa shows Yuriko's address to three passing schoolgirls, who giggle and point up the street. Misa and Keiko walk two blocks, then turn into a side street that leads into a maze of narrow alleys jammed with restaurants, bars, and cabarets. "This is an entertainment district," says Misa.

Approaching Yuriko's place, Keiko first thinks it is a used-furniture store. There is a display window with a red chair backed by a red satin curtain. Drawing nearer Keiko can see above the red chair a single unlit light-bulb, also red, and under the chair a black ashtray filled with lipstick-stained cigarette butts. Keiko notices smudges on the inner surface of the window. She looks closer. Lipstick prints.

Keiko and Misa retreat to a nearby restaurant. A teenage boy comes out. He bows to them, then rides away on a bicycle stacked with wooden trays of fresh noodles. Keiko reads this as a good omen. She takes Misa's hand and together they enter the tiny noodle shop. There are no tables. They sit at the five-stool counter, and Misa looks out the window at Yuriko's place. "Are you sure you want to go in there?"

"No. But I must. Please wait here for me."

Keiko knocks. No one answers. She slides open the front door, steps into the entry, and calls a greeting. A woman in a red and black kimono descends some wooden stairs. Keiko recognizes her from the photograph in Sam's wallet. "You're an hour early," says the woman. "But come in."

Keiko slips off her shoes. "Yuriko-san?"

The woman nods, lights a cigarette, leads Keiko through the empty cabaret, past the tables and bar into an office with bright pink walls. Yuriko sits at a white desk. Keiko sits on a red velvet couch. "You've never done this sort of work before, have you?"

Keiko shakes her head.

"You're a virgin?"

Keiko hesitates. "Yes."

Yuriko draws deeply on her cigarette, smirks. "Technically speaking."

Keiko nods. She feels a blush rise into her face.

"Oh, how the men are going to love you."

"You are Yuriko-san?"

"Of course. Wait a minute . . . you're not the girl . . . who sent you here?"

"My name is Yanagi Keiko. I grew up in Lodi, California, in the United States. I'm a friend of Hamada Isamu-san."

"Oh! Oh . . . I see." The two women stare at each other. After a long pause, Yuriko repeats, "I see."

From a nearby room comes the sound of a child's voice. Keiko turns toward the office's open door. "Is that your son?"

Yuriko hesitates. "Isamu told you everything?"

Keiko nods. Yuriko stubs out her cigarette, immediately lights another. Keiko hears a boy shout, "No! Stay out of my fort." Followed by a girl's voice: "I have candy. Want some?" Keiko's heart aches, and she struggles to keep from crying.

"I think you must have been more than just friends," says Yuriko.

Keiko shakes her head. "No. He's been faithful to you."

"Technically faithful. Well, I've been faithful, too. I've never given my heart to anyone else. But I've had to . . . do things. . . . It was either that or starve. And I had an infant to care for. And medical bills. But in my heart, my love remained pure. I've worked hard, and due to some good luck, I now manage this place for the owner. I wrote to Isamu that I work in a nice restaurant. I was afraid if I told him the truth about this place, he would hate me."

"You're the mother of his child. I think he would forgive you."

"You . . . you're very kind. I can see you would have made him a good wife."

Just then a little girl comes in with tears in her eyes. "Ken-chan hit me."

"You hit me first," says a boy, following her. Keiko notes his reddish-brown hair and pale skin. When the boy turns to look at Keiko, she sees that he is Eurasian.

"I told you children to stay out of my room when I had a guest," says Yuriko.

"But, Mama," says the boy, "she's a lady. You said stay out when men came."

Keiko is baffled. *Mama?* Then her eyes widen, and she sucks in her breath.

When Yuriko sees the change in Keiko's face, something changes in her as well. She feels like her heart is made of silk and it has just been torn in half. "You children, get out of here right now!"

The children stare blankly at her.

"Get out!"

The children scurry away.

Keiko glares at Yuriko. "You lied. That boy's not Sam's."

"You're right. That boy is not Isamu's. But how dare you judge me, you prissy, ignorant little virgin! Your most difficult choice has been which dress to wear. What do you know about the kind of life that grinds flesh and bones into bloody paste?"

Keiko leaves the office. Yuriko follows her out, speaks more softly. "Tell Isamu I appreciated the money he sent. Tell him I wish I could have been the kind of woman he deserved . . . a woman like you. I won't expect to hear from him ever again. But just make sure he understands that I did *truly* love him, and I wish him the best. Tell him I release him . . . from his promises."

They bow stiffly, and Keiko goes out the door. Passing the display window, she sees the children peeking from behind the red satin curtain. Keiko gestures to them as she pulls her Kodak from her purse. When the children see the camera, they giggle and step shyly forward. In her viewfinder, she frames the children and the cabaret's name painted on the wall. Keiko snaps the shutter, winds the film, moves in for a close-up. Keiko is adjusting her focus when Yuriko pulls back the curtain. She is crying. She reaches for the children, then notices Keiko down on one knee outside the window. Just as Yuriko sees the camera, Keiko snaps a picture.

Yuriko jerks as if she's been slapped in the face.

Keiko sees the hurt in Yuriko's eyes. Ashamed, Keiko bows apologetically.

Yuriko steps from behind the curtain. She sits on the chair, puts the boy on her lap, fixes his hair and collar. She tells the girl to stand up straight. She brushes the tears from her cheeks then dips her head toward Keiko. Yuriko waits while Keiko checks her camera's settings and focus. Yuriko holds her head up, looks straight into the lens with sad, solemn eyes.

Keiko holds her breath, fights to steady her trembling hands, and takes the picture. She lowers the camera. Yuriko stands, bows, and takes the children behind the red curtain. Dazed, Keiko turns from the empty window and walks slowly away.

Yuriko appears at the front door. "Wait!" She throws something that glints in the light and lands at Keiko's feet. A man's gold tie clip. "Give that to Isamu-san. He'll understand what it means."

Puzzle Pieces

JULY 1941

KEIKO CATCHES THE NEXT TRAIN BACK TO NAGOYA. WHEN SHE reaches home, the instant she opens the front gate, she senses something terrible has happened. The house is closed and silent, the front door locked. She is searching in her bag for her keys when the door opens a crack and her mother's eye peeks out. "Mama, what's wrong?"

Kuwano pulls Keiko inside and locks the door. She answers in a hushed voice. "The Kempeitai have been investigating us. They've been talking to everyone. All our neighbors are frightened and suspicious. We've done nothing, but no one trusts us anymore.

"They interrogated Dr. Joe's family. He's withdrawn his marriage proposal."

"A good man," says Shoji, coming forward to greet his daughter. "He came here himself and apologized. Said he had no choice; he had to protect his family. Then our go-between resigned. Nobutaro begged her to reconsider, but she was too scared. She just shook her head and ran away. Your mother's been acting crazy. She rages around like a demon, then she hides in the kitchen like a terrified mouse."

"Your father's worthless," says Kuwano. "He just sits with his arms crossed and his mouth shut. Hour after hour, working his jaw muscles in silence like an old bull."

"I've been waiting."

"For what?"

"Kei-chan's return."

"I'm here, Papa."

Shoji smiles. "Yes. I'm so happy you're back."

"I'm happy, too," says Kuwano.

"Kei-chan," says Shoji, "what do you think we should do?"

The gods are handing me the puzzle pieces, one by one. "We're not safe here. And our presence endangers everyone we know. We must not jeopardize Uncle Nobutaro and his family. Let's pack our things. Let's go back to America."

Chills run along Keiko's spine when she hears her mother answer like an obedient child, "Yes, that's a good idea. Let's leave as soon as possible."

Fresh strength and determination flood into Shoji's voice. "*Yoshi! Iko.* All right! Let's go. If we hurry, we can make it in time for the grape harvest."

Briefcase

JULY 1941

TIRED AND DIRTY FROM A LONG DAY IN GENZO'S VINEYARDS, DEWEY and Sam remove their hats, whack their clothes, and stomp their boots on the back porch. Genzo and Al come around the side of the house. Al waves a package. "Mail for you, Sam. It's from Sis." They go in the kitchen and Sam breaks the string, tears opens the brown paper, exposes a bundle of magazine and news clippings, posters and flyers, topped with a pale blue envelope. Sam wipes his hands on his shirt, takes out the letter, unfolds it.

"Whoa!" says Dewey. "Smells like she doused it in perfume."

Sam is reading to himself, eyes widening with astonishment and delight.

"Come on, man," says Al, "what's she say?"

Sam's voice shakes with emotion. "They're . . . coming back to America."

"Who? Mother and Dad?"

"All of them. They're all coming home together."

"What? When?" says Genzo.

"They've already got their steamship tickets. They leave on . . . tomorrow! They're leaving Nagoya tomorrow!"

"This is terrific!" says Al.

"They can stay here," says Genzo, "until they find a place of their own."

"Us guys can sleep in the barn," says Dewey.

"What else does she say?" asks Al. "Did she get married?"

"No. She didn't." Sam removes three photographs that had been clamped to the letter with a gold tie clip.

Dewey and Al crowd around, looking over Sam's shoulder. "Who's that woman? And those kids?"

Sam clears his throat, fights to steady his voice. "They . . . She's an old friend of mine. Someone I knew in Hawaii."

"Yeah?"

Genzo is examining the rest of the contents of Keiko's package. "Sam, look at this! Look! Look at this!"

Sam glances at the papers.

"What are those, Pop? Newspaper and magazine clippings?"

Anxious to divert attention away from the photographs, Sam allows excitement to flood his voice. "Wow! It's Japanese propaganda!"

"Look at the dates on these pages," says Genzo.

"Hey, how about this one," says Dewey. "Looks like she tore it off some wall."

"Sam, you have an essay to write," says Genzo.

They stare expectantly at Sam. "It can't hurt to try," says Al. "No one, not even Professor Knight, has material this recent."

"Do it! Go for broke, man," says Dewey.

"Okay," says Sam, "I'll try."

Al and Dewey whoop and pound Sam on the back, dust clouds rise around them.

Sam takes the letter and photos into the bathroom and locks the door. He holds the pictures under the light and studies them. Clearly, the boy is a child of mixed blood. Keiko's letter states simply, "Yuriko-san told me the boy is not your son. Yuriko-san said to tell you that she releases you from all your promises."

Yuriko's baby is not his. He is free of the promises he made to her. She has returned Papa's tie clip. Keiko didn't get married. She's coming home! Sam feels about to burst into flames of gratitude—the gods are giving him another chance to win the one true love of his life. This time he will not mess things up. At the first opportunity, he will ask Keiko to marry him.

Too excited to sleep, Sam stays up nights working on his essay. Sam pours everything he has into it. He puts Keiko's propaganda collection in the briefcase Genzo gave him, and he carries it everywhere. In the vineyards during lunch breaks, he works on his notes. Some field hands tease him—"Hey, here comes the Briefcase Farmworker"—others take to calling him sensei. But they give him space and even try to keep their voices down while he sits on the dirt and scribbles in his notebook. No one interrupts him when he is writing. Everyone knows he is taking a long shot at a ticket to the big university in Berkeley. And in a sense their own wishes and dreams ride along in Sam's black briefcase.

Kempeitai

JULY 1941

THE YANAGIS ARE PACKED AND READY TO LEAVE. THE BULKIER ITEMS have been shipped ahead. A taxi waits out front. Uncle Nobutaro and Shoji make a final inspection of the rooms. The landlord stands talking with Kuwano.

There is a loud knock at the front door.

Keiko goes to answer it, but before she gets there, the door opens and four men enter. Keiko recognizes the policeman who had caught her with the propaganda poster and the Kempeitai who had been in the car. The other two are huge men, like sumo wrestlers in rumpled business suits. Keiko backs away, dipping her head politely. The Kempeitai does not return her bow, instead he grabs her arm. Keiko smells sake and fish on his breath when he speaks. "Yanagi Shoji, you and your family are under house arrest. Your landlord and brother-in-law are free to go. But no one else in your family may leave this house without my permission."

Uncle Nobutaro stares at the short pear-shaped man, his thick pink lips and Hitler mustache, and says, "This is outrageous! Who the hell are you?"

One of the big bodyguards moves quickly toward Nobutaro, but stops when the Kempeitai raises his hand. "Kempeitai. The secret police."

"Please, Nobutaro-san," says Kuwano. "Go home to your wife and children."

Shoji bows humbly. "Sir, we were just leaving for—"

"I know," says the Kempeitai. "I even know the serial numbers of your steamship tickets. But you can unpack your suitcases. You're not going anywhere."

"My daughter is an American citizen. You've no authority to hold her."

"You have no idea what I can do. I can throw her in prison." He tightens his grip on Keiko's arm. "I can have her tortured then executed as a spy."

Keiko has never seen her father look so desperate nor her mother so afraid.

Trembling and stuttering, the landlord says, "Excuse me, please, sir, but the house has already been rented. The new tenants will arrive at any moment."

"They'll have to find another place."

"But, sir, the renter's an army officer. He's overseas. The house is for his parents and his wife and two children. They expect to move in today." The landlord checks his watch. "I can't turn them away. Please, can't you just take these people to prison?"

Shoji gives the landlord a look of such furious contempt, the man cringes backward and lowers his eyes.

"The new tenant's in the Imperial Army?" says the Kempeitai. "Why wasn't I informed?"

One of the bodyguards pulls out a notebook; Shoji and Nobutaro see the butt of a revolver under his coat. The man leafs through his notebook. "We checked into him, sir. He's a major general currently serving in China. A decorated war hero. Beyond suspicion."

Just then they hear footsteps and voices approaching the front door. Excusing herself, Kuwano goes to answer the knock. Opening the door, she finds B-sensei, the principal, and twenty of Keiko's classmates. Out in the street beside the waiting taxi, a crowd of curious neighbors are gathering. Kuwano begins bowing and murmuring pleasantries.

Keiko thinks, *My God, we're being arrested by the secret police; we face prison, torture, and death, and Mama's worrying about what the neighbors think.* Then she glances at her father and Nobutaro; she notices that they, too, look deeply embarrassed. *Loss of face.*

She checks the Kempeitai and detects a shadow of hesitation in his face.

"Please excuse me." Bowing to him, Keiko slips her arm free and goes to the door. "Please, come in," she says to her classmates. Her mother, shocked and mortified, grabs Keiko's arm, squeezes and shakes it. "Please, come in," repeats Keiko. Her visitors move toward her, but Keiko remains blocking the doorway, and the crowd jams to a stop just outside. Keiko bows. "I'm sorry we have nothing to offer you. We can't even make tea, but since you've taken so much trouble to visit us, please, come in." Keiko waves to the neighbors watching from the street. "Hello! Would you like to come in, too?" Eagerly the neighbors step forward, dipping their heads politely. Keiko bows in return, but she stays solidly in place, blocking the doorway with her mother. Keiko can feel human energy building like an ocean wave in the crowd gathering before her.

Just then the new tenants arrive in a taxi followed by an army truck piled with boxes and furniture. A woman in a formal black kimono gets out of the taxi. She is followed by two children and an elderly lady. From the front seat a white-haired gentleman joins them. The women take the children's hands and lead them toward the house; the old gentleman stays to oversee the unloading of the truck.

"Oh, Keiko . . ." Kuwano utters a soft groan. "This is terrible. To be humiliated in front of all these people . . ."

"Mama," whispers Keiko, " 'Herding Geese, Scattering Geese.' "

Herding Geese? Kuwano stares at the crowd in front of her house. Then she looks sharply at her daughter. *Scattering Geese?* This is no time for *naginata* practice.

Or is it? When a lone warrior finds herself outnumbered but unable to retreat, she must react immediately; otherwise, she will be surrounded and killed. To save herself she must take the offensive, swing around her attackers' flank, herd them together, causing them to bunch up and get in one another's way. On the other hand, when one has superior numbers, but the enemy is more powerful, one must first attempt to scatter them, then surround the isolated elements and destroy them.

Keiko invites their visitors to enter, but she holds her mother's elbow and blocks the doorway. Her words and actions contradict each other. But she continues smiling and waving, and dutifully everyone moves toward her until they are all packed tightly in front of Keiko and her mother.

Keiko glances over her shoulder.

The Kempeitai burns with contempt. What the hell are these two women doing? All their stupid bowing and mouthing of delicate phrases. There is a war going on and these women act as if proper manners still count for something. Keiko waves to him. She and her mother are looking at him. What do they want? The Kempeitai grunts and walks toward them. Just before he reaches them, Keiko and her mother gracefully part, almost like a set of swinging doors.

The Kempeitai is caught completely off guard by the sudden rush of people. The principal enters, followed by B-sensei and twenty uniformed schoolgirls, a handful of curious neighbors, then a handsome matron with two children and an old white-haired lady. They come tumbling in like windblown leaves. It happens so quickly, the Kempeitai never realizes the people are being ever so subtly directed by Keiko and her mother with smiles and bows and graceful little gestures. The Kempeitai finds himself flanked on three sides by schoolgirls, cut off from his bodyguards, who are isolated in separate corners of the entry area. The landlord has been squeezed into a position near the front door. And before the Kempeitai can gather his wits, the new tenants have removed their shoes and taken possession of the "high ground," the tatami area next to Shoji and Nobutaro.

Angrily, the Kempeitai turns, but finds himself looking up at B-sensei and the principal. The Kempeitai raises his voice. "I was about to ask . . ." He looks around for Keiko. "I have some questions regarding a certain 'collection.' "

"What collection?" asks the kocho-sensei.

"I have a list." The Kempeitai holds up several pieces of paper. Keiko recognizes the pages from her notebook. The policeman's face reddens.

B-sensei shoots a look at Keiko. "Is this about the patriotic leaflets? My commanding officer told you to get rid of that . . . stuff."

"Yes," says Keiko. "Please thank him for his advice. My collection's gone."

"If we search, and discover that you are lying . . ."

Again B-sensei looks hard at Keiko.

She smiles at the Kempeitai. "Please go ahead. You won't find anything. Not a trace."

The policeman looks relieved. And B-sensei nods, satisfied. "Good."

The Kempeitai frowns at B-sensei.

After a lifetime spent in teaching, the principal knows a surly face when he sees one. The kocho-sensei glares down at the Kempeitai. The Kempeitai, who in his own secret chambers has made strong men whimper and beg for death, suddenly feels exposed and outnumbered. He looks around for his bodyguards, but sees only the curious, wide-eyed stares of the schoolgirls.

The Kempeitai opens his mouth, but the principal cuts him off by clearing his throat loudly, firmly, and with great authority. Momentarily checked, the Kempeitai closes his mouth, and the principal nods to one of the girls.

"To Keiko-san and her family," says the senior class president, "we extend our humble apologies for disturbing you on such a busy day. Keiko-san, we are very happy to present you with the Student of the Year Award. Keiko-san, you have set a wonderful example for your classmates by showing us the meaning of integrity and perseverance. Please return to America and tell your friends and neighbors that the students of Japan are not hostile toward Americans. The students of Japan do not want to go to war against the students of the United States."

The class president places a blue ribbon around Keiko's neck. Dangling from the ribbon is a bronze medallion. The class vice president hands Keiko a scroll and a bouquet of flowers. Then Keiko and all the girls bow to one another.

Everyone claps. The Kempeitai has no intention of joining in the applause, but one stern look from the *kocho*-sensei and the Kempeitai limply puts his hands together. Seeing this, the bodyguards and the police officer join in. The policeman even gives a little cheer, but cuts it off midway when the Kempeitai glares at him.

There is a gentle rapping at the open front door. The white-haired gentleman pokes his head in and says, "Please excuse us for interrupting you, but could you all kindly vacate the house? We would like to move in now."

"I'm sorry. That's not possible," says the landlord.

"Why?" asks the old gentleman.

From the doorway three soldiers peer over the white-haired gentleman's head. "What's the problem here?" demands one of the soldiers. "We need to unload and return to base."

Timidly, the landlord gestures toward the Kempeitai.

Everyone stares at the Kempeitai.

Keiko holds her breath.

"Let me by." The sergeant steps through the doorway into the crowded entry. He looks toward the Kempeitai. Suddenly, the sergeant snaps to rigid attention and salutes.

B-sensei follows the sergeant's eyes, then he, too, stiffens and salutes.

One by one, the policeman and the Kempeitai's bodyguards follow suit.

The Kempeitai smiles; his heart and head swell with an oily, egotistical pride. *Well, this is more like it!* He returns their salutes, but not one of the men moves. It takes several seconds before the Kempeitai realizes that the men are staring at a spot several feet above his head.

The Kempeitai turns around. At first all he sees are the new tenants and Shoji and Nobutaro. But when those people also turn to look behind them, the Kempeitai finally locates the target of the sergeant's salute.

On the far wall of the tatami-floored room hangs a framed portrait of the emperor.

Mortified to the core, the Kempeitai comes to attention and salutes. He holds his salute while his face turns red and his jaw muscles clench spasmodically. Even after Shoji and Nobutaro turn back to look at him, the Kempeitai holds his salute.

Finally, the Kempeitai brings his hand smartly down to his side. "Yanagi Shoji, I want you and your family out of here immediately. This police officer will escort you to your ship. Between the time you leave this house until you embark from Yokohama, you are not permitted to take any side trips or make any extended stops. Furthermore, you are not permitted to fraternize in any way with any Japanese citizens. If you or your wife or daughter speak a single word to any Japanese citizen, you will all be placed under arrest and brought back to me."

"My wife and I are both Japanese citizens," says Shoji. "Are we permitted to speak with each other?"

Blood-raging madness flares in the Kempeitai's eyes. His voice is like the point of an ice pick scraping glass. "Are you . . . mocking me?"

Instantly, Shoji realizes his blunder. But before he can speak, he feels a powerful blow to his back that drops him to his knees, then a hand grabs him by the collar and forces his head down until his face is pressed against the tatami floor.

"Fool!" thunders Nobutaro. "How dare you repay such kindness with impudence. How dare you insult this gentleman's act of mercy." Then Nobutaro kneels and lowers his own head. "Please forgive my rude, unworthy brother-in-law. He's lived so long in a barbaric foreign land, he's forgotten his place."

"I'm sorry," cries Shoji. "Please accept my most sincere and humble apology. Please forgive my impertinence. Thank you for your kindness and mercy. For the sake of my wife and daughter, please, sir, I beg you to forgive me."

"Well . . ."

Nobutaro says, "Sir, I will personally see to it that my stupid, worthless brother-in-law follows your instructions to the letter. They are packed and ready. Their taxi is waiting. With your permission we'll depart immediately. And I swear that not a single word will pass between them and any Japanese citizens. Except in case of an emergency, I will not even permit them to speak to one another. You have my promise, sir."

"All right," says the Kempeitai, regaining his composure. "You may go."

"Thank you, sir," says Shoji. "Please, sir, may I ask just one favor? With your permission, sir, I would like to thank these people."

The Kempeitai considers the request, clearly enjoying Nobutaro and Shoji groveling before the crowd. "Permission granted. But make it brief. Cross me one more time, disobey or show the tiniest hint of disrespect, and I will arrest the whole lot of you."

With another deep bow Shoji says, "Thank you, sir." Then he lifts his head just enough to show his face. "Everyone, my wife and daughter and I are overwhelmed by your kindness. Thank you for honoring our daughter with this award. Please accept my most humble apology for the discomfort my ill manners have caused you. This honorable gentleman is from the Kempeitai. As you have heard, once we step outside this house, we will no longer be able to speak with you. Please do not interpret our silence as rudeness. As long as we live we will remember your kindness and our debt to you. We will never forget the goodwill you've shared with us today. Please accept our most humble and sincere gratitude." Shoji waves to his daughter. "Keiko, thank your teachers and classmates, and tell them good-bye. And be quick about it. Your uncle and I will load the taxi."

The *kocho*-sensei gives Keiko a letter. The Kempeitai snatches it from her hand and opens it. "It's just a letter of introduction to an old friend and former classmate, now a professor at Stanford University," says the principal.

The letter is written in English. The Kempeitai pretends to be able to read it. He holds the letter and the envelope up to the light and studies them, sniffs them. He takes out his notebook. "This is the professor's name and address?"

"No, sir," says Keiko. "It's this part here." She circles it with her finger.

"Ah, yes, of course." The Kempeitai clumsily records the professor's name and address. He looks at Keiko, and she lowers her eyes. When she peeks at him and realizes that he is staring at her breasts, she feels a wave of nausea and terror. The Kempeitai takes Keiko's hand in his and presses the letter edgewise like a knife blade into her palm. "You may keep this." His hands are icy and damp.

The senior class president gives Keiko a book, which the Kempeitai examines. It is a collection of poetry written by Japanese women. Folded inside are farewell poems written by Keiko's classmates. "This is confiscated." The Kempeitai puts the book and poems in the pocket of his black overcoat. No one dares to argue with him.

"Thank you all for your kindness." Keiko bows to the *kocho*-sensei, B-sensei, and her classmates. "Thank you for everything you taught me. I will never forget you. *Sayonara*."

"Good luck," say the girls. "Safe journey. *Sayonara*. *Sayonara*. *Sayonara*."

A Kiss for Uncle Nobutaro

JULY 1941

ON THE DOCK IN YOKOHAMA BEFORE BOARDING THE SHIP, KUWANO turns to hug her brother Nobutaro.

The policeman thrusts his arm between them. "No contact!"

Before Kuwano can protest, Shoji and Keiko grab her arms, silently shake their heads at her. Kuwano parts her lips.

"Not one word!"

Kuwano looks at Nobutaro's face and the gray at his temples. She knows this could be the last time they see each other. They cannot touch or speak. But they are Japanese, they have a way of communicating nonverbally. Tears streaming from her eyes, she bows to her brother.

Every word unspoken, every touch restrained, all expressed in gently lowering heads and bending backs, Kuwano, Shoji, Keiko, and Nobutaro bow to one another as the policeman stands between them.

Watching the family going up the gangway, Nobutaro feels the policeman lean in close beside him. The policeman whispers, "Forgive me. We're being watched."

Nobutaro shivers and fights the urge to look around.

At the ship's rail, Keiko stands between her parents.

The gangway rolls back, the door clangs shut, sealing the hull. The mooring lines are released. The ship eases away from the dock.

Even so, no one dares the possibility of offending the invisible Kempeitai. They wave, but no one calls a farewell.

Suddenly Keiko leans toward her uncle. She grins like a spunky all-American girl, raises her hand to her mouth, and puckers her lips.

Back on the dock the policeman glances at Nobutaro. "What's she doing?"

Nobutaro sucks air through his teeth and scratches his head. "I'm not sure, but I think it's what Americans call blowing a kiss."

Home

AUGUST 1941

THE TRAIN PULLS INTO THE LODI DEPOT. KEIKO STEPS ONTO THE PLATform. Al and Dewey greet her with huge grins and bear hugs. When Kuwano sees them, she says, "Oh, Papa, look how my boys have grown. They've become real men." Al and Dewey puff out their chests with embarrassed pleasure. Kuwano smiles gently. "Well, *nearly* real men."

"Everyone's at Uncle Genzo's," says Al. "They're fixing a big party."

The boys load the suitcases onto the truck. Keiko and Al ride in the back, Kuwano and Shoji in front. Dewey, behind the wheel, tells Shoji, "Pop's really excited. He's got so many things he wants to talk about . . . couldn't remember 'em all, so he made a list."

"A list?" Shoji laughs. "Ah, I've missed him!" He turns with a grin to his wife, finds her frowning, looking perplexed. "What's wrong?"

"We're home, aren't we? How strange. After all those years . . . longing to return to Japan." They drive by a hardware store with a large red, white, and blue sign in the window: NO JAPS ALLOWED. Kuwano sighs wearily. "Home."

In the back Keiko sits pouting, arms folded across her chest. "Where's Sam?"

"Berkeley," says Al. "He went to show the professor his propaganda essay. Again. The professor keeps making him fix things in it. I don't know how many times Sam's had to rewrite it. The professor's secretary is going to type the final draft."

"I can type."

"They want it to look real sharp."

"I could do that." They ride in silence for a while. "When's he coming back?"

"I don't know."

"Did he get my letter?"

"Yeah. Your propaganda stuff saved his ass. Say, who was the woman in the picture?"

"Sam didn't tell you?"

"He said she was an old friend. Someone from Hawaii."

Keiko nods.

"Well?"

"I met her in Japan."

"Yeah?"

"Al, there's nothing to tell. We met, we talked. I took her picture. That's it."

"I'll bet."

"You're too nosy."

Al shrugs. Keiko grabs him, kisses him on the cheek. "I missed you!"

"Aw, sis . . ."

"Okay. So tell me the news. What's going on with baseball? When are you and Mitsy going to elope? Come on, little brother, talk to me."

"Baseball? Mitsy? Now we've got some things worth talking about."

"Okay!" says Keiko with a delighted smile. "I'm all ears. My God, Al, you can't imagine how good it feels to be sitting here in the back of Genzo's old truck and talking . . . in English." Keiko bursts into tears. "About baseball."

"Aw, sis." Al wraps his arms around her. Keiko is amazed at how thick her brother's arms have grown. His arms and chest are all muscle. She feels so safe. Something breaks loose inside her, and she sobs all the way to Genzo's farm. Al never lets go of her. She expects him to shrivel up and withdraw, but he stays with her the whole way. When they pull into the driveway, Keiko sits up and blows her nose.

"Why do they make girls' handkerchiefs so damn little?" says Keiko. "We've got just as much snot as guys do."

Al sighs with relief. "Now you're talking like my sister again. I thought you'd gone nuts on me. Never seen anyone carry on so at the mention of baseball."

"Oh Al, you big *baka*!" Keiko punches his shoulder.

"Ouch!" He laughs. "Don't call me a fool."

They drive around to the back of Genzo's house, pull to a stop, and a mob surrounds the truck. Keiko hears voices calling her name. She stands up. "Mitsy! Haru!" And just like that, she is crying again.

Her girlfriends reach up and help her off the truck. They put their arms around her. "I'm sorry I'm crying," says Keiko. "I couldn't cry over there, you see. I wanted to, but I just couldn't."

"Of course," says Haru. "You can cry all you want now, Keiko. It's okay."

"Yes," says Mitsy. "You're home now."

Keiko sees her mother bowing to her women friends. They are all crying, too.

And her father and Genzo are hugging each other, squeezing so hard their faces are turning red. They separate. Tears run down their cheeks. Genzo pulls two lists from his pocket.

"*Two* lists?" says Shoji.

"This one's things to tell you. This one's things I want to ask you."

Shoji laughs and hugs his friend again. Keiko hasn't heard her father laugh like that in a long, long time.

Al and Dewey watch their fathers.

Mitsy and Haru are crying.

Keiko looks around and realizes everyone is crying. She begins to laugh, and her laughter is a beautiful musical sound, clear and full of youth and hope and undiluted joy. On the outskirts of the crowd, Genzo's two German shepherds lope first in one direction, then the other, panting and wagging their tails.

Wolf Moon Goddess

AUGUST 1941

GENZO CHECKS HIS LIST AND ASKS HIS FIRST QUESTION. "WILL JAPAN go to war against the United States?"

"It's not what the Japanese people want," says Shoji. "But the combined American, British, and Dutch oil embargo is strangling Japan. What modern nation can survive without petroleum? What would America do if someone cut off her oil supply? Japan feels compelled to strike out against the embargo as an act of self-preservation. I hate to say it, but unless the situation changes, I think war is inevitable."

"Were you mistreated because you'd lived in America?"

Shoji nods. "The Kempeitai came to arrest us. I had to grovel before them."

The *Issei* men gather closer around Shoji.

"What's the Kempeitai?" asks Dewey.

"The secret police."

"Be quiet," says Genzo. "Let the man speak."

"My older brother, Nobutaro, was there," Kuwano tells her friends. "He acted brilliantly. He saved us. It was wonderful to see him and his family again."

"Did you have any marriage meetings?" Mitsy asks Keiko.

"Yes. Three."

"Three? Oh, my!"

Keiko opens her purse, takes out three photographs.

"Ugh! He looks like a frog," says Haru.

"Ooooh . . . but this one's *so* handsome," says Mitsy.

"He's a doctor," says Keiko.

"A doctor!"

"Let's see," says Al, reaching over their shoulders. Mitsy slaps his hand.

"He wanted to marry me, but his mother didn't like me."

"Really?"

"Oh, tell us," says Haru. "And don't leave anything out."

"Yes," says Mitsy. "Start at the beginning. Was he the first one?"

"No. Mr. Frog was. He proposed, but I turned him down."

Keiko's girlfriends squeal with excitement. "You turned him down?"

The party goes all day and long after sunset. Neither food nor conversation runs low. Finally, around midnight, when people realize how exhausted the Yanagis are, the party starts to wind down. The women crowd into the kitchen. Kuwano wants the guests to take food home. The guests insist the Yanagis keep it. Genzo's refrigerator and kitchen counters end up jammed with food.

After the last guests leave, Shoji and Kuwano move into Dewey's bedroom. The room is immaculate. "The boys cleaned it," says Genzo. Dewey and Al stand shyly in the doorway while Kuwano pretends to inspect for dust. She sniffs the air. "They aired it out for three or four days," says Genzo.

"I couldn't have done a better job myself," says Kuwano.

The boys grin proudly. "We moved our stuff out to the barn," says Dewey.

"Oh, how awful," says Kuwano.

"Nah, it's fine," says Al. "We sleep real good with all the fresh air."

"Can I sleep in the barn with the boys?" asks Keiko.

"Absolutely not!" says Kuwano.

"Kei-chan," says Genzo, "you will sleep on the living room sofa."

"Shucks," says Keiko. "Boys have all the fun."

"You wouldn't like it, sis. The first night Dewey and I slept out there, a mouse crawled in bed with Dewey. He screamed like a baby! Sam and I couldn't stop laughing."

"A mouse!" says Keiko.

"When the damn thing bit me," says Dewey, "I thought it was a rattlesnake."

"Sam?" says Kuwano.

"Yes," says Genzo. "Sam's been staying here ever since Mrs. Franklin sold her farm. I don't charge him rent. He needs to save money for college."

"I don't like him," says Kuwano.

"Mama," says Al, "he's almost like an older brother to me and Dewey."

"That's fine for you and Dewey, you're boys. It's Keiko I'm concerned about."

Shoji sighs wearily. "Please, let's discuss this tomorrow."

"Yes," says Genzo. "Time for hot baths and a good night's sleep. Kuwano-san, you've never tried the *furo* I built, have you? It's outside. Shoji-san will show you."

"Your tub is outside?" Kuwano smiles. "How elegant."

"No." Genzo laughs. "It's quite rustic. But it's deep and hot, and you can soak away your weariness while you gaze at the moon and listen to the crickets sing."

Keiko is asleep on the sofa. Sam's low voice pulls her awake. "Keiko." She feels the weight of his hand settle gently on her shoulder. She opens her eyes. Sam kneels beside the sofa. The window above her is open, cricket chirps and moonlight come through the lace curtains. "Oh, Sam," she murmurs, "your face is blue. Beautiful, beautiful blue."

"Welcome home, Keiko," he whispers, offering his hand.

Keiko draws back her blanket. She wears a blue and white cotton *yukata* that she had purchased in Nagoya. Her bare legs flash in the moonlight as she swings her feet to the floor. Holding hands, they tiptoe across the living room. Keiko hears her father snoring in the bedroom. All the windows and doors of the house are open. The air feels cool; a soft breeze stirs the curtains.

"I'm sorry I wasn't here to meet you," whispers Sam.

Suddenly, they hear Keiko's father calling from the bedroom, "Watch out! Watch out for the tree!"

Keiko and Sam freeze. Then Shoji resumes his snoring, and they tread silently into the kitchen. At the back door, Keiko slips her feet into a pair of zori. The screen door squeaks as they step into the moonlight. Genzo's dogs trot up. When Keiko kneels and whispers to them in Japanese, they bow to her. "Want to take a walk with us? Want to hunt rabbits?" Suke-san and Kaku-san wag their tails, and politely refrain from barking. Keiko finds a stick and throws it at the moon, and the dogs sprint across the yard.

Keiko is rising, turning, one hand brushing hair from her face, when she feels Sam's hands on her waist. Still turning, her face comes up as his swings down, and he kisses her. The long, slow, firm kiss of a man moving into a place where he intends to stay.

They pause, listening to their shaking breath. Then Sam kisses her again, more deeply; she feels it penetrating and widening the gates of her heart. It is so forceful and intense, she imagines things crashing all around her. Something stabs her foot. "Ouch!" Keiko pulls away with a jerk. Looking down, she finds Suke-san's paw on her bare foot. He has the stick in his mouth and his tail wags hopefully.

They are standing in the yard barely six feet from the back door. She can still hear her father snoring.

Sam loosens his embrace. And she catches a scent coming up from between them. Their own scent, a warm, delicious, healthy animal scent.

She puts her hand in Sam's, and together they walk into the vineyard toward the full moon. Crickets sing. The dogs lope off in pursuit of jackrabbits. Keiko inhales the sweet aroma of ripening grapes, Concord and Flame Tokay.

The house recedes behind them until the roof sinks below a sea of grape leaves. Sam stops. Keiko is grateful. Under her thin cotton *yukata* she is naked, and her knees are so rubbery she isn't sure how much more she can walk. They kiss, and that wild scent, their scent, blended with the perfume of the grapes, intoxicates her. She doesn't realize how she is moving until Sam says, "Keiko, if you don't stop doing that . . . Please, be still for a moment. Just let me kiss you."

But everything in his kisses urges and dares her to move. And everything in her kisses gives him welcome, gives him praise, proclaims her swooning, melting, joyous surrender.

"Keiko!" Her mother calls from the house. "Keiko, where are you?"

Keiko forces herself to let go of Sam and step away. "I'm here, Mama."

"Where? I can't see you. Are you all right?"

"Yes, Mama, I'm fine. I'm coming." Keiko glances over her shoulder. Sam stands with his arms out, fingers spread wide in helpless frustration.

From the back door Kuwano watches her daughter walk out of the vineyard with the full August moon over her shoulder and two wolflike dogs trotting at her sides. Kuwano is awestruck. She has never seen her daughter look more beautiful, lithe and womanly. She looks like a young goddess.

Keiko brushes past her mother and goes into the house. "I'm sorry if I scared you, Mama. I was so excited to be home. And the moon was so bright, I couldn't sleep. I went for a walk."

"It's not safe."

"I had the dogs to protect me."

Kuwano closes the kitchen door, turns to scold her daughter, when a peculiar feeling silences her. She has just witnessed Keiko as the incarnation of a goddess; the gods might not approve of an old woman criticizing a guest from heaven. Kuwano shuts off the kitchen light and goes into the dim living room. Keiko lies down on the sofa and pulls the blanket to her chin. Backlit with moonlight, the lace curtains look fragile as smoke. Bathed in the pale blue light, Keiko's eyes are enormous and dark. "I'm all right, Mama. Please go to sleep."

To Keiko's astonishment her mother bows, backs toward the bedroom, and answers almost meekly, "Yes. Good night."

Keiko wakes to the sounds of her mother and father talking and moving about in the kitchen. The other menfolk have long since gone to work in the vineyard. Keiko inhales the smell of coffee and bacon. She hears the squeaky springs of the toaster, and her father ordering, "Sausage, bacon, three eggs sunny side up, and hot cakes with maple syrup." Keiko grins and feels like singing. An American breakfast! Now there's something worth getting up for.

After breakfast, Shoji goes into town. Keiko and her mother wash the dishes and clean the kitchen. Later, they prepare lunch and take it out to Genzo and the boys. After they eat, Sam and Keiko walk a short distance from the group. They stand, not touching, in the shade of an oak tree. Keiko's mother watches them. Sam grins, lowers his voice. "Back in Hawaii, we'd say your mama was giving me the stink eye."

Keiko's mother calls to her, "Kei-chan, come help me clean up."

"Keiko, uh, just one more second . . ." says Sam.

"I'll be right there, Mama." Keiko turns, smiling, expecting Sam to tell her another funny Hawaiian expression. But, no, he looks very serious. She watches him draw a huge breath.

"Keiko, will you marry me?"

Keiko is so surprised her mouth falls open.

"Keiko, I love you. Please. Will you marry me?"

Keiko blinks, closes her mouth. Her heart is beating a hole through her chest. Her voice trembles as she answers, "Yes, Sam, I will."

"I'll speak to your parents—"

"No. Wait until they're settled."

"I'll wait until after the harvest."

Keiko's mother glares at Sam. "Keiko!"

Shoji's Hand

AUGUST 1941

THE YANAGIS HAVE ARRIVED IN LODI JUST BEFORE THE START OF THE grape harvest. The Japanese-American community welcomes them home. Keiko's parents return to managing the boardinghouse and reclaim their former rooms. Miyazaki-san, the man who had taken over the Yanagis' restaurant, leaps to his feet, spilling tea on his newspaper, when Shoji walks in the door. "Hey! Good to see you! Heard you were back and looking for work. Let's talk."

The restaurant is across the street from a line of fruit packing sheds; beyond the sheds are the railroad tracks and the Lodi depot. They cannot see the train whistling into the station, but not long after, a gang of farmworkers carrying bedrolls and suitcases strolls through Japantown. Miyazaki-san's waitress stands, pats her hair, tightens her apron, then watches the men pass right in front of the noodle shop, not stopping nor slowing nor even glancing in the window. The restaurant is so quiet, bits of their conversation float in: "... changed owners a year ago ... food's lousy ... damn shame."

Shoji passes his hands over the spotless tabletop and looks around at the newly painted walls and swept floors, Mrs. Miyazaki wiping her hands on her apron in the doorway of the kitchen, the waitress yawning and going back to slowly folding napkins at a corner table. The place smells more of soap than soup, and Shoji can see the desperation in Mrs. Miyazaki's exhausted eyes, and hear the jitters stabbing through Miyazaki-san's embarrassed laugh.

Miyazaki-san and Shoji's friendship goes way back to the days when they, too, carried their worldly possessions in suitcases and blanket rolls, followed the crops, and waited for word from home about picture brides.

"Damn noodles!" says Miyazaki-san. "Flour, salt, and water . . . boiled and dumped in a bowl of broth. I never realized how hard it was to make fresh noodles as good as yours! Customers have been complaining ever since you left. You're looking for work, right? How about cooking for me? No, wait . . . I'm sorry. That won't work. How about partners? You set the terms. My wife and I, we put all our savings into this place. We're in debt and about to sink. Can you help us?" Miyazaki-san and his wife both bow humbly to Shoji.

Shoji returns their bows. He scratches his head in embarrassment. "Don't be ashamed. I understand how hard you've been working. Besides, I'm almost broke, too."

The men gaze steadily into the other's eyes. Shoji puts out his hand. "Partners." They shake hands, sealing their contract. Shoji takes off his coat, unbuttons his shirt, heads for the stairs to the basement. "I'll start making noodles."

The Miyazakis, heads bobbing, smiling with relief and hope, follow him.

"How many waitresses do we have?" asks Shoji.

"Just our daughter."

"Hire five more."

"Five?"

"Just for the harvest. Two girls in three shifts. I was in Genzo's vineyard yesterday. Big crop. Within a week we'll be open twenty-four hours."

Mrs. Miyazaki shakes her head. "But in the middle of the night? Who—"

"Gamblers and card players, insomniacs, musicians, drunk poets, whores . . . lined up, waiting for tables and takeout. Around three-thirty or four, the early risers will start coming in for breakfast. Right now it's a trickle, then tsunami and flood, high water that won't recede, then . . . poof! It'll be over and gone until next year. You'll see."

Lying in bed, Kuwano massages Shoji's aching shoulders and arms. "We were lucky how everything fell into place," he says. "But the restaurant feels smaller to me. In Japan I went for long walks at night. Walked miles in every direction. Here it's not safe for me to do that . . . yet here, the Kempeitai cannot reach us."

"Here in this bed with you, I feel safe," says Kuwano.

Shoji sighs, then begins coughing. "I feel like I'm suffocating."

Kuwano gets up and opens the window. She looks down at the empty street. "Tomorrow, I'll give this place a good cleaning. They really let it go once we left."

"Tomorrow, I make more noodles," says Shoji.

"It's been a long time. Do you still remember how?"

"Hah! I could make noodles in my sleep. Still . . ."

"What?"

"We aren't young anymore. The work will be hard until we get used to it again."

"*Shikataganai*, nothing can be done about it." The bedsprings creak as she gets back under the covers.

Shoji sighs. "I hope our son's as fortunate as I've been . . . to have such a fine wife."

Kuwano blushes.

"Well," says Shoji, "I know it's only work. And we've always worked hard. It's just . . . I feel old and tired."

"It's late," says Kuwano. "We're both tired. As for being old, you're ten times better than men half your age."

"You think so?" Shoji grins. "You really think so?"

"I know so," says Kuwano, thinking how boyish he sounds at that moment.

Shoji chuckles. "We'll feel better after a good night's sleep."

"Yes. Good night."

"Good night." He rolls away from her.

After a moment, Shoji raises his head and speaks over his shoulder. "You know what would make me feel even better than a good night's sleep?"

Kuwano smiles. "I was hoping . . . but I knew how tired you were."

Shoji thinks she sounds almost as shy as a new bride. The idea appeals to him. "Let me show you a few tricks that only old men know," he says with a sly grin.

Then he rolls over and sees the tenderness in her eyes, and suddenly his throat aches with love for her. He puts his hand between her breasts. Her heart is beating so calmly, he cannot feel it. *This is how it is with us. Even when we cannot feel it, our love abides steadily through every moment.*

"I'm waiting . . . for your tricks."

Shoji smiles and slowly lowers his mouth toward her swelling nipples.

Lucky Seven

December 1941

THE GRAPE HARVEST HITS AND PASSES, SAM WORKS AND WAITS, BUT Keiko keeps telling him not yet, not yet. Wait until after Thanksgiving. Wait until December. Three is Sam's lucky number, Wednesday his lucky day, so he is not surprised that on Wednesday, the third of December, Keiko tells him he can speak with her parents. The Miyazakis will be out of town with their daughter. Kuwano and Shoji will be running the noodle shop by themselves.

Hair cut, best clothes cleaned and pressed, stiff as a samurai approaching a castle, Sam walks into the restaurant. Lunch rush over, tables empty, dish clatter and water running in the kitchen. He tells the waitress, "I'm Sam Hamada. I'm here to speak with Yanagi Shoji-san."

She knows who he is, but the formality of his speech and the seriousness of his face startle her. Her eyes grow big. She dips her head quickly and runs down to the basement. After a moment, she returns. "Yanagi-san says to tell you that he's very busy making noodles, but you're welcome to speak with him while he works."

Sam heads for the stairs. Suddenly all the iron in his warrior's heart seems diaphanous as a silk scarf in a typhoon. Sam would trust his martial arts training in a duel with any opponent; but he has no idea how to handle this confrontation with his potential father-in-law . . . to look into Shoji Yanagi's eyes and ask to marry his daughter . . .

Sam's hands are sweating. He can barely breathe.

From the kitchen Kuwano catches a glimpse of Sam passing. Sam is so nervous and preoccupied, he does not see her. Kuwano leaves the kitchen and stands listening at the top of the stairs. She hears Shoji say, "Well, you're certainly all dressed up for a Wednesday. What's the occasion?"

"Yanagi-san, I've come to ask your permission to marry your daughter."

Immediately, Kuwano descends the stairs. "No! You cannot marry Keiko."

Shoji is shocked. "Where are your manners? This man is my guest."

"In Japan, Keiko almost married a doctor." Kuwano looks into Sam's eyes. "She can do better than you—no money, no property. You don't even have a steady job."

Kuwano's words pierce Sam like spear thrusts. All he feels are pain and confusion. "It's true. Everything you say about what I don't have is true. But I have been accepted by the University of California in Berkeley. I hope to begin classes in the spring. I'm determined to make something of my life."

Shoji is impressed. The tone of his voice is apologetic. "Genzo-san told me how hard you worked on your essay. Did you win a prize?"

"No, sir. But I will be doing part-time translation for my advisor."

"Of course he didn't win a prize," says Kuwano. "Do you think they would award money to a Japanese?"

"Don't belittle the boy's effort," says Shoji, his face reddening with anger. "It's easy enough to dream of going to college. It's something else to make it a reality. He's taken on an immense challenge. Don't dishearten him."

"Why do men always insist on climbing distant mountains while their own house is in flames? I know it's a challenge to go to college. But there's plenty of hard work right here. Managing a boardinghouse is hard work. So is making noodles. So is being a farmer. Of course being a college student is more *glamorous*."

"If he was a noodle maker or a farmer, you'd refuse his proposal because you don't want that sort of life for Keiko."

"While the farmers are here playing cards with you, their wives are at home—cooking, cleaning, and raising the children. Farmers complain about how hard their lives are, but a farmer's wife has it even harder."

"If he was a doctor or a lawyer or a scientist or an engineer, then you might consider his proposal."

"Yes. I might."

"He could never become any of those things if he stayed in this town. He must go to college to become any of those. Just like our own son, Al. These boys must go to college or they'll end up like Genzo and me. I know you're blocking this union because you love Keiko. You only want the best for her. You don't want her to suffer like you. But they're both young. Hard work won't kill them. Hamada-san is a better man than any of those rich marriage prospects we met in Japan."

"How can you say that?"

"I've been observing him for years. Because for he and Keiko it was love at first sight."

Kuwano stares incredulously at her husband.

Shoji turns to Sam. "Have you already asked my daughter?"

"Yes, sir."

"And she accepted."

"Yes, sir."

Shoji nods. "She turned down three good men for you. Hamada Isamu-san, you have my consent and blessings. Please take good care of my daughter."

"Thank you, Yanagi-san. You have my word."

"I'm sorry," said Kuwano. "I am truly sorry, but I cannot give my consent. I know it's the duty of a proper Japanese wife to bow to her husband's wishes. But I'm a woman and know what only women know." Kuwano pauses and corrects herself. "I'm an *old* woman, and know what only *old* women know. I regret this, and I mean no disrespect to you or my husband, but I must say no."

Sam braces himself. In a typical Japanese household, such an open display of wifely stubbornness would not be tolerated. Sam is amazed when Shoji smiles. "Well spoken! You see what sort of stock Keiko comes from? My wife never lies to me, even if she knows it will anger me. Honoring herself, she honors me."

Sam is thrown into confusion. For a moment, everything seemed settled; he had won. But now Shoji sounds ready to defer to his wife.

"It's all right," says Shoji. "You and Keiko can get married."

"Are you crazy?" Kuwano asks her husband.

"I trust my own good judgment," says Shoji, "and that of my daughter."

"But not mine?" says Kuwano, heating with resentment.

"You know what your brother told me in Japan? He said he had misjudged me. You and your brother are alike. You don't know how to measure a man's true worth. Your vision is too superficial."

"Superficial? I picked you, didn't I?"

"Yes and no. Your goal was to travel to America. You would have married anyone. You would have married Genzo."

"Yes. I wanted to come to America. But I would not have married just anyone. When I looked at your photograph, I saw a handsome young man with a kind, intelligent face. But it was your letter that won me. It was wonderful. And when you came to Japan to meet my family and take me away with you, you showed up with three hired automobiles. Did you know that was the first time anyone in my family had ever ridden in an automobile? I thought you were wealthy. We all did. You gave my brother Bull Durham. He said it was the finest tobacco he'd ever tasted. I thought you were the most worldly, most handsome man I'd ever met."

Shoji scratched his head with embarrassment. "Thank you for your kind words. But don't you see my point? You were taken by my outward appearance. I saw how you and your family were dazzled. And I was overjoyed, because I knew how little I had to offer, and I didn't want you to reject me. But I tried to be honest. Don't you remember? I tried to warn you about how hard life was in America. I told you the truth and gave you a chance to turn me down. That was the most difficult thing I've ever done. Because with all my heart, I wanted to marry you. But I had to warn you. I had to tell you the truth about myself and how things were, even though I was terrified that I'd lose you forever. The gods were with me that day."

Kuwano and Shoji gaze tenderly at each other.

Sam, embarrassed and touched by what he is witnessing, clears his throat.

Shoji and Kuwano jump. Shoji swings toward Sam. "Why are you still here? I gave you my blessings."

"Yes, sir, but—"

"That's right," says Kuwano. "Let's not be hasty. This is America. You men don't get to decide everything. I haven't given my consent yet. However, instead of no, I'll say maybe. First, I must speak to Keiko, mother to daughter and woman to woman. Come back in three days. Saturday. Noon. I will give you my answer then."

Sam bows to Kuwano. "I know you want what's best for your daughter. That is what I want, too. Keiko is a wonderful, beautiful woman; she could find a hundred men to marry her. But she has only one mother. I love Keiko, but I will not put myself between you. I will abide by your decision."

"Well spoken!" says Shoji.

"You'll not go against my decision?" says Kuwano.

"I will not."

Kuwano appears satisfied and impressed.

Once more Sam bows. "I will return in three days."

Sam leaves and Kuwano goes in search of her daughter. She finds Keiko in the little garden behind the boardinghouse. Keiko's hair is tied back, and she holds a bamboo pole. To burn off her anxiety and focus her *ki*, Keiko has been practicing *naginata*. "Mama, your objections center around Sam's lack of money. Sam has no more to offer than Al does. When Al goes to propose to Mitsy's family, do you want her mother to throw dirt in his face?"

Kuwano recoils. "How unfair! How can you say such a mean thing to me? I'm trying to be practical and realistic."

"You're trying to stand between me and the stove because you don't want me to get burned. But if you don't allow me to take the risk, I'll never learn to cook."

"Kei-chan, you're so young and innocent. I don't want you to suffer all the terrible hardships I went through. You have no idea what it's like to work all day and take care of an infant and a husband at the same time."

"It's true, I don't know. But, Mama, how many young wives have had to contend with that? Women far less able than myself have survived. Surely I won't die from it."

"You don't know about poverty."

"Of course I do. Mama, I've been minding our bank books ever since I could read and write. I remember when our account was down to a dollar fifty-three. I remember the time the banks closed. I remember when Papa went to the store and came back with only half a loaf of bread. I never told you, but I was so worried I used to stay up nights going over and over the numbers. Meanwhile, you and Papa were fast asleep."

"I never knew. . . . You seemed like such a happy-go-lucky child."

"I didn't want you to think I couldn't handle it. I knew you and Papa were working as hard as you could, and I wanted to do my part. Of course I never told anyone. I didn't want to expose our financial problems and cast shame on our name."

"We were poor, but many suffered far more than we did."

"Yes. We were blessed. We were lucky. We survived and prospered because we worked together as a family. And we had a community of friends. We were poor, but we never surrendered our dignity."

"Kei-chan, how did you become this strong?"

"Mama, you're the one who taught me how strong a woman can be."

"I just don't want you to suffer like I did."

"Mama, you can't relive your life through me."

"You think that is what I'm trying to do?"

"Mama, tell me the truth. What is it about Sam that you don't like?"

"I don't trust him. From the moment I met him, I thought he was hiding something, lying about something. And there's a sexual thing. I'm afraid . . . he's just interested in your body. I'm afraid once he's had his fill, he'll play with other women. I'm afraid he'll take advantage of you."

"Sam's had more than one chance to take advantage of me."

Kuwano's eyes widen.

"But I'm still a virgin."

Kuwano seems both relieved and dismayed.

"As for playing with other women, that's probably something no woman can truly know about any man until it's too late."

"Kei-chan, when did you become this grown up?"

"Mama, thank you for your concern. I don't want to fight you. I want us to continue giving each other our wholehearted support. Mama, please, I need your strength. Give Sam your blessings. We love each other. We've loved each other for a long time. Please look at him with your clearest inner vision. If you judge him not by what he has, but by what he is, I'm sure you'll see his goodness. Please consent to our marriage."

The look on her daughter's face breaks Kuwano's heart. She wants to give her consent, but her inner voice will not relent. "I'm sorry, Keiko. I cannot. I don't trust him. He has the eyes of a liar. I think he's hiding something."

"You're right, Mama. Sam *had* a secret."

"I knew it!"

"It was in his past. It was a misunderstanding. I can't talk about it. But it's over and done with forever."

"You're sure? You're certain?"

"Yes, Mama. I checked it out myself, and I am *absolutely certain* Sam Hamada is a good and honorable man. Look into his eyes without prejudice. You'll see he's no longer hiding."

Kuwano sighs, takes Keiko's hand and nods. "All right. *I will look.* And if what you say is true, I'll tell him yes."

"Oh, Mama, thank you!"

Three days later, noon, Saturday, as promised Sam returns. The restaurant is filled with lunch patrons. Keiko's father sits playing cards with Miyazaki-san. The waitress hurries into the kitchen, her too-loud voice announcing, "He's here!" Kuwano and Mrs. Miyazaki come out, followed by the waitress. Kuwano and Mrs. Miyazaki take seats next to their husbands. The waitress stands behind Mrs. Miyazaki.

Thinking it would be easier to charge naked at a battalion of bayonet-wielding soldiers than face these people, steeling himself for Kuwano's hostile gaze, Sam draws a deep breath and walks forward. When he comes to the table, he stops. Mr. Miyazaki turns and looks up at him. Shoji puts down his cards and gestures toward the one remaining empty chair.

Sam's eyes cut quickly left and right—conversation in the restaurant has stopped, all the patrons are staring at Sam.

Sam attempts a smile. Behind Shoji there is a mirror on the wall, and Sam sees himself—stiff, awkward, too much oil on his hair, the part crooked, his collar choking him, tie knotted too tightly and hanging wrinkled from being retied a dozen times, his eyes bloodshot from lack of sleep, cheeks freckled with red shaving nicks. . . . Confronted by his own reflection, as though seeing himself through their eyes, feeling humbled and unworthy, he bows and takes his seat.

Kuwano studies Sam's eyes while she serves him tea.

Sam sits jittery as a stray cat surrounded by dogs. He is so spooked, it takes him a moment to see that Keiko's mother is smiling. Her smile seems nonthreatening, but the weight and clarity of her gaze unnerve him. Sam lowers his eyes. He lifts his teacup with an almost imperceptibly trembling hand. When the hot bitter green taste hits his tongue, it inexplicably triggers a sense memory of old man Fujiwara's bamboo sword tapping his shoulder. With a start Sam realizes he is being tested. This moment—he is being tested.

At the Obon two and a half years ago, Keiko's mother had seen his eyes turn shifty. She had witnessed him slinking away into the darkness. . . .

Sam raises his head. One look at Kuwano's face tells him he is correct. Her smile is like a flower wilting before his eyes. And now she waits, watching to see if he, if his heart, will shift or slink.

Sam puts down his teacup, leaves both hands exposed on the table. He levels his head, looks into Kuwano's eyes, and does not turn away.

Kuwano studies Sam's eyes. The longer she looks, the more she seems to relax. The smile returns to her lips.

Sam is amazed at what he sees . . . Keiko's smile comes from her mother.

"I give you my consent," Kuwano tells him. "And my blessings."

The Miyazakis, waitress, and patrons applaud.

Sam thanks his future mother-in-law with such tremulous relief and joy, Kuwano thinks he might faint or burst into tears. But he soon perks up, especially when Keiko appears from the kitchen, where she has been eavesdropping.

"Come for dinner tonight," says Kuwano. "We'll celebrate."

"Thank you," says Sam. He stands up. Keiko takes his hand.

"Wait a moment," says Shoji, gesturing for Sam to sit back down. "Wife, get a calendar. Let's discuss possible wedding dates. Let's see—"

Kuwano laughs. "Later. We can talk about that later. Can't you see the children want to be alone? Go along now, you two. Tomorrow is Sunday. After the service, Keiko and I will talk with the Sensei and set a date for the wedding. Tomorrow is the seventh. Good. Seven is my lucky number."

Part 4

DECEMBER 1941–JULY 1945

Japs

SUNDAY, DECEMBER 7, 1941

SHOJI IS CARRYING A FRESH BATCH OF NOODLES UP FROM THE BASE-ment, when Al and Dewey rush into the restaurant. "Papa! Haven't you been listening to the radio? The Japanese have bombed Pearl Harbor in Hawaii. It's war."

Shoji puts down his tray of noodles and grabs his coat. "Mama and Keiko are at the Buddhist temple talking to the Sensei about the wedding."

They are heading for the restaurant door, when it opens and four men enter; the first two wear suits, the second two are uniformed police officers. The suit in front flashes his ID. "FBI. I'm Special Agent Wilson. This is Special Agent Fitch. We're looking for Mr. Shoji Yanagi."

"I am Shoji Yanagi."

"You're under arrest." Agent Fitch takes out a set of handcuffs.

"Hey, wait a minute," says Al, "my father hasn't done anything wrong."

Both policemen put their hands on their revolvers.

"Please . . . no trouble," says Shoji, offering his wrists for the cuffs. "No trouble." They leave the restaurant. The cops open the back door of their patrol car, and as they push Shoji in, he calls out sternly to Al and Dewey in Japanese.

Agent Wilson asks, "What'd he say?"

"My father said we are not enemies of the United States. He told us to give you our full cooperation."

"Really? Good." Agent Wilson takes out his notebook. "We're also looking for a man who's been seen carrying a black briefcase. We've been told that the briefcase is full of Japanese propaganda. The man's name is Sam Hamada. Do you know where we can find him?"

Al and Dewey exchange looks. "Yes, sir," says Dewey. "He's at my father's farm."

"Show us the way. We'll follow you."

Dewey and Al get in the truck and start off. The FBI and police follow in their separate cars. Approaching the Buddhist temple, Dewey spots Keiko and Kuwano coming down the steps. He swerves to the curb. Al jumps out and helps his mother and sister climb aboard, then he jams into the seat beside them and slams the door.

Rosy-cheeked with excitement, Keiko says, "We've set a date for the wedding."

"Sis, there might not be one. The Japanese have bombed Pearl Harbor."

"What? I don't understand. . . ."

"War. It means we're at war."

"But—"

"The FBI and the cops are in the cars behind us. They just arrested Papa. They're following us to Genzo's place."

"They're going to arrest Sam. It's that damn Japanese propaganda!" says Dewey. "They think Sam's a Japanese agitator or a spy."

Horrified and speechless, Keiko stares at Dewey and Al.

They park in Genzo's backyard. Kuwano wants to speak with her husband, and Keiko wants to warn Sam, but Agent Fitch orders them to stay in the truck. Keiko looks into the eyes of the lawmen and recognizes a coldness that exactly matches that of the Kempeitai in Japan. She and her family are like cockroaches to these men.

Keiko hears Genzo's dogs barking in the barn. She sees the doors swing open. The dogs come running out, followed by Genzo.

One of the policemen yells, "Ed! Look out!" Both men draw their revolvers.

Suke-san and Kaku-san run barking toward the strangers.

"Wait!" yells Genzo in Japanese. "Wait! Stop!"

The police open fire. Yelping, the dogs tumble onto the dirt driveway.

Genzo staggers forward, drops to his knees, gathers Suke-san and Kaku-san in his arms. "I'm here. Hush now. Hush . . . It'll be all right. The pain will go away. Easy. Easy." The dogs stop yelping and kicking. Panting, they look up at him. "I'm here." Genzo hugs and strokes and pats them while they die. "Good dogs. Good dogs."

Shoji, Dewey, Al, Keiko, and Kuwano watch, frozen in shock and horror.

"Ed! There he is!" Everyone turns to see Sam running from the vineyard. "Gun! He's got a rifle! Get him!" The policemen raise their pistols at Sam.

Keiko screams, "No, don't shoot! Sam, stop! Stop!"

Both cops fire just as Agent Wilson bumps their arms and Sam dives to the ground. The bullets go high; Sam lands low, rolling smoothly to his feet.

"Hold your fire!" shouts Agent Wilson. "Damn it. We want him alive."

"You there," yells the cop named Ed, "throw down that weapon."

"Pruning shears," says Sam as he drops the long-handled shears.

The police handcuff Sam and put him in the car with Shoji. Once more Kuwano and Keiko ask permission to talk with their men, but the FBI will not allow it. The police guard the prisoners, and the FBI search Genzo's house. They come out carrying Sam's black briefcase.

As the lawmen are getting into their cars, Keiko calls to them, "Why are you treating us like this? We're Americans."

"No, you're not." Ed spits on the ground. "You're Japs."

Both cars kick dirt into the air. With Sam's and Shoji's stunned eyes looking out the patrol car windows, the vehicles turn onto the county road and accelerate away, leaving behind the mingled scents of dust, exhaust fumes, and burnt gunpowder.

Running the Course

SEPTEMBER 1942

THE FBI ARE SO HEAVILY BACKLOGGED, EIGHT MONTHS PASS BEFORE they begin checking Sam's background. The essay in Sam's briefcases leads them to Berkeley. Professor Knight explains the reason for Sam's collection of Japanese propaganda, pointing out what a potentially invaluable asset he is. The FBI dispatches a top-priority report to military intelligence concerning Sam's bilingual ability. Sam is drafted straight from his prison cell into the U.S. Army, landing in an all-white infantry platoon for basic training at Camp Robinson, Arkansas.

Delighted to be out of prison, grateful for a chance to prove his loyalty, intrigued by the notion of enrollment in a different school of martial arts, Sam treats his drill sergeant with the same respect he would give to a new sensei. But the sergeant sets out to break the lone Jap boy, dishes a steady ration of insults and curses, KP and latrine duty. On the obstacle course he sends Sam across first, intending to mock him. But Sam runs it with the grace and power of a young tiger, astonishes the sergeant when he apologizes and adds, "I know I can do better, sir. Can I give it another go?"

They hit bayonet drill and hand-to-hand combat. They call Sam out, intending to give the Jap a beating. Instead Sam throws down the sergeant and the two rock-hard instructors one by one, gently, politely, almost apologetically, like an uncle playing with his favorite nephews. The two instructors take Sam aside—that's when they learn Sam is a black belt, that he completed his basic training years ago in Hawaii. That he has been practicing and working out on his own ever since. They return to the training area, position Sam in front of his platoon. Sam wonders if he is about to take them all on. Instead, the lead instructor announces that Sam will assist them with a knife-fighting drill. Without another word both instructors whip out practice blades and leap at Sam. The vicious precision of their attack allows Sam no margin for gentleness. A sudden cyclonic blur and *wham! wham!* Sam drops his assailants so hard, he nearly breaks the second instructor's arm. Grim-faced, the lead instructor retrieves his knife and rubs his elbow. Sam starts to apologize, but the instructor gruffly cuts him off. "Good job, soldier."

The next day, without explanation, Sam is made assistant instructor of hand-to-hand combat.

Now they have to run his course.

That's when they begin to understand how difficult their mission will be, how tough and skilled the enemy. Sam keeps his lessons brutally simple, teaches them how to break bones, to use their hands and feet to kill, to de-fend and shield their bodies' vulnerabilities.

He watches the men in his platoon practicing the alien moves. When they begin to get it and, drunk with a new sense of power, they laugh and joke, he throws them down like puppies, grips their throats, glares until their eyes turn cold sober. He tells them, "Fooling around today could cost your life next month. I want you to survive. I want you to live." That's when they be-gin to understand that Sam Hamada is an American, that he is on their side, that he is a gift and a treasure. He ends his first class by teaching everyone, including his sergeant, how to bow.

Ball of Yarn

OCTOBER 1942

THE FBI HOLDS SHOJI FOR ELEVEN MONTHS. THEN THEY TRANSFER HIM from one kind of prison to another. Two military policemen escort Shoji from his cell and put him in a jeep. When they bypass Lodi, Shoji politely mentions they missed their turn. "Nah, your family don't live there any-more. Ain't no Japs left in Lodi."

The jeep stops at the San Joaquin County fairgrounds. A young *Nisei* greets Shoji. "Hello. I'm Tad Nomura. Welcome to the Stockton Assembly Center. I hope your family's still here. Most of the people have already been transferred to relocation centers. After the seventeenth, this'll be a ghost town." They trudge between empty tar-paper barracks, cross a plank over an open trench, hold their noses at the stench rising from a broken sewer pipe. They pass a barrack where a classroom of children sing their ABC's. They pass more blocks of empty barracks. "A couple months ago we had over four thousand people here." Tad stops and checks his notes. "You're in luck. All the families in this block are due to leave this afternoon."

"Leaving? This afternoon? I don't understand. Leaving for where?"

"The camps . . . Rohwer or Jerome for this group."

"Camps?"

"You made it just in time to join them. Go down there to the third door on the left. Those are your family's quarters."

"Third door on the left. Thank you." Shoji goes slowly down the path. On his right is one of the standard tar-papered barracks. The older structure on the left is different. And it stinks! Horse urine. His family has been housed in converted horse stalls. He goes to the door, hears no sound within. He panics. They've already been sent away. How will he find them?

Shoji pounds on the door, uses too much strength; the booming startles a flock of blackbirds into flight.

Something scrapes against the floor inside. Then his wife's voice: "Hello? Who is it?"

Shoji wants to shout his name but chokes, and cannot utter a sound.

"Who is it?"

He opens the door.

Kuwano sits on a stool made from scrap lumber. She has been knitting. When she sees her husband, she stands up, and a ball of sky blue yarn drops out of her lap and rolls toward him.

Still unable to speak, Shoji picks up the yarn and carries it to her.

Tags

OCTOBER 1942

GUARDED BY AMERICAN SOLDIERS WITH FIXED BAYONETS, THE CROWD of Japanese-American men, women, and children board the train.

Shoji coughs.

"That doesn't sound good," says Genzo.

Shoji drops his cigarette, grinds it with his shoe. "My lungs are healthier than yours. I outran you when we were kids. I still can."

"You never did! You barely kept up."

"Ha!"

"I'll race you around the depot," says Genzo. "Come on. Let's go. *Iko! Iko!*"

"*Yoshi!* All right." The two old men grin at each other.

"I won," says Genzo. "Just now when you blinked, I ran three times around the depot. But I was so quick, you never noticed I was gone."

"Liar."

Genzo takes a book from his pocket. "This anthology of American folk stories is filled with feats like mine. They aren't lies; they're called yarns and tall tales."

Dewey and Al hurry by carrying an invalid on a stretcher; the boys' faces are flushed, their shirts dark with sweat. "Please don't wander off. Your numbers will be called soon."

Shoji checks the tag pinned to his coat: *Family No. 29969. Id No. 1358.*

A commotion erupts as national guardsmen move to block the end of the platform. A woman angrily demands that they get out of her way. Genzo recognizes her voice and rushes forward. Shoji follows. Keiko runs after them. Genzo and Shoji are stopped by a wall of soldiers, rifles and bayonets aimed and ready. Coming up behind Genzo and her father, Keiko grabs their arms, feels their tensed muscles.

On the other side of the line of soldiers, Mrs. Alberta Franklin repeats her demand. "Get out of my way!" And she raps her cane on the rifles crossed in front of her face.

A baby-faced lieutenant hurries up to Mrs. Franklin. "I'm sorry, ma'am, but you're not allowed to mingle with the Japs."

Mrs. Franklin turns and stares for a long moment into the young lieutenant's hazel blue eyes. Then she says, "Don't I know your mother?"

The lieutenant blinks; sweat pops out all over his face.

Mrs. Franklin leans close to the lieutenant and her voice, while still firm, becomes much quieter. "I'm not here to cause trouble. I came to say good-bye to my friends." She holds out a covered basket. "You see? I brought them fruit and sandwiches."

The lieutenant reaches out.

"Are your hands clean, young man?"

The lieutenant's hand hovers momentarily in midair. "Yes, ma'am." Using only the tips of his thumb and forefinger, he lifts a corner of the red-and-white-checkered napkin and peeks into the basket. Then he says, "As you were, men. Let the lady pass."

Mrs. Franklin steps forward with her basket just as Genzo and Shoji hear their numbers called. They have only enough time for Genzo to bow and thank her, while she shakes everyone's hands and says good-bye. Apologetically, Keiko tugs at Genzo's and Shoji's sleeves. "Mrs. Franklin, thank you so much for coming to see us off. We wish we could speak with you, but they've called for us to board the train, and we must hurry because we're holding up the line."

Bowing and waving, they back away from Mrs. Franklin. Genzo almost trips over a little girl sitting on a leather suitcase. Beside the child is an enormous pile of luggage and duffel bags. Tied to a buttonhole of her pink sweater is a tag bearing her number. Genzo reaches into his basket, gives her an apple, tells her that it's from Mrs. Franklin. The little girl's face lights up, and she waves shyly to Mrs. Franklin.

Mrs. Franklin waves back, then quickly turns and walks away before the child can see that she is crying.

Rohwer

OCTOBER 1942

KEIKO RIDES IN A TRAIN WITH BLINDED WINDOWS. THROUGH THE Sierras, over the Rockies, and across the wide hostile belly of America. Sleeping to the rhythmic sound and motion, she has a dream of riding in a taxi through the rain. She looks out at an immense green lawn where thousands of soldiers stand in formation. Her taxi rolls slowly past the front ranks. The soldiers are all Japanese-American. Al, Dewey, Sam, and the *Nisei* boys from her high school are among the troops. They gaze at her as she goes by. No words. Just their faces, mouths, and eyes, solemn and soft. Rain streaking and dripping off their olive green helmets, beading on their overcoats. Still and silent soldiers on a gently sloping lawn. Huge oak trees spreading wide their branches as if to offer them shelter from the rain.

"Wake up, sis, we're here."

They gather their luggage and shuffle off the train, then along a corridor of armed troops to a line of buses and trucks. "Al, where are we?"

"Arkansas."

The convoy leaves the railroad station and drives along country roads. Through her bus window Keiko sees they are approaching a town—a tall smokestack rises above an orderly sea of identical roofs—some kind of factory town. Then she notices the guard towers and barbwire fence surrounding the perimeter. The road parallels the fence; Keiko gazes through the wire and down avenues of newly built black tar-papered barracks. Ahead she sees the line of buses turning off the road and driving through the main gate. Her bus follows, dust billowing as it jerks to a stop before a pole flying an American flag.

Keiko helps her mother and father step down. The driver keeps the engine running, and the dust and exhaust fumes choke them. Keiko hears the distant racket of men hammering and sawing, building more barracks.

Outwardly, Keiko appears calm and controlled like everyone else. She watches Al and Dewey hurrying away to unload the trucks. Everyone seems eager to be helpful, hardworking, and efficient. Inwardly Keiko feels like confetti in the wind. *This is insane. This is not happening.* Clutching a slip of paper with their new address—*Block 23, Barrack 10, Apt D, Rohwer Relocation Center, McGehee, Arkansas*—Keiko leads her parents away from the vehicles and into the maze.

She walks, but not with her own legs.

She finds their room, but it isn't her hand that opens the door.

It isn't she who steps aside to let her parents enter.

When she closes the door, sets down her suitcase, and sits on the edge of a cot, Keiko does not feel her fingernails biting into the flesh of her palms, not even after her father says, "Oh! Kei-chan, your hands are bleeding."

Paul Bunyan-san

NOVEMBER 1942

GENZO AND DEWEY LIVE TWO DOORS DOWN IN THE SAME BARRACK. Soon after their arrival, Shoji catches a cold, and Genzo visits with books to read aloud. Cheerfully, Genzo remarks on how grateful he is that they now live so close to each other. Kuwano produces a deck of cards she had packed back in Lodi. Shoji and Genzo have just dealt their first hand, when a gang of men knock on the door. "We need volunteers to go into the forest near the camp and cut trees for lumber. People are arriving daily. More barracks are needed."

Genzo leaps up with such enthusiasm, he scatters cards all over Shoji's blanket. "*Iko!* Let's go!" says Genzo. "I know all about cutting trees. I read a book about Paul Bunyan-san and Babe, his blue ox."

Keiko laughs. She can imagine Genzo in the forest lecturing the men on how Paul Bunyan-san could fell a tree with one swipe of his huge ax.

"I'd like to join you," says Shoji, "but I really don't feel up to it. Maybe tomorrow or the next day."

"*Yoshi.* All right. You rest." Genzo heads for the door. "I'll tell you about it when I get back." Genzo looks excited as a boy heading out on an adventure.

"Genzo, be careful. Pay attention. Watch out for the trees."

Genzo waves, joins the group outside, and launches into the story of Paul Bunyan-san. The men walk away, and Shoji overhears an *Issei* man calling Genzo a liar. "Who the hell ever heard of a blue ox?"

When the men return from the forest late that afternoon, they carry Genzo's body, his head, shoulders, and spine crushed by a falling tree. The accident occurred midmorning, and the men worked all day to free his corpse.

Shoji hears the news from Keiko, dresses, and goes to the infirmary. Al and Dewey stand next to the table. Genzo's body is covered with a blood-stained sheet. Shoji reaches out, but Dewey stops him. "Please, don't. The tree messed him up awful. I don't think he'd want you to see him like that."

Shoji nods. He feels under the sheet for Genzo's hand and slips Buddhist prayer beads around Genzo's wrist.

Cloak of the Goddess

November 1942

That night Shoji tosses, delirious with fever and grief. He dreams of walking for miles through a burnt, smoldering forest. He is searching for Genzo, but there is no sign of his friend nor any other living thing anywhere in the charred landscape. When he sees someone standing among the rocks at the base of a dry waterfall, he rushes forward. "Genzo!"

As he draws closer, Shoji realizes that it is not Genzo, but a stone statue of the goddess of mercy. Shoji kneels before the statue. He puts his hands together and bows. "I've lost my best friend. Please, can you help me find him?"

In Japan, people often drape cloth around sacred stones and statues. Shoji finds himself staring at the cloak this stone goddess wears. At first it appears drab and tattered, but upon closer inspection, the surface of the cloth seems to shimmer and move. The cloak is woven of threads of water mixed with dust, and every thread is alive and slowly moving. Plants, animals, fish, birds, people, each warp thread is an individual life pushed by its past, pulled by its future. Each weft thread is a cross-life. Over and under, touching, knotting and breaking, the patterns changing continuously as each thread affects the path of every other thread. Holes appear and disappear. Sometimes the gaps seem part of the design, sometimes not.

Shoji shakes his head. *How can this be?* The fingertips of the statue's left hand peek from beneath the cloak. The fingers are living flesh. The statue of Kannon-sama has come to life. Shoji bows, forehead to ash-covered earth, then with great humility, he raises his head. So radiant is the light, he cannot see her face.

Loosely knotted at Kannon-sama's throat, the ties of her cloak are strands of pearls, but pearls of smoke dissolving into mist, rising wisps, stroked with iridescent rainbows, evaporating in shafts of sun. All around, the burnt forest miraculously healed and green, cloaked with pearl gray mist. Hearing gurgling water, Shoji turns, recognizes the forest, finds himself kneeling beside the stream below his childhood home, birdsong and wind in the treetops.

Shoji awakes to whispering voices, sees his family huddled in the corner of the room. "What's wrong?"

"Papa," says Keiko in her gentlest voice, "the camp authorities have a rule against mass gatherings. They're afraid of riots. They say we can't hold a funeral."

Shoji's feet thud against the floor. "Wife! My clothes. I'll go talk to the man in charge of this place. Al, Keiko, you translate for me. Genzo will have his funeral, or I will tear this camp apart with my bare hands! No, wait . . . that wouldn't work. They would just shoot me or throw me back in prison. Wife! Get me a knife. Keiko, you tell them that I humbly request that Genzo be allowed a proper Buddhist funeral. If my request is denied, I'll commit seppuku on their doorstep. That will guarantee a riot."

"Papa, please—"

"Do as I say!" thunders Shoji. "Genzo will have his funeral, or I will join him. I have spoken, and my word will not be broken."

Genzo has his funeral outdoors under an overcast sky and watchful guard towers. When it is time for Shoji to speak, he stands and faces the mourners but finds himself unable to utter a word. Finally, he takes a deep breath and says, "Those of you who lived in Lodi, you all knew Genzo. He would not be stuck like this. He would reach in his pocket and take out a long list of things he wanted to say."

Gentle laughter ripples through the crowd.

"Matsuyama Genzo unwrapped each day of his life as if it were a gift. Wherever his spirit is now, I know he's looking around with his eyes full of delight. Taking note of each new thing. Reaching out to touch, sniff, and taste everything. I can see him . . . as he was when we were boys. Happy. Impatient. Full of energy. Eager and ready to run. '*Iko!*' he says. '*Iko! Iko!* Let's go! Let's go! The adventure awaits.'

"*Yoshi!*" Shoji raises his hand. Then so softly, only those closest to him can hear, Shoji says, "*Ike.* Go."

Bowstrings

NOVEMBER 1942

Basic training completed, Sam's platoon marches off to war, leaving him behind. Abandoned without explanation, unable to sleep that night, Sam practices his martial arts exercises. In his underwear he moves barefooted across the wooden floor of the darkened barrack, back and forth along the main aisle between the empty bunks, through shafts of pale blue moonlight coming in the windows. Sam punches, leaps, spins and kicks.

The moonlight reminds him of Keiko. He hasn't heard from her. He's sent a dozen letters to her boardinghouse and her parents' restaurant in Lodi. He hopes his mail has been forwarded . . . maybe the letters haven't caught up to her yet? Where is she?

He readies a punch, but doesn't throw it. Instead, he reaches into the darkness and imagines he is drawing Keiko into his arms. Then he waltzes up the aisle . . . imagining Keiko in his arms. He smiles. The music from Mrs. Franklin's Victrola drifts into his mind, and then the old lady's voice: *When you dance the waltz, you must open your heart. You must be like a house with all its doors and windows opened wide so the music can flow through every room like a warm breeze. . . .* Sam stops. Stunned. Mrs. Franklin's words were like an English translation of a lesson in *mu* and *ki*.

Emptiness . . . a house with all its doors and windows open . . . so the *ki* can flow . . .

Sam wonders how, where, and when he will be tested in combat. Then he hears a sound, not waltz music but a drumming like distant tramping feet. It comes from the shadows in the corner of the room. The headlights of a passing jeep flash across the windows, sweeping back the darkness, revealing nothing there. Ghosts. How many of the boys who walked these floors and slept in these bunks were already ghosts?

Yin and yang, compassion and bloodlust. Half of Sam's heart aches for all the beautiful places of the earth in flames. For all the wailing women and doomed children. For all the virgin troops, their cheeks pink with pride, their bodies pumped full of bravado, who believe they can march forever, can shout forever, their young male voices shaking the trees of heaven. The other half of Sam's heart pounds like a Japanese *taiko* war drum. The sinews of his hard young body strain like bowstrings pulled and held taut, impatient for the command to loose the arrows of first combat.

But am I ready? Will my aim be true?

In the barrack, everything lit by the moon is a different shade of blue. In the dense blue black shadows in the corner of the room, something listens to his thoughts. Demon or angel? *What if I raise my rifle, and the Japanese soldier in my sights is my younger brother, Bunji? I haven't seen Bunji in almost thirteen years. Would I even recognize him? What if the Japanese soldier attacking me looks like Papa or Fujiwara-san? An instant's hesitation could be fatal.*

How, where, and when will I be tested?

Here and now, his old sensei would have answered. You are being tested here and now. Are you paying attention?

Savage

NOVEMBER 1942

SAM REMAINS ALONE IN HIS EMPTY BARRACK, TAKES HIS MEALS IN THE crowded mess hall, but sits apart, speaking to no one. All around him troops continue training and shipping out. Then one morning two MPs come for him. Sam grabs his gear, and they drive him to the railroad station. Thirty *Nisei* soldiers wait there—the first Asians Sam has seen since he left prison. The train takes them north out of Arkansas. At stops along the way they pick up more *Nisei* soldiers. The group tops out at eighty Japanese Americans with a young Caucasian lieutenant in charge.

Someone says the main junction is at St. Louis. "If the train turns east, we'll be fighting in Europe. If the train turns west, we'll be sent to the Pacific."

The train reaches St. Louis, keeps traveling north.

They are all perplexed until someone recalls there is another junction at Chicago. East at Chicago means they'll be shipped out of New York. West will mean San Francisco.

They head west from Chicago. But at Rockford, Illinois, the *Nisei* troops are ordered off and bused to Camp Grant, a medical facility where doctors and nurses train for combat duty.

At Camp Grant the *Nisei* take a battery of Japanese-language tests. Sam's final examiner is an army major who says, "All right, soldier, you're a keeper. Pack your gear."

"Where am I going, sir?" asks Sam.

But the major waves him off and calls in the next *Nisei*.

It is snowing when Sam leaves Camp Grant. Just he and an armed escort, a sergeant, who drives Sam to the railroad station then boards the train with him. The train rolls north into Wisconsin, then crosses into Minnesota. Every time Sam leaves his seat to use the toilet, the sergeant follows. "Sarge, are you worried that I'm going to try to run away or something?"

"Hell, no, son." The sergeant pats the .45 on his belt. "I was ordered to protect you at any cost."

In the middle of the night, they get off the train. An army jeep picks them up and takes them to a military base called Camp Savage. Sam is let off, and the sergeant rides away into the night. Sam goes up the steps to his barrack and opens the door. The place is empty, no heat, no blankets. Sam keeps his clothes on, sleeps sandwiched between two mattresses. During the following week, more *Nisei* GIs arrive, filling Sam's barrack and the ones adjoining.

Savage is a military-intelligence language school. When Sam arrives, the instructors number nineteen in uniform and twenty civilian. The curriculum is spoken and written Japanese with emphasis on military terminology. The atmosphere is electric with urgency. Seven hours of classroom work each day, two hours more in the evenings, exams on Saturdays. After lights out, men cram with flashlights.

Those who make it through the eight weeks of intensive training are formed into teams and sent to the Pacific. The graduates are told, "Whatever happens, do not under any circumstances allow yourselves to be taken prisoner. Not only your fate, but those of any relatives you have in Japan, will be more terrible than you can imagine."

Sam graduates at the top of his class, receives the three stripes of a tech sergeant, and is pulled from the ranks to remain at Savage as an instructor. The army assigns him to a classroom where he begins teaching the vocabulary of war.

His students, all Japanese-American GIs, call him Sensei, and after they graduate, they embark for Burma and New Guinea and places with names none of them has ever heard before, names that will later appear in newsreels and history books: Kwajalein, Tarawa, Lingayen Gulf, Saipan, Guam, the Marianas, Bougainville, Guadalcanal.

When the post office is finally able to forward Sam's letters to Keiko, he writes that he has been assigned to serve out the war as a language instructor and confesses the mixed emotions of watching his students march off without him. She writes back immediately, telling him that she is applying for a pass to leave Rohwer. She is coming to Minnesota to marry him. Sam reads her letter and whoops for joy. But his celebration is cut short by the loud rumble of trucks approaching his barrack. Sam opens the door. Rain glitters and streaks in the headlights as three trucks pull up and a new bunch of *Nisei* GIs jump down and run toward him. Jostling past him into the barrack, someone knocks the letter loose. Before Sam can retrieve it, Keiko's dove gray stationery is rain soaked and printed with muddy boot tracks.

Omamori

APRIL 1943

ALMOST THE ENTIRE JAPANESE-AMERICAN POPULATION OF LODI AND the surrounding area were sent to Camp Rohwer or Jerome in Arkansas. The same week Mitsy, Haru, Al, and Dewey receive their high school diplomas in the mail from Lodi, an army recruiter visits Rohwer. He gathers the young

Nisei men in the mess hall. Guarded by a rifle squad, he announces that the army is building an all-volunteer Japanese-American combat team, and is therefore reopening its ranks to nonaliens of Japanese ancestry.

Many of the *Nisei* listen in hostile silence. Al asks, "How come you call us 'nonaliens'? What the hell's a 'nonalien'? Why can't you just say 'American citizen'?"

"I'm reading it exactly as it appears on this official government document."

Another stands up with a newspaper clipping. "Last week General De-Witt testifying before the House Naval Affairs Subcommittee in San Francisco was quoted as saying: 'A Jap's a Jap. You can't change him by giving him a piece of paper.' How can you expect us to volunteer and maybe end up serving under a man who feels like that?"

Hands shoot up around the room, and the lieutenant, realizing he is about to become entangled in a debate, waves off further questions and calls for volunteers.

Al, Dewey, and seventeen others stand up.

Contempt darkens the officer's face.

Al feels like punching the young lieutenant. "Sir, just give them time. A lot of guys haven't made up their minds yet. We're the first wave; others will follow. As for those refusing to serve, well, sir, they're just taking a stand for liberty and justice in a different way."

In preparation for Al and Dewey's departure, Kuwano sews two matchbook-size silk envelopes, tied shut with thin silk cord. Each contains a piece of paper with a religious inscription written by one of the camp's Buddhist priests. The Japanese call these good luck charms *omamori*. Dewey puts his in his shirt pocket. Al gives his to Keiko. "Here, sis, keep this for me until I get back."

"But Al, Mama made it for you."

"Come on, sis. You know I'm always misplacing things. If I lost this out there, I'd be so rattled I might forget to pay attention. This way I'll know it's safe, so I'm safe and keeping you safe at the same time. That way we won't worry about each other."

Keiko smiles bravely. "Okay. I'll hold it for you."

Al grins. "You're so pretty when you smile. Say, this is a good idea. Can't have too much good luck, right?" He takes some change out of his pocket. He picks out a nickel and two pennies. "Here, Mama, lucky seven. Please hold these for me until I come back for them, okay? They'll keep both of us safe."

Kuwano stares down at the seven cents in her hand.

"Don't spend them on anything," says Al.

"Don't be silly," she scolds. "You think I'm a fool? I'll make an *omamori* for them and wear them around my neck until you come home."

"Good," says Al. He takes out his fountain pen. "Here, Papa, would you please take care of this for me?"

"I will," says Shoji solemnly.

Al breathes a huge sigh. "Well, I must say I've never felt so well protected." He laughs. It sounds almost convincing.

Dewey looks a little forlorn.

Shoji puts his hand on Dewey's shoulder. "I have two sons now. When you write to me, I would be pleased if you called me Pop. You and Al are brothers. Look after each other."

Dewey gets so choked up, all he can do is nod and croak, "We will."

Red Peonies

NOVEMBER 1943

KEIKO'S PASS IS FINALLY GRANTED, AND SHE LEAVES ROHWER FOR MINnesota. She travels with a woman named Mildred Yamashiro who is married to a GI also teaching at Savage. The train pulls into the station. Sam and Mildred's husband, Paul, are waiting on the platform. Both men hold small bouquets of hothouse roses in their hands.

It is snowing, and Keiko wears a navy blue raincoat suitable for California. When Sam puts his arms around her, Keiko feels an upwelling of tears. But she fights them down. The station is crowded, and their four Asian faces are drawing stares. Sam and Paul are in GI uniforms; nevertheless, Keiko does not feel safe.

Sam's hug is warm and genuine, but Keiko feels the tension in his body—he, too, feels constrained and ill at ease. They release each other and step apart. Neither makes a move to kiss the other. Sam hands her the bouquet of roses. She puts them to her nose then looks up and meets his eyes.

Sam's smile is so gentle and full of love, it melts Keiko's heart. For a moment it's as if everyone and everything else in the world has disappeared. What Keiko feels coming from Sam is sweeter than words and potent as the most fervent kiss. Plain and simple, he adores her.

But when she does not lower her eyes, when she boldly holds his gaze, Sam's smile broadens, and something else comes into his face. Suddenly the air between them seems to crackle with electricity. Paul grins and slaps Sam on the back. "Hey," he whispers, "save it for the hotel. Another ten seconds of this and they'll hit you with the fire hoses."

Keiko and Sam are married at the Hennepin County courthouse. Mildred and Paul stand beside them as witnesses. After the brief civil ceremony, the justice of the peace tells Keiko, "If you're out alone and someone asks your nationality, say you're Chinese. The Chinese are allies. Don't let anyone know you're a Jap."

Keiko smiles sweetly. "Yes, sir. Thank you, sir. I won't."

The four go to a hotel. They dine together then go up to their rooms.

Sam wants to share a bath with his new bride, but Keiko feels overcome with shyness. She insists Sam go first. While Sam splashes, Keiko unpacks her suitcase.

Snow and wind buffet the windows.

Keiko sits on the edge of the bed. She stares at the buckled and faded print of roses over the headboard, the three ugly lamps, the hissing radiator. The room smells stale and stuffy. Keiko closes her eyes and tries to remember the night she returned from Japan, the night she and Sam walked in Genzo's vineyard. The warm breeze, the perfume of Tokay and Concord grapes.

She opens her eyes, looks down at her chapped icy hands, flexes her fingers, brittle as bird claws. Keiko listens to the wind moaning, feels the sound enter her ears and coil itself around her heart. She shivers and hugs herself.

Sam comes out of the bathroom. "I'm sorry. I didn't have time to buy pajamas. I hope you don't mind." He wears GI underwear, dog tags around his neck. He walks quickly across the floor and throws back the covers, his posture and the jerkiness of his movements betraying his nervousness. Suddenly, he stops.

"What's wrong?" says Keiko. "Why are you staring at me?"

"I was so busy with myself, I didn't see the colors in your . . . I didn't see you."

Keiko makes a face. She feels so ugly, she actually feels a surge of intense self-loathing. "Please, stop it. Don't stare at me."

"You look tired and cold. Maybe a long hot soak will make you feel better."

Keiko grabs her nightgown and cosmetic bag and goes into the bathroom, her joints creaking and rattling like an old ladder folding and unfolding. In the bathroom mirror her eyes look dull, sunken; she's seen better-looking prunes.

What's wrong? What's happened to us? Then she recalls the night she taught Sam to dance. She remembers how awkward he had been and how angry and disappointed she had felt. *So, here it is again—all that fuzzy-focused romantic Hollywood stuff versus real life. It's my wedding night, and I feel like week-old fish on ice.*

She opens the bath oil Haru and Mitsy gave her back in Rohwer. She runs a steaming-hot bath, and while the tub fills, Keiko scrubs the makeup off her face. Her reflection in the mirror scares her. *My skin and hair look like they belong in a nursing home.* Shoulders slumped, she turns to the tub of rose-scented bubbles. *How strange it is to be here. After traveling so far. Waiting so long.* Her damn wedding night, and she's so tired she's falling asleep on her feet.

Whoa! Hot! Hot water! Keiko clenches her teeth and eases down, inch by painful inch. *No icebergs in my bed on my wedding night. No, sir.* Keiko sinks to her earlobes, closes her eyes, breathes deep. *Thaw. Damn it. Thaw . . .*

With a start Keiko opens her eyes. She has fallen asleep in the tub. Haru's voice rings in her head. *Keiko, you idiot, what if you overcooked yourself and got hives or something? That would* really *ruin your wedding night.*

Smiling, Keiko rises glistening pink from the tub, draws the thick white towel across her skin, wipes a clear spot in the mirror—her eyes still look tired, but not so bad. Mitsy would probably put on fresh makeup, but Keiko can't stand the idea.

She dabs perfume behind her ears and on each breast just above the nipples and one last touch on her belly below her navel. She puts on her nightgown. *Well, I guess this is it.* She takes a deep breath and opens the bathroom door.

Sam has turned out all the lamps except for one. Covers pulled to his chin, head propped on two pillows, eyes closed, in the center of the bed.

"Are you asleep?" she whispers as she slips under the covers.

He opens his eyes. "I was meditating." He smiles. "Praying." He moves aside. "Here, I warmed a spot for you."

Keiko nestles into the space he has vacated.

"Keiko, I'm so glad you're here."

"Me, too."

"Keiko, I love you." Voice low and trembling, he caresses and kisses her. Repeating his love over and over, softer and softer. His voice a fading mantra of wind, her heart wild grass shivering to the root tips.

"Sam, I crossed an ocean for you." And she holds him as the earth cradles the sea, cups every calm and stormy part of him. Holds him while he washes every shore of her with wave after wave of rough-edged tenderness, touching, tasting, savoring her without hurry, lingering in each place that draws her sighs and moans, his fingers and tongue exposing and polishing pearls, triggering sensations like filigrees of silver and gold lightning, drawing forth a sweet molten ache. Ah! This is what Misa once mentioned on the ship—*the dance of rain clouds over the earth* . . . this readiness, this!

Sam, hovering like a cloud, opens, lets every guarded part of himself fall, and as rain to waiting earth, his words and eyes and hands and tongue and mind and heart and hard, lovely penis, penetrate her.

Keiko weeps, sobs with joy, as her virginity blossoms into the red peonies of womanhood.

Monsters

OCTOBER 1944

Orange and white hot against gray green, another German artillery shell explodes in the treetops. Shrapnel and jagged timber fragments hurtle down on the Japanese-American GIs hunched below, snapping branches, tearing holes through rain-soaked foliage and living flesh.

Screams.

Al scrambles forward even before the voices yell, "Medic!" He kneels beside a man lying facedown. "Okay, Tosh. I'm here." Tosh's pants ripped, right buttock sliced, bloody meat curling like a filleted fish, shrapnel like the dorsal fin of a shark diving toward Tosh's testicles. "Hold still." Al works his fingers into the wound. Tosh stiffens, cries, curses. Al feels around the jagged edges, grabs it, pulls it out, flips the bloody chunk of iron still hissing hot into the mud, then digs in his pack for bandages.

The guy next to Tosh has been hit square in the back, jacket and shirt blown to tatters, half his spine gone, shattered rib cage exposed to the gray morning light. The cold rain splashes and dilutes the blood and washes bits of dirt and flesh off the bones. "Aw, shit, Doc, it's Hiroshi. Hiroshi's dead."

A machine gun burrs not far ahead of them. Instantly, they recognize it as German. "Go on, Doc," says Tosh. "They need you up there. I'll be okay."

Al sees two guys with a stretcher running toward him. "You're in luck, Tosh."

"Thanks, Doc. Go."

Al squeezes Tosh's shoulder and sets off through the forest toward the machine gun. He tops a rise, slips in the mud, bounces hard on his side as bullets whiz overhead. "Hey! For Christ's sake, I'm a medic!" Al grabs his helmet, raises it high to show the white circle and red cross emblem. Bullets whip past his helmet.

"Shit!" The branches above him crackle as the bullets chew lower; the gunner has the range and is determined to cut Al to pieces. Al tears off a fingernail clawing the wet, rocky ground as he tries to dig in.

Al hears a grenade explode. The machine gun stops. For a brief moment there is only the blessed music of rain falling in the forest. Then off in the distance, the popping of small-arms fire. And Dewey's voice. "Al? Al! You hit?"

Al spits dirt, puts on his helmet, yells that he is okay. He spots Dewey and his platoon stalking around the smoking machine-gun nest.

Far off to their right more enemy artillery shells explode in the treetops.

Al works his way through the underbrush. Up ahead the guys drop to their bellies. They have advanced into the interlocking fire of two more machine guns.

"Medic! Medic!"

Al scrambles forward, grunting and panting, puffing steam. Two guys drag their wounded buddy behind a fallen tree. By the time Al gets to him, he is dead. Al leaves him to look after another soldier with a gaping stomach wound. Al recognizes him: Frank Enzo from the Big Island, the one everyone calls Fish Mouth.

"Medic! Medic!" Another man down, ahead to the right.

Al digs in his pack for morphine. Rain drips off his helmet onto Fish Mouth Enzo's face.

More treetop bursts, moving closer from the left. German mortar rounds landing short to the right.

"Medic!"

Fish Mouth grabs Al's arm. "Please, don't leave me."

"Medic!" This one from somewhere straight ahead.

"Medic!" Another one.

"I'll be back as soon as I can," says Al, knowing he will not, knowing Fish Mouth will be dead in minutes.

"No! Doc, don't leave me. Please! Please, don't leave me." Even as Fish Mouth speaks, the strength melts from his grip as the morphine takes hold. "Wait . . . Tell my mom . . ."

"I'll tell her," says Al, already crawling away.

Fish Mouth alone now, gazing up into the rain. Choking and gurgling, sinking like a drowning child. "Mama. Mama."

One month ago the Nazis seemed to be in full retreat through the French Biffontaine forest, northeast of Belmont, fleeing for the German border. American field officers wanted to pursue with caution, but they were overruled and pushed by their division commander.

Suddenly, the melting Nazis line closed in behind the advancing American infantry. And part of the 1st Battalion, 275 GIs, found themselves in a perfectly engineered and executed trap.

U.S. intelligence reported that Hitler had sent an elite force trained in mountain combat to annihilate the 1st Battalion. As repeated American rescue attempts failed to break through, war correspondents began reporting the story. Because the 1st had originally been part of a Texas national guard unit, some journalists called the trapped soldiers the Texas Battalion. Other writers gave them the name that stuck.

The Lost Battalion had been under siege for almost a week when the *Nisei* troops of the 100th/442nd Regimental Combat Team were ordered to go in and rescue them. The moment the *Nisei* soldiers entered the fog-shrouded forest, they found themselves in a human meat grinder.

The route to the Lost Battalion led through merciless German artillery and rocket fire, minefields, hidden bunkers, camouflaged trapdoors that sprang up behind the advancing *Nisei,* exposing them to machine-gun fire from the rear.

Now, around noon on day two of the rescue mission, the forest is so dense and the overcast and rain so unrelenting, Al can barely see twenty yards in front of him.

In the dim light he treats wounds as much by touch as sight.

The dead and wounded mount. Al works, numb as a drone on a factory line in hell.

He finds a man with his arm blown off below the elbow. Al applies a tourniquet. The man refuses morphine. "Help me up."

"Are you nuts? Just lie still."

"If I stay here, I'll die. It's too dark. Too cold. Too many bodies. Underbrush too thick. I'll be dead before anyone finds me. Help me up."

"No. Listen—"

"Damn you! I'll do it myself." The soldier tries to stand; he slips and falls, screams and sobs in agony and fury.

Al helps him to his feet, and the man staggers toward the rear. Al watches him disappear into the gloomy forest. *A monster.*

Al looks down at his gory hands. *We've all become monsters.*

Owl

OCTOBER 1944

Aʟ ꜱᴛᴀɴᴅꜱ ᴏɴ ᴀ ᴅᴇꜱᴇʀᴛᴇᴅ ʙᴀꜱᴇʙᴀʟʟ ᴅɪᴀᴍᴏɴᴅ. Hᴇ ꜱᴛᴀʀᴇꜱ ʙᴇʏᴏɴᴅ ᴛʜᴇ outfield fence at an impossibly huge tree silhouetted against a fiery-orange sunset. A white owl launches itself from the tree and flies silently toward him. Al expects the owl to veer away, but it does not. At the last minute Al ducks, but the owl strikes him in the face. Al falls on his back, and the owl sinks its claws into Al's chest. Al feels an excruciating pain, but thankfully it lasts only for a moment.

Then the owl slowly sweeps its wings back and forth above Al's face. The undersides of the wings are pure white. Al sees with microscopic clarity the exquisite structure of each feather quill, each filament of down. The wings grow enormous, and Al feels himself lifted into their updraft. He floats into radiant white softness. Peace and ecstasy flood his heart.

Al opens his eyes. The Biffontaine forest is shrouded in moonlit fog.

His back pressed against Dewey's back, Al huddles cramped and shivering in their foxhole. They are ankle deep in water. When he moves, ice crackles on the surface of the water. "Dewey?"

"Al? What's wrong?"

"I had a dream. A good dream."

"Yeah?"

"Yeah."

"Okay. Go back to sleep."

October 29, 1944. Day five of the rescue mission.

"Retreat! Retreat! Retreat!"

Dewey and his squad tumble down to the base of the ridge.

Nazis are dug in at the top. The ridge drops steeply on both sides; flank attacks have failed; the only route to the Lost Battalion is straight up the middle. The Germans have already repelled several assaults; bodies of *Nisei* soldiers litter the rocky ground.

Dewey looks back and curses. Al has not retreated, he is in the open, scrambling from one wounded man to the next. "Al! Al, get the hell out of there!"

Al hears Dewey calling to him and all the different sounds of the bullets ricocheting off the rocks and whizzing and whining and whooshing past him in both directions—German bullets trying to kill him, American bullets trying to protect him.

The man he is tending says, "Thank you," and Al feels him die, feels the man's living spirit slip through his hands with the calm sure grace of a cat.

Al raises his head, looks over his shoulder, sees Dewey's anguished face, and in the instant their eyes meet, knows what is about to happen.

They both know.

Dewey hears the first bullet shatter Al's right arm, then sees three quick explosions of blood burst through Al's torso and hang momentarily as a thin red mist in the air.

Dewey leaps to his feet and sprints toward Al. A German bullet knocks off his helmet, but Dewey keeps running. He wants to die. Feverish with exhaustion, he thinks that if Al is checking out, he wants to go with him.

But when Dewey grabs Al and drags him back to the base of the ridge, Al sputters fiercely, "Go the distance. Home plate. You got to make it home." A medic shoves Dewey aside and tears open Al's bloody shirt. "Dewey! Tell Mitsy I love her."

"Fix bayonets!"

Dewey hears voices passing the command along the line. "Fix bayonets! Fix bayonets!"

He stares at Al's wounds, knows there is no hope and no time left.

"This is it, boys. No retreat. Go for broke!"

The cry ignites Dewey's blood. He feels all the hatred and murderous rage of hell rush into his heart. He picks up his weapon, affixes his bayonet, his hands sticky with Al's blood.

He does not feel patriotic or pure or good. He feels crazy, lost, and damned. Dewey rises and starts running toward the Nazis. Soul-sick with grief and despair, he runs through the ugly buzz of bullets passing his bare head. He feels the icy wind in his greasy sweat-soaked hair. Mixed with the screams of men, explosions of grenades, and gunfire, he hears wind washing through the forest and across the ridge.

More than any other sound, it is the wind that defines this moment for him—feverishly, he thinks the sound comes from tree goddesses hissing and sucking in their breath, twig-thin fingers trembling before their eyes; sister goddesses in the earth dragging their long stony sleeves in front of their faces and turning away in horror as the line of men charges.

Keeping Score

OCTOBER 1944

SAM HAMADA CLIMBS ABOARD A MINNEAPOLIS TROLLEY. IT IS A STRUGgle because he is carrying a collapsed baby crib. Hands reach out to help him. As the trolley gets under way an old lady asks, "Is this your first child, Sergeant?"

"Yes, ma'am."

"How old is your baby?"

"Hasn't arrived yet."

"When's your wife due?"

"Around the middle or end of January."

The lady smiles and nods.

When Sam reaches their tiny studio apartment, he finds Keiko sobbing. "I was taking a nap, and I dreamt Al was dying. The place was an old French church filled with wounded. A doctor was there, but Al knew he couldn't be saved. Al told the doctor to go and help someone else. The doctor seemed relieved and grateful. He left Al. I was kneeling on the floor beside Al. I called out and tried to make the doctor come back.

"But Al said, 'Let him go, sis. He's got work to do. And he's so tired and heartsick. Let him go.'

"I started crying and Al said, 'Sis, don't cry. I'm going to be safe now. No one can ever hurt me again.'

"Al stood up. He had on a white T-shirt and jeans. He wasn't bleeding. I was so happy. He wasn't hurt at all. When he began walking away, I said, 'Al, wait. Where are you going?'

"He said, 'Baseball practice.' He opened the church doors, and the sunlight outside was so bright, it blinded me. Al was outlined in light.

"I said, 'Have fun, Al.' And he laughed. You know? That beautiful, beautiful laugh of his. He went out and the doors closed behind him, *boom*. And I woke up."

October 30, 1944. Day six of the rescue mission. B, I, and K companies break through to the Lost Battalion. Normally an infantry company has between 180 to 200 men. After their six-day push, K Company's 186 men have been cut to 17; of I Company's 185 men, 8 surviving members reach the Lost Battalion.

An hour after the route is secured, the soldiers of the Lost Battalion walk down from the hill. They are met by the division commander and a group of war correspondents. While the survivors of the Lost Battalion eat and take hot showers, the exhausted *Nisei* are ordered to continue their advance. Under constant Nazi artillery and rocket bombardment and heavy troop resistance, day after day, they fight their way forward. The weather goes from rain to snow. Misdirected American artillery shells hit them. Even so, their orders do not change: Advance.

There are more Nazi prisoners than *Nisei* GIs; no one can be spared to escort prisoners to the rear. All companies are so depleted, they can barely function as fighting units. The *Nisei* crack under the strain. Enemy shelling intensifies, but the word from division is the same: Advance.

Finally, the *Nisei* are moved back to a position near Bruyeres. Ten days after they rescued the Lost Battalion, the order comes for the 100th/442nd

Regimental Combat Team to leave the forest and descend from the hill.

Three days later, the 100th/442nd is assembled. The general looks over the troops standing at attention and says, "I ordered that *all* the men be assembled."

"Yes, sir. All the men are what you see."

Among those missing from the ranks are Corporal Al Yanagi, dead, and Sergeant Dewey Matsuyama, wounded. The 100th/442nd entered the Vosges Mountains four weeks earlier with 2,943 men. Standing before the general are fewer than 750 men.

The Lost Texas Battalion began with 275 men; 211 survived.

In November, Sam and Keiko receive a letter from Kuwano informing them that Al was killed and Dewey wounded. In January, Dewey sends Sam and Keiko a letter from a hospital in England. He tells them how Al died, and he mentions that his arm was injured but gives no further details about his condition.

On January 28, 1945, Keiko gives birth to a boy. They name him Alexander Genzo Hamada, but almost never speak his given names. Keiko calls him Sweetie or Ink-Pink; Sam calls him Little Buddy.

The day Sam and Keiko leave the hospital with their new baby, it is snowing lightly. They stand waiting for a trolley. Sam feels his son suddenly wiggling in his arms. He looks down and sees that a snowflake has landed on the baby's nose. He seems to like it.

Sam has a momentary urge to take his wife and baby and start running. But he lets the useless impulse pass. He knows life offers no exemptions from pain. Looking up from the baby in his arms, he gives Keiko a reassuring smile.

Keiko sees through Sam's mask, reading mirrored in his eyes the truth they share and need not speak: *Only Al, playing baseball, and Genzo, reading, talking, making lists, and keeping score in the bleachers, are beyond all suffering.*

Ink-Pink

MAY 1945

ON MAY 7, 1945, GERMANY SURRENDERS, AND THE WAR IN EUROPE IS over. The crosshairs of the entire Allied war machine turn toward Japan.

Yearning to test himself in combat, but resigned to serving out the war in his classroom, Sam digs in and puts all his energy into training his students to be the best linguists in the army. Then one day he sees a report and photograph of a *Nisei* translator captured and tortured to death by Japanese troops. The body in the photo is barely recognizable as human, but the name leaps out at him—the soldier was a former student. That night Sam calls an unscheduled meeting. He shows his students the report and picture. Then Sam gives his men a martial arts lesson that none would ever forget—it concludes with instructions on how to kill themselves. Leaving the classroom, the students bow solemnly to their sensei.

Thursday, July 26, 1945, 1:30 A.M. Sam and Keiko are awakened by two military policemen pounding on the door of their studio apartment. The baby wakes up and starts crying.

While Sam gets dressed, the MPs stare at Keiko.

She picks up the baby, rocks and gently bounces him in her arms. Turning her back to the MPs, she coos to the baby. Reciting his favorite nonsense jingle, "Ink-Pink, you stink, Ink-Pink, you stink," she offers her breast, and the baby settles down. Wrapping her robe around herself and the baby, she whispers, "Sam, what's wrong?"

"I don't know. Some kind of emergency at the base."

"How long will you be gone?"

He kisses her. "I love you."

"I love you, too, Sam. Please be careful." Sam is halfway to the door when Keiko calls, "Wait!" She goes quickly to the dresser. Then she runs to Sam and thrusts an *omamori* into his hand. "Take this. Don't give me any arguments. Just take it."

Sam and the MPs walk through a drizzling rain to the jeep double-parked in the street. Sam looks up and sees Keiko silhouetted in the apartment window. They wave. When Sam climbs into the jeep, he finds that someone has packed his duffel bag for him. "What's going on?"

The first MP shrugs. "No idea. That your wife, Sarge? She's real pretty."

"What'd she give you?" asks the second MP.

Sam holds up the matchbook-size silk packet. "It's a good luck charm. Her mother made it for me."

"Yeah? What's your secret? My mother-in-law hates me."

Sam pulls out his neck chain and hangs the *omamori* next to his dog tags. The amulet is a wedding gift from Kuwano, the pale blue silk cut from the hem of Keiko's favorite dress.

A military DC-3 waits on the ramp. As soon as Sam's jeep appears, the plane's twin engines sputter to life. Sam grabs his duffel bag and climbs aboard. Even before the door swings shut, the plane is rolling. In the dim red light, Sam realizes there is only one other passenger. Sam snaps a salute.

"Relax, Sergeant. My name's Jack Wright."

"Colonel Wright, may I ask what's going on, sir? Where're we going, sir?"

"Albuquerque, New Mexico. Get some sleep. We've got a long ride ahead."

The DC-3 pauses in Albuquerque for fuel and a civilian named Abe Berman—slender, thinning hair, horn-rimmed glasses, friendly, eager to talk, but the colonel orders him not to. Abe shrugs and gives Sam a helpless smile, crosses his arms. Sam studies Abe's tweed jacket, elbow patches, breast pocket full of pens and pencils, a small slide rule.

In Los Angeles they transfer to a gleaming new B-29 Superfortress. Abe eyeballs the wingspan. "I'd estimate you could just barely squeeze two of these monsters side by side between the goal lines of a football field." They are issued parachutes and life vests. The bomber takes off, carries them out over the Pacific Ocean. Sam, Berman, and Wright sit on the deck in the waist cabin. The only seats available are taken by the three gunners and radar observer.

After flying for several hours, the bombardier sticks his head into the cabin. "The captain sends his greetings. Says you're welcome to come forward one at a time and check the view out the nose. It's not every day you get a ride in one of these babies."

Colonel Wright goes first, then Abe. Abe is gone for over an hour, and the bombardier gets impatient. "Hey, Sergeant, go tell your buddy his time's up."

Sam climbs into the crawl tube that connects the waist cabin to the nose. The tube is about three feet in diameter, lined with blue fabric. Bundles of cables and wires run along the sides of the crawlway.

Sam enters the nose cabin, makes his way past the radio operator, navigator, and flight engineer. Ahead of the pilot and the copilot, Abe Berman sits in the bombardier's seat. The nose of the B-29 is like a round greenhouse. For a moment the sunlight pouring into the greenhouse blinds Sam. He squints, and Abe's body, silhouetted against the black curving frame lines of the nose canopy, looks like a giant spider in the center of a web.

The copilot greets Sam. Abe looks around and reluctantly vacates his seat. Sam squeezes through the opening between the pilot and copilot's instrument panels, then slides into the bombardier's seat. He is riding high above the clouds. In formations all around him are more B-29s, gleaming in the sun, trailing lines of white vapor.

They fly through turbulence, and Sam feels an odd bouncing sensation travel out to him along the forward body of the B-29. He feels like he is perched on the tip of a tree limb dipping up and down in the wind.

They refuel in Hawaii. Sam heads for the hatch. He wants to climb down to the tarmac. He knows it would look bad if he bowed, but he wants to at least turn his face toward the Big Island and the old cemetery where his brothers' and Fujiwara-san's ashes are interred. But Colonel Wright won't allow him to leave the plane. "You, me, and Abe need to remain out of sight. No one except for our flight crews can know that we exist."

At Iwo Jima, Colonel Wright, Sam, and Abe Berman transfer to a twin-engine PBY Catalina flying boat. Once airborne, their seaplane is joined by a fighter escort of six P-38 Lightnings, and they continue westward toward the setting sun.

"Wake up, Sergeant," says the colonel, "it's time to get ready. We're almost there." The colonel strips and begins putting on combat fatigues. Sam opens his duffel bag and follows suit. The colonel throws a uniform to Abe.

"I don't want it," says Abe.

"Once we're in the combat zone, anything unusual will draw immediate attention. Your civvies could make you the target of a Jap sniper."

"Okay, you've sold me." Abe holds up the shirt. "What's my rank?"

"Private first class."

"Both you fellows outrank me."

"That's right, college boy."

Okinawa

JULY 1945

THEIR SEAPLANE SPLASHES DOWN OFF THE WEST SIDE OF A LARGE ISLAND.

Once ashore, they are met by a young marine lieutenant and a rifle squad led by a short, cigar-chewing sergeant. "Gentlemen," says the lieutenant, "welcome to Okinawa. I'm Fred Loganberry, and this is Sergeant Clay."

Sam notes Loganberry's clean-shaven face and spotless uniform. The sergeant and the marines in his rifle squad are filthy and unshaven. They hang together, and though they say nothing, the contempt and hostility coming off them is as daunting as the odor of their unwashed bodies.

Sam puffs out his chest and tries to stand tall. Then he notices Loganberry, Wright, and Abe Berman are doing the same. Sam almost laughs. The new guys are hoping they will measure up. They all want to make the team.

"We should get going, sir," says Loganberry. "It's a couple hours to the cave."

Loganberry and Wright lead the way in a jeep. Sam, Abe, Sergeant Clay, and his squad follow in a truck. They roll inland through beautiful patch-work fields of ripening rice and barley. An endless line of trucks passes, go-ing the other way, carrying wounded down to the beach and waiting hospital ships.

For several miles they make good time, then they catch up with a supply convoy. Vehicles close the gap behind them, and they are stuck in the long procession crawling toward the front.

They crest a rise. Far off to the right, smoke billows from the southern hills. Sam hears the faint thump of bombs and heavy artillery shells ex-ploding. Ahead of him, the line of vehicles descends into a shallow, bowl-like valley with a village crossroads at its center. He sees thatch-roofed houses and a barbwire compound of Okinawan peasants guarded by American soldiers. At the junction the supply column turns right and goes up and out of the little valley. The barley fields surrounding the village are pale, almost white. Here and there patches of yellow flowers brighten the landscape.

Sam is looking at butterflies when enemy artillery shells suddenly fall whistling from the sky. The first volley, four shells, lands in the fields a hun-dred yards from the road. The convoy grinds to a halt. The second volley hits thirty yards closer.

Birds fly from the barley. Soldiers jump out of their vehicles. The last one off his truck, Sam slides into a ditch beside Abe. Sam's heart pounds furi-ously. Another four rounds land close enough to shower him with dirt and rocks. Helplessly, he presses himself against the earth.

Silence.

The enemy shelling has stopped. Someone yells, "Let's get the hell out of here." The men scramble back to their vehicles, and the convoy begins mov-ing again. But now, instead of seeming relaxed and leisurely, the pace feels like torture.

Nearing the village, Sam feels himself sucked toward the center of a giant bull's-eye. In the village at the barbwire compound of Okinawans, a *Nisei* GI translator is yelling in Japanese for people to get down and stay down. Sam does not recognize the *Nisei,* but he assumes the man received his training at Camp Savage or Fort Snelling.

At the village crossroads, Loganberry points left, and their jeep and truck split off from the convoy and head north at top speed. Just as they clear the outskirts of the village, the Japanese artillery fire resumes. This time shells drop like a cloudburst. The section of road leading south from the crossroads disappears under flames and smoke—a truck takes a direct hit and disintegrates, pieces flying high in the air and raining down onto the barley and yellow flowers. Explosions engulf the screaming villagers.

"My God!" says Abe Berman. "I guess we've arrived at the front."

"Hear that? He thinks this is the fucking front." The marines laugh.

Abe blushes, stares down at the toes of his shiny new boots.

Yae-dake

JULY 1945

THEY DRIVE NORTH-NORTHWEST ONTO THE MOTOBU PENINSULA. THE day fades into a gentle pastel twilight—blue, lavender, and pink. Darkness falls; they turn on their headlights and continue on to the big craggy hill called Yae-dake. Sergeant Clay tells Sam and Abe that Yae-dake had been the stronghold of some two thousand Japanese troops assigned to northern Okinawa. Their mission was to delay and divert the Americans from the main Japanese force in the south. One month earlier, two regiments of U.S. Marines, the 4th and the 29th, had paid dearly to take the hill. "Now there's just one pocket of resistance left."

The jeep and truck climb through woods, skirt the sides of steep ravines. The marines in the truck stub out their cigarettes. They grow silent and watchful. "Snipers," says Sergeant Clay as the road snakes up the slopes of Yae-dake.

Through breaks in the trees, Sam can see the full moon shining on the ocean. He smells charred wood. They come out of the forest and enter a burnt and broken landscape.

They park. Dry ash billows from under the tires, puffs from under their boots when Sam and the marines jump down from the truck after Sergeant Clay. Lieutenant Loganberry whispers, and Sergeant Clay and his squad move out. As he goes by Sam and Abe, Clay puts his finger to his lips. They hike uphill. Several times the men freeze, crouch and listen to the night sounds surrounding them. Sam sees strange shapes in the shadows. When he thinks he sees a Japanese soldier with three foxes, one on each shoulder and one atop his head, he realizes that he is so tired that he is dreaming on his feet.

Out of the darkness ahead a voice calls, "Duke?"

"Ellington."

"Sarge?"

"Relax, son."

"Hey, Sarge. Welcome back."

"Any action?"

"Nah, they're still in there. How'd it look down south?"

"Like there was a war going on."

When they reach the marines' camp, Loganberry and Wright disappear into a tent. Sam and Abe are handed K rations. They eat sitting with their backs against a burnt tree. The wind carries a foul odor. Sam assumes it comes from the latrine trench.

Wright and Clay come out of the tent. Sam and Abe are asleep. The sergeant nudges Sam's boot to wake him. Leaving Abe snoring softly, Sergeant Clay leads Sam and the colonel through the camp of sleeping marines. The slope steepens. They hike up through loose rock and boulders toward a ridge silhouetted black and jagged against the night sky.

The smell, more sickening than any latrine, is growing worse.

At the ridge crest, they come upon a line of marines. "Keep low," says Clay. "The moon's almost directly behind us. Go up real slow and don't stay exposed too long. The snipers in the cave have their sights ranged for this ridgeline."

They drop to their bellies and crawl the rest of the way. Gingerly, they raise their heads. The other side of the ridge drops away into a ravine, the bottom hidden in darkness.

An overpowering stench rises into their faces. "Jesus!" says the colonel.

Sam gags and grits his teeth against a wave of nausea.

"Rotting corpses," says Sergeant Clay. "Mostly Japs. Some of our own . . . down there." He dips his head toward the black shadows within the ravine.

They look across the ravine and up a steep crumbling slope to a cave whose mouth is on a level about ten yards higher than the tops of their helmets.

Cautiously, they lower their heads. They retreat, moving away from the stench and the line of dug-in marines, to where they can talk without being overheard. "Sergeant Clay," says Colonel Wright, "go get some sleep. I need to talk to Sergeant Hamada alone."

"Yes, sir."

"Sergeant Hamada," says Colonel Wright in a soft, low voice, "our objective is in that cave. What we're after is something so secret, so important, that we've been ordered to secure it at any cost."

"What is it, sir? What are we after?"

"I can't answer that, Sergeant, because I don't know. I don't know if it's written or drawn on paper or a machine or if it's in the head of one of the Japs in the cave. That's why we can't blow the cave or burn them out. We need to get everything and everyone out intact."

"Sir, I don't understand. If we don't know what we're looking for, how will we know when we've found it?"

"Abe Berman will know. That's why we've brought him."

"What am I supposed to do, sir?"

"Your mission is to get the Japs in the cave to surrender without a fight. Then you will translate every word we find in there. If what we're looking for is not on paper, then we'll need you to interrogate each of the prisoners."

"Won't they have destroyed all the code books and important papers by now?"

"I hope not."

"All right, sir. I'll do my best."

The colonel gazes wearily at the starry sky. Then he turns his eyes southward. "Two more things, Sergeant. First, we're working against a ticking clock. The main battle line is in the south. Our ground forces need the fire support of the offshore fleet to take this island. But Admiral Nimitz is being hit hard by kamikaze attacks. Nimitz doesn't want to hold his fleet here any longer than necessary. He's pressuring the ground troops to get on with it. Our guys are giving it everything they've got. Casualties are horrendous.

"We have two companies of marines securing this one little cave. They're needed for the fight in the south. Our marines want to blow or burn this cave and go. But they've been ordered to give us complete cooperation. They hate sitting here, and we can't even tell them about our mission. It's top secret. No one knows what we're doing here. And that's the way it's got to stay. You understand?"

"Yes, sir. But if time is so critical, why'd you take the trouble to bring me all this way? You must have other translators here."

"We do. And they've done a terrific job. But this mission is special. Out of all our translators on Okinawa, we selected our two best guys. The first stripped bare-ass naked except for his dog tags and boots so the Japs could see he wasn't armed. He crossed the ravine and went into the cave. After about ten minutes the Japs told him to leave. They let him get as far as this ridge, then shot him in the back. Before he died, he gave as much information as he could to his partner. He told his partner we should get you. Apparently, you were his teacher back at Camp Savage."

"What was his name, sir?"

The colonel pauses, then says, "Sorry. It's slipped my mind. I'm not real good with Japanese names. Actually, you see, I wasn't here. I was trying to conduct this operation via radio messages relayed from stateside.

"The second translator decided to give it a try. He also stripped and went out carrying a white flag, but they shot him before he even reached the cave. His body is down in the ravine."

"Sir, you said there were two things. What's the second?"

"We've got a prisoner, a captain, the commanding officer of the unit holding the cave. When the marines fought their way up this hill, the Japs were dug in along that ridge. When the marines finally took the ridge, the Japs fell back to the cave. That night the Jap captain led his men in a banzai counterattack and pushed the marines off the ridge and down into the trees where their camp is now. Some of the Japs were suicide men with land mines wired to their bodies. One took a direct hit from a machine gun. His mine exploded and the concussion knocked out the captain. The captain couldn't believe it when he came to and found himself a prisoner. Other than two black eyes, he didn't have a scratch on him.

"Usually, a banzai attack means the entire Jap unit fights to the death, but just before the captain went down, he had ordered a retreat. The Japs fell back to the ridge. In the heat of battle and the chaos of the retreat, they didn't see their captain go down.

"After two more days of hard fighting, the marines recaptured the ridge, and the Japs retreated to the cave. The marines were all set to burn out the Japs with flamethrowers when I ordered them to cease fire."

"Sir, where's this Japanese captain now?"

"Down there in camp."

"Sir, did our translators talk with him before they went into the cave?"

"Yes. But he refused to cooperate. That's why our translators had no choice but to appeal directly to the men in the cave."

"Does the captain know what we're after?"

"I don't know."

Sam gazes up at the moon. He is exhausted. He thinks if he allows his eyes to close for more than a blink, he will fall asleep.

"Sergeant, we must get those Japs to surrender. We need them alive. And we've got to get the job done as soon as possible."

"Sir, you said the first translator gave a report before he died?"

"Yes. It's not much. The notes are back at camp."

"Let's go look at them, sir."

Shogi

JULY 1945

IN A TENT AT THE MARINES' CAMP, SAM READS THE ENTRY SCRIBBLED IN a bloodstained notebook.

> *"Troops in cave determined to fight to the death. Sergeant Itsuo Nagata, highest surviving rank. 37 able-bodied well-armed troops. 18 wounded. Fresh water spring in cave. THEY ABSOLUTELY REFUSE TO SURRENDER. STRONGLY SUGGEST BRINGING IN HAMADA-SENSEI FROM SAVAGE."—Preceding report given by Sergeant Kinji Yamamoto, recorded by Sergeant Calvin Hirata, 25 July, 1945. I am going to attempt to talk the Japanese troops into surrendering. If I don't make it, note that I concur with Sergeant Yamamoto—advise headquarters to bring in our former instructor, Sergeant Sam Hamada from Camp Savage.*

Calvin and Kinji—two of Sam's best students. Dead. The colonel allows Sam a moment, then asks, "Does the report give you anything you can use?"

"I'm not sure. The highest-ranking soldier in the cave is a sergeant named Itsuo Nagata."

"Another unpronounceable Jap name."

"Itsuo is a name given to a fifth son."

"Yeah, so what?"

Sam shrugs. "Perhaps he's more comfortable following than leading. Or maybe he's sick of taking orders; maybe he's enjoying being the top dog. I guess it depends on how his father and older brothers treated him." Sam leafs through the notebook to the interrogation sessions with the captured Japanese captain. The pages are blank except for a single notation—the officer's name is Sadamichi Oshima.

The colonel checks his wristwatch. "Let's grab a couple hours of sleep. We'll start the interrogation at 0700."

At 0640 in the morning, Sam follows Sergeant Clay to a heavily guarded tent. "If that Jap gives you any trouble, turn him over to me. I'll have him talking a blue streak." Clay pats the hilt of his K-Bar knife then lifts the tent flap.

Colonel Wright sits at a table next to the pole in the center of the tent. The prisoner stands in front of the table. His eyes narrow when they meet Sam's.

Sam lowers his head to enter the tent. He turns the movement into a graceful bow.

Automatically, Captain Oshima begins to bow in return. But he catches himself and lifts his head in a way that conveys his defiance and contempt.

The morning is overcast and muggy, the air inside the tent hot and stuffy. But there is something else that brings an immediate sweat to Sam's skin.

Danger. Imminent danger. Sam feels it radiating from Captain Oshima. Oshima's hair is graying, but his body is lean and taut as a Zen archer's bow. Within his invisible core, Oshima's fighting spirit is as lethal as a fully drawn arrow, silent and still and totally alert.

"Gentlemen," says Colonel Wright, "let's get started."

Sam never takes his eyes off Oshima's. "Colonel, leave this tent now."

"What did you say, Sergeant?"

"Sir, this man is a martial arts expert. He can kill you with his hands tied behind his back. As long as you're in this tent, you're his hostage. Leave now, sir. Otherwise, most of my energy will be spent protecting you."

The colonel puts his hand on the Colt .45 on his hip. He glances at Sam.

In that brief moment of distraction, Captain Oshima steps closer.

It is only because he has been warned that Colonel Wright notices Oshima's form shift almost imperceptibly in the corner of his eye. The colonel leaps up, knocking over the empty ammo crate on which he had been sitting.

As the colonel backpedals and fumbles for his sidearm, Sam moves into position to intercept Oshima.

But Oshima stands absolutely still. He ignores the colonel. His eyes never leave Sam's.

At the entrance to the tent, Colonel Wright pauses. "Under different circumstances, I'd gladly take this guy on. But a fight would screw up our mission. Sergeant, I'm going to give you some time alone with the captain. Try talking to him Jap to Jap." Wright backs out of the tent, and Oshima gives a snort of derision.

"Captain Oshima," says Sam in Japanese, "shall we sit down?"

"Who are you?"

"Sergeant Hamada Isamu."

"I don't sit with sergeants, and I don't talk with them, either."

"Not even your own sergeant, Nagata Itsuo?"

"How do you know his name?"

Sam sits down. He waits silently. Finally, Captain Oshima sits facing him.

"Where did you learn the name of my sergeant?"

"In the report given by our translator, Yamamoto Kinji."

"I told both your translators not to go to the cave. No one under my command will ever surrender to the Americans."

On the table are a pad of lined paper and several pencils. Suddenly, Sam has a crazy idea. He picks up a pencil and begins drawing a large grid on the pad. In sullen silence, the captain watches him. Sam tears off the sheet of paper and puts the finished grid in the center of the table. Then he rips off the next blank sheet and begins tearing it into small, neat squares. He counts out twenty pieces, pushes them over to Captain Oshima along with one of the pencils.

Oshima glares at Sam. "I will not divulge unit locations or map coordinates."

"That's not what I had in mind."

"Then what's all this for?"

"Captain Oshima, how about a game of *shogi*?"

"*Shogi*?" Sam's offer of a game of Japanese chess takes the captain completely by surprise. Oshima cracks a tiny smile. He picks up the pencil and begins inscribing his pieces.

Sam observes him for a while, then writes out his own.

Placing their pieces on the grid, Oshima asks, "Why were you staring at me? Had you forgotten the names of the pieces?"

"No. I was studying your hand . . . your calligraphy."

Again the captain is surprised. "And what did you deduce?"

"Intelligent, well-educated, artistic, sensitive . . . a delicate touch."

Oshima smiles. "Sergeant, you're an interesting fellow." Oshima narrows his eyes and studies Sam's writing. "Energy, strength, confidence, but somewhat rigid, or perhaps controlled would be more accurate."

"Since you're the guest," says Sam, "please, take the first move."

Very quickly Sam realizes Oshima is a superb player. Oshima first thinks Sam is an overly aggressive player who survives on luck. Then he sees Sam as a brave mouse who enjoys dancing close to the cat's mouth. In the final stage, Oshima finds himself fighting with all his skill to survive. The game, which takes just over thirty minutes, ends in a stalemate. Oshima laughs. "Good game."

Sam says nothing.

"We're well matched," says Oshima.

Sam keeps his eyes lowered. "I couldn't decide whether to beat you or let you win," he says. "My sensei would not be pleased with me."

"Are you saying you weren't playing your hardest? How rude."

"Forgive me. I didn't mean to insult you. Sometimes I'm too blunt. I don't have your aristocratic background. I'm the son of a poor Hawaiian plantation worker. My manners aren't refined like yours."

"Let's play another game," says Oshima, replacing his pieces on the board. "And this time, give me your best."

"You'll lose."

"We'll see."

Wager

JULY 1945

SAM AND CAPTAIN OSHIMA FACE EACH OTHER ACROSS THE MAKESHIFT Japanese-chess board. "How about a wager?" says Sam.

"What sort of wager?"

"Let's play for the lives of the men in the cave."

"Their lives are not mine to bet. They belong to the emperor and the nation of Japan. However, if you wish, we can bet our own lives—yours and mine."

"The lives of your men belong to the emperor, yet you can bet your own?"

"I am a prisoner. Which is . . . intolerable! If I die fighting, I would be absolved of my shame. If I take your life, that would be one less American soldier."

"Your bet's worthless. As our prisoner, you already belong to us."

The captain growls and tenses, preparing to leap at Sam.

"You want my life?" says Sam. "I'll bet it against the lives of your men."

"I told you—their lives are not mine to wager."

"Officers have always wagered the lives of their men. The reason you don't like the bet is because it doesn't offer anything you really want."

Captain Oshima stares at Sam with a new respect in his eyes.

"Let's make a *real* wager," says Sam. "Let's ask for what we truly want."

"I want to die with my men."

"Good! Spoken from your heart like a man. All right. If you win, I'll see to it that you're allowed to die with your men."

"They'll never come out of the cave," says the captain. "That means you must allow me to return to them."

Sam grimaces as he realizes he's been outmaneuvered.

Captain Oshima smiles. "Are you a man of your word?"

"If I allow you to return to the cave, it would only be under the following conditions. You must take me with you, and allow me to speak freely with your men, then return safely to my own lines. Also, you must promise not to attack us. My commanding officer would never agree to a deal that might cost the lives of his men."

Oshima shakes his head. "Sergeant, I wish it could be so. But let us not confuse a chess game with the realities of war. You could never talk your commanding officer into allowing me to go free."

"You saw how I convinced him to leave this tent."

"He left because you told him that I could kill him."

Sam notes something odd in the way Oshima says that. *This man understands English.*

"I recognize a martial arts expert when I meet one," says Oshima. "We're like tigers, you and I. Your colonel and those marines who think they're guarding me—they believe they're tigers, too. But we know they're merely farm boys, laborers, and store clerks who happen to be in uniform and armed with lethal weapons."

Sam and Oshima gaze intently into each other's eyes.

"Sergeant, do you honestly believe you can convince your colonel to honor the wager if you win?"

"Yes."

"Then I'll take the bet. You know what I want—if I win, I will be allowed to die with my men. Now tell me what you want."

"Your wholehearted cooperation," says Sam.

"What?"

"If I win, you will give me your wholehearted cooperation."

"You ask for the impossible," says Oshima.

"For one day. Twenty-four hours."

"No."

"Twelve hours."

Oshima breaks into a grin and shakes his head. "Sergeant, you're a very unusual man. All right. If I lose this game, I'll cooperate with you for one hour, as long as I'm not required to do anything dishonorable."

"Cooperate wholeheartedly."

"As wholeheartedly as I can."

"All right."

Oshima sets up his pieces. His eyes are deadly serious. "I will not allow you to win." He emphasizes his words with a slashing motion of his hand, as if he has just cut Sam with an invisible sword.

Sam smiles, but his eyes are just as serious as Oshima's. "You can't win against the puppet masters of fate."

Oshima frowns.

"I'm sorry. My lack of manners is showing again. I'll try to make it up to you. Would you care for some tea?" Sam turns. "Guard!" he calls loudly in English. The tent flap jerks to one side, and a marine corporal comes in with his rifle held at the ready. A second and third guard appear right behind the first. "Do we have any tea?"

"No, Sergeant. But we've got some hot coffee."

"I suppose that'll have to do." Sam turns back to the captain. "Sir, would you like a cup of coffee?"

"Yes, please."

Sam had asked the question in English. And before he could catch himself, the captain had answered, also in English.

"Corporal, please bring us two cups of coffee and inform Colonel Wright that Captain Oshima understands English."

"This Jap speaks English?"

"Yes."

"Right away, Sergeant."

Oshima frowns. "You're beginning to aggravate me, Sergeant. Let's stop all this talk and begin the game."

"Captain, with all due respect, our match started quite some time ago."

"Eh?" Then Captain Oshima begins to laugh. He raises his head and roars, "Damn it, Sergeant, I like you. *Yoshi!* From this point on, I'll show you no mercy." The captain puts out his fist. Sam mirrors him, and they play rock-paper-scissors. Sam chooses scissors. The captain's hand remains a fist. Oshima leans forward and makes his opening move.

"Where did you learn English?" asks Sam as he moves a piece.

"Before Pearl Harbor, I served for three years at our embassy in Washington, D.C. I took classes in Washington and at Columbia University in New York. I loved New York City. I used to—" Abruptly, Oshima stops himself.

"Is something wrong?"

"Talking will distract us from the game."

"Talking is part of the game."

"Is it? Sergeant, your interrogation techniques are so clumsy and transparent."

"I'm just trying to be polite." It's a lie. And both he and the captain know it. Sam retreats, and they play in silence.

When the guard comes in with coffee, he hands Sam a note. Sam reads it and frowns. "Tell the colonel I understand, and I'll do my best."

The guard leaves. Oshima sips his coffee. "What did your colonel have to say? Is he afraid to step into this tent again?"

Sam stares at Oshima for a long moment, then passes the note across the table.

Oshima reads it aloud in English. " 'Bad news. Marines on alert. They have been ordered to use flamethrowers against cave, then head south to reinforce Twenty-ninth Division at Sugar Loaf Hill. Will try to buy us time. Cave burn-out set for 0930.' "

Sam checks his wristwatch. "We have an hour and thirty-seven minutes."

"Sergeant, I want to die with my men."

"The only way you can do that is if you win this game."

Captain Oshima and Sam ponder the *shogi* board. Oshima appears to hold a slight advantage, but the game could still go either way. Oshima makes his move. His voice suddenly turns steel-hard and razor-sharp. "Sergeant Hamada, how can you stand being a soldier in such a dishonorable army?"

"I don't understand what you're talking about." Sam moves his *shogi* piece, then looks up, frowning, into Oshima's eyes.

"When I regained consciousness after our banzai charge, I was tied to a tree and had a close-up view of how things are in your military. I witnessed a marine urinating into the mouth of a dead Japanese soldier. I saw another marine use his bayonet like a chisel to extract gold teeth from a man who was not yet dead. The dying man was my nephew."

"I'm sorry." It is all Sam can think to say.

"I watched the marines haggling over something. I ignored them until I realized they were auctioning my sword. My sword! You know what that means? It had been the soul of our family for over three hundred years. The highest bidder took it for a cheap camera, a little money, and a deck of pornographic playing cards."

Captain Oshima's *shogi* pieces have begun a powerful slicing attack. Sam's countermoves appear weak and desperate.

"Earlier you said you wanted a conversation. But you with your freshly laundered uniform and your eager puppy-dog innocence . . . What do you know of real life? What talk can you offer that could possibly hold my interest? Shall we speak of war and combat? Answer this: an infantry soldier, after his basic training, after the speeches and parades, after the final exhortations from his commanding officer, down at the level of whistling bullets and fixed bayonets, down in the mud where he crouches awaiting the signal to advance, what fire burns at the secret core of his terrified heart? Tell me, Sergeant Hamada, do you know?

"Do you know how it feels to share a hole in the mud with another man, unable to sleep while your own artillery shells fly overhead toward the enemy? Your terrified and murderous heart sucking hope from the sound of your shells ripping across the sky. Do you know what it takes to leave the pathetic safety of your hole and advance against enemy fire?"

Sam does not answer. His *shogi* pieces are being scattered and decimated.

"The obscene truth," says the captain, "is that nothing's more horrifying or sublime than combat. Nothing's more frightening in its total barbaric insanity. Nothing's more challenging or thrilling or intoxicating or addictive. That's why you're willing to bet lives on this chess game. You want to feel closer to the jaws of war.

"Combat soldiers bond with one another. They belong to a fraternity in the school of war. Those who survive are forever changed. Even the most compassionate humanitarian among them has a part of his spirit that views the unbloodied with disdain. Sergeant, you don't have to tell me. I know you've never been in combat."

Hesitantly, Sam moves a *shogi* piece and looks up. He is startled to find Oshima waiting, eyes clear and sharply focused, channeling all his *ki*, his total inner strength, into his next move and words. "You feel what all virgin soldiers feel. Fear, uncertainty, shame, and curiosity. You, Sergeant Hamada, like to think of yourself as a warrior. But you're just a frightened boy who's never been tested."

Sam is dumbfounded; Oshima has read his soul. "Your move," says Oshima.

Off balance, floundering, Sam has trouble focusing on the *shogi* pieces. He feels dizzy, hypnotized. Outclassed and panic-stricken, Sam treads deep water.

Oshima circles calmly as a shark.

Swimming

JULY 1945

I THOUGHT YOU WANTED TO HAVE A CONVERSATION," SAYS OSHIMA.

A memory flashes into Sam's mind—the time he swam across Awaopi'o Cove. Sam hears his own frightened, childish voice ask, "What happened to the current?"

"I beg your pardon?" says Oshima. "The current?" His voice is soft, but his *ki,* all the focused energy of his warrior's spirit, thrusts like a spear toward Sam's heart.

It's wearing us like a tattoo. That's what old man Fujiwara had said.

Sam feels a lethal current rushing powerfully toward him from Captain Oshima. Sam has been bucking it with all his strength. Suddenly, he gives way, swims with it.

Sam raises his eyes and focuses on the varied colors of Oshima's face—bruised yellowish purple across both cheekbones, white hairs scattered through the black, unshaven stubble, hints of amber brown where the light dips into the blackness of Oshima's eyes. "You're right about me," says Sam. "I've never been in combat. I feel inadequate and afraid to speak. I must seem shallow and childish to you. But . . . please continue. I'm fascinated by your words."

Oshima smiles and leans across the table. "You flatter me."

"No. It's the truth."

Oshima knows it is. He gazes calmly at Sam.

They had challenged each other with their *ki.* Oshima's mature power almost smashed Sam like a moth against a wall. But Sam had survived by transforming himself into smoke.

The men hear a huge crackling explosion. Instinctively, they hunch their shoulders and duck. Then they realize it is thunder. Rain begins drumming on the tent. It grows rapidly louder. Sam gets up and opens the tent flaps. The marine guards are pulling on ponchos. The air feels cooler and less oppressive.

Sam returns to the table, and the game continues. Now they play in silence with total concentration. Immersed in the game, both men lose track of the time until, finally, Oshima leans back and crosses his arms. Sam has been playing wide and open, as though ignorant of any form of strategy. Now Oshima sees that Sam has gained the advantage. Oshima's eyes widen and his lips part slightly as he realizes that it is more than an advantage.

Sam has won.

Sam checks his wristwatch. "Your men will be dead in thirty-five minutes."

"I really wanted to win."

"Time to pay off your bet."

Captain Oshima nods grimly. "All right. Your one hour of wholehearted cooperation begins now."

"Good," says Sam, standing up. "Let's go."

"Where?"

Sam takes a deep breath. "To the cave."

Ravine

July 1945

Sam and Captain Oshima leave the tent. One of the guards runs to inform the colonel and Sergeant Clay, the rest follow Sam and Oshima up the trail toward the ridge. The rain is so heavy, water streams down the trail. Sam inhales the scent of wet ash and charred vegetation. Big raindrops strike his shoulders like repeated taps from Fujiwara-san's bamboo sword. *Isamu, are you ready to be tested?*

Sam licks rain from his lips. He revels in the subtle watercolors tinting the sky, earth, and distant sea. Sam and Oshima hike through the remnants of a pine grove—shattered, burnt, and ashen, a few bright green tips sprouting amid wilted bronze needles. Water—streaming down the trail, pooling in boot prints and treadmarks too wide for a jeep or truck—swirls into an iridescent petrochemical question mark in a widening puddle of yellow ochre mud. All his senses are open, and he inhales deeply, down to the tips of his toes. Sam smells the tank before they see it parked at an angle, gun turret pointing up toward the ridge.

As they approach the marines along the ridge, Sam says, "Captain Oshima, call to your men. Tell them to hold their fire. You and I are going into the cave together."

Without hesitation Oshima stands exposed at the top of the ridge and shouts to his unit.

Sam climbs up next to Oshima. Suddenly, Sam inhales the awful stench and gags. He looks down. "Oh, my God . . ."

Corpses litter the slopes of the ravine, the bottom is a mass grave—over two hundred bodies tangled and twisted atop one another. He spots one corpse naked except for boots—the *Nisei* translator Calvin Hirata, his former student. Sam staggers away from Oshima and the marines. He bends over and vomits.

Sam takes off his helmet and lets the hard cold rain beat on his hair and scalp. Closing his eyes, lifting his face, feeling the rain striking his closed eyelids . . . he sees Keiko sitting with their baby. They are wrapped in a purple and gray quilt, surrounded by warm muted lamplight. Sam hugs the image to his stunned and shriveling heart. How can he remain open in this place of absolute horror? Mu . . . *must throw myself away.* With trembling hands he puts on his helmet and returns to Oshima's side. He draws a shallow, wary breath. "Let's go."

Oshima and Sam descend slipping and sliding into the ravine. Avoiding the corpses as best they can, but finally forced to step on them, they cross the ravine and climb the far slope to the cave.

When they reach the mouth of the cave, the captain enters, and Sam pauses to look back at the ridge. He sees Colonel Wright and Sergeant Clay just arriving there. Sam shouts, "Colonel, were you able to buy us any time?"

"No! The burn-out's still on for 0930. You've got twenty-seven minutes."

Sam turns and faces the cave. Darkness ahead, gray light behind. Hard rain soaking through to his skin, chilling his body to ice. Nauseated and terrified of losing his wife and child, of failing his mission, of failing what could be his final test, Sam walks into the cave.

Cave

July 1945

The stench of urine, feces, rotting and gangrenous flesh burns Sam's nose and eyes.

The troops stand at attention. "Sergeant Nagata," says Oshima. "Status report."

"Yes, sir! Eight dead. Ten wounded. Of the wounded five have gangrene. Thirty-seven able-bodied men remaining, sir. Medical supplies gone. Ammo low. Less than three grenades per man. Two knee mortars intact, but no shells left. Water supply good, but no food for the last two days." The sergeant's voice trembles and cracks. "Sir, when you called to us just now, we were debating whether or not to cook and eat the flesh of our dead comrades."

Captain Oshima addresses his men. "In twenty minutes the Americans will attack. As you know, we were never expected to prevail over them. Our main forces are making their stand in the south. Our mission was to act as a diversion, to engage and delay American troops here, relieving pressure on our forces in southern Okinawa. Therefore, we will hold this position to the last man. We will not surrender."

Oshima's men stare at Sam, waiting near the cave entrance. "This is Sergeant Hamada Isamu. He wishes to speak with you."

Sam advances until he stands next to Captain Oshima.

"We don't want to listen to him! We have no respect for any Japanese who allows himself to be used as a pawn of the Americans. We killed the previous two dogs."

"Sergeant Nagata, you will give this man your full attention. I gave him my word that he would be allowed to speak to you." After that no one speaks. Even the wounded listen. But all they can hear is the sound of the steadily falling rain. Sam has gone absolutely still. The captain feels waves of energy rippling like heat off Sam. *He's diving,* thinks Oshima, *diving to the deepest center within himself.*

Finally, Sam speaks, and his voice is clear and resonant, yet so gentle that it takes the men by surprise. They strain to catch his words. "If I wanted a bowl to hold water, I would use porcelain, glass, or metal. I would use wood or waxed paper or even my hands. But never in a million lifetimes would I think of using smoke. To use a cloud as a vessel to hold water . . . the vessel itself is made of water. Just listen to this rain. How could any cloud hold so much water?

"You men are like clouds. You've been asked to hold on to yourselves. To hold on, and hold on, and hold on. I see the exhaustion in your eyes. You have performed far above and beyond the call of duty. You're all heroes. You deserve to let go. You've earned the right to release all the tension you hold. And rest.

"What Captain Oshima told you about the Americans preparing to attack is true. The marines have been ordered to burn out this cave. There is a tank positioned just beyond the ridge. Instead of a cannon, its main weapon is a long-distance flamethrower. It can shoot a stream of burning liquid one hundred yards.

"As part of my duties I go to hospitals and interrogate wounded prisoners. Last month I spoke with a Japanese soldier captured at Iwo Jima. He told me that when the tanks burned his bunker, the men in his unit died without inflicting a single wound on an American. He was the only survivor. He said the sound of his friends being killed was like chicken frying.

"When I was young, I studied the code of the samurai warrior. I understand Bushido and the significance of dying honorably. Most Americans have never heard of Bushido. They do not understand why Japanese soldiers are so willing to sacrifice their lives. They do not see you as human. They do not understand the pain and sorrow in the hearts of Japanese soldiers ordered to die. I do. My flesh and blood and bone are just as Japanese as your own. I know that we are as sensitive to fear and pain and grief as any other human. I know how I would feel if I had to sacrifice my life. That is why I respect you for the iron in your spirits."

Sam turns and looks straight into the eyes of Captain Oshima. Sam does not raise his voice, but he pours all the strength of his *ki* into his words. Not the *ki* of a lethal spear thrust, but the *ki* of compassion, one's purest empathy with the heart of another. "Sir, with my deepest, most profound, and humble respect, I make this offer: if you and your men lay down your arms and leave this cave with me, I promise that you will all be allowed to die with honor.

"You will be given food and water. You can bathe and wash your uniforms. Your wounded will be given medical treatment and painkillers. You will be allowed to put pen to paper. Then to die by your own hands. You may have seconds to minimize your suffering.

"After the war, I will deliver your ashes and your letters to your families in Japan.

"If you remain in this cave, you will all be burned to death. You will never receive proper burial. Your families will never know what became of you.

"Your mission was to divert and engage the marines for as long as possible. If you're burned in this cave, your mission will be over. However, if you surrender, the marines will be forced to guard you. Their medics will treat your wounded. You will be keeping them occupied for as long as you remain alive. And if you all go to your deaths like true samurai, your story will be passed from marine to marine until every American soldier on Okinawa carries your memory in his heart and mind. You could win a great moral and psychological victory."

The captain has difficulty speaking. "I am deeply touched by your kindness."

"Don't trust him, sir!" screams Sergeant Nagata. "He's lying. We'll all be tortured and killed like dogs."

"Silence!" says the captain. "Sergeant Hamada, are you sure you can convince your commanding officer to honor your terms? I don't mean to sound ungrateful or cynical, but your terms are so . . . kind and generous. And from their behavior and all the conversations I overheard, I know the marines hate us. Why would they give us what we want most?"

"You're not cynical, Captain. It's true, no American GI feels kindly toward Japanese soldiers. But you must bear in mind that to the Americans, my offer to allow you to kill yourselves will sound like a terrible punishment. My commanding officer hates all Japanese. He won't think of seppuku as a kindness. He'll think of it as a mass execution."

The captain nods thoughtfully.

"Sir," says Sergeant Nagata, "let's not wait for their attack. Let's attack them immediately. Even though we're all killed, at least we'll die fighting. Let's kill this American dog and attack at once. Sir, please, lead our final charge."

"That is not an option." Sam checks his watch. "Captain, the hour you owe me is not yet up. If you decide not to surrender, you must return with me as my prisoner. The only way that you can die with your men is if you accept my terms."

"What?" Sergeant Nagata raises his rifle. "You can't take away our captain!"

Instantly, all the soldiers aim their weapons and surround Sam. Men grab him from both sides, their fingers gaunt as animal claws. They hold him so desperately that they tear open the front of Sam's shirt.

Sam gazes steadily past the ring of bayonets pointing at him. "Captain Oshima, I'm allowing you one minute to make your decision."

Oshima stares at Sam's torn shirtfront, at the blue silk *omamori* dangling alongside Sam's dog tags. "What kind of man are you?" says Oshima. "Born of pure-blooded Japanese parents. Yet you wear an American uniform and make war against Japan. I don't understand what goes on inside you."

Without a moment's hesitation, Sam repeats an ancient quotation, one which every Japanese student learns. *"Ko naran to hosseba chu naran; chu naran to hosseba ko naran."* The words belonged to a samurai named Taira-no-Shigemori. If Shigemori wished to give his parents filial piety, he would have to be disloyal to the emperor; and if he was loyal to the emperor, he would have to go against his parents. Sometimes a person faces terrible choices because of a conflict of loyalties. Every soldier in the cave understands what Sam is trying to say, and they all hear the sincerity, pain, and resolution in his voice.

Captain Oshima says, "Sergeant Hamada, I accept your gift. On behalf of my men and our families, I thank you. I realize that you may have great difficulty convincing your commanding officer to honor the terms you've offered us. Please do your best on our behalf. I place our lives and honor into your care."

The Japanese soldiers release Sam. Sam salutes to Captain Oshima. The captain and all his men return Sam's salute.

"Lay down your weapons," says Sam. "Small arms and bayonets here. Grenades there. The marines will search you. If they discover any weapons on you, they'll think you're trying to trick them. Once outside the cave, be careful with your wounded. The ground is slippery because of the rain. Form two lines. Wait here. When I call, come forward without hesitation."

Sam goes to the cave mouth. "Colonel Wright," he shouts, "the Japanese troops have surrendered."

"Surrendered?"

"Yes, sir. They're ready to come out now."

"Hot damn! Good work, Sergeant."

"Colonel, make sure our men hold their fire."

"You got it, Sergeant. You men hear that? Hold your fire! Hold your fire! The Japs are surrendering."

Sam listens to Captain Oshima addressing his men. "We are about to present ourselves to the enemy. We will go forward with dignity. We will show these Americans how Japanese face death. Understood?"

The Japanese troops—filthy, hollow-eyed, and gaunt, half-crazed from exhaustion and starvation—do their best to shout in unison, "Yes, sir!"

Captain Oshima turns to Sam. "We're ready."

Sam nods.

Oshima gives the order. "Forward march!"

Test

JULY 1945

THE JAPANESE TROOPS MARCH OUT OF THE CAVE INTO THE RAIN. WATER cascades down the sides of the ravine around rocks and tangled corpses. Fighting his nausea, Sam remains at the bottom of the ravine to help carry the wounded.

Stumbling and sliding, Oshima's men climb toward the waiting marines. Suddenly, Sergeant Nagata, partway up the slope, slips and falls facedown onto the decomposing corpse of a Japanese officer. Nagata struggles to get up. But the more he thrashes, the more the corpse disintegrates. Horrified, Nagata begins screaming.

"Hold your fire! No one moves!" Sam shouts the order in both English and Japanese as he climbs toward Nagata. Sam takes off his helmet, lets it drop rolling into the ravine. He strips off his shirt and undershirt, throws them aside. He removes his dog tags and *omamori,* slips them into his pocket.

Screaming continuously, Sergeant Nagata grabs a sword and a grenade from the body of the dead Japanese officer. Nagata is dead, too, but he doesn't know it. His lungs still draw enough air to feed his throat-scraping screams, but all along the ridge the marines level their sights on him. Colonel Wright and Sergeant Clay yell repeatedly for everyone to hold their fire. Nagata's life hangs by a spider's strand. One snap and he joins the corpses in the ravine.

Sam has trouble seeing Nagata through the heavy rain until he is very close. White froth bubbles from Nagata's mouth. Mud and gore smear his uniform. Rotting flesh and wiggling maggots stick to his face. Screaming, Nagata slashes the air with the sword. Sam stops just beyond the whooshing arc of the blade. Nagata pauses for breath, and Sam calls out, "Itsuo!"

"What?" Nagata squints through the rain. "Who said that? Who's there?"

"*Omae no aniki da.* It's your older brother."

"*Niisan?* Older brother?" Nagata's voice cracks. "*Oniisan,* save me! Please, please, save me."

"Itsuo, you must be tired. I'll carry you the rest of the way." Smoothly, with infinite gentleness, Sam turns and crouches in front of Nagata.

Naked back exposed and vulnerable, Sam closes his eyes and waits. In the deafening rain, Sam throws himself away, empties himself, becomes *mu.* Hears, but with more than just his ears, Nagata's awkward, hesitant footsteps drawing closer, stopping. Senses, but not with any bodily sense, Nagata raising the sword to strike, the heat of Nagata's eyes focused on the back of Sam's neck.

No hint of fear or tension in his body, Sam waits, full moon on lacquer black pond, absolutely still. He opens his eyes and inhales the colors spread before him. So many colors. Rich, subtle, glistening with rain.

Life, death, the gods roll the dice . . .

No one moves. There is only the sound of wind and rain and running water.

Then Nagata climbs onto Sam's back. With the sword still clutched in one hand and the grenade in the other, Nagata throws his arms around Sam.

"Hold on tight, Itsuo." Sam straightens his knees and lifts Nagata off the ground.

Nagata begins sobbing. The razor edge of the sword trembles within an inch of Sam's left jugular. The grenade is jammed against Sam's right ear.

Bent forward, eyes on the ground, one careful, fully conscious step at a time, Sam carries Nagata up the slope to the ridge.

Gently, as if retrieving toys from a sleeping child, Captain Oshima disarms Nagata and passes the sword and grenade to a totally dumbfounded Sergeant Clay.

Manuscript

JULY 1945

THREE HOURS LATER IT IS STILL RAINING.

Sam, Abe Berman, and Colonel Wright sit in the interrogation tent. Assembled on the table are all the documents retrieved from the cave. Sam has been translating them for Abe and the colonel. Maps, the unit's tactical logbook, and the communications log are all intact. Sam thought they had captured a treasure trove, but so far neither Abe nor the colonel has shown any interest. They finish skimming through the military papers. Now, only the Japanese soldiers' personal papers remain—wrinkled and stained letters from home, a few notebooks and diaries.

Sam unties a silver-gray silk cord and opens the waterproof canvas wrapping the captain's personal diary. He takes out a photograph of Oshima's wife and two children.

Abe fans the diary pages. "Nothing." He passes it to Sam.

"You're going so fast," says Colonel Wright, "how can you be sure?"

"It's not in there."

"Look again."

"I'm sick of this."

"Damn it, Professor, we're all just as tired as you are."

Sam glances up. Colonel Wright appears to regret what he has just said. Frowning, he lights a cigarette.

Sam studies Oshima's notebook. "This isn't really a diary. These aren't daily entries. Several short essays. But mostly, it's poetry." Sam comes to some loose pages, watercolor sketches, scenes of a city: streets, people and shops, a park with tall buildings in the background. "This artwork was done by a friend of his. This is a manuscript. A collaboration. A book of paintings and poems. Apparently Captain Oshima wrote these poems during the three years he lived in the United States."

"How do you know?" asks Colonel Wright.

"According to the captions, the drawings are of New York City. And so are all these poems."

"I told you it was nothing," says Abe.

"They were going to title their book *The Manhattan Project*."

Abe and Colonel Wright both jump as if hit by an electric shock. "That's it!"

Sam is thrown into utter confusion. "What?"

Without offering any explanations, Wright orders Sam to begin translating.

"I walk through the winter rain. It's night,
and I'm alone. The rain speaks a familiar language,
but this is not my home. I think of the village of my birth,
of forests of bamboo and pine, green rice bowing under
slanting gray rain. Here I smell coffee, and I hear a flute.
Not shakuhachi—*this music is bright as polished silver,*
and the melody doesn't follow the logic of my childhood. But
I understand the feelings in that silver voice. It says: 'I'm alone.
I hurt.' The language of the human heart needs no translation.
It says: 'I miss those I left at home. I'm poor and struggling.
But, Mother, do not weep for me. I am young and
full of dreams in this city of chances and choices.
Someday I will return with gifts for you.' "

Sam turns the page and continues translating.

"I walk everywhere. On my face I show nothing.
But as I inhale the electric air, I feel it glowing in me
like sunlight in the eyes of trees. I love this energy!

I love this feeling—delicate as the songs and
shadows of tiny birds—it wraps around my throat
like a scarf ready to fly at the slightest start.
As if to weight it to the earth, the buildings they call
skyscrapers stand like stone gods or demons—"

"That's enough, Sergeant," says Colonel Wright. He takes a notebook from his pocket. "On April thirteenth, our offshore listening posts intercepted a radio message sent by Captain Oshima."

Sam flips through the pages of the Japanese communications log. "April thirteenth, 1945. Final transmission to headquarters: We will die gloriously for—"

"Skip that part. The last two lines contained a personal message."

"Yes, sir," says Sam. "I see it. It's to someone on Colonel Yahara's staff. The message reads: 'We should have completed our Manhattan Project sooner. I'm grateful we were able to take it as far as we did.' "

"Who was that message sent to?" asks Abe. "Does it say?"

"Captain Tamura Yasuji."

"And is he the same man who did the artwork in Captain Oshima's journal?"

Sam checks. "Yes, you're right. Here it is. Tamura Yasuji."

Abe Berman and Colonel Wright grin at each other. "All right, Sergeant," says the colonel. "That'll be all. You can go and get some rest."

"Yes, sir. But when do you want me to finish translating these papers?"

"We're done here, Sergeant. We'll be leaving within the hour."

"I don't understand, sir. Have we found what we were looking for?"

"I believe we have." The colonel looks at Berman.

Abe Berman nods. "Yes. I think this is it."

Sam stares at Abe and the colonel, at their satisfied smiles and obvious sense of relief. "You're telling me that Kinji and Calvin died for these drawings and poems?"

The smiles disappear from Abe and Colonel Wright's faces.

"This whole thing was a big mistake, wasn't it?" says Sam.

"I'm sorry, Sam," says Abe Berman. "But you must believe us. We had no choice. We had to check this out. We had to be sure. If the Japanese knew about our Manhattan Project or had one of their own—"

"Stop!" says Wright. "Not another word. Sergeant, everything you've seen and heard on this mission is absolutely top secret. You will take it with you to the grave."

"Sir, I don't understand."

"Believe me, Sergeant. Someday you will."

"Yes, sir." At the entrance to the tent, Sam pauses. "Sir, have you decided what to do about Captain Oshima and his men?"

"They'll be transferred to a special POW camp where they'll be kept isolated for the duration of the war."

"But I promised they'd be allowed to die honorably by their own hands."

"I'm sorry, Sergeant. I can't allow it. My orders were to get everything and everyone out of that cave intact. Orders from the highest level. I don't have a choice in the matter. Once headquarters sees Captain Oshima's notebook, I'm pretty sure that'll be the end of it. However, just in case HQ orders further interrogation, those prisoners must be kept alive, even if we have to chain them hand and foot, and feed them through intravenous injection."

"Sir, they'll feel betrayed. They might even stage an uprising."

"Then you'd better talk to them, Sergeant. Listen, I want you to know that I understand their desire to die honorably. When I was at West Point, I had a class in Oriental history. I have a soldier's respect for the code of the samurai. However, in this situation my orders leave no room for personal discretion. The stakes are too high. Honor is a luxury none of us can afford. For us there is only duty. And duty is something every Japanese soldier understands. I know you've given your word. I'm sorry. You're just going to have to swallow your pride."

"Yes, sir."

"Sergeant," says Abe, "please, try not to be upset. Because you're Japanese American, you're able to see and understand both sides of this war. If anyone can explain things to Captain Oshima and his men, it's you."

Sam nods, thinking that being Japanese American did not make his task easier. *Because I not only see both sides, I feel both sides.*

Honor

JULY 1945

Sam walks through the rain to where the prisoners are being held. Surrounded by marines, the prisoners sit eating K rations under several large tarps. Sam motions to Captain Oshima. They stand at the edge of a tarp just out of the rain. "I'm very sorry to tell you this. My commanding officer cannot allow you to commit seppuku."

"Cannot or will not?"

"He's under orders to keep you alive."

"For later execution?"

"No. You're to be sent to a special POW camp."

"We'll resist."

"It's useless."

"Back there in the cave, you said your commanding officer hated us. You weren't lying. He knows our humiliation will be a terrible form of torture."

"No, sir. Truly, he understands your wish to die with honor. But he has no choice. He must follow his orders. Besides, I think the colonel's a good Christian."

"And Christians abhor suicide."

"That's right. They consider it a sin."

Oshima recoils, offended and hurt. "Sin?"

"Captain, embrace your fate. Let the boys return to their mothers and fathers. You and the rest of the husbands go home to your wives and children."

"Sergeant, my men deserve to die with their honor intact. Without honor, their lives would be like broken cups, useless to hold the sweet, pure water of an honest life. They deserve to die as good and honorable soldiers."

"You all deserve to live as good and honorable men."

Captain Oshima's face reddens. His voice grates with anger. "If we don't commit seppuku, we will lose our honor."

"To honor death is easy. To honor life is hard. To live with shame . . . To live with the shame of defeat and surrender, to return and rebuild Japan . . . the gods could not give you a greater challenge. If you cannot see what a sacred gift this is, then all your training and your search for meaning in life have been for nothing. Captain Oshima, I know how hard this is for you. But do not take the easy way. Truly, your real test is just beginning."

Oshima shakes his head, dazed, suddenly uncertain. "My test? But honor—"

"Honor? Captain Oshima, when you began your training and committed yourself to the path of the samurai, did you ever think that it would lead to what's in that ravine? We can smell it from here. Maggot food."

"Their spirits are at peace."

"Their spirits are lost in the flames of hell! Their spirits wail over how their lives were torn from them so far from home."

"How do you know?"

"I felt it when I walked among them. Didn't you?"

"All my life I was trained to fight. To the death."

"I thought that, too. It wasn't until today that I realized all my training and discipline have been about how to live with awareness, courage, and compassion. I'm lucky my sensei was a patient man. I've always been a slow student."

Oshima nods. "Me, too." He lowers his voice to a whisper. "I'm afraid to go home."

"When the war's over, Japan will have urgent need of you and your men. Show mercy to the families waiting for your return. Be compassionate to yourself. Do not die here. Go home, work hard to repair the damage of the war. Die of old age in your own bed."

"But how can I live with my shame?"

"I think when you go home and see your wife and children, your joy and gratitude will far outweigh your shame."

"I think you're right. I think your words are true and wise, but what if you're wrong?"

"You can always kill yourself. You don't have to do it today."

The captain flinches with shock, but he detects no hint of mockery in Sam's eyes, only compassion. "I will think about this."

"Good. At least wait until the rain stops. The men can't build funeral pyres in this downpour."

Now Sam is joking. Captain Oshima smiles and relaxes. "I was going to ask if you would act as my second."

"I would have considered it an honor."

"We could still—"

"No," says Sam, "I'm sorry. I know I gave you my word, but I cannot go against the direct orders of my commanding officer."

"I understand. It's a matter of priorities."

"Yes. I've no choice but to live with the shame of having broken my word."

Captain Oshima nods. "I know how much that pains you. So I release you from your promise." After a grave silence, he continues. "And having done so, my men and I will have to live . . . with our fate."

Sam nods. "Thank you, sir."

"I said some rude, harsh things to you in the tent during our *shogi* game. I thought it would shake your concentration and help me win. I apologize. Perhaps we can play another game. And this time I really would like to have an honest and open conversation with you."

"I'm sorry, sir. I would like that, too, but I have to leave."

"Well, then, good luck. I hope you survive the war. I will never forget your kindness, Sergeant Hamada. Thank you and *sayonara*."

First Sam and Oshima salute each other and then they bow.

"*Sayonara,* Captain Oshima."

Sam walks away. Oshima calls out, "Sergeant Hamada."

Sam turns.

"Your sensei would be proud of you."

Hometown

July 1945

Homeward bound in a B-29 over the Pacific, Colonel Wright asleep, Abe asks, "Are you married, Sergeant?"

"Yes."

"Any children?"

"A son. Six months old."

"Say, that's terrific. Where're you from, Sergeant?"

"Right now, I'm stationed at Camp Savage and Fort Snelling in Minnesota. Before Pearl Harbor, my wife and I were living in Lodi, California. That's a little town near Sacramento."

"Were you born in California?"

"No. My wife was. I was born in Hawaii."

"Is that where your parents are?"

"My father's dead. My mother and brother and sister are in Japan."

"What are their names?"

"Their names?"

"I enjoy learning new languages. I like the sound of the Japanese." Abe grins.

Abe reminds Sam of his uncle Genzo—full of curiosity, always hungry for a good conversation. Sam smiles. "My mother's name is Ohatsu. Bunji is my younger brother, and my little sister is named Akemi."

"Ohatsu, Bunji, and Akemi."

Sam is impressed by the quickness of Abe's memory and his ability to pronounce the names almost perfectly on his first try.

"You must miss them."

"Yes. I haven't seen them since I left home at the age of nine."

Abe takes a map of Japan from his jacket pocket. "I got this from a bomber pilot on Iwo Jima. He had three copies. This one's brand-new. I traded a Zippo lighter and a Timex for it. Show me where they live."

Abe and Sam unfold the map. "In the last letter I got from my sister, Akemi said my brother had been drafted and sent to Manchuria. I don't know if he's still alive. So in the house in Honura village where I grew up, there are only my mother and Akemi."

"Honura," says Abe. "Never heard of it."

"I would be very surprised if you had. Actually, Honura is what Americans would call a district or borough. I've always thought of it as my little village, but many years ago Honura was swallowed up by one of Japan's larger cities."

"Which one? Show me."

Sam touches a circle on the map and lovingly pronounces the name of his hometown.

"Hiroshima."

Part 5

JUNE 1945–JUNE 1947

Bunji's Ashes

JUNE 1945

SITTING ON THE TATAMI FLOOR OF THEIR HOUSE IN HONURA, AKEMI listens to her mother and brother arguing over why the B-29s have spared Hiroshima. "Tokyo, Osaka, Yokohama, and Kobe have been bombed repeatedly. Over sixty of our major cities have been destroyed. Even Kure, only twelve miles away, has been bombed." Bunji coughs then continues. "The Americans know Hiroshima is an industrial and military center. But they've never touched us. Why? Because they are saving Hiroshima for a special weapon's test."

Mama shakes her head at her son's cynicism. Ohatsu believes that her weekly visits to the temple of the goddess of mercy give them divine protection. "Every time the bombers fly over Hiroshima, Kannon-sama spreads her cloudy white veil over the city, and the pilots and bombardiers can't see us."

Bunji coughs and spits blood. A month ago he returned from Manchuria carrying tuberculosis and a package for headquarters. The package contained a status report and letters from his unit. Bunji knew the letters were last words, and that he, too, was terminal. The doctors had no cure to offer beyond an admonition for complete bed rest. The military hospitals were so overcrowded that Bunji was given a discharge. Everyone understood that he had been sent home to die.

As a last resort Bunji decided to self-medicate his TB with the locally favored folk remedy: tobacco. Akemi knelt beside her brother, and while he coughed and spit blood, she lovingly lit cigarette after cigarette for him. When he became too weak to keep one going, Akemi put them to her own lips and alternated puffs with him.

On Thursday, June 21, 1945, in the evening after a blistering-hot day, Bunji succumbs to his tuberculosis. Akemi and her mother place Bunji's white porcelain jar of ashes with his father's under the gravestone behind the little temple dedicated to the goddess of mercy.

Akemi visits often with flowers and incense. One day in July she is in the cemetery when the air raid sirens wail. She looks up and sees a hundred gleaming B-29s flying through a cloudless sky. She cringes among the gravestones like a trapped animal. But the bomb bays remain closed. On that day the planes are hunting other people in other places.

B-San

AUGUST 1945

DURING THE NIGHT OF AUGUST 5, AKEMI AND HER MOTHER ARE STARtled by two air raid warnings; the first at nine and the second at eleven, both false alarms.

In the morning Ohatsu awakes at six as usual and prepares vegetable soup for breakfast. A half hour later Akemi gets up and dresses for work. They are sipping their soup when the sirens wail and Radio Hiroshima broadcasts another air raid warning. The women don their padded cotton air raid bonnets and hurry to the neighborhood shelter. An old man arriving after them says, "Don't worry. There's only one B-san up there buzzing in circles like a dragonfly."

A group of men and boys venture out to check. "He's right. What a waste of time." By the time the all-clear sounds, Akemi is walking across a bridge halfway to work, and her mother is home, washing the breakfast dishes.

The lone plane that triggers the 7:09 A.M. alert is the *Straight Flush,* a weather scout, piloted by Captain Claude Eatherly. At 7:24, Captain Eatherly sends a report: "Cloud cover less than three-tenths all altitudes. Advice: bomb primary."

The message is received by three B-29s: the *Enola Gay,* the *Great Artiste* and *Number 91.* In her bomb bay the *Enola Gay* carries a slender uranium bomb named "Little Boy"—the nine-thousand-pound child conceived by the Manhattan Project.

The three B-29s approach Hiroshima from the northeast at 330 miles per hour. From six miles up no one on board can see people or even cars below. What they see shining in the morning sun is a city built on an alluvial fan divided by a river that splits into seven fingers draining into the calm waters of the Inland Sea.

The *Enola Gay's* bombardier, Major Thomas Ferebee, hunches over his sight and zeros in on the Aioibashi, the one and only T-shaped bridge in Hiroshima. At 8:15 A.M., "Little Boy" is released from the belly of the *Enola Gay.* The pilot, Captain Paul W. Tibbets, banks hard and heads away. The second plane, Captain Chuck Sweeney's *Great Artiste,* drops radio-transmitting measuring instruments that float down on parachutes. The third plane, Captain George Marquardt's *Number 91,* lags behind. Its role in the mission is to photograph the event.

Forty-three seconds after its release "Little Boy" detonates at its preset altitude, 1,890 feet above the ground.

Captain Tibbets reports that shortly after detonation, he feels a tingling sensation in his mouth and notices a taste of lead.

The *Enola Gay's* tail gunner, Staff Sergeant George R. Caron, his eyes protected behind heavy dark glasses, witnesses a pinkish-purplish flash. After the initial flash, he removes his glasses. One minute later, nine miles away, he spots something huge chasing the aircraft. Heat, condensing moisture along its face, makes the shock wave visible. He watches the wave, traveling at twelve hundred feet per second, overtake and hit the plane. The *Enola Gay* bucks and rattles as though struck by an enormous fist. A second, lesser shock wave hits the plane shortly after the first.

Two gentle love pats from "Little Boy."

Behind them a purple mushroom cloud rises to 45,000 feet. A bubbling purple-gray mass of smoke with a fiery red core. Down at the spreading base, the smoke is so dense it looks like boiling tar. All around the base, flames are shooting and springing up.

In the *Enola Gay* the captain lights his pipe.

Flash

AUGUST 6, 1945

AT THE CENTER OF THE NUCLEAR EXPLOSION, THE EPICENTER, THERE IS a blue-white flash, as a star pulses into being for an instant. For a single beat, the heart of that star is a million degrees Fahrenheit. Energy blasts outward in every direction. Directly under the epicenter, the point called Ground Zero, or hypocenter, two hundred yards from the T-shaped Aioi bridge, is the courtyard of the Shima hospital. At this point the temperature hits eleven thousand degrees Fahrenheit. The downward pressure reaches eight tons per square yard. The only things that remain upright are the concrete pillars at the clinic's entrance. And these are driven into the earth like giant tent pegs.

Out to six hundred yards from the hypocenter, ceramic roof tiles with a melting point of 2,300 degrees Fahrenheit dissolve.

To one thousand yards, the surfaces of granite building stones melt.

Bridges sag under the weight of "Little Boy," then buckle when the shock waves hit the surface of the rivers and rebound against the undersides of the bridges. No engineers in their most drunken, insane nightmares could have imagined such loads imposed upon their bridges from below. Steel girders snap and bend like licorice sticks.

A half mile from Ground Zero, the flash of the bomb's single heartbeat burns the silhouette of bridge posts and railings onto the road—like a photographic negative—an eerie white shadow of posts and railings against a black, charred road surface.

All buildings, except for a few ferroconcrete structures, within a radius of one mile are destroyed.

Wooden buildings two miles out burst into flames.

Roofs blow off houses five miles away.

When the shock wave reaches eight miles, it still has enough force to shatter windows facing the hypocenter.

In Kure, twelve miles from Hiroshima, people think an ammunition dump has exploded.

The shock wave ripples outward in concentric rings. Then it reverses direction and sucks inward toward the hypocenter, creating a whirlwind.

When they left the bomb shelter that morning, Akemi had said, "Mama, don't forget I won't be home for dinner. Tonight is Makio-san's birthday party."

"Give your fiancé my best wishes. And tell him I said he should spend time with his guests and not devote all his attention to you."

Akemi blushed. Her marriage had been arranged in the traditional way. However, due to the uncertainties of the war, Makio and Akemi had decided to postpone the wedding. On the one hand, Akemi felt a sense of urgency, which she traced to a fear of loss. On the other, she savored the delay, because it prolonged the romance of premarital courtship.

When Akemi arrived at work, her department head asked her for some information from an account that was over five years old. The older files were stored in the basement. Akemi opened the door and started down the narrow staircase when a coworker called to her. Akemi turned. Her boss was waving a folder and smiling sheepishly. He stood near the large plate-glass window that looked onto the street. Through the window, Akemi could see people walking and a trolley rolling—

A flash of light.

So brilliant it obliterated every shadow, overpowered every eye, left nothing visible except itself. Absolute white light.

An instant of wonder.

Everyone in the office turned toward the window.

Blinded by the flash, Akemi stumbled, bumping her shin on a stair. Regaining her balance, bent over in pain, she was reaching down to rub her leg when the shock wave hit, shattering the window, blasting away the front of the building, the walls, desks, chairs, people, everything.

Black Rain

AUGUST 6, 1945

AKEMI HAMADA REGAINS CONSCIOUSNESS.

She opens her eyes, blinks repeatedly, touches her face.

Absolute darkness.

Akemi thinks she has gone blind. Then she hears the scream of nails pulling loose and wood cracking overhead. With a tremendous crash the basement ceiling gives way, and a mangled trolley car drops through, nearly crushing her. The rear of the trolley settles to the floor of the basement. The front remains snagged on the joists of the floor above. She thinks she must be mad or dreaming—what monstrous hand could have lifted the trolley from its tracks and tossed it through the front of the building into the center of her office?

Like an ant on a cracker box, using the trolley as a ramp, Akemi crawls up the side of the trolley, out of the basement toward daylight. All the trolley windows are broken. She glances inside, sees blood-splashed seats, crumpled, mangled bodies. She looks away, keeps crawling, hears metal creaking and glass crackling beneath her hands and knees, but not another sound.

She stops. Absolute silence.

How can there be such unearthly stillness in a city of 400,000 people?

Then she hears the soft *snap* of burning wood, smells smoke, and she crawls faster, exits through the jagged hole into the smoldering rubble that was once her office, small flames and smoke sprouting like weeds all around. Wind growing.

She looks up at a monstrous pillar so dark and dense she does not recognize it as smoke. Cannot comprehend the hellish cobra, 100,000 souls just swallowed, still hungry for more, roiling purple-black body veined with orange fire, writhing toward the sun, spreading, blotting out the perfect August sky, casting her into darkness and howling wind.

Makio-san! Akemi heads for the center of the city to find her fiancé.

She reaches a bridge. Halfway across she sees a man on a bicycle, apparently exhausted; he leans against a lamppost. But, no, he is dead, his burnt body black as a statue made of melted tires, body and bike welded to the lamppost and bridge railing.

Floating on the river, bodies and parts of bodies, up and downstream, as far as she can see. The narrow banks crawling with the wounded, burned, and bleeding, dragging themselves to water, drinking and splashing, slipping, falling, drowning before her eyes.

Someone bumps her shoulder—a man dressed in a suit of tiny mirrors stumbles past her on the bridge. No. Not mirrors. Shards of glass, the man's naked body is impaled by a thousand splinters of glass.

Akemi continues across the bridge, now jammed with people moving against her. All naked and burned. Akemi wants to run, but her legs begin to shake. She looks down and finds her clothes are tattered rags. She has lost her shoes. A piece of metal juts from her right thigh. She pulls, and it slides out easily as a knife drawn from a sheath.

She limps up a street of smashed houses, many burning, the rest beginning to smolder. A woman and two children are pinned under shattered beams and roof tiles. People stand watching helplessly; the flames are so hot, no one can get close. Akemi puts her hands over her ears to block the screams of the burning mother and children.

She comes to a broken, burning temple, sees people gathered around a large granite cistern in the yard. She has never felt her throat so parched. When Akemi goes to dip her hands in the water, she finds half the people draped over the lip of the cistern dead, the rest terribly wounded. Naked, floating face-up in the water, a dead pregnant woman. Other than a tiny cut in the corner of her mouth, there seems to be no marks on her pale body.

Akemi cups her hands and drinks the water.

She stares down at the reflection of her face. A long deep gash runs across her left cheek. She hears footsteps on gravel, turns as a woman approaches, a teacher leading the survivors of her classroom—all young girls, naked and burned, staggering, elbows bent, hands extended, the flesh of their hands and arms melted like candle wax, bones bared in the flickering firelight.

Akemi leaves the temple yard. A wall of fire rolls toward her like a tsunami. Akemi has come as far as she can. She cannot reach Makio-san. She must turn back or die. Already the street behind her is partly blocked by flames. The burning temple collapses onto the cistern. Standing in the roasting wind, Akemi hears inhuman screams. A white horse runs across the temple yard and into the street. Eyes crazed, mouth frothing, hooves clattering on the pavement, the horse twists and kicks, trying to buck the monkey-demon flames clinging to its back.

Akemi feels something cold and wet strike the top of her head.

Rain.

Drops larger than grapes.

Blacker than ink.

Black rain.

Akemi follows the flaming horse. Threads her way around piles of burning rubble, the wide street shrunken to a crooked footpath through a forest of fire. Her spirit separates from her drenched and shivering body, swirls upward like a scrap of paper into the tumbling smoke, hot wind, and icy black rain. She looks down through the dying light, sees herself fall, and a hunched figure, back cloaked in raw burnt flesh cracked open to the bone, stooping and kneeling beside her, gently taking her elbow, helping her up, then both staggering forward, joining the procession of ghouls slouching through the man-made hell.

Atonement

AUGUST 1945

RETURNING TO MINNESOTA FROM OKINAWA, THE WORDS *HUSH-HUSH* stopping all questions about where he has been or what he has been doing, Sam resumes his teaching duties with renewed fervor, taking great satisfaction from the progress of his students. But everything changes with the news of the bombing of Hiroshima. Sam absorbs it—piece by piece over the following days, the reports and pictures deceptively simple yet barely comprehensible—the horror of America's latest weapon.

Sam takes it personally. Hiroshima is his hometown. When he reads "destruction beyond a ten-mile radius . . . estimates of 100,000 killed by the blast, tens of thousands more dead and still dying of injuries, burns, and radiation," the words pierce him like snake fangs. Each dose of new information injects fresh poison into his soul.

Keiko tries to help him, but he blocks her out, locking his emotions inside, his face distorted by migraines and nightmares. He never misses a day in his classroom. But Keiko sees the hellfire of Hiroshima glowing in Sam's eyes.

One night he brings home a map and a bottle of whiskey. She has never seen him drink alcohol before. He once told her he never did because of his father. She serves dinner, but he ignores her. She eats alone and watches him drinking and staring at the map with its concentric rings indicating degrees of destruction.

She leaves dinner on the table for him, washes her dishes, and takes care of the baby. Their studio apartment feels claustrophobic. When she says good-night to Sam, he does not respond. She tucks the baby in his crib, and drops into an exhausted sleep.

Keiko wakes in the middle of the night. Sam is hunched over the map. His bottle is almost empty. Gently, she calls him to bed, but he does not acknowledge her. Instead he rises and staggers into the bathroom to throw up. Keiko covers her ears and shuts her eyes. She hides her face under the covers to muffle her sobs.

Instead of bed Sam returns to the map. He compares it with an aerial photograph taken from a B-29. He recognizes the hills and rivers, the bridge where he fished, the shallow place where he learned to swim. His eyes follow a street line on the map, and he sees himself walking home from school . . . to his mother's house . . . within the ring two and a half miles from Ground Zero. *Destruction beyond a ten-mile radius. 100,000 dead.* His mother, brother, sister, former classmates and teachers, neighbors, shopkeepers, every face, every name, the entire population of his childhood before Hawaii, all dead.

Finger-snap deaths, he prays, hard but quick.

Bottle empty, so drunk and exhausted that he can no longer focus on the map, soaked in sweat and stinking of vomit, he finds himself in the cockpit of a B-29. He pushes and pulls, twisting the controls like taffy, but the plane remains on course. He hears the bomb bay doors open. He punches and kicks, shattering every instrument, but nothing he does stops the bomb from slipping out, and he feels the plane suddenly lift, freed of the enormous weight.

And then he is the bomb plummeting toward Hiroshima.

He sees the split-fingered river and Ogonzan hill and the forest where he played soldier with his friends and the dirt path to the cemetery and the temple of the goddess of mercy. He sees the tile roofs of Honura, his school, his street, his house.

No! No! No! His house. His house. His house.

In the garden his mother's face looks up at him. "Isamu!"

Crippled with a death-wish hangover, shaving in the morning, Sam finds his reflection hideous. The mirror steams over, obscuring it. He does not rub a clear spot. Instead he raises a finger and begins drawing lines on the hazed glass. Sam tallies the promises he has broken—one: when he was in Hawaii; he wrote his family and told his friends that he would stop working for Fujiwara-san. Two and three: He promised to send for Yuriko and marry her. Then he broke his promise to Fujiwara-san when he told Keiko about Yuriko and how Bidwell died. He promised Captain Oshima and his men that they would be allowed to die honorably by their own hands. . . . Did that count as one broken promise or one per Japanese soldier?

Sam had been raised to live according to an ancient code of honor. Thrown like a spear all the way to the mainland, planting his family's crest on American soil, Papa's winning lottery ticket, eldest son sworn to protect and care for his mother and siblings, Sam feels like every hope and promise in his life has been betrayed, perverted, and defiled.

He draws two more lines for the mother and sister he has failed to protect.

Coming out of the bathroom, Sam cannot meet Keiko's eyes. He leaves without eating, without touching or speaking to her or the baby.

Two days after the bombing of Hiroshima, Nagasaki receives the second A-bomb. One week later, Emperor Hirohito's voice, announcing Japan's surrender, is broadcast over the radio.

Keiko is overjoyed. She immediately begins planning their return to California.

Her spirit revives like a seedling reaching toward the light. Sam's is like a rock plummeting into the blind darkness of a deep-sea trench. In the weeks following Japan's surrender, Sam's depression grows more and more unbearable. Each time he reads or hears *Hiroshima,* another face or name from home—a relative, a teacher, classmate, or friend—swims before his mind's eye. Sam buries the dead in his heart, buries them deep, covers them with silence and stone. He feels damned, knowing the corpses will fester and rot, ooze poison into every cell of his body, pollute and quench every color in his soul of lights.

Whenever he speaks, he smells death on his breath, the unforgettable stench of the ravine in Okinawa. He carries it like a disease. Cancer at his core, inoperable.

Inoperable?

Perhaps not . . . perhaps there is a way. He begins to fantasize about seppuku, ritual disembowelment. From the first millisecond the idea occurs to him, it seduces him. Then as heroin does to an addict, it caresses him with each pulse in his veins.

Haunting him are the arguments against suicide that he offered to Captain Oshima. Every word had come from his heart. But now Sam realizes how easy it had been for him to challenge Oshima to live with his humiliation and pain. Breaking on the rack of his shame, learning that he is his own most diabolical and merciless torturer, Sam finds himself willing to do anything to stop the pain. Anything.

Seppuku. The idea becomes an obsession. One cut, and he will hurt no more.

His rational mind submits the word *atonement*. A good reason. One that any Japanese would respect as valid. Because to Japanese, shame is contagious. And one person's sacrificial act of atonement can cleanse the entire group, the family, of shame. Death's morphine voice whispers to Sam that Keiko would be better off without him polluting her life and the future of their innocent baby. Of course she would grieve, but then she would move on, ultimately feeling relieved and happy that his pain was over and that his shame had been cleansed. Seppuku—for one attuned to the code of a Japanese warrior, an honorable path out of an unlivable life.

Only two questions remain. When? Where?

Sam decides he will resettle Keiko and the baby in Lodi. Once they are safely home with family and friends, he will carry out his act of atonement. His decision made, Sam treats Keiko with infinite gentleness.

But Keiko doesn't fully trust it—something about Sam reminds her of the days when he was hiding the secret of Yuriko and the baby. He is sweet, but never fully present. His eyes seem cloaked and evasive. There is a numbness in Sam's voice. His skin feels different. Even his smell has changed. She tells herself these are symptoms of his terrible grief. But subconsciously, she senses his soul yearning for release from this plane of existence.

She begins to suspect the path Sam has chosen, but she cannot risk asking him; she fears that speaking of suicide might plant an idea that isn't there, except in her fears. So Keiko finds herself inwardly preparing for the awesome test that every wife of every samurai most dreads—the possibility that her love and loyalty will demand the unwavering acceptance of her husband's seppuku.

Bewildered and helpless to change or save him, Keiko concentrates all her energy into getting them home to California as quickly as possible.

Haircut

November 1945

Dewey arrives at Rohwer, his face and body aged, left arm encased in a cast and carried in a sling. He gives Al's bloodstained pocket diary to Shoji and Kuwano. "I've come to escort you back to California. Pack your things. We're going home. Keiko and Sam are already in Lodi. They've opened the Buddhist temple as a halfway house."

Shoji puts on his suit. Kuwano her best black dress, black hat, and black shoes with the thick high heels. They board a train in Little Rock and ride out of Arkansas into Texas. They stop at a station in a small town where they have to change trains. "We will wait here for about an hour," says Dewey as they cross the platform and look into the waiting room. Seeing no Asian faces in the crowd, Kuwano says she prefers to be outside in the fresh air. Dewey and Shoji put their luggage against the station wall near a bench in the shade. There are no empty spaces on the bench, but when Kuwano approaches, two big husky men in army uniforms stand and offer their seats to her.

Kuwano stares with astonishment into their gem blue eyes.

The two soldiers keep smiling and gesturing toward the bench until Kuwano bows to them and sits down. The space the men vacated is big enough for her and Shoji and Dewey, but only Kuwano sits.

"Pardon me, Sergeant," one of the men says to Dewey, "would you by any chance have served with the 100th/442nd?"

"Yes, I did."

"Well, sir, we . . . both of us . . . we were members of the Lost Battalion."

"That's where these folks lost their son," says Dewey. "And where I was wounded."

Both soldiers take off their hats and face Shoji and Kuwano. "We're very sorry about your son. We owe our lives to him."

Shoji's face pales at the mention of his son. Kuwano speaks, and Dewey translates. "She's happy her son made it possible for you to return to your mothers."

The soldiers nod. "Yes, ma'am. Thank you very much, ma'am. Sergeant, there are a few other guys from our outfit in that bar just across the street. We'd sure be grateful if you'd allow us to buy you a drink. I know the guys would be sorely disappointed if they missed a chance to meet you and shake your hand."

Dewey explains to Shoji and Kuwano. They both smile and tell him to go with his friends. Shoji watches Dewey and the two soldiers leave the station. Shoji notices a barbershop next to the bar. "I think I'll get a haircut to celebrate our going home. Will you be all right?"

Kuwano nods. "Don't worry about me. I'll stay and mind the baggage. I'm very happy sitting here in this lovely breeze on a bench that's not moving."

When Dewey returns thirty minutes later, he is accompanied by a half dozen soldiers. They are all laughing and talking loudly. Dewey is wearing a white cowboy hat and smoking a cigar.

Shoji's and Kuwano's faces are filled with hurt and anger.

Immediately, Dewey asks, "What's wrong? What happened?"

"Nothing," says Shoji.

"He couldn't get a haircut," says Kuwano. "The barber said, 'No Japs allowed.' "

Dewey's face turns red.

"Sergeant, is something wrong?"

Dewey explains.

Very gently, one of the soldiers, an officer, takes Shoji by the elbow. "Sir, please accompany us back to the barbershop. There's been a misunderstanding. We'll set things right, sir."

Shoji shakes his head. "No trouble."

"You go with them!" says Kuwano in Japanese. "Enough is enough!"

No one needs a translation. They can read the tone of her voice. Several men tip their hats to her. "Yes, ma'am, we'll take care of it right away."

"Don't worry, ma'am, we're gonna make sure your husband gets the best damn haircut of his life."

"Please, sir, come with us."

Kuwano watches the men go back across the street. Dewey and Shoji look so small next to the six big Texans. One soldier opens the door of the barbershop. The officer enters, then Shoji and Dewey, then the rest. Kuwano is surprised that all the men are able to squeeze inside the tiny barbershop.

The barber is sitting in his chair with a *Life* magazine. When the major enters, the barber looks up and smiles. The smile evaporates when Shoji and Dewey come in. The barber's expression changes to bewilderment when he sees the rest of the soldiers jam into his shop.

Without a word the soldiers surround his chair.

Then the major speaks. "Mister, this gentleman would like a haircut. Now, seeing as this is your shop, and this being the United States of America, I suppose it's your right to refuse service to anyone you choose. However, we've decided to give you a chance to reconsider."

One of the men, unable to restrain himself, blurts, "Or we're gonna bust everything in this place and stomp you right through the goddamn floor."

"My boy died at Iwo Jima," says the barber.

"We're all truly sorry to hear that," says the major. "You and this old gentleman have something in common. His son died in France."

"Died saving our lives," says another soldier.

"I didn't know," says the barber. "I thought he was just one of them damn Japs."

"We're Japanese Americans," says Dewey.

The barber looks confused.

"Why don't you give the gentleman a haircut," says the major. "And while you're at it, we'll tell you the story of how a bunch of Japanese-American boys busted through the German lines to rescue an outfit of Texans."

The barber stands. The major helps Shoji into the chair. Shoji slumps miserably. He hates being the center of all this attention. He feels totally humiliated.

The barber shakes out the white apron, then hesitates.

"Shoji-san," says Dewey in Japanese, "Al and I fought our battles. This one's yours. *Shikkarishite kudasai.* Be brave and resolute."

Shoji nods. He sits up straight and lifts his head with dignity. He looks into the barber's eyes. "My son and your son, both American soldiers . . .

both dead. I am very sorry about your son. If you do not want to cut my hair, it's okay. I know how a father feels."

"I'll cut your hair, sir," says the barber, throwing the white apron over Shoji. "I apologize if I offended you. I turned away several Japs before you ... I mean, Japanese ... I mean, Japanese Americans. Hell, I don't know what they were. But, anyhow, I turned them away because of my boy. I guess in my heart I knew those men had nothing to do with my son's death, but I'm just so angry and bitter ... because the war's over, and all the boys are coming home. All except my Jimmy."

"My son's name was Al."

"Al?"

"Al loved baseball. Did your boy Jimmy play baseball?"

"Oh, hell yes! He was the shortstop. And he was the best damn hitter on his high school team. They won the league his senior year."

"My son and your son are on the same team now. They play baseball all the time."

The barber brushes away some tears. "Yeah, that's right. They're up there right now playing baseball."

After his haircut, Shoji steps from the barbershop, and the barber follows him outside. "Mr. Yanagi, I'm sure glad you came in for a haircut. And I'm grateful these boys gave me a second chance with you. God bless you and your wife, sir. I can't tell you how much talking with you has comforted me." He offers his hand.

Shoji gives it a firm shake. "Good-bye, Mr. Baker. Thank you very much."

Shoji starts to walk away. Then he turns back. "The war is over."

"Yes, the war's over."

Shoji puts his hand flat on his chest. "It is time now for you, me, everybody, to heal."

"I hope so, sir. I hate feeling this way."

"First grieve. Then heal."

The barber nods in agreement. The two men shake hands one more time, then Shoji leaves and rejoins his wife.

Letter

APRIL 1946

Dᴵᴬᴸ ɢʟᴏᴡɪɴɢ ᴏʀᴀɴɢᴇ ᴏɴ ᴛʜᴇ ᴋɪᴛᴄʜᴇɴ ᴄᴏᴜɴᴛᴇʀ ᴏꜰ ᴛʜᴇ Lᴏᴅɪ Bᴜᴅ-
dhist temple, the Philco is tuned to a news broadcast. Walter Winchell announces, "In Tokyo the Allies have indicted Hideki Tojo with fifty-five
counts of war crimes and plotting to rule the world." Listening, Sam lies flat
on his back, his head under the sink and a pipe wrench in his hands. Sitting
on the floor beside him, his fifteen-month-old son plays with tools from a
red toolbox. Sam has just finished replacing the drainpipe when Keiko
comes in. "Sam, Mrs. Franklin is outside. She wants to see you."

"Ma-ma!" The boy stands and toddles toward his mother.

"Oh, Sam . . . Look!" As he swings out from under the sink, Keiko observes Sam's face. Watching their son taking his first steps, Sam's expression
is a blend of joy and sorrow. *It's all right,* she thinks, *just as long as he feels
something. Every word, every smile, every step the baby takes leads Sam out
of his inner darkness and into the light.*

The boy raises his arms and continues unsteadily forward. Keiko catches
her son as he turns and falls, grinning proudly at his father.

"Hey, Little Buddy, good for you!" *He's doing fine,* thinks Sam. *Keiko
and her parents need a place to live. But once that's taken care of . . .* "I'm
done here." Sam stands and turns on the water. He washes his hands then
takes the baby from Keiko's arms. "Come on, let's introduce you to an old
friend."

Mrs. Franklin, now seventy-nine, is a bit more stooped, but still carries
herself with dignity. Her eyes, clouded with cataracts, brim with tears when
she hugs Sam and Keiko's baby. Driven to the Buddhist temple by her
daughter, Mrs. Franklin has come with a letter for Sam. The soiled envelope

bearing multiple postmarks—Tokyo; Bern, Switzerland; Washington, D.C.;
San Francisco—contains a single torn notebook page with a penciled note:

November 2, 1945

Isamu-san,

*I hope you are well. I have prayed for you every day of this wretched
war. Our brother Bunji died of TB this year on the twenty-first of June.
Mother and I survived the A-bomb. But we are both sick and desperately need your help. Today—just now—I met a Japanese-American
nurse wearing a red cross. As she kindly waits for me, I am hastily
scribbling this letter. I will give it to her with the hope that it will
reach you. If you are alive, please help us.*

With my most loving and humble prayers, Akemi

Mrs. Franklin offers to loan Sam the money for a steamship ticket, but
none is available. It is 1946 and Japan is a former Axis nation under Allied
military occupation, not a tourist destination. It occurs to Keiko that Sam
could reenlist. She hates the idea, blaming the army for the death of her
brother and for Dewey's injury and for the evacuation and the camps. But after the A-bombing of Hiroshima, returning and struggling to get resettled in
Lodi, Sam has been like a zombie. Akemi's letter has rekindled a soft flicker
of life in his eyes. Hoping to fan it, Keiko offers her suggestion. "Sam,
maybe if you reenlisted?"

"Yeah . . . I've been thinking about it."

Keiko nods. "Being in uniform might be the quickest way for you to get
to Hiroshima."

"And you and the baby would be safe here with your parents and friends."

"Once you're there, you could sign up for married-dependent housing
and send for us."

"But if anything happened to me . . . you two would be okay."

"What do you mean? The war's over. What could happen to you?"

Hearing the alarm in Keiko's voice, Sam smiles reassuringly. "Nothing.
I'm just saying, you know, you and the baby would be safe."

"It's bad luck. Stop it." She frowns at the sudden cold glint in Sam's eyes.

He lowers his gaze. Seppuku. The word gleams like a naked blade in the forefront of his mind. In the uniform of an American GI, he will return and apologize to his mother and sister in Hiroshima. He will present himself in disgrace before the gravestone of his father. Then—

"So it's decided."

Sam raises his head, his eyes murky and distant. "What?"

"You'll reenlist."

"Yes. It is decided."

To everyone's amazement, Sam flunks the physical. "Flat feet," says the doctor.

"They've been good enough for the past four years."

"Sorry."

Sam writes a letter to a newly starred general named Jack Wright. Dewey sends a half dozen telegrams to Texas. Sam passes his second physical without removing his clothes. The doctor tells Sam that he received a telegram from the governor of Texas, and a general called from Washington. "He really chewed me out. Said they needed you as a translator at the war crime trials in Tokyo. You should have told me."

"Sorry."

American Trash

SEPTEMBER 1946

SERGEANT SAM HAMADA IS ASSIGNED TO ESCORT TWO COMPANIES OF infantry to Japan. He takes charge of them at Camp Stoneman in Pittsburg, California, marches them down to the docks and loads them aboard a barge tug-hauled through the Carquinez Straits and across the bay to San Francisco, where they board a navy troop transport and steam out through the Golden Gate.

During the two-week crossing, Sam gives a series of informal lectures on Japanese history, customs, rules of etiquette, and classes in basic conversation. Most of his troops are green, a friendly, cheerful bunch of boys on their first grand adventure. However, there are a few combat vets in the group. These men, especially the ones who fought in the Pacific, harbor a certain amount of resentment toward their Japanese-American sergeant. They are wary and aloof. Sam worries about how these men will behave once they reach Japan. He wonders if they might be tempted to settle old scores against ex-soldiers and innocent civilians.

The ship docks in Yokohama. Sam transfers his troops to a battered Japanese train with broken windows in every car. They roll slowly from the waterfront toward Tokyo. Sam had expected to see bombed and fire-gutted buildings, so the massive destruction does not startle him. What touches him most profoundly is the appearance of the Japanese people. As Sam and his men leave the docks, he sees a gang of Japanese workers pushing a stalled flatbed truck. The men are emaciated, and they grunt and pant for breath. They seem to be straining with all their might, but they are so weak, the truck is barely moving.

The train passes shantytowns where ragged people wander like stunned fish floating on the surface after an underwater explosion, people staring with glazed and dead eyes at the American troops. The train stops at a bomb-gutted station. A crowd of children appear outside Sam's glassless window. Filthy, clothed in rags, silently they hold out their hands and wait.

Sam grabs his duffel bag and opens it. He has some oranges, Wrigley's spearmint gum, a few Hershey bars, and a carton of cigarettes. He doesn't smoke, but he knows American cigarettes can be bartered. He'd purchased them aboard ship, thinking packs of cigarettes would make good gifts. He stands and calls to the children in Japanese. They come closer. Sam leans out the window.

Suddenly, someone grabs his arm. A very young, very green lieutenant begins yelling at him. "Sergeant, what the hell do you think you're doing? American soldiers are not allowed to fraternize with Japanese nationals."

"But, sir . . ." says Sam, "they're just children."

"No, Sergeant. They're Japanese nationals."

The train whistle sounds; the car jerks and begins moving.

Sam looks from the lieutenant to the faces and outstretched hands of the children.

"Sergeant, I'm ordering you to sit down and put away all that stuff."

Sam feels paralyzed. The train is rolling slowly, and the children are walking alongside, their eyes on his face. "Yes, sir," he says. And then Sam throws everything out the window.

"Sergeant, what the fucking hell—"

"Sir! Just getting rid of trash, sir. My duffel bag was too heavy, sir."

"Bullshit, Sergeant! You've just disregarded a direct order. Consider yourself on report. I'm going to bust . . ." The lieutenant's voice trails off. Sam hears a rustling and rattling commotion behind him, and the lieutenant's face registers such surprise that Sam turns to see what is going on.

The troops Sam has been escorting are at the windows. "I ain't gonna carry this shit no further," says one as he throws out gum and chocolate bars.

"Me neither." Out goes more gum and a box of Cracker Jacks.

"Stuff's too damn heavy," says a fresh-faced recruit as he throws two Superman comic books and a pack of Lucky Strikes out his window.

"I'm throwing out this candy," says another. "It's wrecking my teeth."

"Rotten," growls a veteran of Saipan as he gently tosses an orange into the hands of a little girl. When he sees the astonishment and delight on her face, his eyes well up, and he shouts, "Rotten fuckin' garbage! Rotten! Rotten!" and carefully tosses out three more oranges.

Outside the train the children are crying, *"Arigato gozaimasu. Domo arigato gozaimasu.* Thank you! Thank you very much!"

More children are running toward the tracks as cigarettes, candy, and gum continue to fly out the windows. Sam sticks his head out. He shouts in Japanese, "We're sorry! We don't mean to be rude, throwing things at you this way. Don't fight. Be decent and share everything equally."

The children are stunned. One of the older boys yells, "Are you Japanese?"

"Yes. Japanese American." Sam pulls his head back in.

The young lieutenant, red-faced and speechless, storms off to sit in another car. Sam looks at his men. To the last man they are all grinning at their Japanese-American sergeant. Sam doesn't care if he loses his stripes; he has never felt so proud to be an American.

And for a brief moment he forgets how close he draws to the end of his chosen path.

Gold

December 1946

Sam delivers his troops to division headquarters in Tokyo and puts in for a furlough to visit his mother and sister. In December when his furlough comes through, Sam's commanding officer calls him in. "Sergeant, it's been over a year since the A-bomb, and there are still people dying in Hiroshima from the radiation. Two months after the bomb the number was around a hundred people a day. The last report I heard was five to ten deaths a day. When you get there, you may discover relatives or friends suffering from radiation poisoning. And they may tell you about the American medical station in Hiroshima. Don't go there demanding treatment for your relatives. The facility is for research, not to render care. The truth is, no doctors anywhere in the world know how to cure radiation poisoning. It's too new. That's why our government's studying the victims of the bomb.

"Do you understand what I'm saying? There's no cure for radiation sickness. We're not set up to care for A-bomb survivors. Your relatives are on their own."

Tokyo station. A morning of wind and heavy rain. Grease- and grit-smeared snow mush on the pavement. Steam billowing from iron grates. Rivers of black umbrellas, buildings like cliff walls blue-black in the downpour. Yellow headlights as a U.S. Army jeep pulls up. Sergeant Sam Hamada gets out from the passenger's side, struggles with his duffel bag. It snags. The driver jumps out and helps wrestle the bag from the jeep. They carry the load like a body bag up the steps to the mouth of the train station. The driver gripes, grunting, cursing, sour breath barbed with resentment. "Damn, Sarge, what the hell you got in there?"

"Gold." Sam lifts the duffel bag, gets it balanced on his right shoulder, and walks quickly away. His left hand waves farewell, sinks and disappears into a sea of Japanese faces, a fresh tide of arrivals, black umbrellas uncurling, rolling toward the exits, forcing the driver to backpedal, sweeping him out into the rain and his jeep.

Sam moves along the platform between two waiting trains. He passes car after packed car, taped, broken windows rain-beaded and steamed with breath and body heat, glassless windows filled with eyes, staring, curious eyes, eyes intrigued, perplexed, envious, hostile, a gauntlet of eyes piercing him—*Who is this lone soldier sharing our face, this man with the samurai eyes and ugly American GI uniform?*

Honura

DECEMBER 1946

SAM STANDS ON THE CRACKED STEPS OF HIROSHIMA STATION.

On the day he left for Hawaii with his father, Sam had paused on this same spot. He had looked upon a beautiful city. Now he sees a village of ugly shacks scattered across a wasteland of bone white rubble stretching from the hills to the Inland Sea. Here and there a cracked and gutted ferroconcrete building remains standing. Wind blows little whirlwinds of dust through the streets. A single old badly dented taxi waits at the curb. A smokestack protruding from the trunk emits blue-gray smoke—gasoline being unavailable, the taxi has been modified to burn charcoal. Sam hoists his duffel bag onto the backseat then climbs in after it. The upholstery is shabby, spotted and stained.

The taxi moves very slowly, and people stare as Sam rides by. They stare at his U.S. Army uniform and his Japanese face. There is nothing Sam can do or say to explain who he is and how he feels. Part of him feels like cringing and lowering his head in shame. Another part insists that he is innocent of what happened here. He clenches his teeth, wraps his arms around his aching stomach, forces himself to meet their eyes.

Sam's home in Honura is only two and a half miles from the hypocenter. Between Ground Zero and his house there is a long low hill called Hijiyama. Beyond Hijiyama is the larger hill called Ogonzan on which are located an ancient cemetery and the temple of the goddess of mercy. Nestled in a cove-like space at the foot of Ogonzan is the district called Honura. The Honura village of Sam's childhood.

The taxi rounds the first hill, and Sam is amazed to find most of the houses of Honura are still standing. Hijiyama and the curving arm of Ogonzan had deflected the A-bomb's shock wave.

The streets become too narrow for the car. The driver pulls up in front of the Buddhist temple where Sam first learned to read and write. Sam pays, delighting the driver with a generous tip—five Lucky Strike cigarettes.

With a grunt Sam shoulders his duffel bag. Bent under its weight, he walks up a deserted street between silent houses.

This is the street he used to take every day to and from school.

His shadow ripples across the same high walls, now cracked and dilapidated.

He turns the corner and startles a flock of sparrows from the gate to his front yard. His father's name is no longer on the post. Sam puts out his hand and touches the white plaque inscribed with his own name. As the eldest son, he is the master of this house. He pushes open the gate and walks up the path through the garden.

He stops. *How can I face them? How dare I come home wearing this uniform?* He steadies himself with the thought that he only needs to endure his shame a little longer. His time for atonement has finally arrived. Today is the last day of his life.

He grits his teeth and slides open the front door. And it speaks to him with the same squeaking, rattling voice he knew as a child. He steps into the entry, puts down his duffel bag, his throat so choked he cannot speak.

"Who is it?" a young woman's voice calls from the kitchen.

Sam recognizes something in that voice; he hears an echo of the sister he left on the Hiroshima station platform so many years ago. "Akemi!"

"Isamu?"

Memories flash through him—the feel of her chubby arms around his neck as he carried her on his back up Ogonzan hill; the vision of a little girl twirling and dancing under the first soft snowflakes of winter.

Akemi, now twenty years old, walks out of the kitchen. She walks with a pronounced limp. She wipes her hands on her apron, and stares at Sam's face and uniform. "Isamu." Tears flood her eyes and run glistening down her cheeks.

Sam hugs her. *Bones.* Like embracing a skeleton.

And yet her voice rings with sweet music. "I'm so happy, Isamu. I'm so happy."

Sam smells metal and blood on her breath. "Akemi, I'm sorry. I'm so sorry. . . ."

They go into their mother's room. Covered with a quilt, Ohatsu lies absolutely still, eyes closed, face like a mask molded from gray and yellow candles, hair completely white, patches bald from radiation.

"Mother, it's me. Isamu. I've come home."

"Isamu?" Her eyelids flutter open. "Oh, Isamu . . . just look at you. You've grown up." Her voice is full of love and joy and unutterable sorrow. She opens her arms wide, hands trembling as she reaches out to him.

Survivors

December 1946

While Akemi tells Sam about Bunji's final illness and death, Sam unpacks his duffel bag: a hundred-pound sack of rice, canned ham, Spam, coffee, canned pears and peaches, sacks of sugar, chocolate bars, gum, cartons of cigarettes, nylon stockings. Akemi divides the rice into fifty-two portions to be shared with relatives, friends, and neighbors. It will be Sam's homecoming gift to them.

"I had just finished washing the breakfast dishes," says his mother. "The sliding doors were open. Suddenly, there was a bright flash. All the colors in the garden turned white. Then something huge hit the side of the house. The outer doors banged off their tracks, and the heavy roof tiles clattered furiously. I flew against the wall and lost consciousness."

"Since our house survived," says Akemi, "we were filled with wounded and dying, many burned so badly they no longer looked human. We had nothing for their pain. One burned boy—his grandfather came looking for him. When his grandfather tried to pick him up, the boy's arm disintegrated. He screamed, and he begged his grandfather to kill him. Finally, the old gentleman borrowed one of our swords and ended his grandson's suffering."

Sam's mother says, "I'm going to have all the swords in this house broken and made into sashimi knives."

"Black rain fell," says Akemi, "and Hiroshima burned for days. As soon as I could, I went into the city and searched for my fiancé along endless lines of the burned. Most could not speak. The ones who could talk, I had to put my ear close to their mouths to hear them; all they said was: '*Mizu . . . mizu.* Water . . . water.'

"I saw soldiers using long pikes to skewer and throw corpses onto a truck. The soldiers wore gauze masks because of the smell. Just before I reached them, the soldiers started the truck, and it passed in front of me. Burnt bodies were piled like rotting garbage, and I saw . . . I saw a man's eyes blink. He was still alive.

"My fiancé was a trolley driver. I walked his route until I found the burnt remains of his trolley. Searching through it, I found this. . . ." Akemi goes to the family altar, returns with a matchbox and hands it to Sam.

Sam opens the box and stares at a scarred, warped, melted piece of gold engraved in English with his father's initials. "Papa's belt buckle."

"I had given it to my fiancé as an engagement present."

Sam closes the matchbox. "Akemi . . . I am so sorry."

Mama turns her head, leaving a patch of white hair stuck to her pillow.

Sam's voice scrapes, dry and raw in his throat. "Radiation . . ."

Mama begins with a tiny smile. "It made my morning glories grow . . . unbelievably lush and wild." Her smile fades. "But other plants and animals . . . dwarfed, deformed. Frogs with eight legs and no mouth, human babies . . ." Mama closes her eyes.

Akemi strokes her mother's hand. "Well . . . that's what people say. I saw the flowers. But not the frogs or babies. People are afraid that the bomb poisoned the air, water, and earth. Last month the weather turned unseasonably warm. Plants began budding, and I saw birds gathering nesting material.

People blamed the bomb for the false spring. I think perhaps human dread can be almost as toxic as the radiation. People—" Akemi's eyes well up, and she looks away. "No one wants to come near us survivors. They're afraid we're contaminated. We're treated as lepers, as untouchables."

"Perhaps in time," says Sam, "people will forget."

Akemi shakes her head. "You know they won't. No man will ever love me again. No one will ever marry me."

Akemi leaves to distribute the rice. Sam offers prayers and incense at the Buddhist altar in the corner of his mother's room. He is puzzled when he notices that the brass candleholders, bell, and old cast-iron incense burner are missing. "Mama, what happened to your *butsudan*? All the metal trimmings are gone. Did you sell them in order to buy food?"

"No. The military took all the metal and melted it down for war materiel. None of our temples have bells now." She reaches out.

Sam takes her hand. *My God . . . it's just a bundle of cold twigs.*

"Does the presence of death frighten you?"

"No." But listening to her, he shivers. Not from fear but because her voice, once clear and musical as birdsong, reminds him of dry leaves scratching across a dark and windy street.

"Death is an honored guest in our house. After the bomb, I watched him guide many to their final sleep. Now, he waits for me."

And me. Sam bows. His GI dog tags slip against his chest, and he feels like a murderer wearing the evidence of his crime. He feels so heartsick, he can barely speak. "Mama . . ."

"He is patient. Free of anxiety or urgency." She closes her eyes, drifts off to sleep.

For a long time Sam sits holding his mother's hand. He cannot hear her breathing. The only sound is the ticking of her clock. Hanging in the alcove beside their Buddhist family altar is a scroll with a single *sumi* ink character that reads "serenity" or "peace." Beneath the scroll is a rack holding his grandfather's set of two swords. *The military took all the metal from our family altar, but they left the swords. To them, the swords were more sacred.*

Gently, Sam lets go of his mother's hand.

He reaches out and grasps his grandfather's *wakizashi*, the short sword a samurai would use for beheading an enemy or for his own ritual disembowelment. Seppuku. With trembling hands Sam shoves the ancient weapon under his belt, tight against his waist. Then he takes his father's prayer beads, a roll of incense sticks, and a box of matches from the altar.

He drops the matches on the floor, and his mother awakes. She reaches for her glasses and looks once again at the photograph Sam has given her. "I dreamt that your wife and son were here. Akemi and I sat at the table drinking tea and talking and laughing with your wife. You and your son were taking a bath together. I could hear the hot water splashing as you rinsed off the soap."

She turns her head. Again Sam sees clumps of her hair stuck to the pillow. He bows. "Mama, I'm going to the cemetery. Please, try to rest."

"Your father and Bunji will be so happy to have you visit them. Please tell them I'm not ready to join them yet. First, I want to meet your wife and my grandson." Her voice shimmers with a fresh clarity and joy.

But the light in her voice is so weak, the color in her gaunt face is so pale, so translucent, and Sam's blood is thundering in his head. Closing his eyes, he rubs the leaden ache in his temples. "Rest, Mama. I will deliver your message."

Shugyo

December 1946

SAM WALKS UP OGONZAN HILL, NOW RAVAGED AND STRIPPED OF THE forest where he played soldier as a child. The sun settles, and the cold air smells of wood smoke. He climbs the terraces of the cemetery to the row of his ancestors' graves.

It is the eighth of December, five years and a day after the attack on Pearl Harbor. Sam Hamada, eldest son, the family's winning lottery ticket, dressed in the uniform of an American GI, lights incense and bows before the stone shared by the ashes of his father and brother.

"Papa, Bunji, I have returned to join you."

Sam apologizes but does not ask for forgiveness. Face, mind, heart, and spirit cold and hard as the gravestones surrounding him, he refuses to cry. He must not cry. He fears that if he allows himself to start, his sobbing will break his bones.

Sam leaves the gravestone and walks to the temple of the goddess of mercy. It looks tiny to him. The shattered doors, lifted from their tracks, rest propped against one side. Sam removes his shoes, enters the bare one-room interior, kneels, and spreads his handkerchief on the dusty wooden floorboards. He takes the *wakizashi* from his belt, unsheathes the blade, places it on the square of white cloth. He pulls off his shirt and T-shirt. The cold air raises gooseflesh across his chest and belly.

He sits formally, legs folded, spine straight, head level. Ready for atonement.

He waits with his back to the doorless entrance, the world of the living receding behind him, in front only the blade and the blank wooden room, like staring into an unlined coffin.

He cannot see Hiroshima, but it bites into his soul like broken glass into bare feet, and he knows no penance can wash away the stains of his shame. There are no tears in his eyes. He is lost, doomed without hope, damned beyond forgiveness or salvation.

He waits for a sign from the goddess, a sign of mercy to free him from the agony of his shame. He has carried his burden as far as he can. He does not have another step left in him. He breathes, but he is already dead. He sits, but he is already gone. Ashes scattered to the wind.

And then he hears the voice of his old teacher Fujiwara-san. *Someday . . . when you are beaten and exhausted and all is lost . . .*

Sam blinks.

He feels like he is waking from a drugged sleep. He has been sitting with his eyes wide open but totally blind. Now he looks at the unpainted wooden walls grayed with age, the world outside reduced to blurry green and brown slits between the shrunken planks. There are several open knotholes, and he imagines a child's eye peeking in at him. But, no, there are no witnesses or intruders. Sam is alone.

Mu . . . He sits in absolute renunciation of life, as if he has already died, relinquished and thrown away everything: himself, Keiko, his son, his mother, sister, friends . . . the whole world. He has stepped off the path of earthly striving. Here, now, he sits while the river flows by. And now he truly understands the Bodhisattva's choice: whether to remain one with the void or to return and be reborn among the suffering, amid the strife and vanity, to once again become just another bobbing head in the loud, messy, jostling herd.

When one reaches the point of *mu* . . . the void. Nothingness. Then? Sam's eyes widen. He feels himself breathing the chill air. He feels *ki* pulsing through his body.

Seppuku—ancient samurai ritual, proud and unyielding—waits for Sam to keep his word. He feels tears welling in his eyes, an ache growing in his chest and throat, and he realizes that the act means little unless the individual feels the enormity of all that is being sacrificed.

Sam picks up the blade, aims the tip at his bare belly.

And now he feels himself awakening more . . . vulnerable, hypersensitive, like after a fever has broken. He looks down at his grandfather's *wakizashi*. Helplessly, he admires its handcrafted beauty. The lethal gleam coming off it shaves away at his numbness, awakening him even more. And it comes to him that seppuku might erase one layer of pain only to expose a far deeper level of pain hidden beneath. That whatever resolve and strength it takes to commit seppuku, it might require an equal degree of both to break this final promise. That this moment's test might not be about measuring his strength, but his gentleness. Not about rules or promises to keep or break, but about acceptance of human fallibility, human imperfection . . . and forgiveness.

Sam sits absolutely still. He has never felt so completely awake. He breathes.

And once more he hears Fujiwara-san's voice. *Someday . . . when you are beaten and exhausted and all is lost . . . you will hear my voice in your ear. "Isamu, go the distance."*

Whoosh . . .

Something whips past Sam's ear. The blurred sound followed almost immediately by a sudden urgent cry of birds.

Sam looks up, sees a nest in the rafters, a flicker of wings as a female sparrow lands briefly then flies away, her babies immediately silent.

Whoosh! Another bird, the male, flits in with a pink and purple worm wiggling in his beak; the squawking babies tear the worm to pieces, and a bit as long as the tip of Sam's little finger drops to the floor, writhing.

The father sparrow lands on the floor, hops forward on one foot; the other foot is crippled, claws curled under and back like a tangle of black fish hooks. With a sharp peck the father retrieves the worm, flies to the nest, and stuffs it down the throat of one of the screeching babies. Then the sparrow drops backward from the edge of the nest, rotates in midair, spreads his wings and flashes out the doorway.

Sam thinks of Akemi, scarred and lame, Dewey with one good arm, the returning troops and those freed from the camps . . . all hurt, even those with no outward injuries, carrying wounds invisible within.

Survivors. Shattered, fragmented, torn. Crippled.

But alive. Living with their pain. Caring for the children.

Sam lowers and sheaths the blade.

He puts on his shirt and his shoes. Outside the temple, he holds up his grandfather's *wakizashi,* looks at it one last time, then drops it clattering through the slot into Kannon-sama's wooden offering box.

Sam walks to the small wooden bell tower. He is surprised and disappointed to find the old bronze bell missing, until he remembers his mother telling him how the military took the metal. Sam gazes out beyond the empty bell tower, over gravestones and tree stumps, downhill to the immense swath of rubble—Hiroshima, mirror image of his soul, wasteland without, wasteland within. He notes the confetti flecks of color scattered throughout the ruins of the city—rooftops made from scraps . . . poor and humble seeds of a new Hiroshima.

Sam grips the hemp rope, swings the log forcefully into the space where the bronze bell used to hang, the void his old sensei might say is now filled with *mu,* with nothingness. It is a spontaneous gesture arising from his feeling of utter powerlessness.

But then from within his heart's deepest memory, Sam hears the ancient voice of Kannon-sama's bell. Hears it as he did so many times as a child, hears it ring with such resonance and clarity that it dissipates the murk clouding his mind; it lights the darkness, warms the chill, calms his soul into pure stillness.

Sam closes his eyes, sees himself as a boy with his mother. It is almost midnight, Bunji and Akemi are asleep, Papa is off drinking with friends. The next morning Sam and his father will leave for Hawaii. Sam is writing farewell and thank-you notes to his teachers and classmates. His mother finishes sewing buttons on a shirt that she has made for him. She dips a brush in ink, writes something on a piece of paper. "Isamu, can you read this?"

He shakes his head.

"*Shugyo.* It means to thoroughly train oneself. To study very hard. To practice asceticism."

He nods uncertainly.

"When a Buddhist monk, samurai, artist, or poet sets off on a journey of self-discovery, that's *shugyo*. When a calligrapher repeats the same strokes over and over again, when an athlete, musician, dancer, or writer spends years practicing, that's *shugyo*. It is never an easy practice, never an easy path. It means dedication, sacrifice, and suffering. It is a path that hurts. But it is also a path with heart. The goal of this kind of training is spiritual enlightenment."

Sam nods. "I think I understand."

"Some might say that you're only nine, too young to leave your mother. But your father has made up his mind, so we cannot dispute him. You must be brave, resolute, and persevering. Isamu, tomorrow you begin your *shugyo*."

"I can do it, Mama. I'm strong. And smart."

"Yes. I know you are."

"Tomorrow," he whispers, "tomorrow I begin my *shugyo*."

Sam opens his eyes, looks out at the ruined city and gently glowing twilight. Tears roll down his cheeks; he licks his lips and the taste of salt fills his mouth. Turning from the empty bell tower toward the small, dilapidated temple of the goddess of mercy, he puts his hands together and bows.

Feeling reborn, *ki* coursing through him like a school of pilgrim salmon scenting seawater for the first time—the river walls and bottom dropping away into a vast mystery—gliding into the *mu* . . . A new circle beginning, humble and flawed bodhisattva reentering the labyrinth of life, husband, father, son, brother, and friend heading home to his place in the world, Sam Hamada walks down from Ogonzan hill.

Epilogue: *Torii*

JUNE 1947

KEIKO REMEMBERS . . . THE MAY MORNING, ONE MONTH SHY OF A year ago, when Sam left Lodi for Japan . . . his good-bye kiss fading from her lips, but his gaze steadily holding hers, his right palm pale as the moon in the train window. She remembers how she held the baby and waved until the caboose passed in front of her like the edge of a steel curtain opening . . . to reveal a mirror of her soul: the vacant rail yard with scattered bits of paper trash, parched, sickly weeds, and rows of tracks gleaming on beds of grimy stones.

Then—as she and her parents, Dewey, Haru, Mitsy, and a dozen other friends and well-wishers left the station and walked across the tracks and rounded the fruit packing sheds and were just entering the main street of Japantown—they heard crows cawing at them.

Papa stopped, squinted up at four big birds perched on four thin power lines, black on black, against a bright ash-white overcast sky. Papa sighed, and they all resumed walking in silence. Four: the Japanese word for death. Black and white: the colors of a Japanese funeral.

One of their group would die soon.

Keiko hugged the baby, hunched her shoulders, raised her hand to shield his face from the crows' glittering eyes and menacing beaks, but the crows flew cawing after the train.

When Sam's letter arrived from Tokyo, saying his furlough had been approved and he was packing for Hiroshima, Keiko understood that he was going home to commit seppuku. She held the letter to her heart and remembered the day he told her she was a samurai woman. His words had given her such a sweet sense of pride. But here was the biting, astringent other half of what it meant to be this samurai's woman. She read the letter again, as good wives have always been able to do, not the words on the surface, but through them, to the heart of her husband. Cleft by gods or fate, the path forked here. Keiko put away the letter and made her choice. Whichever path Sam walked, she would journey with him to the final gateway. If they were together . . . if he asked her for the blade, she would carry it to him without hesitation, offer it to his hand like a sacred object. He would die in Hiroshima, and she would care for their child. Someday she would visit his grave to offer incense and prayers. She would meet his eyes without reproach or shame in the next world.

When the next letter arrived, postmarked Hiroshima, Keiko gathered her family and friends before she opened it. Not because she was afraid to face the news alone, but because she assumed it contained Sam's last words, his farewell to them all.

Keiko unfolded two blue-ruled pages torn from a pocket notebook. *Dear Keiko, I arrived in Hiroshima yesterday . . .* Then her hand rose to her mouth, and her eyes flooded with tears. When she looked up and saw the anguished faces of her parents and friends, she realized that they, too, had understood how terribly Sam had been suffering. They, too, had been preparing for the death the crows had foretold.

Keiko lowered her hand and smiled. "Sam's okay."

Hanging between hope and disbelief, Dewey stared into Keiko's eyes.

"He's applied for married-dependents housing. He says he'll send for me and the baby as soon as he has a place for us. He wants us to join him in Japan!"

Teeth clenched hard, Dewey swiped his face with the sleeve of his good arm. Mitsy and Haru leaped forward to hug Keiko. Mama whispered prayers of gratitude. Papa breathed a huge sigh of relief, coughed, and rolled a cigarette.

Now, a month shy of one year later, Keiko thinks . . . once again she has crossed the ocean for Sam. After two weeks at sea, steaming into Yokohama harbor this morning, she recalled her arrival in this same port seven years ago, a wide-eyed schoolgirl coming to Japan in search of an arranged marriage.

Now, shortly before noon, she stands immobilized and entombed in steel—thick steel plates underfoot and overhead, windowless, curving, riveted walls. People are jammed against her in the stifling heat. Sweat trickles down her neck, soaks into her collar. Her vision begins to blur and flutter around the edges. In her arms, slumped heavily against her shoulder, her two-and-a-half-year-old son fidgets in his sleep.

A loud *clang*.

Startled awake, the boy begins to whimper as a big steel door rumbles open, admitting gray light and muggy air that smells of diesel fumes, seawater, and creosote.

The crowd sighs in unison and shuffles forward to disembark. Momentarily stopped at the doorway, one hand on the thick steel hull, Keiko looks out and sees the backs of the people descending the gangplank ahead of her. Suddenly, a visceral wave of panic hits Keiko so hard that she staggers backward, bumping the passengers behind her.

It is the sight of slowly herding people . . . like when she got off the train and the bus in Arkansas. The sensation of being hemmed in, caught in the current of a human river. Keiko's eyes dart and roll, escaping toward the open sky. But then she catches sight of the Yokohama dockyard. And her breath snags in her throat.

Rubble. Low hills of rubble. Sparsely forested with, not trees, but twisted, rusting steel. At the foot of the wharf, several rows of Quonset huts, shaped differently, but arranged like camp barracks. A line of waiting buses. Chills shoot through her. Beyond the docks she sees a junkyard city—shanties, shacks bearing crude bar and shop signs, street vendors and raggedy, maimed beggars, prostitutes . . .

People jostle her from behind. On numb, stiff legs Keiko cautiously descends the gangplank. Beyond the shadow of the ship, she is fully exposed to the sun and humid summer heat. Seeking to reclaim her stunned heart, Keiko concentrates on the comfort of simply being outside, freed from the ship's stifling hold. Telling herself nirvana must be an open path. Never looking back. Leaving all life's pain behind and forgotten. Heart, mind, and spirit growing more transparent with each step, until you are completely gone, pure light into Pure Light.

Once on the dock with the enormous gray bulk of the ship looming behind her, she veers unsteadily for the edge of the crowd. Ahead she sees the passengers flowing around and through a wooden gateway like the ones that mark the entrances to Shinto shrines and other sacred spaces. From the high crossbeam of the reddish-orange *torii*, someone has hung a signboard, English block letters painted black on white: YOKOHAMA—GATEWAY TO JAPAN. In the lower left corner the sign painter, apparently an American GI, had signed his work with a little cartoon head and the name Kilroy.

What am I doing here? Tattooed on both cheeks: American and . . . arriving with another shipload of Allied occupation forces. With her American passport and clothes, her American shoes stepping onto a shattered and prostrate Japan. Her Japanese name and face permanently disfigured by the memory that in America she had been branded *Jap* . . . distrusted, despised, imprisoned.

Watching the ship from the dock, Sam stands in the semicircular shade at the end of a U.S. Navy Quonset hut. He is alone but he feels the presence of guardian spirits. *Papa, Bunji, Fujiwara-san, Uncle Genzo, and Al . . . Thank you. Keiko, Shoji, Kuwano, Dewey, Mrs. Franklin, Captain Oshima . . . thank you all for being my teachers. . . .* It comes to him that they are not done teaching him, and they will be joined by other teachers he has not yet met. Sam gives thanks for every promise he kept or broke—lessons and tests of honor and mercy, each part of a larger one. And it comes to him that we swear an oath before we are born: *To cherish and savor the gift of life. To honor the sacredness of all living things. To be honest and kind. To be gentle and forgiving.* And then we arrive here and learn how difficult it is to follow our oath. Confronting us, challenging our hearts, is the question: *How do we preserve our purity and wholeness in a world so desecrated by human madness and cruelty?*

He sees Keiko coming off the gangplank. She maneuvers crookedly to the edge of the crowd and stops. She is wearing a white summer dress and carrying their baby. Sam draws a deep breath as he pushes away from the Quonset hut and dives into the oncoming stream of disembarking passengers.

Keiko spots Sam striding toward her. He moves with powerful, masculine grace . . . so handsome in his U.S. Army khakis, his smile filled with tenderness, eyes shining with love and happiness. Her own spirit fragmented and unbalanced, Keiko turns the baby, holding him as if she needs to offer her husband proof of her identity. "Look, it's Daddy." She scarcely has the words out when she feels Sam's arms around her and his kiss on her mouth. There is something so solid and real, so welcoming and safe about Sam's hug, Keiko feels the tears starting.

She does not want to break down in front of all these people. She tries to speak. She will be all right if she can just think of something to say. Simple, true, loving . . . something not about fear or pain or uncertainty or sorrow. Looking into Sam's eyes for the first time in almost a year, Keiko remembers seeing him when he had shameful secrets or unbearable pain locked inside, when he was preparing to die. Looking now, she can tell that his dark eyes hide no part of himself. But she is caught off guard by the sense of mystery, of yet unknown possibilities in his gaze. She reads Sam like a beloved old book she knows intimately . . . only to discover that, suddenly, now, finally, the book lies open to the first page of its real story.

The crowd of disembarking passengers flows around them. Whatever words Keiko might have spoken are lost, spinning leaves and sunlight flickering downstream.

Sam kisses the baby on the forehead. "Hey . . . Little Buddy."

At the sound of Sam's voice, the boy tips his head back, black hair gleaming, brown-black eyes staring at Sam's face.

Keiko draws a shaky breath, blurts without thought: "His nickname is Ink."

"You mean Ink-Pink?"

"No. Just Ink."

"Ink Hamada? Okay." Sam grins and lifts the boy from Keiko's arms.

A feeling of weightlessness spreads through her. Followed instantly by a desire to hold on to something. Keiko grabs Sam's arm, and they start walking.

As they pass through the vermilion gateway, Keiko and Sam dip their heads, bowing in awareness and acceptance of their sacred path.

Then Sam feels her hands trembling, and he stops, brow furrowing with concern. "Keiko, are you all right?"

Sam's face has aged. That which she once saw as granite is still there, but now no longer sharp-edged and brittle. His face has more character; like weather-beaten stone it speaks of endurance. And the other quality that she always loved, his gentleness, seems to have grown as wide and deep as the sea.

Sam and Ink are both staring at her.

Meeting their eyes, recognizing so much of her husband and herself in their son, Keiko's heart shivers, bamboo forest in the wind, shaken by fear, uncertainty, and immeasurable love. Wonder. And joy. *How strange indeed to be here. On this path of many turns, of so many sorrows and blessings. Here at the gateway—*

"Keiko, are you okay? Can you walk?"

Keiko is overwhelmed with gratitude for the path given to her and the forks she has chosen. *Whatever's going to happen next, I'm ready.* She squeezes Sam's hand and releases it. Squares her shoulders, lifts her chin, and tosses her hair. "I could walk forever, Sam. Let's go."

DATE DUE

GAYLORD   PRINTED IN U.S.A.